A Step Too

❄

For Verity

Copyright © 2021 Hazel Beecroft

Editor: Jessica Runyard, Runyard Editorial Services

Cover Photograph foreground 2019 by kind permission of George Parish

Cover Photograph background 2017 by kind permission of Annie Spratt

❄

Natalie woke with a start. There it went again. She breathed in sharply through her teeth. It must be the booze, or perhaps the two a.m. kebab. She could have bet that the meat had gone off. She had been prone to a dodgy stomach recently so she should have known better and shouldn't have risked having it. It had looked questionably grey whilst rotating on the counter, pivoting slowly enough that she imagined a fly could land on it, but she had ordered it regardless, ignoring her suspicions and in need of sustenance. She moved her hand to her stomach and was puzzled to feel a dead weight above the duvet. Then she remembered.

Slowly, quietly, so as not to disturb, she eased her hand out from below the covers and gingerly lifted his arm from her chest. She peeked at him, afraid that his eyes might flicker open. There was a pool of drool on the pillow. What had she been thinking? Why had she finally relented? He wasn't her type, but he had fancied her from the very start and she had decided to say yes just to keep the peace. At the time she had been tempted, she supposed, because she had been drunk, but right now she was disgusted with herself. She should have stayed strong and said no.

He would have gotten over it. There had been a fleeting few moments when she had found him attractive last night but looking at him with sober eyes confirmed what she had always thought about him; he would be disheartened to learn that it couldn't happen again, ever, even if they were drunk, they could only be friends.

She shifted her weight so that she could sit up which then set off another cramp. Swinging her legs out of the bed she felt something wet on her thigh. Great, I'm also covered in his semen, she sighed, pushing herself onto her feet and staggering towards the bathroom and ignoring the beginnings of a hangover. She dropped onto the toilet and stared at the grubby wall in front of her. She wished they had chosen to spend their one and only night of regrettable passion in his dorm instead of hers. She would have to wash the sheets now. She would also have to wait for him to wake up and make awkward conversation until he took the hint and buggered off back to his own dorm. She didn't have it in her to be frank and ask him to leave. She massaged her temples. They were supposed to be just friends, and they could hopefully remain just friends, last night would be nothing more than a small and unspoken blip in their friendship. He was going to be crushed when he learned that friendship was all he was going to get. If the sex had been great then she might have been able to reminisce, but it had only been mediocre, which she shouldn't blame entirely on him because they had both been too smashed to put in a good performance, and a cramped single bed stuffed into a dingy room was far from a romantic setting. She could hardly remember it, so it can't have been earth-shattering. With a bit of luck, he would regret it too and would never want to speak of it again, let alone re-enact it. With a lot of luck he might not remember it at all.

It was the weekend so she couldn't even pretend she had an early morning lecture to attend. What if he tried to kiss her with his rank morning breath? We didn't even use a condom, she sighed, looking down at her leg. She started at the blood smeared over her skin. Standing up in a panic, more liquid started trickling down her inner thighs, splashing into the toilet bowl and around the seat, dripping onto the faded linoleum floor. It was pink, diluted blood.

'Doug,' she cried automatically, her voice ashen. She now found that the boy she had just shuddered over was also the person she was now in desperate need of. Then she questioned what had happened last night. Had she misremembered? Was she bleeding because he had forced her? It wasn't as concentrated as blood, so perhaps she had been so paralytic that she had just wet herself?

'Tally?' He staggered into the room, brushing the mop of dark hair from his face. He was the sweetest guy she had ever met. He looked at her with those puppy-dog eyes, at her legs, at the floor, and from the sheer panic and confusion spreading across his innocent face she knew he would never – could never – hurt her in any way. Not every man was like that. That's why she had tried last night, because he would be a keeper – a safe bet – if only she was able to feel the same way about him as he so clearly felt about her.

'What's happened? Are you okay?' He rushed towards her. It was something most other boys would not have done in this situation, upon seeing streaks of bloody urine running down a girl's inner thighs. He didn't know what to do. 'Here,' he said finally guiding her into the cramped shower cubicle.

'Argh.' Tally doubled over, bracing herself against the wall for support as another twitch of pain travelled through her body. More blood splattered at her feet, mixing with the water from the shower head that Doug was holding. He tested the temperature, because even through his panic he didn't want it to freeze or scald her.

'It's alright,' Doug said in a shaky voice, as they both stared at the liquid leaving her body, wondering if it really was alright. 'Your period?' he suggested hopefully.

'No,' Tally gasped, clutching her stomach as another wave hit her. It was painful, but it also wasn't. It was there and then it was gone, all memory of the pain disappeared when the cramp ended just as quickly as it had arrived. She racked her brains once she was able to think again, in-between the surges of pain. Her period must be due by now, overdue. She couldn't even remember when she had last had one, but then they had always been sporadic. It must have been sometime last month, perhaps. He must be right.

Humiliation flooded Tally as she considered how she must look to an outsider. She decided that if anyone other than Doug had witnessed the scene she would have been permanently mortified. He was a true friend and they had been stupid to sleep together and potentially ruin that friendship. They would have to ensure that their friendship survived the accidental sex - they could laugh it off in years to come, hopefully. As for what was happening right now, well it would be too much to ask Doug to ever find any humour in it.

The running water from the shower head magnified the amount of blood, that was swirling around her feet until it was nearly up to her ankles in the small square shower tray she stood stooped over. Doug aimed the flow at her hips, washing her lower half clean, and she was grateful for the warmth, it eased the cramps somewhat.

'Shall we call someone?' he asked, choosing not to say 'ambulance' in case it alarmed her.

'No, I'll be okay, it'll pass, it was the kebab,' Tally managed through gritted teeth as another wave of pain hit her, taking her focus away from the room, from the world. Somehow she had been attacked by a bout of food poisoning at the exact same moment her period had started. That was the only explanation she could think of right now, as disgusting as it was. *At least I haven't been sick yet*, she thought, waiting for her stomach to start bubbling.

She refocused on Doug and tried to ignore her embarrassment at standing in front of him naked. Her top half shivered with cold while he hosed her bottom half down to wash away the blood and ease her cramps. He was naked too and she did her best to not look below his waist, hoping that he was also returning the favour. When it returned, the pain was so severe that she didn't have room to feel humiliated any longer, the pain blocked out every other possible emotion.

He asked her a question that she simply couldn't understand. 'What?'

The wall was slick with steam and the hand she was using to brace herself against it slipped. As he caught her, Doug dropped the shower head and showered them both with a warm spray as it jerked around on the end of its leash and jettisoned water in all directions. She collapsed to her knees because the pain returned, twisting in her abdomen, curling around her spine, and taking her breath away. It felt as if someone had just hit her in the back with a shovel. Doug knelt down in front of her and firmly took hold of her arms, ignoring the running water. His grip persuaded her to look into his eyes and listen carefully to his next sentence. Despite the ludicrous words he seemed serious, stern, as if he actually believed what he was saying.

'I said: I think you're having a baby.'

'I don't understand,' Tally repeated, wrapped up in her dressing gown, clutching Doug's hand as if it held all the answers. 'I'm not pregnant, I can't be.'

They were in the back of an ambulance, travelling at speed. The red patch between her legs was growing, every time the paramedic checked on her Tally couldn't help but glance down in disbelief. Doug had managed to convince Tally to let him call the emergency services, and he had then been asked some difficult questions during a rushed telephone conversation with the switchboard operator, including 'Have a look and tell me what you can see'. Although Tally remained doubtful, Doug and the ambulance dispatcher agreed she was in established labour, and so the ambulance had been dispatched immediately, with lights flashing and sirens wailing to punctuate the severity of the situation.

The vehicle juddered along in a hurry, yet the paramedics inside made a big play on how there was no real need to become hysterical. They were going further than the city hospital because they needed a neonatal intensive care unit apparently. Tally's blood pressure had been checked twice already and there was a contraption on her finger to measure her oxygen saturation. The trolley Tally was lying on rattled away and everyone else was forced to brace themselves as they turned corners, which set Tally on edge because it highlighted how she had become the centre of an emergency situation. Tense reassurances and suggestions that she should try to relax were thrown at her through tight lips although it did very little to actually reassure her.

'We'll be there in just a few minutes.' The paramedic said with a well-practiced smile. She had now given up trying to convince her patient that she was in the late stages of labour, and close to delivering a baby in the back of a speeding vehicle. She had quickly discovered that her patient was in complete denial of her predicament, which at least meant that she appeared to be relatively composed. *If it was me*, the paramedic mused, *I would be starting to twitch*.

'My dad is going to kill me,' Tally said flatly as she began to consider the possibility the paramedic might be correct about her alleged pregnancy.

'Just focus on your breathing,' Doug encouraged, having been the only one of them who had listened to anything the paramedic had said. The paramedic gave him a proud nod.

'What does that even mean?' Tally snapped, before another contraction hit and she was yelping. 'Mum is going to kill me right after Dad does,' she added as an afterthought, as soon as she was able to speak again. 'She's going to revive me just so she can kill me all over again.'

'Try to remain calm, it'll help. Relax your jaw,' the paramedic reminded her as she prepared for a speedy disembarkment. She didn't want to clean up the extra mess a baby would produce, especially when Accident and Emergency was so tantalisingly close. She was determined the baby would remain on the inside of her patient until her patient was outside of the ambulance.

The vehicle finally lurched to a stop and the paramedic flung open the back door to the welcome sight of a midwife standing next to a porter with a wheelchair. It was a relief that they had been able to assign one to Natalie at such short notice; it must be a quiet night on the labour ward. They were going to have to fit her in regardless of the lack of warning anyway because this baby was nearly here.

'We're here,' Doug announced gleefully, as if they had just rocked up to Disneyland.

'Are you going via A&E?' the paramedic asked the midwife, suspicious of her intentions as she saw her hiss an instruction into the porter's ear.

'No, straight up. I'll deal with it,' the midwife said in the clipped tones of someone who was not prepared to waste any time arguing.

'You know that's not protocol.'

'Do you want to help me deliver this baby?' the midwife asked curtly, as Tally doubled over in agony once again, only just able to get off the trolley in time to lean over it and ride out the contraction from a more comfortable position than lying flat on her back.

'She's all yours,' the paramedic mumbled, deciding to deal with the agro of breaching protocol later. From what the paramedic had seen, there was undoubtedly a baby on its way, and it would definitely need the neonatal unit more than the accident and emergency waiting room. Neither the paramedic nor the midwife were going to let protocol risk the life of a new-born baby. They would rather face a slapped wrist from the boss than have to explain to Tally or Doug why the baby hadn't quite made it.

Doug helped Tally stagger down the ramp. When she got near the bottom she had to lean on Doug to endure another contraction. It was less than two minutes apart from the one before, which caused the midwife to flash the paramedic an 'I told you so' glare. As Tally stepped off the ramp, the paramedic breathed a sigh of relief. Although she was going to get a kicking for allowing the midwife to kidnap her patient, at least she was able to avoid mopping up a placenta.

'I've got it from here,' the midwife confirmed with a wink, not missing the change in her counterpart's expression. She ushered Tally into the chair whilst making the necessary introductions, then they began the controlled rush up to the labour ward.

'Are we sure about this?' Tally asked through gritted teeth, still questioning whether it wasn't a burst appendix or something like that. She didn't see the bemused glances shared above her head as they hurried along.

'We've got a birthing room on Delivery Suite ready for you, and a neonatal team on standby.'

'Birthing room?' Tally scoffed, as if the whole concept of her giving birth was ludicrous. She was still partly convinced it was the kebab. How on earth could she be pregnant?

'Have you contacted her parents?' the midwife asked Doug, sensing that he was at least accepting of the fact his girlfriend was about to give birth.

'No!' Tally interjected, before taking a sharp intake of breath as another wave of pain hit.

'She thinks they are going to kill her, one after the other,' Doug explained.

'I think it might be prudent to call them regardless,' the midwife urged, ignoring the childish explanation. They were entering the lift now, which had been held open by another, much younger, midwife who looked almost as panicked as Tally and Doug did.

'She doesn't have a green book,' the new midwife said, her tone somewhere in between disbelief and horror.

'We'll muddle through,' the older midwife replied, shooting her assistant a hard look for appearing so nervous.

'My dad *will* kill me!' Tally insisted, wondering why no one was taking the threat to her life seriously.

'He's going to have to wait until I've delivered your baby,' the midwife muttered.

'We know, you said,' Doug pointed out to Tally, 'and then your mum will.' He was trying not to freak out at the idea of walking on to a labour ward at least ten years earlier than he had ever imagined he would. Although it was completely irrational all he kept thinking was that he was somehow the father because they had slept together last night. 'If you give me their number then I can call them.'

Calling a stranger in the middle of the night to tell them their daughter was not only pregnant, but also about to have a baby – no wait – *actually having a baby* - was not something he was keen on doing, but what other choice did he have? He was aware the midwife was keen for her parents to know because this was going to be a risky birth. There was a reason they had rushed to this specific hospital on the outskirts of the city. No one knew how old the baby was. It was probably premature. Tally was hardly waddling around with a gigantic bump. She wasn't even particularly fat, which made her ability to hide an unborn baby, from not only the world but also herself, seem that bit more plausible, yet here they were. Tally's flat denial was definitely convincing.

'Natalie, please could you hop up onto the bed? Would I be able to examine you?' the senior midwife asked, anticipating consent while she snapped on a pair of gloves. The junior midwife flapped around in the background, preparing equipment that Doug didn't have the courage to look at. 'I'll need Dad to work with me on keeping Mum calm.' She nodded to Doug who looked back blankly.

'Mum?' Tally's eyes blurred at the new label she had just been given.

'I'm not the dad!' Doug cried when he realised that she had been addressing him. His paranoia at potentially somehow being the father caused him to protest a little bit too sharply.

'You need to keep her focused on her breathing.' The midwife accepted his non-dad status with the blink of an eye, because it really wasn't important who he was right now. The dad not being there was not unusual, it was the way he acted with Natalie that had convinced the midwife that he must be the father. She felt silly for making the assumption and told herself she should have known better than to assume.

'Lie back darling, we're just going to measure your bump.'

'I don't really have a bump,' Tally said, still adamant she could convince them she was on the wrong ward.

The two midwifes exchanged glances as the tape was stretched across Tally's relatively flat stomach. That was one of their worries. 'Let's get them up here,' the first midwife suggested after reading the measurements, keeping her tone light when it was so obvious that they had something that was a cause for major concern. The way the second midwife rushed over to the wall and pressed a giant red button confirmed those fears.

'We're just going to get some extra help for the baby,' the first midwife soothed as the alarm started booming. The midwife was talking evenly because she was used to appearing calm in a crisis, however, this was the most uncertain birth she had encountered in a long while. Underneath her composed veneer her palms were starting to sweat. Once again, she glared at the junior midwife who looked like she was about to hyperventilate. 'Now, is it okay if I internally examine you?' she asked patiently.

'Err, okay,' Tally agreed despite not wanting this lady anywhere near her, especially not internally. Then another wave of pain hit her, and it really didn't matter anymore. She turned towards Doug as the midwife stuck her hand inside her, and he was staring back at her, his horrified wide eyes a reflection of her own.

'Right,' the midwife said, in a tone that meant business, 'You're ten centimetres dilated, that means Baby is ready. You're doing so well, Natalie, believe it or not you're nearly there.'

Natalie did not believe it, not one bit. Nearly there? Nearly there to what? Becoming a Mum? Tally didn't know what being ten centimetres dilated meant, she could barely even remember her sex education classes from back in school.

'Do you mind if we listen to Baby's heartbeat?' the midwife asked as her assistant sidled up with a hand-held Doppler.

Tally nodded; the power of speech having momentarily left her. It was pretty weird to think she had been smuggling a second beating heart around in her belly for the last however many months and she hadn't even realised it.

'The next time you feel the urge to push, during the next contraction, I want you to go with it,' the midwife continued, as people entered the room. One was wheeling a trolley with a plastic box on top of it. Tally was left to process the instruction, wondering how to comply when she didn't know which muscles to push with.

'Your body knows what to do,' the midwife reassured her.

'What's this?' Doug eyeballed the group of people who had bundled into the room.

'After birth, Baby may need some extra help on our Neonatal ward,' the midwife said breezily, as if it was something quite normal and wasn't a cause for concern.

Tally felt another contraction coming and, with the midwife nodding encouragingly at her, she pushed as hard as she could, allowing her body to take over and work out what it had to do.

'Good work Natalie,' the midwife encouraged, taking a look, 'I can see the head'.

'It's Tally,' Tally insisted. She would prefer the midwives to use her nickname since they were insistent on hovering around and she hoped it might help her to feel like she was still the same person from yesterday, from her previous life. The news that there was a head emerging from her body was mind-boggling. The twitchy team of people watching didn't even register with her.

'Okay, Tally, during the next contraction I want you to really go with it, give me two big pushes, but I need you to pause in-between them to take a deep breath, okay? We need to give your skin time to stretch.'

Tally nodded, unsure if she would have the capacity to follow the instructions, and gripped Doug's hand as she prepared to give birth to a baby she had only just discovered existed. It hadn't dawned on her yet that the challenge of bringing a baby into the world would be dwarfed by the upcoming task of holding one in her arms and coming to terms with the idea that it was hers. Tally, the carefree and single university student, was now a mother, now responsible for a helpless baby. She wondered later as she gazed into two small, half-closed, steely blue eyes if she should start answering to Natalie after all. She also wondered if she should feel something, anything, other than sheer shock and panic.

❄ Before Baby ❄

She turned her face towards the window to escape her body. Snow was falling in a blur behind the mottled glass. She tried to pick out a single fleck as it darted its way from top to bottom, disappearing as quickly as it had appeared, but it was always too fast for her, as fleeting as her hopes and dreams. Something else caught her eye, offering another distraction, as her mind searched for a way to pretend this was not happening to her. She turned her head slightly, and winced at the disembodied face staring back at her. Its hollow eyes and tombstone teeth mocked her with an open-mouthed grin. That leering expression, of spite and morbid fascination, was going to haunt her forever. Look back at the snow, she silently instructed herself, lose yourself in the way it tumbles. She tried to find joy in the dancing of each snowflake. How could anything contain joy ever again? She was jealous of the snow, of the carefree fancy that it portrayed, and the way it fluttered oblivious to her, enjoying the freedom that existed outside of this room, refusing to help her. She resented how it didn't even notice it was tumbling towards the floor, to land on a heap of bodies and inevitably melt.

This never happened to me, she vowed, blinking back the tears before they fell, refusing to cry because that would be proof that it had. I am as carefree as that snowflake; I am not trapped inside this room. This was not my fault – not the punishment I deserved. I am behind the glass, outside the window, floating on the wind. I am not lying on this floor, I am tumbling.

❄ After Baby ❄

'Michael, get the bags,' Helena instructed with a level of authority that only a mother possessed. She straightened her shirt, tucking it in and smoothing down the creases caused by the long car journey. Packing something that required ironing had been a mistake. For Helena, looking good usually helped her to feel better about pretty much anything, but today it wasn't working. Today she remained overwhelmed and no amount of lipstick was going to restore her sense of control. Barking orders at her son wasn't helping like it usually did, either.

Michael jumped into action, relieved to be put to work, momentarily out of excuses – or any desire to even fabricate an excuse. He was unable to just stand there and gawp as Helena guided his little sister up the steps into their family home. He glanced at the bundle in her shaking arms as she passed him and although he could only see blankets, his heart skipped a beat. There was a tiny human somewhere in there, blinking against the cold light and he wondered if it was as shocked as they were by its unscheduled appearance into the world.

'Where's your father?' Helena hissed as Michael closed the front door, the bags an ominous pile at his feet. His mother never travelled. She had borrowed Michael's sports bag for the unexpected trip and was still complaining that it had made all her things smell like socks. She didn't really care about the stench, but it had been a welcome reason to complain about something other than how she had just gained an unexpected grandchild. How could she begrudge the little thing now that she had met her? How could she ever forgive her nineteen-year-old daughter for getting pregnant? How could she *not* forgive her now she had gifted them all with something so precious?

Michael stared at Tally as she stood in the middle of the reception room, turning her unseeing eyes about the place, searching for something normal to grasp on to. The way she pivoted on the spot, her arms clasped tightly to her chest as if fearful she might drop her new baby, he was for once unable to find something sarcastic to say to her. For once he was a nice person, the older brother he should have always been, shepherding her to shelter and carrying her bags.

'Not sure,' was all he managed as he continued to stare at Tally. He knew exactly where their father was. Charles had announced he was going to his study for a bourbon six hours ago, during breakfast, and had not yet resurfaced. He had risen from the table, leaving his poached eggs on toast untouched, and hadn't even looked at Michael as he had slouched away, showing no hint of embarrassment at the early hour in which he had decided to start drinking. Anna had raised an eyebrow at Michael, she had been midway through pouring orange juice, and Michael had reassured her that he would have two glasses and she was not to worry about the wasted eggs. He only hoped his father had not drunk himself to death during his quest for solace because he would be the one to find the dead body slumped in the chair. Charles wasn't going to find a solution to this new predicament at the bottom of a glass; drinking hadn't solved the last predicament either.

'Darling, not that way.' Helena tottered over the parquet flooring in her signature heels.

Tally turned slowly, one foot on the bottom of the staircase, still avoiding eye contact with her brother.

'There's been a bit of a reshuffling,' Helena explained, her voice sing-song and light, as if it had been a wonderful idea – *their* idea.

Michael snorted. Tally was not going to buy that. Nothing in their home had changed in their entire lifetime. Even the hideous ornaments had remained the same, never moving an inch in all those years of futile yet dutiful dusting that was carried out by Anna. The only reshuffling he could think of was the seasonal erection, decoration (using the exact same dated ornaments), then dismantling of the Christmas tree, always purchased from the same farm, always dragged across the house to the biggest sitting room leaving a trail of persistent pine needles and an exasperated Anna in its wake, always burnt on the bonfire and bid a ceremonial adieu.

'Your new room is at the back, overlooking the orchard.' Helena smiled encouragingly, as if the prospect of having rear garden-facing views was wonderful. It sounded like it should be, surely a sea of apple trees would be a welcome sight to wake up to, but Tally knew this house, and the back quarter Helena was referring to was redundant for a reason. It was basically falling down; there was nothing 'new' about it.

Michael waited for his sister to flinch, to question the change, and to have the same temper tantrum that he had, but she simply stepped back down off the bottom step and turned down the hallway, unaffected. He remembered the bundle in her arms and that there was nothing else that really mattered right now, because she shouldn't even be here, holding her new-born baby, it shouldn't have even been born.

That was when it truly hit him. He had a niece. His sister was a mother. His mother was a grandmother. There was going to be a little baby girl living in their house. Her cries would echo around the walls. He was going to have to look after them, especially if his own father was refusing to wake up from his alcohol-induced haze. He was going to have to stop dicking around for once in his life and pretend he was getting it together for the sake of the rest of them. He was going to have to settle down, grow up and be a man – all at once. He exchanged glances with his mum and from the desperate look on her face he knew that he had realised all of this a little bit too late.

Helena was watching Tally with disbelief, taking a small moment to reveal her true shock and confusion, allowing herself to indulge in the panic she was feeling whilst her daughter's back was turned and she thought no one was watching her mask slip. His mother was about to snap under the strain of carrying it all alone.

Michael put an arm around her shoulders. 'Shall I make a pot of tea?' he suggested hopefully, thinking it may be the right thing to do, imagining this was the right way to go about fulfilling his newfound responsibility.

'Don't be ridiculous, Michael,' Helena scoffed, thwarting his attempt at being empathetic, despite her usual desperation over his childishness. 'You wouldn't even know where to find a pot.' She regained her usual cool demeanour in an instant and pattered across the entrance room to catch up with Tally, already over her uncharacteristic blip before she had even given it the chance to truly take hold.

Michael sighed, and bent down to pick up the bags. His mother was right, so it only stung a little. A kitchen symbolised work and preparation, and they had Anna for that sort of thing.

Opening doors and carrying bags would have to be enough. Maybe after this short burst of chivalry he would have a lie down and smoke a joint instead. He wanted to ignore the ominous thoughts swilling around his head and get back to his original self, because the last thing anyone needed around here was another unnerving and incomprehensible change. As quickly as he had decided to step up, he was back to making excuses again.

Although her initial instinct was to be surprised at the way her room looked like her room yet wasn't her room, she didn't even blink. A rickety single bed had replaced her super king, and a writing desk was lined with her transposed belongings, all cramped between walls much closer together than before.

'I thought we could move this chair out and put the cot here,' Helena said helpfully, pointing at the chair, despite it being the only chair in the room and it not needing to be singled out for clarity. Helena hadn't even bought a cot yet. She pulled out her phone to text Anna, who had been barraged with similar instructions over the last few days, but then remembered they had no signal in this derelict portion of the house. As if to reinforce the point, a gust of wind rattled the single-pane window. 'We'll change that,' Helena automatically promised, realising that with winter approaching this room was not nearly warm enough for a baby. She was going to have to text Anna about that, too. She was going to have to momentarily forget they couldn't afford a new cot or a new window, and that it was unfair to delegate every single problem to poor Anna.

'Where *is* your father?' she asked with despair, not really asking, because Tally hadn't seen or heard from him for weeks, she had only just re-entered the county.

Tally ignored her, knowing she would not be expected to answer, unable to even contemplate facing her father – glad that she hadn't had to do so yet. She approached the writing desk and did not recognise the face in the photos, the face of a smiling Tally, laughing at the ease with which she had sailed through life up until now, when the ceiling had come crashing down on top of her. There was a photo of her sitting astride Match, her dotty grey Connemara horse. He had been scrubbed clean for the competition at which someone had taken his photo, however, he still looked slightly grubby owing to the brownish colour of his flecks. He was standing proudly with dark-tipped ears pointing towards the camera. His eyes were big, deep, honest pools, ready to accept whatever the world threw at him with a calm acceptance and underlying faith in humankind. The stranger on top was grinning, as if horse riding was her everything, and it had been. Match had been her superstar, but then she had decided to go off to university because she thought she ought to get away, because that's what teenagers did. Running away from her life had seemed perfectly plausible until now.

She looked away from the photo, because giving up horse riding so she could sit in endless lectures and then go out drinking with people she didn't really know had not been worth the sacrifice.

Escaping hadn't worked because she was back here, exactly where she had started, only now she was back with a baby to look after as well. She had put Match on loan to her best friend for her anticipated three years of study. He had remained on site but was now exercised by Leila, who was therefore likely to have mixed feelings about Tally's unexpected return.

She had agreed to Tally riding him on the university holidays, but right now she couldn't really contemplate climbing onto a horse, so Leila would still have him exclusively to herself for a few weeks. Tally would be unable to dedicate herself entirely to riding anyway, even after she had healed from childbirth, what with being stuck with the baby, so perhaps Leila could stay. There was always Peter, Michael's old horse, who they used to share whenever they decided to ride together. It was too soon to worry about it. Her horse would still be there tomorrow, in the stables outside the house; she could just start with going to see him and take it from there. Tally would talk to Leila tomorrow. The thought of having to explain the baby to another person, to so many more people, was unnerving. At least Match wouldn't say a word, or think those unavoidable thoughts, like 'How could she be pregnant and not know it?' and 'She must be lying' and 'But she's still a baby herself'.

Another of the photos had been taken only a few months ago, yet she looked years younger than she now felt, standing here now in old leggings and a baggy jumper, still sore and uneasy on her feet. She recognised the background; she could pinpoint the exact location from the shape of that particular tree. The Polaroid had been snapped in their grounds during one of their signature grand family parties. The guy with his arm around her, Andrew, was her childhood sweetheart. They were smiling at the camera and pretending the summer didn't have to end, and they didn't have to go to university. They were pretending their relationship wasn't about to fizzle out over the course of a few half-hearted phone calls and messages, the way most long-distance relationships did. They were embracing the bubble, buying into the lie that youth lasted forever, and no one would ever have to compromise.

He wasn't going to like the reason she had returned home either. It wasn't his baby. He was away, at his own university on the other side of the country, pursuing his dreams. If she had let him, he would have married Tally and given her children. He would have been willing to wait university out. He might even have taken on the baby in the knowledge she wasn't his, but the love he had for Tally had all but disappeared now, because she had driven him away. She had never loved him back, despite trying to. She had been too young to be in love. Helena had always liked Andrew and she would have loved for the baby to be his.

A sudden noise interrupted Tally's rumination. She looked towards the source in surprise, momentarily confused. She saw a pink, scrunched up face with tightly screwed up eyes and it shocked her. Her arms jerked and that only made it scream louder. She looked towards her mother, pleading for help.

'She's hungry,' Helena encouraged, gesturing for Tally to sit on the edge of the bed.

Hesitant to comply, Tally slowly sat down, wincing more in anticipation than actual pain; the few stitches she had – probably inflicted when she had forgotten to take a deep breath between those last few pushes - were healing well.

'Now, lift your jumper,' Helena coached, copying how the midwife had helped at the hospital, putting on her newfound 'Everything will be okay' voice. 'Let her latch on like they showed you,' Helena reminded her daughter, praying the little thing would follow her instinct to nurse. Helena had never been expected to breastfeed and it hadn't even crossed her mind that she should try. Her own mother had seen to it that someone else fed the baby, Helena remembered having to fight just to keep Natalie in her arms, away from all of the helpful intruders.

'That's perfect,' Helena smiled, as she watched the baby settle onto her mother's breast, pretending this moment was as magical as it ought to be, as three generations sat huddled together, when all Helena could really think was 'I'm far too young to be a grandmother'.

The echo of water droplets hitting a metal bucket interrupted their sanctuary, squashing the moment. She pulled a grimace, catching Tally's questioning face as she noticed the bucket in the corner of the room. 'We'll fix it,' Helena nodded, 'that's just a temporary measure.'

Even in her baby-haze state, Tally had assumed a bucket standing in the room was never going to be a permanent fixture, yet she still did not ask why this was now her room, and why her plush four-poster bed sat empty in the other, leak-free, double-glazed, wing of their family home.

The ramshackle section of the house symbolised why they were here, and highlighted exactly why they had no choice, not that Charles accepted it. Charles was still trying to blame Helena for everything. She wondered if it would also be her fault that their innocent daughter had just given birth. It probably was. Helena had probably spoilt them both. Michael probably had a swarm of illegitimate children somewhere out there and she wouldn't be surprised if one of them rang the doorbell right now. Bad news comes in threes, so there must be something else on the horizon. Then she looked at her granddaughter and corrected herself. She wasn't bad news, not really, she was the best news ever, a guiding beacon of light in amongst the gloom.

After feeding, the baby continued to cry. Tally frowned down at her, wondering why a full tummy had not solved the predicament.

'She must need changing,' Helena said, looking around as if there might be a handy pack of nappies already in place, or perhaps even a plush changing station. She shook her head, remembering she had not had a chance to prepare, not even a whisper of forewarning, and the others had then let her down when she had hastily left to support Natalie.

The phone call had come during the early hours, and Helena had answered in a panic, fearing the worst, glancing towards the unfriendly digits on her bedside clock. A frightened boy, someone called Doug, was rambling away. His tone provided no respite from the terror that gripped Helena as she imagined her daughter's body cold on the pavement, perhaps hit by a car, or on the sticky floor of a toilet, convulsing from a drug overdose. And then he had said the word 'baby' and everything had turned on its head. Now it was not her daughter's life in question, but that of a child, of Helena's grandchild. A premature baby was fighting for its right to stick around for more than a few moments, having only just been gifted a small chance of survival in the outside world. Helena's heart had pulsed and a whole new piece of it emerged, blossoming in an instant, wrapping itself tightly around a tiny unknown person who only seconds ago had never, to her knowledge, even existed. The rush of love she experienced for someone she hadn't even met yet had been overwhelming, it was almost painful.

She had spent a week in hospital, sitting next to Tally's bed on a hard, uncomfortable pea-green chair, walking down bleak corridors and avoiding eye contact with strangers, gazing into the clear plastic cot, trying to ignore all the tubes and the bleeping sounds. Then they had finally been told that Tally would be okay, and the baby would be okay, that they were both allowed to go home, and now they were here, muddling through because they were expected to care for the tiny human without any help, to replace a team of around the clock staff and all their machines and monitors. After the rest of the family had enjoyed a week of warning there were still no nappies, because no one had thought about that. Not even the amazing Anna had pre-empted the need to keep a baby's bum dry, because she had her hands full enough as it was with the half-mad father and his irresponsible son, and the ongoing battle with the unwelcome house guests, and she wasn't even being paid this month because there was nothing left to give.

'I'll tell Michael to go.' Helena rushed out, glad to have been given something productive to do, and Tally listened as her heels clattered on the stairs, wondering for the first time ever if her mother even owned a pair of slippers.

She held on to the wriggling, bawling baby and was engulfed by a sudden panic at being left all alone with it. She remembered there were a few nappies left in the bag of emergency supplies her mother had bought in the pokey hospital shop when it had been announced the baby was going to be discharged. She looked hopefully at the door, but Helena was long gone. It was pointless trying to run after her because she knew from experience just how long it took to locate people in this maze of a house. Michael could be anywhere, in a proper room or hidden away in one of his many hideouts dotted around the house, most of which Tally had managed to discover over the years. She made a futile attempt to shush the baby, wishful that she may be able to stomach the crying before Helena returned, but then realised she was going to have to attempt a nappy change all by herself.

    She carefully lay the baby down on the thin and wiry carpet, remembering the plush carpets in her old bedroom. This new room stood in sharp contrast to the surroundings she had expected to encounter upon returning home. The space reminded her more of her university halls than her family home. She didn't have the capacity to wonder what had happened just yet. The baby flailed its limbs around, but otherwise remained immobile on the floor, unable to do anything but cry and thrash in protest. It struck Tally again that she was such a helpless little thing, programmed to elicit all the assistance she needed from her mother. Tally crouched down, and pulled open the poppers of the sleepsuit. Although it was in tiny baby size, her little rat-like baby was far too small for the baggy garment. She undid the next layer of clothing, another gift from the hospital staff which had been buttoned up by a friendly midwife. She pulled the clothing away from the baby's bottom half and braced herself to open the nappy. She unpeeled the tabs then gingerly folded down the front. Immediately, the baby started weeing again, as if to teach Tally a lesson for not tending to her sooner, and it sprayed over the edges of the nappy and onto the cheap carpet that Tally had been scrutinising. Tally instinctively tried to stop the flow with her fingers but ended up making more of a mess, covering her hands in urine. She looked around desperately for wipes even though she knew she didn't have any. There was a scarf on the chair. She grabbed it and pushed it onto the baby to stem the flow.

'Oh dear,' Helena said upon her return from dispatching Michael to the shops. She had also remembered the nappies in the hospital bag. She pulled out some wipes and a clean nappy, then held them out for Tally.

'You do it,' Tally mumbled, drying her fingers on a dry section of the scarf. It was going to need a good soak, or perhaps she would just chuck it.

Helena ignored how her daughter currently refused to care for her own baby and knelt down to take over, cursing as the seams of her fitted shirt strained and a few threads tore. She was going to have to start dressing like a grandmother, in oversized woollen cardigans and pleated brown skirts that hung down to an unflattering mid-calf length.

Once the baby had a fresh nappy on, she settled down. They both stared at the wet patch on the floor. 'We need a changing mat,' Helena said, adding another item to the ever-growing list of baby essentials.

'Does Anna do babies?' Tally asked.

'Anna has enough on her plate,' Helena said sternly. Anna probably did do babies, as Tally had put it, but that was not something they were going to ask. Although Helena respected Tally as the mother and would support her to the utmost degree, she was not prepared to stand back and allow the parenting of the baby to fall to anyone else. That was what she had done, and as a result she hadn't really got to know either of her children, she was too distanced from them by the rules and restraints of a well-to-do society. This was her chance to remove the barrier that existed between the generations within her family.

'Anyway, you've got an important decision to make.' Helena held out the baby, passing her back to her mother.

Tally took her reluctantly, watching as she stretched her arms and legs, going rigid for a moment and then relaxing. She turned her head into Tally's bosom, closing her eyes for another nap. She let out a little content sigh, the wet nappy and the scratchy floor already forgotten. She had never questioned the tubes and lights, and now she didn't question the lack of them. The baby just let life happen to her, and allowed the drama to wash over her. She accepted things for what they were, something that Tally was struggling with. As Tally stared at the helpless thing in her arms, wondering what she felt, she prepared herself for her mother to ask her if she was keeping it. They hadn't discussed that yet. They hadn't discussed anything. Tally hadn't had to face any difficult questions because up until this point there had been other more pressing matters, like whether or not the baby was going to survive. They could hardly consider if they wanted it when they didn't even know if it was going to live.

'What?' Tally asked, buying another second or two before she announced her decision.

'What are we going to call her?' Helena beamed.

Tally looked down at the little girl, noticing how her dark hair was already starting to rub off at the back where she usually rested her head, realising that Helena was far too much in love to allow anyone to even speak of getting rid of her. Tally didn't have the energy to fight her on it, and didn't completely trust her empty heart, so that was at least one decision already made.

'I just can't believe it,' Michael shook his head as Tally entered the sitting room. He raised a glass to his lips and hid a mischievous grin behind it. His mother was on high alert, but he was unable to resist. 'You went and got yourself knocked up and didn't even tell us.'

'That's enough, Michael,' Helena warned, her tone indicating that she was not going to put up with their bickering tonight.

Tally clenched her jaw. The baby had been put down for a nap, so she finally had some time to herself. She had managed to carefully transfer her into an empty storage box that would serve as a makeshift cot until someone went shopping. She didn't want to sit in her room and stare at it whilst it slept, so she had been forced to find somewhere else to go and for some reason this was the only room available to her. Every door leading back into the decent part of the house had been locked. Ignoring Michael's eyes on her as she crossed another hideous carpet, she lowered herself cautiously into the softest chair she could find, still wincing despite taking it slowly.

Michael was watching her candidly with an eyebrow raised, as if he didn't quite believe it.

'I don't get it,' he pondered, his drink having loosened both his nerve and his filter, 'How did you manage to hide being pregnant for nine months?' He sauntered over to the drinks cabinet.

'Michael!' Helena snapped, not wanting this to be discussed here and now, with Tally still reeling and Michael half-drunk. He was turning into his father and she had expected better of him.

'I didn't know,' Tally said in a small voice, blushing at the way her older brother had asked her outright, but also knowing that she should have expected just as much from him. He had always been a pig-headed bully and his show of chivalry from earlier was already over by the looks of it, now the initial shock had worn off.

'Yeah, right.' Michael poured himself another glass, shaking his head in total disbelief.

'It's possible,' Helena interjected, supporting Tally's story, even if she couldn't quite believe it herself. The midwives had played along as if it was perfectly normal to give birth out of the blue and Helena had not managed to work out if they genuinely thought it possible or if they had decided to support a patient who was in total denial. 'And she didn't carry the baby full term, she was estimated at eight weeks premature,' Helena added, because that made Tally's story a little more likely.

'How can someone not notice they've got a human being growing inside their belly, even if *only* for thirty-two weeks?' Michael scoffed.

'I thought I still had my period,' Tally said, hoping talk of menstruation would shut him up. She had spotted intermittently over the past few months, enough to make it appear as if she had been on a cycle of sorts.

'Sometimes,' Helena started, ready to launch into the 'ghost period' explanation offered to them by a sympathetic midwife, but Michael waved her attempt at an explanation away, scrunching up his face in disgust. He didn't want to hear about his little sister's period, even if he deserved to be made to squirm.

He fell quiet for a few seconds as he leaned against the dark wood of the cabinet and swilled his drink thoughtfully. Tally hoped his attack on her was now over. She wished she had stayed in her room, even if it had meant staring at the walls or the baby. He made a show of shaking his head again, unable to let it lie. He refused to hide his opinion – that there was no way Tally had not known, regardless of how early the baby had come, regardless of a mistaken period every now and then. He took another large gulp of whisky. 'Is the baby alright in the head, with all the drinking and drugs?'

'Stop right there!' Helena slammed her book down, having had quite enough of his cheek. She wished her children would just get along, at least occasionally. She had been stupid to think that becoming an uncle might have made Michael a nicer brother – or human being for that matter - instead he was using it as a new source of ammunition to hurl at his sister, whose lack of retaliation was worrying. Tally used to come back at him with a sharper tongue to put him in his place. He was running rings around her tonight, and their father – the only person on earth ever able to discipline them – was still nowhere to be seen.

'I didn't do drugs,' Tally protested, but her cheeks went a deeper red, because although she had never touched drugs, she had been drinking without restraint, living it up like a clichéd, non-pregnant university student. She had been poisoning her unborn child.

'You've been at university for an entire year, how could you *not* have done drugs?' Michael was seemingly disappointed she hadn't been putting her body – and her baby – at risk by taking recreational drugs. 'You were always such a bore, a secret pregnancy is probably the most interesting thing that's ever happened to you.'

Helena put her head in her hands, exasperated with Michael's attitude.

'It wasn't a secret,' Tally persisted, 'because even I didn't know.' If she had the energy she would get up and hit him even though he was much stronger than her. Growing up, she would always lose the physical fights, but now they were adults Michael couldn't hit her back anymore.

'Well, you picked a bloody wonderful year to bring home a dependant.' Michael made his way to the door, gesturing at the room they were in, which was dark and dingy and cold, 'As you can see, this place is completely baby-proofed.'

Tally had never even sat in this room before. In her mind, the only purpose of this part of the house had been for childhood adventures, conducted when Michael was in one of his rare sociable moods. They would sneak around pretending they were on a grand exhibition through mystical ruins, or ghost-hunting in a haunted house. Their parents didn't let them back here because it was in such awful disrepair, so they used to sneak in when they could play together unnoticed. The state of the section of the house they were now occupying had worsened significantly. Why her mum was currently curled up on an aging sofa and struggling to read in the half-light, Tally had no idea. They had a choice between two gorgeous gigantic sitting rooms on the other side of the house.

'I assume you noticed the bucket in your room,' Michael grinned falsely, laughing at the ridiculousness of it all, 'well I've got three. I swear I'm going to wake up one morning and see daylight peeping right back at me. We are the richest people in the county and yet we're living in the biggest shithole for miles. Ironic considering it's a 'must-see'.' He waggled his fingers sarcastically, and Tally frowned at his choice of words.

'I'm going to the pub,' he announced, despite having had more than enough to drink already. He glanced at Helena as he walked past, 'You can tell her.'

Tally watched her mother expectantly, waiting to hear what on earth was going on, but then the baby monitor she had placed on a rickety side table flashed. She braced herself and sure enough, the wailing that followed meant Tally was going to have to get back on her weary feet and try to figure out what could be wrong this time.

'Do you want me to help?' Helena asked, lowering her magazine in anticipation of an affirmative reply.

'No, I'll be okay.' It wasn't that Tally particularly wanted to tend to her baby on her own, it was just that she didn't want to listen to her mother coo and babble at the thing, as if she was completely demented.

Tally knew that she wouldn't be able to avoid her father forever. Her pulse quickened when he entered the kitchen. They would usually take breakfast in a large dining room, lined with full length windows looking out over the terrace, across their rolling gardens. Now they were on a cramped round table wedged into the same room as the kitchen. Anna was flipping eggs self-consciously, not used to the family sitting at such a close proximity, watching her cook. Michael was opposite Tally, wearing dark glasses because that's what they did in the movies. His mammoth hangover had quelled his aggression, so far all she had received from him was a stuck out tongue to which she had responded with a mature two fingers. No matter how old they were, they were always going to bicker, which Helena had finally accepted, so she just pretended not to see because she didn't want to start the day by scolding them.

'A bloody joke,' Charles muttered when he entered the room, looking about as if he still couldn't accept where they were eating.

'Oh, get used to it, Charles,' Helena snapped, almost completely out of patience despite it not even being nine in the morning. She was fed up with his constant barrage of snide comments. She proceeded to spread butter onto her toast with enough vigour to poke the knife straight through.

'It's like living on a battery farm. I'm an abused chicken.' Charles sat down with aplomb and Tally and Michael exchanged wry glances, smothering their involuntary smiles, because siblings could switch from enemies to best friends within seconds, no matter how crushing their previous insults may have been, and their father was hilarious, despite how terrifying he could also be. Charles had always been prone to his outlandish metaphors and it was at least comforting to know that this dire situation had not quelled his temperament. Although it sounded like he was jesting whenever he said anything like this, over the years they had discovered he really wasn't, he wasn't even aware he was being funny, and they had to ensure he never saw them laughing.

'Would you like to meet your granddaughter?' Helena asked pointedly, since Charles had not even acknowledged the baby in Tally's arms. He hadn't even said hello to Tally, acting as though it was perfectly normal for his daughter and her baby to join them at the breakfast table, when she should be half-way across the country preparing for her first lecture. She had been expecting an argument, so being overlooked was welcoming yet it was also unsettling. She coughed self-consciously when he finally regarded her.

'Shouldn't you be at university?' he asked her finally, ignoring the question, and the baby, acting as if no one had filled him in on the accidental birth scenario.

'I had to quit.' Tally looked to her mother for help.

'She can't take a baby into lectures, darling,' Helena sighed, wondering if her husband was finally becoming senile. This was the point in her life when she was going to regret marrying a much older man. He was going to lose his marbles and she wouldn't have the luxury of doing it with him. She was forty-one and he was seventy-four. The poor children were going to have to watch him crumble much earlier than most children would, and she would be expected to pick up the pieces. The manner in which he was drinking himself away didn't exactly help matters either. No one would thank her for holding it together whilst he degenerated, either. She had no option but to take drastic measures in order to save their family home, and neither Charles nor Michael were grateful. They openly blamed her, as if she hadn't been forced to take a raw deal. They hadn't realised just how close they had all been to leaving their family home completely and moving into a tiny bungalow in a grotty town somewhere.

Anna dished out the eggs, so everyone went momentarily quiet, even though she would still be able to hear every syllable uttered when she went back behind the kitchen counter because it was about three-foot away. Out of habit, they still waited patiently for her to finish her task. It was polite to save their bickering for when she had turned her back.

'I always thought it was a stupid idea, anyway, gallivanting off to university.' Charles said into his eggs.

'I remember,' Tally replied dryly, ignoring Michael's wiggling eyebrows. It had been a horrendous argument at the time and now it all seemed so pointless, a complete waste of energy, since she was stuck back here anyway, and no better off.

'I told you not to bother, what does a female need an education for?'

'Charles that is an outdated concept,' Helena warned, but Charles characteristically ignored her.

'Women are just here to *have babies*, right Father?' Michael winked at Tally.

'They are supposed to marry respectable men first.' Charles finally glanced down at the sleeping thing in Tally's arms, as if it was a flea-infested dog that had just snapped at his ankles. 'I don't suppose she came from a respectable man, did she?'

'Another outdated concept,' Helena interjected, taking the floor so that Tally didn't feel the need to respond to his question. Of course, they all wanted to know who the father was, but Tally was unlikely to divulge that information, especially around the breakfast table. It was possible she didn't have a clue who had fathered the baby. Helena had initially wondered if it was Doug, but soon discounted that upon meeting the soppy fellow. Her bets were elsewhere.

Tally was grateful for support. She knew her mother agreed with her husband, that marriage before babies was ideal – proper - but it was touching how Helena was not going to let the men put her down even if privately she was equally as disappointed with how her daughter's life was turning out. It also helped that Helena was completely besotted with the accidental baby.

'As much as I would love to see how this conversation plays out,' Michael said, standing up and wincing, 'I better get going.' He shot Tally a narrow-eyed look, perceptible even through his dark glasses, 'Apparently someone needs a shit load of baby paraphernalia.'

Tally looked at her mother questioningly as he left. 'I've sent him into town with a shopping list,' Helena explained.

'He's actually going for you?'

'He's going for you,' Helena replied, cutting into her egg, satisfied with the way the yolk escaped and soaked evenly into her damaged toast. It seemed there were still small victories to be had in life. 'Despite the despicable way he behaves, he'd do anything for you, Tally, and for your little baby now as well, so just take all his bullshit with a pinch of salt.'

Tally looked down at the bundle in her arms. She rarely heard her mother swear and it had momentarily thrown her, as had the concept that Michael potentially cared about the little human being in her arms, let alone her. She swallowed hard. 'Edith,' she said, after swilling the name around her mouth for a few moments, silently testing it one last time before she committed to it.

Helena paused, and the piece of egg half way to her mouth fell off the fork with a splat, sending droplets of yolk into the air.

'I've decided to call her Edith,' Tally repeated with growing conviction.

❄

'Excuse me, you can't go in there.'

The voice startled Tally, and her jolt woke up the baby. Edith was pressed to her chest, wrapped in a material sling, another generous gift from the hospital. Until Michael returned from town with a push chair it was the only method of baby transportation she possessed besides her aching arms.

'Brilliant, thanks for that.' Tally turned to face the stranger, wondering why some random bloke was standing on her yard, telling her she couldn't go into her own tack room. He was not much taller than Tally; stocky like a rugby player, with shortly cropped thick hair. He was wearing a dark burgundy fleece and faded jeans. His dark eyes were framed by long lashes. He had a wide-set jaw, and his nose was slightly ridged, as if he had broken it once in a scrum and had been lucky in the way it had healed.

'Oh.' The sight of a baby halted him in his tracks, 'I didn't realise you had a…' he seemed incapable of saying the word and Tally tried not to feel judged, not by some ignorant twit who was roughly her own age. 'Is it yours?'

'Well, I didn't steal it,' Tally hissed back, affronted that it could be so difficult to believe that the baby was hers. She agreed she didn't look fit to be a mother, it was an almost laughable concept even to herself, but she didn't exactly want everyone else to notice it so easily.

'Sorry.' He looked down at his feet, realising his question had been insulting and she was hardly going to have anyone else's screaming baby strapped to her chest. He was still compelled to ask the next, more pertinent, question. 'What are you doing here?'

'I want to see if Leila has nicked my jump saddle,' she explained whilst rocking from one foot to the other, attempting to settle Edith, shooting him a cold accusing glance for waking her. She wondered why she had felt the need to explain herself to him, when he was the trespasser. She should be asking him what he was doing here.

'I'm sorry, but members of the public have to wait for the tour to see the yard, if you purchase a ticket and,' he paused, processing her words. '*Your* jump saddle?' he asked, his brow creasing. This wasn't just a nosy visitor.

'Yes, for my horse.' She pointed at the grey nose sticking over the stable door. 'That horse, right there.' She had visited Match and enjoyed their reunion. He had briefly sniffed the baby but otherwise accepted it without even a blink, and then he had nudged her impatiently, asking to be let out into his field. As soon as I can bear it, I'll ride you again, she had promised, her spirits lifted as she considered Match as the silver lining to her being home without a degree, with a baby, whilst now being up to her eyeballs in student debt and with no real life prospects anymore. She pushed away the odd phrase he had used when he called her a 'member of the public'.

'Where's Grampy?' Tally asked the stranger, 'Is he off sick or something?' She continued to bob up and down as she spoke, thankfully Edith was quietening. 'It's not his arthritis flaring up again, is it?'

Grampy was the estate's handyman and had been tending to the horses as well as the gardens, and pretty much every other outdoor job that needed doing, for the last forty-odd years. He wasn't their real granddad, their grandparents were all dead, but since he was the closest thing they had, Michael and Tally had called him Grampy from the moment they could talk.

'You mean the ancient guy who used to work here?' He rubbed his chin, 'He quit. Something about being outraged. They would have fired him anyway to be honest, he could barely walk.' He had the decency to stifle laughter at the memory. Gauging her expression, he did not expect she would find it quite as amusing as he did. How the old and decrepit man had even managed to push a wheelbarrow still baffled him.

Tally frowned. Grampy had quit? And who were 'They'? She watched him walk across to Match and pluck his headcollar from a hook next to his stable. 'Hang on, what the heck are you doing?' she balked at the way Match welcomed him with a traitorous snuffle, as if he knew this stranger. 'Where's Leila?' she wondered if this was a boyfriend or someone else that she had roped in to help. Perhaps Leila was feeling sick and didn't want to come to the yard today. They had Grampy to do all the chores, but Leila still liked to get her hands dirty and help to look after the horses, just like Tally always had.

'Leila can only ride out of hours,' he explained, talking in riddles again. From the way he said her name it didn't sound like he really knew her, not enough to be a boyfriend of any sort. In fact, he uttered her name with disdain, as if she was just another inconvenience to him, just like Grampy, and just like Tally was being right now.

'Out of hours? And who are 'They'?' Tally asked, assuming all this oddness was connected. What exactly had Grampy been 'outraged' about? She hoped it was nothing Leila had done. Although her best friend could be a total cow, there was no way she would have done something to upset Grampy, she loved him as much as they did, having known him since she was eleven.

'Before nine and after five,' he said, glancing at his watch, 'It's twenty past nine, you're too late I'm afraid. I need to get him turned out and mucked out before the first tour at ten thirty.'

'Tour?' Tally looked down, because Edith had gone back to sleep. She still continued to rock on the spot, just in case. She was so used to jiggling around that she sometimes found herself doing it even when Helena was holding the baby. She lowered her voice as much as was possible whilst she was losing her patience with the guy. 'Can you just wait for a minute and tell me what the hell is going on? Who actually *are* you?'

He paused whilst mid-way through opening the stable door. Match boffed him with his nose, eager to escape his stable. 'I'm Simon,' he said, 'I'm with British Estates.'

'What?' Tally asked automatically, flinching at the last two words, not fully understanding him. But then she recognised the name, and the logo stitched on to his corporate fleece, and even before understanding had sunk in, she was hit with terror. She thought back to the magazine Helena had been flicking through last night. I should have known, she shuddered, because Mum only ever reads trashy novels with half naked, beautiful people on the cover.

British Estates was a business that owned a nationwide portfolio of stately homes and gardens. They opened the doors of once private gigantic houses for nosey visitors in order to generate an income. Most of their estates were gifted due to the owner's inability to maintain the expensive upkeep or they were left to them in wills when there was no obvious beneficiary. Surely, they weren't one of those impoverished families? Surely they hadn't been forced to give away their family home?

'Where are you going?' Simon asked as she turned and marched off, realising he hadn't even found out her name. 'You can't go that way,' he called after her feebly, stuck holding the horse, unable to stop her from meandering from the designated footpath.

'It's my home,' she called back, too enraged to remember that she was supposed to be keeping her voice down so she would not wake the baby, 'I'll go wherever I bloody well want!'

Tally found Michael in her room.

'Before you have a go at me, I'm only here to build this stupid cot,' Michael said defensively, holding up a screwdriver and pointing to the flat pack on the floor. 'By the way I had to tie it to the roof and it nearly slid off halfway home and killed a bunch of people, myself included.'

'Have you seen this?' Tally held up the magazine she had located in their new, gross sitting room. She had thumbed through it until she found the article that she had suspected was hiding in there. A four-page spread on their home, complete with a smiling picture of Helena who looked thrilled to be handing six generations of family history over to some corporation. There was a load of waffle describing the 'must-see' aspects of their house and gardens all typed up in a gigantic maroon font. 'What the fuck is British Estates doing here?' Tally exploded, glad to have finally found someone to vent her shock and anger at. She looked down at Edith, and then decided she didn't have to censure her language around her, not yet anyway. This was a justified excuse for expletives, anyway.

'Thank God, they finally told you.'

'Mum and Dad didn't tell me, some bloody idiot called Simon did! He told *me* to get off *my* yard. He said we can only ride outside of visiting hours. What the hell, Michael?'

'I know, it's crazy. That's why we're stuck in here, in the servant's quarters.' Michael pointed at the bucket, which, just to highlight their predicament, was holding a good inch of rain water.

'Why did no one tell me?'

Edith started crying, properly awake this time, probably because Tally swore, so Tally extracted her from the sling and sat down on the edge of the bed.

'I guess they thought they could wait until you got back from university before telling you,' Michael shrugged. 'Obviously they weren't expecting you back home before Christmas.' He glanced at the baby, and then saw Tally was lifting her top. 'Don't get your boob out in front of me,' he snapped, horrified, 'I'll actually be sick.'

'Oh, grow up, I've got to feed her,' Tally argued back. She was choosing to ignore his quip about her returning home long before the Christmas holidays.

Michael pointedly turned away and busied himself with extracting the cot from the packaging and figuring out how it went together, deciding it was too early to admit defeat and glance at the instructions.

'Okay, so why didn't *you* tell me? You've got my number, right?' Tally raised an eyebrow. As much as they hated each other half the time, they were still supposed to be a united front when it came to battling their parents. 'Maybe we could have done something? By the way you can't see any boob now.'

Michael cautiously turned and was relieved to see her jumper and the back of Edith's head blocking any sight of his sister's breast. 'I went through it with Mum. There was literally nothing else we could have done, getting to stay here is already a huge compromise in their minds. Inviting those bastards in was the only way we could keep living here.' He paused, and used the silence to locate a screw. 'I guess I just didn't know how to tell you.' As much as he pretended to be strong, losing their childhood home had been a huge blow. He didn't know how he was going to be able to put it into words and tell his little sister without breaking down; crying in front of her just wasn't an option.

'How on earth did they let it get this bad?'

Michael shrugged. They both knew. Their father. He had no concept of money, or bills, or even consequences for that matter; he enjoyed living the high life and Helena was unable to control his spending and was also guilty of her own excess. His drinking had steadily increased over the years, which probably fuelled further spending habits, and the household took more money to run than Charles could even comprehend. The regular expenses of both Anna and Grampy's wages had steadily drained their reserves, and no one had given a thought to ever topping them back up. Despite never mentioning it, the family had noticed the general upkeep sliding, as the house threatened to become dilapidated, but because the degeneration had occurred so gradually it had almost gone by unnoticed. It had certainly never been mentioned. It wasn't until they had all stood back and took a long cold stare at their affairs - the way British Estates had done when considering their final offer - when they had realised just how poorly the estate had been managed, and just how much their blinkered living had contributed to the loss of wealth, control and autonomy.

When it came to lack of available funds for maintenance and repair, Tally's horse and university education probably hadn't helped. In the end, Helena had been forced to approach British Estates and practically beg them to step in and save them, which hadn't started off negotiations from any position of strength. The out of hours rule had been an imposition placed on the family, and the only basis upon which British Estates would allow them to remain on site.

'Don't worry, I've got the stupidly expensive car and have never worked a day in my life. I've never contributed anything, this wasn't exclusively your fault,' Michael said, seeing her blaming herself and taking a rare time out from making fun of her to instead try to make her feel better.

'They should have said something.' Tally shook her head. They had assumed the family money was unending, but she supposed the simple maths of it just didn't add up. They had been blissfully ignorant and assumed it grew on the trees in the orchard. The income sitting in inheritance pots was finite, and the outgoings just continued to pour. Their only real wealth was the estate itself, and that was why they had been forced to offer it to British Estates in order to keep a portion of it over their heads.

'It was too late by the time we bought the horse and the car, anyway. They don't have cash, that's the key issue. They've got all of this,' he pointed through the window, at the acres and acres of rolling land, 'but nothing to put into keeping it going.'

'Which is why the roof is leaking.' Tally looked at the bucket.

'Yep. The nice part of the house is for the visitors, and if they weren't paying to snoop then that roof would soon be leaking too.'

'Is this why Mum and Dad are arguing?'

'He blames her because she arranged it all. He can't understand that British Estates saved us from having to leave. That's why his drinking has become even worse.'

Tally bit her lip. To have to leave the property would have hurt them all far deeper, but her father was never going to see it like that because he lived in a dream world just like they both had, where money was no object, and a distinguished family history triumphed every hurdle.

'And Grampy?'

'He couldn't face being told what to do, and they were going to fire him anyway. He's way beyond retirement age, they just saw him as a relic.'

'I heard,' Tally said darkly, remembering the way Simon had found it funny how their beloved Grampy worked on the estate. He had no heart, and no understanding of what his stupid company had taken from them.

'How is he going to cope?' Tally found her lip quivering.

'He's doing alright.' Michael started screwing a piece of the cot together. 'It's not like he ever needed the money, he just worked here for the love of it.'

'That's what worries me, is he going to be okay without us? Without anyone?'

'He's only in the village so he's not going to be without us. I visit him every Wednesday. You two should come along next time.'

Tally smiled at her brother's back. Although he was a horrible selfish twit sometimes, he did occasionally surprise her.

'Hey, at least it means the heat is off you for this latest fuck up.' Michael grinned at her, winking at the baby, making Tally recoil as he referred to Edith as a 'fuck up'. She immediately regretted her kind thoughts about her brother, even if she couldn't exactly disagree with the sentiment. Edith was, technically, the biggest fuck up of her life.

'I can see why Dad's angry, but it's not Mum's fault.' She looked down at Edith as she suckled, oblivious to their predicament, unable to appreciate that despite appearances, the family she had been born into was dirt poor. 'I mean, are we actually going to adhere to these out of hours rules?'

Michael laughed, picking up the next piece of the cot, still being stubborn about his decision to ignore the instructions despite being unsure about where the piece he was holding actually went. 'What do you think?'

'Oh. My. God.' Leila halted Match, and Tally was sad that she had stopped riding. It was lovely to watch her horse being put through his paces, even if she did envy Leila for being able to just get on and ride whenever the fancy took her, not encumbered by a baby, or stitches. 'That is *your* baby?' Leila stared down at the pair, over the fence of the arena. It was beginning to get dark and the floodlights were on, causing Edith to blink up towards the towering horse with uncertainty.

Leila was also restricted by the new situation; she could now only ride 'out of hours'. It didn't seem to faze her, because she had a nine to five job anyway. In her mind, Tally was still the rich kid with the amazing facilities, and whilst Leila loved her oldest friend dearly, she wasn't about to start feeling sorry for her, or her family, on the basis that they were now supposedly poor.

'Meet Edith,' Tally smiled, trying to ignore the general shock and horror that every introduction to a teenager's surprise baby was certain to evoke. It would be nice if someone actually looked pleased to see her, rather than gobsmacked.

'So, you like, gave actual birth to it?' Leila's eyes were giant orbs as she considered this with morbid fascination, and Tally groaned inwardly at the realisation she would have to share all the gory details with her at some point.

'Yes,' Tally said, mentally replacing the 'it' with a 'her', because although she was still adjusting to the idea that she had given birth to another human being, Edith was not going anywhere – Helena had made that much clear - and no matter how strange and unwelcome Tally found motherhood, Edith was a little girl and not an inanimate object.

'And you, like, didn't know you were pregnant until it finally came out?' Leila narrowed her eyes, because if Tally *had* known then surely she would have confided in her best friend. Because Leila couldn't face the prospect of Tally keeping something like this from her, and because *someone* had to have Tally's back, Leila was fully prepared to believe her crazy story.

'Something like that,' Tally shrugged, impatient to get these questions out of the way. It was going to be so tiresome having this conversation over and over again, each time never really convincing the other person that any of it was true. She had to prepare herself for more adverse reactions than Leila's fairly kind, albeit shocked response. Her best friend was duty bound to take it all pretty well and at least try to believe her. Leila hadn't asked for details on the sex that must have led to the baby yet, which was a relief because Tally wasn't prepared to share that with anyone, not now and probably not ever. That was something she wasn't even willing to face herself.

'And you're home now, for good?' Leila asked, pausing slightly as she decided how to frame the question.

'Yes,' Tally replied carefully. Leila's hesitant tone suggested that it was difficult for Leila to accept her unexpected return home as entirely good news. 'Although, I'll still need your help with Match, so don't stress about losing him.' Tally guessed it was the threat of another horse rider that was giving Leila a cause for concern. Leila would now have to share Match again, and compromise by riding old ploddy Peter, like she was forced to do before Tally had left her in peace.

'Oh, I wasn't thinking about that,' Leila said, although Tally couldn't help noticing how she had visibly relaxed. 'I'm sorry you had to leave university. But it isn't all that special to have a degree these days, things will still work out.' She said with an encouraging smile, pretending her friend hadn't just royally fucked up her entire life prospects. Leila knew going away to study had been Tally's dream throughout secondary school, so her words were hollow. Someone had to gee up her friend, though.

'Thanks.' Tally appreciated the attempt Leila was making at smoothing it all over. Leila had shared the exact same perspective on university before Tally had announced she wanted to study. Leila saw a giant mansion and figured Tally didn't really need to do anything with her life, as if it was already perfect. She was of the same ilk as Tally's father when it came to life planning, which was probably why she worked in a local café for pittance and spent literally all her money on shopping and partying. She was basically the female version of Michael, without the nastiness.

'Do you want a go?'

Tally glanced down at Match, who was trying to sneak in a doze.

'He's nicely warmed up for you,' Leila added, wondering why Tally hadn't jumped at the chance.

'The midwife said I would have to wait six weeks,' Tally said, her voice wavering. She hadn't really considered getting onto Match this soon. Logistically, riding was going to be tricky for her from now on because every time she wanted to ride she would have to ask someone to look after Edith. She guessed that Helena would be a willing volunteer since she was smitten with her new grandmother duties, probably partly because Edith gave Helena a break from the rest of the household and was the only family member who didn't hold her personally responsible for losing their family home. Tally knew that Helena would jump at the chance for some uninterrupted time with her granddaughter, and she now wondered if she would be able to start riding regularly. The therapy aspect of horse riding could help her to process all the other mess she had to deal with whenever she was out of the saddle; it could be a good distraction for her, a way to rediscover herself. It wasn't going to solve anything but carving out some time for herself away from the drama of new babies, drunk fathers and uninvited management teams might make her feel better.

'Yeah, but your midwife didn't consider one thing,' Leila said, kicking her feet free of the stirrups, apparently already over the baby interrogation because talking about horses was so much more interesting.

'What's that?' Tally asked, smiling at her friend, because it was a relief not to feel like they should dutifully discuss babies. She wanted to talk about horses too, and she could tell Leila was about to say something silly from the cheeky grin on her delicate face as she launched herself out of the saddle and landed nimbly at Match's shoulder.

'You're a horse rider. You're as hard as nails.'

Tally laughed, remembering how it still hurt a little to sit down or go to the toilet. Screw it, she decided, accepting the hat and passing over the baby, which Leila was prepared to stomach holding awkwardly, just for now, out of stanch loyalty. Tally took the reins and bounced on her toe, anticipating the smack of pain to come. One, two, three, and she was up, and problems like lost houses and unplanned babies seemed smaller than they just had, as her problems always did when she was sitting astride a horse.

✻

Tally stared at the baby as it wriggled around in the cot, screaming. She was in a daze, numbed by lack of sleep and all out of ideas. Helena staggered into the room, the door now permanently open as Tally accepted that she needed her mother's help more than she needed any privacy. The concept of personal space had gone out of the window the moment the paramedic had asked Doug to 'take a look down there' and again when the midwife had casually asked for permission to examine her internally.

'Hungry?' Helena asked, tightening the silk tie on her impractically thin dressing gown before reaching down to scoop up Edith. Tally didn't bother pointing out she had only just put her down, because rocking her in her arms had not worked. Desperately telling Edith to shut up hadn't worked either and had only resulted in her feeling guilty as well as exhausted. Their bedrooms had been so far apart previously that Helena wouldn't have heard a baby crying from Tally's room. Living practically on top of each other had altered things, and whilst Helena found it handy to be sleeping so close to her darling grandchild, Charles and Michael were unimpressed by the regular awakenings.

'She doesn't want to latch,' Tally shrugged. She hadn't laid down all night. She had been sat up in bed, attempting to feed, rocking Edith, intermittently placing her down in her cot then picking her back up again because she refused to settle. A few times Edith had nodded off whilst in Tally's arms, but then Tally had slipped into a doze and woken shortly afterwards with a start, slumped over the baby, aware of how dangerous it was to fall asleep like that.

'I just want to lie down,' Tally complained, her voice cracking, 'I want to go to sleep.' She crawled into bed, leaving her mother to calm the baby.

'I think she's got a bit of colic,' Helena said to the shape of her daughter below the covers, 'this phase will pass, I promise.'

Right now, Tally couldn't imagine an end to the current cycle. As far as she knew, colic happened to horses, not babies. 'How did you do this?' she muttered from below the duvet, knowing this selfish time out would have to end in a moment, because her mother was not going to just stand there and rock her baby while she slept.

'The same way you are, I just gritted my teeth and somehow got on with it.'

'That's not true.' Tally sat up reluctantly and held her arms out to take the baby. 'You had lots of help.' She could remember a nanny, who used to not only care for them but who also used to play with her and her brother, until they were too old to want to play with grownups.

'Things were different back then,' Helena admitted, regarding the cramped bedroom, wondering once again how they had ended up in this ramshackle section of the house, then reminding herself this had all been her doing. 'I missed out on this.' She looked back down at the baby, somehow smiling sweetly as if Edith was not purple from all the bawling, 'I want to treasure it this time around.'

'Be my guest,' grumbled Tally, opening her dressing gown to try to quieten Edith with milk again.

Edith decided that in fact, she did want a drink, probably because she had worked up an appetite with all that crying, so there was a moment of calm where the walls fell silent and the house seemed to take a deep breath during the interlude. Helena sat down on the bed, and Tally could see her shoulders drooping.

'I am terribly sorry about all of this,' her mum said. She wished Edith was in the purpose-built nursery in the main wing of the house, and that Tally was enjoying the luxury of her old room and giving herself some much-craved space. Helena sensed the baby was exposed to the tension they were all experiencing. The family had endured the fall out of being up-rooted from their home, and then tortured by having to live on the fringes, watching from a distance as other people poked their nose around, waiting for the daily curfew to lift which even then did not permit them full access to the house. Helena worried that it impacted Edith somehow, and that the stress reached down even to her small shoulders.

'It's not your fault, Mum, no matter what Dad says. You didn't really have a choice. Michael knows it too, despite his stupid remarks.' Tally looked at her mother's tired face and reflected that she was not used to seeing her without makeup. Without the usual war paint on, her mother seemed smaller, older, and more vulnerable. The weight of the rest of the family on her small shoulders was visible tonight, reflected in the small brown age spots starting to appear on her once sun-kissed cheeks.

Helena carried her own guilt for spending so recklessly, on new shoes and handbags and ornaments and whatever else it was that she fancied at the time. The endless extravagant parties she hosted with aplomb seemed such a waste of time and precious money now all those supposed friends had disappeared back into the woodwork upon the news of their now lowly status; they had all gone back to their own secure houses to smirk.

'It's not exactly ideal for raising a child though, is it?' Helena looked over at Edith, thinking she deserved better, embarrassed that her generation had let Edith down by frittering away the last of the money. Helena was afraid her granddaughter would resent her one day, just like the others did now. She should have dealt with it sooner, on her own terms, and been a bit smarter about it all. Perhaps she could have opened up the house without British Estates. Being a lady of leisure, she would have had time to put in all the research on running a business. All those years of family money and it had run out before reaching their first grandchild.

'Hey, between five and nine she's got it all,' Tally joked dryly, thinking of their stupid curfew designed to ensure they didn't bother the visitors.

'You really helped me out, you know, by not having a tantrum like the other two. I appreciate it.' Helena reached over and squeezed Tally's leg through the covers.

'I could hardly take the moral high ground,' Tally pointed out.

Her mother hadn't lost the plot at discovering Tally had given birth, so Tally owed it to her to keep her cool over this disastrous news. The only thing she couldn't hide was her disappointment at not having an inkling about their financial predicament. 'You could have told me sooner, I thought we told each other everything?' Tally had been home for the summer holidays not long before the acquisition had taken place, and yet Helena had continued to throw lavish parties as if money was no object. Tally had thought she knew her mother pretty well, but she hadn't noticed a change in her demeanour, she had no inkling as to what was about to happen to their home.

'I just didn't know how to phrase it.' Helena looked down at her manicured toenails. The last party of the summer had been held as a private goodbye to her old lifestyle, partly out of futile defiance but mainly through nostalgia and a smidge of denial. It seemed pointless to try to save the last dregs of cash when the paperwork was signed, and the news was waiting for them on the horizon. Helena had been basking in the eve of summer, deciding that tomorrow when the last guest had gone she would face up to the idea that winter was coming. 'Besides,' she nodded towards Edith, 'some things are harder to tell than others, wouldn't you agree?'

Tally bristled, because that was the first time Helena had hinted that she thought Edith was not quite the surprise Tally had insisted. Rather than protest and repeat her story, she simply blinked and pretended Helena hadn't said anything.

'Will we have to sell Match?' she asked, worried he was another expense they could do without. They weren't exactly charging Leila to horse share, and she wouldn't be able to afford it even if they tried. Tally didn't want to risk losing her best friend over money.

'No, we can't,' Helena said firmly, 'Match is family, and we don't abandon family.'

She looked back to Edith and Tally got the distinct impression she was thinking about the way Tally had been unsure of the baby. I'm still unsure of the baby, Tally corrected. She was connected to the little thing but she was also struggling to see her as anything more than a thing. She would look down at her and feel nothing, besides a gripping fear that she was stuck with the infant forever. She watched Helena's eyes light up with love at just the sight of Edith and wondered why her own eyes remained distant when they should be programmed to shine just as brightly. Helena's heart would visibly swell whenever she picked up the child, but Tally's would remain deflated.

'I don't know if I love her,' Tally whispered, ashamed of her own thoughts and feelings.

Helena's grip tightened on her daughter's leg as she finally admitted what Helena had been fearing. 'Give it time,' she pleaded, 'you're still adjusting.'

Tally looked down and wondered if time would help. Edith had stopped feeding and was finally asleep, with her small steel-coloured eyes only half closed. Tally carefully detangled herself from the bedding and lowered her gently into the cot, reflecting that despite the lack of feeling, she was still determined to care for her, to go through the motions of being a committed mother, for Edith's sake. Helena also needed the baby here. Tally set her mind to mothering as if it was employment, not instinct, as if she was doing it all for Helena as some kind of favour.

'When are you going to talk to Andrew?' Helena tilted her head.

'Andrew?' Tally was surprised by his mention. But then, it was only natural Helena would assume. If anyone had to gamble, then the odds would be very much in his favour. Tally was going to have to face him at some point and present him with the baby. 'I'm sorry, Mum,' Tally shook her head sadly, wishing things were different and she didn't have to disappoint her mother all over again, 'he's not the father.'

❄

'Grampy, what happened to your garden?' Tally stared out of the kitchen window at the tangled mass of greenery. It was beyond chaotic and wouldn't even pass off as an informal cottage garden. It made her wonder if the wildflower borders back home were merely accidental and were not actually carefully contrived. Perhaps Grampy really was a feeble old man and they had all been kidding themselves that he would be able to keep up as their handyman.

Tally had joined Michael on his weekly visit. His stupid sports car only had two seats, so there was no chance they were going to get a baby in the back. Being his usual selfish self, Michael had driven ahead and left Tally to push the pram along the winding road from their estate into the village, trying to make her feel better by pointing out she only had a pram because he had bought it for her, even if it had been under duress from their mother. It hadn't even occurred to Michael that he could have offered to accompany his sister and new niece for the walk.

Grampy chortled as he stirred the cups. 'Do you think I ever felt like gardening here after a whole day of it at your place?' He shuffled back and forth to the table, bringing one cup at a time. It made Tally realise how much he had given to their family, how much of his life he had dedicated to them. He had gone above and beyond the role of an employee and had become family himself, as his longstanding nickname suggested.

'I suppose you can crack on with it now then, eh?' Michael winked, before taking a noisy slurp of his drink.

Tally frowned at him, unable to appreciate the joke, even though she knew he was only making light of the situation in an attempt to cheer up Grampy.

'Who's this then?' Grampy leaned over the pram, causing Edith to promptly burst into tears.

'Sorry, she's not used to strangers.' Tally catapulted into action, mortified that her baby had reacted so badly to Grampy. She supposed being unexpectedly loomed over by an unknown person was rather daunting. 'Her name is Edith.'

'Ah well, I guess I will be a stranger to her, now that I've been sacked,' Grampy sighed, sitting down with grim acceptance of his enforced retirement. 'I once courted a lass called Edith,' he wiggled his finger at the baby in a futile attempt to stop her from crying, 'she wasn't as pretty as you though.'

'I hope she had more hair!' Michael exclaimed.

'She must have got her hair from you, Tally, because you were nearly bald until you were a year old, everyone that met you mistook you for a boy.' Grampy smiled at the memory, and the memories of both children running around his ankles whilst he pretended to be annoyed that they were disrupting his planting, or his leaf sweeping, or whatever else he had been up to.

'Do you miss it, Grampy?' Tally asked, trying to steer the conversation away from genetics. She couldn't bear someone mentioning the father, and what Edith might have inherited from him. The idea of her looking anything like him frightened her. Grampy confirming Edith had hair like Tally's was a relief, but there were still eyes and lips and so many other features she might have got from 'him'.

'Every day.' Grampy pursed his lips together forlornly.

'You couldn't do it forever though, could you?' Michael pointed out. 'You had to retire at some point.' He watched as Grampy lowered his drink onto the table with shaking hands.

'You know, I remember you two when you were that age,' he said, allowing himself another few seconds to indulge in the baby, before tackling Michael's question. 'I knew it wasn't going to last forever. It would have been nice to leave on my own terms though.' His eyes darkened, and Tally wondered if he blamed Helena, too.

'Well, it's not the same without you, Grampy,' Tally said, whilst rocking the pram back and forth in an attempt to quell Edith's crying. 'We don't like your replacement very much.'

'That strapping young fellow, he could carry a hay bale under each arm.' Grampy looked down at his wrinkled hands and accepted that it was the end of an era.

'Yes, but I bet he doesn't have any magic plasters,' Michael said, remembering the way they would always run to Grampy when they were kids, seeking his help when one of their epic adventures went awry.

Tally was surprised he would even admit to remembering the magic plasters Grampy used to give them whenever they presented him with a grazed arm or a bashed knee. From what she could recall, the only magic thing about them was the star pattern, other than that they were ordinary plasters. Something about the way Grampy put them on and distracted them from their injury had convinced them both they possessed magic. It was actually Grampy who was truly magical.

'Match doesn't like him half as much,' Tally lied. Match didn't seem to mind that Grampy had been replaced, because Simon still fed him at regular intervals.

Grampy grunted, doubting Match's loyalty. 'As long as you kids remember I'm here, I'll be alright, especially if you bring this little treasure over to visit.' Despite the baby's wary stare,

Grampy smiled warmly at Edith, 'That garden could do with some attention, it'll keep me busy for a while.' He turned his head back out of the window. 'And go easy on that new kid, he's just trying to do his job.'

'He didn't even care that it was our home,' Tally complained, remembering how Simon had sneered at the idea of Grampy mucking out. It was pretty hard to believe when you saw the wizened old man, but somehow, over all these years, the stables had remained impeccably clean, and the hedges had remained neat, and the flower beds were permanently weeded. How he had juggled it all, whilst keeping one eye on two children, Tally couldn't even begin to fathom. Simon didn't deserve to have Grampy sticking up for him, and Tally refused to accept that Grampy didn't have much left in him. Just like the house, no one had noticed him deteriorate over the years, nor had they seen his standards of workmanship start to slip.

'We love you, Grampy.' The sentiment burst from her chest as she revelled in what it had been like to be young and naïve, not having to worry about the world. Grampy symbolised a time of blissful naivety, constant protection and no knowledge of all the hurtful things the outside world could bring. Sitting here in his kitchen with nothing to do except tend to his own small garden was evidence that change was inevitable, and all good things had to come to an end.

She was gripped with an overwhelming fear of mortality, for not only herself but also for everyone around her who she loved. She looked at Edith and it perplexed her to think that one day, she must die too. She wished she had never bothered going to university, because she had lost an entire year – the last year - of enjoying her family home. University had been a complete waste of time. She had expected the house to just sit there and wait for her, for things to remain perfect and unchanged forever. Instead, events had gone spinning out of control, and it had all started with that awful, unspeakable night.

Edith finally stopped looking at Grampy with mistrust and dropped off to sleep, turning her head into her pram and smacking her lips with content. *It's not your fault*, Tally thought, surveying the baby as she succumbed to sleep and her face went still, oblivious to the critical stare, *you can't help what you symbolise.*

'I love you too, both of you.' Grampy looked from Tally to Michael. He then glanced at Edith before locking his eyes onto Tally. 'You must learn to love little Edith too, because she needs it.'

'I do,' Tally said automatically, surprised by what he was insinuating, scared he had seen right through her. Of course, he had, he always did.

✻ Before Edith ✻

Tally stretched her limbs out, enjoying the heat as it soaked into her skin. It would be unbearable soon, but the pool was only inches away, promising to cool her down whenever she needed it, which allowed her to withstand a little more heat than usual. The inviting water lapped against the tiled wall, making gentle slapping sounds, threatening to lull Tally off to sleep. She was lying on the wide white perimeter stones, choosing proximity to the water above the comfort of the sun loungers. She tried not to move too much, because the untouched stone was painfully hot. Leila was perched on the adjacent side, sitting on the short edge and dangling her legs in, kicking her feet backwards and forwards, creating the mini waves that splashed by Tally's ear.

'The weather is getting more extreme,' Leila commented, shielding her eyes so she could look accusingly towards the sun, as if she might be able to see the additional weather bearing down on them. The heat wave had been forewarned and there were hopes – and fears - it would last all summer.

'You're so British,' Tally exclaimed, laughing at the banal choice of topic. She couldn't blame her friend, though, because both of their brains were fried from a heady mix of scorching sun and the aftermath of exam season. She didn't even open her eyes as she spoke. It would be indulgent to have a nap now, in the early afternoon. They had only recently finished school, and not just for the summer, but forever. The holiday stretched out ahead of them, bringing a sense of excitement for the freedom and peace at the idea of three months with nothing to do but ride, swim and relax. This was their last summer as adolescents and they were determined to enjoy themselves, considering it as the calm before the storm; the last big hurrah before new challenges would begin.

They certainly deserved the break; both of them had been studying hard and had then taken a string of exams. After weeks cooped up in their bedrooms revising, they were now indulging in some well-deserved rest. Tally was pretty confident with her results, but Leila was not so sure. Of the two girls, Tally had always been the most academic and usually had to force Leila to work alongside her, always wasting energy refocusing her on the task at hand. Leila needed the direction and was more than happy with just scraping by. Without Tally, she would have probably flunked. Leila already knew what she was going to do with her life. There was a small café in town that needed a waitress and the job was as good as hers, all she had to do was drop by with her CV. Although, because Leila was Leila, she hadn't got round to it yet and that didn't worry her.

The only real thing concerning them about their future, the blip on the horizon, was the distance between their chosen places for the next few years, and coming to terms with how they would not be able to live in each other's pockets forever. Leila would be staying at home, as she lived within walking distance of the prospective café, whereas Tally was about to relocate to the other side of the country. Tally tried not to think too hard about September, when she would be starting university and moving far, far away from Leila and Match - and everything else she knew and loved. She only thought about today, and perhaps tomorrow, and ignored anything further ahead.

'We watched a documentary on it last night – climate change.' Leila seemed determined to continue the mundane subject, unwilling to accept her friend's lack of interest. Tally couldn't be bothered to muster a response. 'You know, some people think it's a myth.'

If Leila really thought Tally had the energy for a serious conversation about climate change, then she was going to be sorely disappointed.

'My dad has a name for those kinds of people,' Leila said sternly, determined to keep the one-sided conversation going. 'You can't ignore these hotter summers and the wetter winters.' She looked around, as if the day offered all the proof you could ever need. 'I mean, it's *boiling.*'

Tally spent a few moments imagining all the possible choice names Leila's father might have for the ignorant people out there, and the way the three of them had probably discussed this last night whilst huddled on their sofa watching the documentary. Any debate they were about to have would be unfair because Leila had the advantage of cherry picking from the conversation with her parents. Tally had sat her maths A-level just two days ago, and business studies the day before that, so the last thing she needed was to be presented with any more information. She was tired of learning and unsure if her mind had the capacity for any more facts, figures or statistics. It was difficult to consider the glorious weather as a bad thing; if Leila was right about the hotter summers then global warming was going to result in a nice tan.

'Is this the real reason you made friends with me?' she asked finally, opening her eyes a fraction to take in the clear sky above them. If humans were to be blamed for that expanse of blue then it was hard to begrudge them. She dropped her right arm into the cool water to exaggerate her point.

'I didn't make friends with you just because of your pool!' Leila said, with mock horror, 'What kind of person do you take me for?'

Tally's smile grew wider because she knew what was coming.

'I'll have you know,' Leila continued, the laugh already on the edge of her voice, spoiling her mock outrage, 'I made friends with you because of your *horse*!'

Tally chuckled. Her horse, Match, was grazing peacefully nearby, in the giant paddock next to the garden, munching grass side by side with her brother's horse, Peter. Michael didn't ride anymore so, whilst Leila preferred Match, Peter was always available so they could ride together. Everything Tally could ever want was right at her fingertips, and some days she would pause for a moment to pinch herself. Despite growing up with it, and not knowing anything different, she was still aware of her privilege, something her brother accepted with a lot less humility than she did. She allowed Leila to joke about it, because she could trust her motives. On that first day of secondary school eight years ago, Leila had plonked herself onto the plastic seat opposite Tally and outright asked her if she could sit there, with no clue of the family riches, and no plan of moving her bum in the unlikely event Tally said no.

Tally turned her head to appraise her oldest friend. She hadn't really changed over the years, except for the addition of small breasts that were currently proudly on display in her string bikini top. She complained about them, especially when comparing herself to Tally's generous curves, but they suited her petite build perfectly and besides, they were much more practical when it came to all the swimming and horse riding. Leila's hair was long and dark – almost black - and so naturally poker straight it was difficult to believe she hadn't achieved the style with hair straighteners. Once again, it was in sharp contrast to Tally's bouncy curls, although they did share a similar hair colour, with Tally's slightly lighter, more chocolate in hue. Leila's eyes were as wide and curious as ever, with her petite face never really having caught up with them, and the freckles on her cheeks made her look much younger than she wanted to be regarded, especially now they were old enough to consider sneaking out to procure alcohol.

Tally had normal sized eyes, clear normal skin, and generally regarded herself as the least exotic of the pair. Leila caught the attention of boys. Tally would just make do with the cast offs, or the less attractive best friend. It was a miracle Andrew had chosen her first and was also probably the main reason Tally had allowed him to hang around. That was all fine; she had never really had much interest in boys, not until the last year of school at least, and Andrew was there to scratch her itch, even if she was aware that he liked her a lot more than she liked him. They were genetically programmed, she supposed, to stop thinking about horses and start thinking about sex around about now.

Leila's moving into the village and asking to become Tally's friend had been a turning point for Tally. All the other kids knew about her rich parents and the nearby mansion, sitting on the outskirts of Fenson, set inside acres and acres of grounds, and being little kids, they saw her differences as a barrier rather than an interest. Rather than rush to be associated with her, she had been singled out as the odd one, teased for being a snob despite her never displaying any snobbish tendencies. Leila had not been at the same primary school, so she had viewed Tally with fresh, objective eyes. On their very first day of secondary school, Leila had spotted Tally sitting all alone in the lunch hall during those awkward few moments of turning, laden tray in hand, to pick somewhere to sit. She had seized the opportunity to be partnered up, even if her instinct had told her there must be a reason Tally had been rejected by the others. With no other options, and her usual state of innocent optimism, she had bounded across the squeaky floor regardless, and upon learning the reason for Tally's isolation, she had decided the other kids were stupid.

It had been Tally and Leila against the world since then, inseparable and laughing, because they were the ones enjoying the pool and the horses. According to the other children she had not been worthy of association, and during those lonely lunchtimes before Leila, Tally would have been grateful to be befriended just because of the pool or the horses. At least her reward for being patient had been a genuine friend. Unlike her older brother Michael, who was treated like a celebrity by his peers and had never paused to question the motives behind his countless friends; Tally had grown up as the black sheep. Leila entering her life had saved her from enduring years of solitude as she worked her way towards her A-levels, and freedom, where she planned to disappear to university and never mention the house, or the horses, or the pool, to anyone.

Some days, she would look at Leila and wish she had chosen to stay, but changing her plans for a friend was a risky strategy. She was playing the long game and banked on their friendship surpassing small hurdles such as distance. Her experience of the last years of school told her they would blink, and then university would be finished, and they could regroup and make another plan, perhaps this time together.

'You think too far ahead,' Leila said when they were discussing their options one evening before their last week of exams. She hadn't seemed too fazed by Tally's decision to go to university miles away, possibly because she possessed the same unwavering faith in their friendship, and because Leila struggled to worry about anything, even the things that probably should concern her, like the café job that was likely to get snapped up by someone else who had also just finished their exams and was looking for employment.

'But wouldn't it be great, to live together one day?' Tally gazed up at the poster on her wall, reflecting on the fact she didn't really listen to that band anymore. She was going to have to change her room completely if she was going to grow up this summer, it still smacked of little girl when it needed to suggest sophistication.

'You would leave all of this?' Leila pointed towards the window, then the ceiling, then the opposite wall.

'I can't stay here forever,' Tally sighed, although she was certain that was what her brother was planning to do. He had been accepted into three prestigious universities and had turned the offers down, choosing to stay home and take a college course he didn't much care for just so he could justify staying where he was, and get his parents off his back. Now he had scraped by, barely passing his course after a number of re-takes; he lounged around and made no real effort to find suitable employment. He laughed at Tally's high aspirations and said she would soon be back, making a dark crushing prophecy then turning away, distracted by his next adventure.

'Why not? I'd never leave.' Leila sighed happily, unable to comprehend why Tally would even contemplate leaving the house and everything it had to offer for university. She hadn't thought about how, when Tally was gone, she would be limited in what she could do, confined only to the stables if she was to continue exercising the horses. Leila and Michael were so similar in their attitude that it made Tally think perhaps she was the strange one, for actually aspiring for something in this life. Leila didn't concern herself with unnecessary worries, hence why she had never studied too hard, or partied conscientiously. Tally couldn't decide if her best friend was an extremely good or devastatingly bad influence on her strict self.

'Oh, look who it is,' Leila said, her smile audible, bringing Tally back to the present, to the hot weather and the swimming pool.

Tally lifted her head and then quickly lowered it back down again. Michael was here, which was annoying, but she could forgive him because he had brought her favourite friend along with him. The way this boy made her feel proved Andrew was not the one for her, but he was so far out of her league she was better off sticking with a safe bet, unless she wanted to remain single. There were four older boys approaching them, so both girls quickly sucked in their stomachs and rearranged their sweaty hair, with Tally discounting her oaf of a brother and Leila under strict orders to do the same.

'We were here first!' Tally cried, anticipating her brother's hostility, unable to avoid sounding like the shrill, younger sister.

'We're not here to swim,' Michael replied, defensively, wishing that his sister wasn't dressed so scantily and didn't have the physique of a grown up. He could feel his friends' eyes roam all over her and he didn't like it one bit. His opportunity to enjoy the sight of Leila in just her bikini only lessened his annoyance slightly. Tally had made it clear to him that Leila was off limits, and for once Michael was going to respect her wishes. He was as aware as Tally was, however, that Leila wouldn't forever be in Tally's shadow, and he considered her fair game as soon as his sister disappeared off to university.

Tally propped herself up onto her elbows, curious at his response. She ignored the searing sensation as her skin touched new sections of the heat-soaked stone. Michael would usually want to swim in this weather, especially if it brought the satisfaction of kicking his sister out of the pool. Despite all the space, he usually wanted to be exactly where Tally was just so he could exert his older brother influence and send her packing. The weather tended to drive them towards the same spot on the property. It was too hot to play tennis so the pool was the current location of choice. The stables remained solely Tally's sanctuary since Michael had stopped visiting as soon as he had stopped riding, not even remotely interested in caring for Peter anymore.

Tally's eyes met Brad's, who was holding a big box stuffed with an array of colourful props. He gave her a half smile before Tally's brother stepped in front of her view.

'What's that?' Tally asked, craning her neck, enjoying the way she had just been given a legitimate reason to openly stare at Brad. He was Michael's most attractive friend, and he also reminded her of her brother the least. Brad always smiled back at her and he didn't laugh whenever Michael poked fun at her. She had always had an odd feeling towards him, and something about the way he occasionally looked at her made her wonder if perhaps he was interested in her too.

'Decorations,' Brad said, and he looked directly at her, as if he had said something much more intriguing.

'What for?' Leila asked, saving Tally from her frozen state, unwittingly covering the way she had suddenly forgotten how to speak after being addressed by Brad.

'The party,' Michael said, able to answer Leila with more kindness and information than he would have ever offered so easily to his little sister. He wished Brad had kept his mouth shut, because he didn't want them to wind up at his party.

Tally registered the word 'party' but was too consumed by the way Brad was still watching her to notice the implications. 'What party?' she asked, her concentration finally dragged away by the concept of a party.

'You're not invited,' Michael snapped automatically, anticipating her request. He avoided eye contact with Leila, because it would be too tempting, and it wasn't worth the penalty of his sister hanging around.

'I live here, I can't *not* be invited if you're holding it here,' Tally pointed out.

'You should just stay in your room and play ponies,' Michael said, remembering Tally and Leila used to do just that when they were younger. He had once purposefully snapped the leg off her favourite plastic horse and she had never forgiven him. Anna had glued it back together, but the joint was visible and the pony had never been the same again – permanently lame. He still felt mildly guilty about it, and just now he was certain his comment had evoked the memory in her.

'We're busy tonight, anyway,' Tally said loftily, hoping her mysteriousness would intrigue Brad. She dared a sideways glance at him, and he was still watching her. She wondered if he looked a little bit disappointed at her declaration.

She felt Leila tense besides her, ready to protest. She didn't speak out in front of the others. As the boys busied themselves with setting out the party paraphernalia, with Michael satisfied by Tally's declaration of being busy, Tally winked at Leila, and Leila understood.

❄

'He's going to spot us at some point,' Leila said, ducking down behind someone so Michael wouldn't notice them as he walked past, too distracted by slapping some tarty girl on the bum to notice his sister and her friend had crashed his pool party.

'He's far too drunk and more interested in chasing girls.' Tally observed his behaviour with an exasperated sigh, before taking a large slurp of her drink, already feeling the effects. 'Besides, he can get lost if he thinks we're leaving. We deserve this party – we've worked for it!'

'Plus, it took too long to do my hair to leave early,' Leila fingered a curl that was already dropping out, attempting to revert back to its usual straightness despite her best efforts. Tally, on the other hand, was constantly smoothing hers down, hoping it would stay straight after all the hot ironing, praying it didn't start fluffing up. It was kind of silly how they had both attempted to fight their natural styles.

'Mum said that as long as we don't argue or drown then she will have our back if Michael sees us and kicks off.'

'Your mum is awesome.' Leila eyeballed the talent clustered around the pool. They were glad the boys were all older than anyone they knew, and therefore were supposedly more mature. As one dive bombed into the pool fully clothed, however, they doubted their maturity. Although the sky was darkening, the air was still warm and with the added help of alcohol, some brave people were still frolicking around in the water, screeching and splashing about as if they were in an American frat movie.

'She's clever. She knows we are going to do stuff like this, she's been through it all before with Michael, so she would prefer we got drunk here, at home, where we're safe.'

'I don't think you're safe,' Leila laughed.

Tally frowned, confused by her friend's odd comment. She turned to ask what she was talking about and was perplexed to find her ally had melted away into the crowd like a genie.

'Can I get you a drink?' a voice asked.

Tally started. She recognised his voice but had not been mentally prepared for him to actually use it to talk to her. She swallowed hard and then turned to face him, hoping Michael wasn't anywhere nearby. In the dim light, he was even more alluring, as shadows danced across his face and emphasised his features. His eyes were darker, and his lips were fuller. The stubble across his chin reminded Tally of how much older he was, which was exciting to her. She rolled back her shoulders and stuck out her chest, trying to show him she was a grown up too, no longer just Michael's kid sister he had seen around from time to time. Although they were crashing this party which was supposed to be for over eighteens, Tally and Leila were nearly there, on the cusp of adulthood.

'Sure,' she replied as casually as possible, glancing down to see her plastic beaker was nearly full. That was awkward. As he turned away to get a new one, she quickly gulped down her drink, and then stifled a burp before he was back, extending an arm towards her, offering her another as the previous one still slid down her throat. She didn't know if she could stomach another one, but she was hardly going to turn down his offer, and it also gave her something to nervously clutch on to.

Her mind was already clouding, unused to drinking this much, let alone this quickly. She was usually too busy with the horses, or relaxing with Leila, or more recently revising, to bother with alcohol. They were never really invited to parties, and even if they had been, they would have been unlikely to go. As they often remarked, what more did they need than each other? The truth was they were still in exile, with Tally never being accepted into the fold by her old primary school classmates and Leila was guilty by association. Andrew had been there, on the fringes, and Tally had only spent time with him instead of Leila with a sense of reluctance. Right now, however, Tally was looking up at exactly what else she thought she might need. Right now, Leila didn't matter at all. What she would actually do with him if she ever got him, she was not certain. The idea of kissing a boy with tongues was terrifying, let alone doing anything else. And Brad would have experience with older girls. Brad would have expectations. She took another sip of her drink, realising he had given her spirits. She tried not to cringe at the taste of it on her tongue, unable to even recognise what it was and fearing it was a dangerous concoction.

'How did your exams go?' Brad asked, as if he wanted to have a proper adult conversation.

Tally was surprised he had asked such a genuine, sensible question, and it fuelled her attraction even more. 'Fine, I should get my predicted grades.' She decided not to play down her ability. Although she had been considered a geek by her peers, she was well aware that once she transitioned to university, things would turn upside down. Achieving high scores would become the new cool and failing would be an embarrassment. She hoped he would think her sophisticated for being proud of her intelligence, and besides, Brad knew she was a book worm because Michael had sneered about it in front of him before.

'I can't believe you're going off to uni.'

Tally smiled into her cup, because Brad seemed dismayed at the prospect. Also, he had been paying close enough attention to learn about her plans, it would seem. She wondered if he had asked Michael outright, or if the information had been offered up in passing. She hoped it was the former. Perhaps he did fancy her and this was not just a dream invented by a hopeful teenager. She wished she had revealed her feelings towards Brad to Leila now, because she might have been able to provide some advice. Leila had at least kissed a boy before, and Tally therefore considered her a source of valuable knowledge on the inner workings of a boy's brain. I should have asked Leila for help with my snogging technique, Tally thought, as she stared at Brad's lips and wondered how it was going to work without clashing teeth.

'I've still got the summer,' Tally invited, attempting a coy smile, emboldened by the buzz of the alcohol. She was reminding him that she would be here, if he wanted her, and he smiled back, interpreting her comment as the offer it was supposed to be. The possibility of going to university no longer a virgin was suddenly very real, and it both thrilled and terrified her in equal doses. Brad was a much better prospect than Andrew. It was a big step up from kissing, that much she was sure, and Leila would have nothing to offer on that because she was just as inexperienced as Tally when it came to sex.

'We better make the most of it, then,' Brad said, making his intentions clear.

Tally blushed, but before she could think up an appropriately flirty response, she was grabbed by the arm.

'What the actual fuck are you doing here?' Michael asked, eyeballing Brad with suspicion, momentarily outraged. He looked her up and down, not liking the amount of make-up or cleavage on show.

'Get off.' Tally smacked his hand, wincing at his vice-like grip. She was embarrassed to be treated like this in front of Brad and hoped it wouldn't put him off. Michael had popped her bubble of sophistication. She looked back towards Brad to gauge his reaction, maybe even hoping he would stick up for her and call her brother off, but he had gone, possibly to avoid being accused of trying it on with Michael's sister. She was disappointed, but also a tad relieved. Things had become too intense too quickly and the reality was she had no idea what to say or do next. She was desperate to find Leila and tell her the news, but first she had to shake off her brother.

'I told you not to come to this, I thought you were busy.' Michael let her go, calming down, realising he had potentially overreacted. His sister was rubbing her arm and the thought of hurting her made him feel guilty, as much as he declared a strong hatred to her face most days.

'Our plans fell through,' Tally lied, 'Besides, Mum said we could come.'

'Oh my God, you're such a loser. You spoke to her about it?'

'Yeah, just so you can't dob us in for staying.' Tally stuck out her tongue, immediately switching to bratty little sister mode when she should be channelling refined young woman.

'Leila's with you?' His eyes lit up for a fraction of a second.

'Yes, obviously.' Tally narrowed her eyes, hoping that spark hadn't been any kind of sexual interest. Michael knew the rules and so did Leila. She had faith Leila would not break them, even if she doubted Michael's self-control.

'Just don't talk to any of my friends,' Michael warned, 'especially Brad,' he added, shooting her a cold glare that portrayed his seriousness.

'That would mean not talking to anyone else here, except Leila,' Tally protested, ignoring the emphasis on Brad, deciding to disobey him if the opportunity arose once more.

'Exactly,' Michael said triumphantly, and then turned away, apparently granting her permission to stay, albeit on his unrealistic terms.

Tally muttered something to his retreating back and then ambled around in an attempt to find Leila, conscious that her clumsy legs were giving her more of a stumble than a saunter.

❅ After Edith ❅

'Can you believe this?' Charles stormed into the kitchen, waving a box above his head, shaking it like a rattle.

Anna was scrubbing the hob with her usual dedication and Helena was knitting in the armchair they had taken from Tally's bedroom to make room for the cot. Helena had decided to take up residence in the small space between the kitchen table and the window because the sitting room was too dingy for her to see what she was doing. Tally was placing Edith into the pram, and shot her dad an annoyed glance for making her jump and nearly drop the baby.

'This is ridiculous!' Charles continued to wave the box around his head, threatening to throw it somewhere, hopefully nowhere near the pram.

Helena slowly lowered her latest project, careful not to let her husband distract her so she messed it up. She was working on a baby blanket for Edith, to keep her warm when in the draughty bedroom, and her knitting skills were rusty. She recognised what he was holding and sighed. She had been hopeful he would not have discovered those for a while.

'What is it?' Tally asked, tucking Edith into her pram so she would be adequately prepared for the walk she was about to take. It was nearly five o'clock and so soon she would be 'allowed' out into her own garden for some exercise and escape.

'Fudge!' Charles cried, 'Bloody fudge!'

Tally had not been expecting fudge. She wondered why he had taken such offence to a box of sweets. Then she recognised the picture on the front of the box. It was a photograph of their home, of the front of the house taken square on, portraying the grand steps, the ornate windows and deep red brickwork. The edges were adorned with trees, and Tally couldn't tell if they were real or had been photo-shopped into place. She certainly didn't remember such voluptuous bushes framing the house, but then, perhaps that was another thing she had taken for granted all these years, until they were snatched away.

'Since when did we promote fudge?' Charles continued, outraged. He then turned on his wife, 'I assume *you* allowed this to happen.'

'It is part of the marketing package; they sell it in the gift shop.'

'Gift shop! There is a gift shop!' Charles shouted in case no one had heard the first time around. 'They this and they that,' he fired, accentuating each word with a formidable shake of the box. 'What about *us*? What about what *we* want?'

'You can't have what *you* want any more Charles!' Helena shouted back, unsettling the baby, and letting her knitting needle slip so it lost the yarn. 'When are you going to wrap your fat head around that?' Helena stood up and let her knitting drop completely to the floor. She marched out, throwing a 'Sorry,' towards Tally and the baby, who was now screaming, perceptive to the anger pulsating around the room.

The silver lining to the crying was that it gave Tally a valid excuse to also make a swift exit outside, leaving poor Anna to pacify Charles, and pick up the scattering of fudge that had exploded from the box and sprayed itself all over the room like sugary shrapnel. They would probably be finding little bits of it for weeks. Tally wanted to laugh at the way her mother had called Charles a 'fat head', something she would never have imagined coming from her polite and reputable lips, but Edith was screaming which denied her any comic relief. She would have to glean some joy from the retelling of the episode later when she found Michael, once Edith was calm.

Pushing away the echoes of Charles' continued rant, that showed no sign of quelling even after his wife had snapped at him and dramatically left the room, Tally breathed a sigh of relief as the back door closed behind her. Poor Anna deserved a pay-rise for the extra ear-bending, although according to Helena she had actually taken a cut now so the family could keep her on. She would be mad if she wasn't currently looking for a new job. It would be no great shock if they woke up tomorrow to find the help swiftly departed and Tally had no idea how they would cope with their father without her. They would never be able to hire a new housekeeper. A new baby had not softened him, and being a granddad appeared to have no real impact. Tally was not entirely sure that he hadn't completely forgotten about Edith, with him being too distracted by the house controversy and his drinking addiction. Tally supposed it wasn't unexpected; he had never been an overly invested Dad. He had an old-fashioned attitude towards children, considering them to be the domain of the mother – or the maid.

'Are you okay?'

Tally's eyes snapped open. He was interrupting her moment of respite. She was leaning her head back against the cold glass of the door she had just closed behind her to contain the madness, and was taking a couple of breaths of the dusky evening - the cool calm - shutting out the cries of the baby for just one second. Now she looked like a terrible person, like a mother prepared to leave her baby to cry out in the cold. She was certainly not okay. And it was mainly his fault.

'Can you go away, please?' Tally picked up her baby despite having spent forever tucking her into her pram. She did it to make a show of appearing busy, like an attentive mother.

'Can I help?' He dropped the wheelbarrow of weeds he was pushing and approached her.

'No,' Tally replied coldly. What exactly it was this boy thought he could do to help her or her baby she could not imagine. She was hardly going to hand over control to a stranger, even if she did need a break, a moment to be herself, to be just Tally and not Tally plus a dependant.

'Are you sure?' He continued to walk closer.

'Of course, I'm sure, what is your problem?' she bit back, and then she realised she was crying, almost hysterically; that tears were streaming down her cheeks, and she hadn't even noticed.

He got closer still, his features blurring behind her tears. Rather than take the baby, because that was not going to fly with Tally, he gently rested a weather-worn palm on her arm, and despite her humiliation, it calmed her. They stood for a while, until she finally sniffed, breaking the spell, causing him to drop his hand before it became too awkward.

'See you,' he said, and he walked back to his wheelbarrow. He was unable to decide how he should be acting around the client that was not a client, the new mum who was still really a child, not much younger than him.

She stared after him, watching his proud swagger, and was jealous that he appeared to be so comfortable in his own skin. *Why aren't I like that?* she asked herself: *why aren't I free to just walk away?* Of course, the answer lay in her arms, and in her past.

❄

'Just go,' Helena instructed as Tally wavered, almost changing her mind. Tally was standing in the kitchen wearing her riding gear. 'She's fed, so I can handle everything else. Go!' Helena shooed her daughter away, looking forward to some time alone with her new granddaughter almost as much as Tally was looking forward to some time alone with her old horse.

Tally took a deep breath and turned away. She hoped it would be easier to deal with the streak of guilt and anguish of leaving Edith once she caught sight of her friend and the two horses. It should be easy, she told herself, because you don't even want a baby, remember? Leila was already at the yard, and the horses were already groomed and tacked up ready to be exercised.

'You didn't need to do that,' Tally said, realising she was later than planned due to a dirty, over-spilling nappy, and then her hesitation at leaving the house alone. She hastily pulled on the riding hat Leila had unearthed for her.

'It's fine, I enjoyed getting them ready.' Leila wiggled her eyebrows.

Tally frowned, wondering why Leila was making eyes at her, and then Simon appeared, wheeling a barrow of horse feed. Did he ever put down that barrow? He looked up and his face altered when he caught Tally's eye. He must feel weird about last time, Tally thought. Crying in front of him had certainly made her feel weird.

'Why do you do all the horse chores?' Tally asked Simon.

He lowered the wheelbarrow, and the two horses perked up. They recognised the bags and sniffed the air eagerly. 'It's in my job description,' he replied carefully, wondering what she was getting at.

'It's not exactly essential property maintenance, it doesn't impact the visitors. Shouldn't we be mucking out?' Tally challenged.

'Watch out or you'll talk yourself into more work,' Leila exclaimed, trying to make light of the situation. She was perplexed at the conversation Tally had just instigated. She thought they were going to share a girlie giggle over the cute new guy, but instead Tally had launched into a line of questioning that was heading towards an unprovoked attack. Leila welcomed Simon; he was attractive, young and useful. It was bizarre that Tally was complaining, and it was also awkward for Leila. She had been pleasant with Simon ever since he had started working there, before Tally had returned home, and now she might have to pick sides.

'We took over the running of the yard as part of the deal.' Simon lifted the handles of the wheelbarrow, keen to get out of there. It was just after five and he was running late. He shouldn't be talking about work anymore. He was on his own time and there was a cold beer waiting in his fridge. He could sense they were on the cusp of an argument, and he was as keen to avoid it as Leila was. He regretted his decision to unload the bags of horse feed from his car; he should have waited until the morning.

'Oh, I see.' Tally put her hands on her hips, her tone accusing, 'It was just a sweetener, something to make it easier for my mum to agree to give you this place.'

'Look,' Simon started, lowering the wheelbarrow again, accepting he wasn't going to get to leave as soon as he hoped, and that this crazy girl had returned from wherever it was she had been hiding with more emotional baggage than he was prepared to handle. One minute she was blubbering, and the next she was biting his head off. He couldn't keep up. It irked him that Tally made it sound like they had simply gifted the house to British Estates, for free with no strings attached, when in reality Helena had instigated the handover and begged them to save her family home. Tally obviously didn't appreciate the huge risk British Estates had taken, and how without the financial support from the company her family would not be able to live in her precious home.

'I don't want to talk about it,' Tally cut him off, turning back to Peter, deciding she couldn't even look at him, and everything he represented. 'We don't have much light left for riding,' she added, finding a suitable excuse to giving him the cold shoulder. Peter nosed her, checking her annoyed mood was nothing to do with him. She had agreed to let Leila ride her horse, and she would take the happy hacker. Peter was too old and a little too stiff to do much demanding work, but as promised previously, Tally coming home was not supposed to impact Leila's time with Match.

'I don't know,' Simon said, deciding he didn't mind being late home if it cleared the air, and that it wasn't going to be up to her to abruptly end every exchange they had. 'You're acting like you want to talk about it – shout about it.'

'Well, what do you expect?' Tally cried, turning away from a bemused horse and flinging her arms out, unable to control her outburst, because she needed to let rip at someone, and Simon was preferable to Leila, and he was also wearing one of those hideous British Estates fleeces. 'You have ruined *everything.*'

'Me? Personally? I've ruined your life then, have I?' he challenged back, defiant now that she had decided to make it personal. If she thought she could talk to him like he was a bit of muck on the bottom of her shoe just because she had moved back home to find things not to her liking, then she was sorely mistaken.

He dropped the wheelbarrow again, but this time with a force and a clang that made the horses jump. He was damned if he was going to let this girl blame him for everything that had recently gone wrong in her life, because it was pretty obvious that nearly losing her family home was not her major issue.

Tally stopped in her tracks after this comment, because she could see what he was implying. British Estates were not responsible for putting a baby inside her, it wasn't their fault she had just been forced to abandon her university course and move back home, two years too early and without a degree. She clamped her mouth shut and worried for a moment she might cry in front of him again, as a wave of humiliation fought against the anger nestled in her gut. She should have left it. She had just marred her rare chance of freedom from the baby by going and upsetting herself with a pointless argument. Was nothing sacred anymore? Was she destined to mess up absolutely everything in her life from now on?

'I know you're looking for someone to blame but it's not me. You're targeting the wrong guy,' he continued, noticing her pink cheeks but deciding she deserved the retaliation. He picked up the wheelbarrow and this time he did not look back as he pushed it towards the feed room, trying to shake off the guilt of potentially going too far with his last sentence.

Tally stared after him, her breath hot and fast as she processed his words. As much as she hated to admit it, Simon was right; he was not the guy who had ruined her life. Helena had been forced to make the devastating decision about their home, and if anyone was going to pick a fight with British Estates it should be her.

'Shall we get going?' Leila asked cautiously, unsure what else she could say to help. 'You're right about the fading light,' she pointed out helpfully, hoping that getting on Peter would soothe Tally's mood. Even Leila knew, however, that there were limits to horse therapy. When she got off in an hour, she would still have the same smashed up dreams.

Tally grunted then let Peter free from his headcollar. She didn't care about the light, she would ride in the dark if it meant some time out, away from the rest of the household, and all of the mistakes. She would rather be alone, without Leila, but that was not going to happen. She at least had the common sense to avoid turning on her only friend, so she kept her mouth shut, mounted the horse and let Leila chat to her in a pointless attempt to cheer her up. She admired her ability to at least pretend everything was alright, Tally had lost the ability to look on the bright side of life; everywhere she turned it was dark.

❊ Before Edith ❊

'Have you got anything?' Andrew asked, breaking away from nuzzling Tally's neck.

'No.' Her voice was hoarse from having to shout over the music earlier. It was hardly the girl's job to bring the condoms. Her heart sank as she realised this would be it, they would have to stop, all because stupid Andrew hadn't had the forethought to bring protection. Surely he knew there was a chance this could happen tonight and they could be alone, hidden away in a back room, taking advantage of their last opportunity to have sex before she returned to university to finish the final term of her first year. She was hoping to return no longer a virgin, and Andrew was about to screw that up. She wondered if it was perhaps a blessing in disguise because, try as she might, she had not found a way to properly fancy him yet. He was *okay,* but were you supposed to make love to someone who was just okay? If you wanted to get it out of the way, then she supposed the answer was yes, so she remained disappointed in his failure to prepare for their night of passion.

'Shit, shall I go and ask someone?' Andrew sounded as disappointed as she felt, as he fumbled to pull up his trousers.

Tally sighed and sat up, pulling her bra and top straps up as she did so. It was freezing, and the absence of his body heat made her skin go instantly goosepimply. The moment had passed, and she was unsure if she wanted to continue. Whoever Andrew went to ask would work out who it was Andrew was about to bang, because they had been dancing and drinking together all night, for everyone to see. She didn't want it to be instant public knowledge when she lost her virginity. She had drunk too much, and her head was starting to spin. The anticipation of tonight, of sleeping with Andrew, had caused her to have one drink too many. He was a lovely guy, albeit a tad too wiry, but she considered him the best of a bad bunch. He would have to do for her first encounter.

There wasn't exactly anyone else in the village she could imagine sleeping with. Leila said Tally should follow her lead and find an older guy, but that was easy for Leila to say, she didn't have an older brother who warned everyone else off of his sister in some outdated and futile attempt to shelter her from the opposite sex. Brad had been evidence enough of that. She hadn't been able to talk to him properly in months, despite all of the flirty glances and silent promises made across rooms whenever they were thrown together; always in the presence of Michael. If it wasn't for the fact he was messing up her chances of graduating to proper adulthood Tally might have found her brother's protective manner kind of sweet.

Leila thought it should be easy to blag a guy outside of Michael's wide circle of influence, but she was forever an optimist, and also appealed to older guys with her classy look, Tally on the other hand still had the unkempt hair and the puppy fat of an adolescent. Her pool of likely candidates was extremely shallow, since Michael scared away anyone who was willing to overlook Tally's inadequacies. Leila would scold her for thinking that and encourage her to consider herself as windswept and curvy, like a real woman, but Tally knew she couldn't always trust kind words said to her by her best friend. As for the guys at uni, she hadn't clicked with anyone yet – except Doug who was firmly in the friend zone no matter how hard he tried. She didn't want to sleep with a random guy from a drunken night out because she considered herself to have some standards. Andrew was her best bet, so she was going to have to let him go off in search of a condom whilst she tried to talk herself in to waiting for him.

Andrew winked at her, thinking everything was fine and she was still completely up for it, then left the room to scrounge. Tally let him go, too hesitant to tell him the truth. She had acted like she was in love with him for such a long time now, it was a hard tradition to break. The reality was, however, that she was debating whether or not she should stick around. She could blame it on the drink and say that she needed to go and lie down. Andrew would forgive her, he was too infatuated to begrudge her for making excuses, even if it would still disappoint him. She glanced up at the walls and it took her a moment to recognise which room they had staggered into. It was right at the back of the house, in a bid to keep out of sight from anyone else who could be stumbling around drunk. The last thing they would have wanted was another horny couple falling through the door on them, and seeing far too much. Tally hadn't been in this abandoned back bedroom for years.

She crept into the corridor and spotted the ajar door of a bathroom. She decided to go for a wee, to empty her bladder just in case she did decide to sleep with Andrew, if and when he returned with his prize. She almost laughed at Andrew's disappointed face upon realising that they would need a condom, and that he hadn't brought one. He must be kicking himself, she mused as she lowered herself onto the dusty toilet seat, wincing as the cold surface touched her skin, and lamenting that the winter had lasted far too long. She wondered if the water would even be turned on back here, even if it was on she could imagine the pipe would be frozen in this snowy weather. Although they had an awesome house for partying, living with so many rooms was impractical when there were just the four of them – five if you counted Anna who only left the house to feed her cat and sleep. They only tended to heat the rooms that they used.

At least Michael had allowed her and Leila, plus some of their friends including Andrew, to come to this party without a fight. He had finally accepted his little sister had grown up, and also realised some of her friends might actually be attractive girls. He was still warned away from Leila, so opening up the invite to others was his way of rewarding himself for allowing his sister – and her unofficial boyfriend - to tag along.

She thought about all the events she and Leila had crashed over the years, just so they had an excuse to dress up, drink alcohol and practice flirting on Michael's seemingly mature and gorgeous friends. She realised now that they had been impatient. They should have treasured their tender years. Their youth had been precious and innocent and then passed by almost without warning. They had been in such a hurry to grow up that they had sometimes forgotten to relish the present. Now she was already into her first year at university, where you could party every night if you wanted to, where deadlines were demanding and teachers didn't give you a pat on the back just for trying. She was back home for the Christmas holiday and there was another party, when all she really needed was her old bed and a home cooked meal. Being grown up wasn't always that much fun, it certainly wasn't as amazing as you imagined it to be when you were young. There was so much pressure to do everything, and be everything, that you didn't have much time just to sit still and *be*.

A movement caught Tally's eye, putting an abrupt end to her pondering. The door knob was turning. 'Hang on, Andrew,' she called, rushing to pull up her underwear. Although the plan was that Andrew would be taking it right back off again, she didn't want him to see her like this, it wasn't exactly sexy.

Andrew ignored her and pushed the door open, making it squeak on its rusty hinges. 'Wait,' Tally said, not even having a chance to flush the loo. She stopped in her tracks at being presented with someone who was not Andrew, and who was not expected at all. 'Oh,' was all she could manage. She recognised those eyes, those lips and that five o'clock shadow. 'Brad, hi.' He had been hanging around the party, but it was pointless trying to speak to him. Michael would notice, not to mention Andrew as well, and she had long ago understood that wanting to be with someone like Brad was just a school-girl's pipe dream. She was over it now, content that it was never going to happen.

'I'm sorry,' he said, eyes glinting, not at all sorry, 'have I interrupted something?'

'I was having a pee,' Tally replied, feeling it was unnecessary to discuss what she was doing next to a toilet, taken aback by the way he had bowled confidently into the bathroom, without even flinching to find it occupied despite the door being unlocked. Something in his manner set off urgent warning bells in Tally and despite everything she had thought about him before this moment, despite all the steamy scenarios she had played in her mind, her intuition was screaming at her to get as far away from him as humanly possible. Unfortunately, with him standing in the doorway, the possibility was pretty low.

'I've been looking for you.' He pushed the door closed behind him, looking extremely proud of himself at having found her, as if it had been a big party game and he had simply forgot to tell her she was playing. The ominous click of the latch echoed around the room.

'Andrew will be back in a minute,' she said, feeling it important she make the point that she was not here alone. She wished she had said second instead of minute, because a lot could happen in a minute.

'The skinny chap? I told him you'd given up on him and gone back to the party.'

'Oh,' Tally said, looking desperately over his shoulder, hoping that Andrew had not believed him so easily.

'He asked me for a condom,' Brad said, smiling in a way that made Tally shudder. 'Was that for you?' He stepped closer.

'No,' Tally said automatically, her neck now getting hot. Why was he asking her that question? Why was he looking at her like she was something to eat? She dropped her eyes to the floor in a panic, unable to look at his hungry expression any longer. *How could I have ever found him attractive?* she asked herself, feeling sick at the way she had fantasised about him before. In her imagination, he had never been like this.

'Michael knows I'm in here,' Tally tried, realising she sounded desperate. From the quiver in her voice he would know she was afraid of him, and had an idea of what he wanted to do to her.

'Nice try,' he chuckled darkly, reaching out for her wrist and wrenching her towards him. She turned her face away from his in disgust, unable to avoid his stale beer breath as it hit her. She looked to the window, to the soft snow falling through the mottled glass, and she longed to be outside; free, spinning with the snow. 'He's with that slutty friend of yours. She was practically begging him for it, just like you did with me.'

He grabbed her other wrist and Tally was overwhelmed with the strength he had over her, his frame much larger and containing the power of a grown man. He was capable of restraining her, she didn't have a chance against him and it wasn't even worth the struggle, not now his motives were clear. Tally had never practically begged Brad for anything and Leila was not slutty. Brad clearly had a certain way of thinking about women, and had somehow let everything get twisted in his mind.

Tally swallowed and focused on the snow, trying to single out a lone flake so that she might be able to distract herself from the next thing he did to her. She tried to pretend she was the snowflake and not herself, that she was outside of the bathroom and not trapped inside with Brad. She was pushed back roughly, onto the seat of the toilet, and then dragged down onto the grubby floor. She hit her head on the edge of the seat, and then the floor, but he didn't care. She wished it had knocked her out so the world could go black for what she was sure was about to happen to her. I hope it doesn't hurt too much, she prayed, searching for the strength to endure it. He didn't even have to worry about the noise he was making since they were so far away from the others, nestled at the back of the house. The music was turned up too loud for anyone to hear her shout. Even if he hadn't locked the door, no one was going to try the handle. Andrew must have believed his stupid story and she hated him for that, for letting Brad convince him that she had abandoned him so quickly. You were thinking of abandoning him, though, she thought, blaming herself for the way she must have made it apparent to Andrew that he wasn't as important to her, when all along she thought he had never noticed their uneven relationship. Perhaps I brought this upon myself, she added, wishing she could have been more grateful for the affection of a boy who wouldn't ever dream of hurting her like this.

From where she lay, smothered by Brad, she could see the garish face of an old Christmas decoration. It had been hidden away in here, years ago, to gather dust and would now look over the events with sinister, unblinking eyes. Santa was watching her with a twisted, mocking smile and she willed him to look away, so there would be no witnesses to the scene. If no one else had seen what had happened, not even the ugly ornament, then perhaps Tally could convince herself it had just been a terrible dream. Some snowflakes touched the window and slid slowly down the glass, instantly changing from delicate dots to ugly water drops, as if bearing witness to the attack had killed their innocent spirit and quashed their carefree downward spiral.

I can't believe Leila broke her promise, was all Tally could think, despite what was happening to her, as she stared out the window, and pretended this small bathroom didn't exist.

❄ After Edith ❄

'Stop crying,' Tally pleaded, keeping her voice low so as not to attract Grampy's attention. He was busying himself with the tea, standing with his back to her no doubt to give her a moment, so she wouldn't feel pressurised or embarrassed at the way her child was kicking off. It wasn't working; she still felt pressurised and embarrassed.

'Don't you worry about her,' Grampy said kindly, as he eventually turned with the brewing pot, 'I can just turn my hearing aid off if it gets too much.' He placed the pot down and then busied himself with arranging biscuits on a plate, so Tally had a few more seconds to recompose herself.

Tally bounced Edith up and down on her hip in a concentrated effort to soothe her. She had tried to feed her, but she was refusing to latch, and waving her nipple about for Grampy to see was not exactly her idea of fun. He had of course averted his eyes but it was still pretty awkward, no matter how much he pretended not to notice. Tally sniffed Edith's bum but was not offended by the aroma and couldn't believe the nappy was already soaked through after having changed her before setting off on her visit to Grampy. The only other potential causes of Edith's discontent were tiredness and colic, neither of which Tally could do much about, so she continued to shush her in the hope it might eventually work.

'You know, there's a group in the village you could join.' Grampy casually lay a leaflet down in front of Tally, as if he had just happened to find it lying around somewhere and had not been waiting for the opportune moment to produce it. Tally eyed it with suspicion, and then him. Someone must have told him she was struggling. It was Thursday, so it must have been Michael during his regular Wednesday visit. She didn't realise Michael had even noticed how newfound motherhood did not really suit his little sister.

'Thanks.' She pocketed the leaflet to be polite. She had absolutely no intention of meeting another bunch of slobbery babies; one was enough. The mums would all be perfect and married, and probably in their late twenties or early thirties, all safe and secure. They would judge Tally before she even sat down, and sneer at Edith too, thinking how unfortunate she must be to have a slutty single mum who was still technically a teenager. Tally could not bear the silent criticism.

'It won't be like that.' Grampy said, guessing her thoughts and as perceptive as ever. Although his hearing and eyesight was fading, his sixth sense of knowing exactly what Tally was thinking was as sharp as ever.

'Hmmm,' was all Tally could say as Edith let out an impolite burp and then quietened down, now relieved of the trapped gas. With the baby calm, Tally was able to pour herself a cup of tea one-handed, proud of her astonishing new skill of using only half her body to do most tasks. She didn't want to argue with Grampy because he was only saying it to encourage her to go, but the truth was he had no idea what the other mums would think. If she had learned anything from having horses, it was that most horse owners imagined everything outside of the actual competitions to also be a competition, from which saddle and horse they had to which lorry they drove or how much they spent on jodhpurs. Tally suspected motherhood was similar and she didn't have the inclination or energy to start comparing herself, or her premature baby, because they would both lose.

'What else will you be doing next Tuesday, eh?' Grampy encouraged, refusing to let it go.

'Thanks for the reminder that I now have no life.' Tally rolled her eyes. She *should* be in a lecture a hundred miles away. She *should* at least be allowed to ride her horse if she was at home. But she had nothing to do most days, except avoid her crazy father, strained mother and selfish brother, not to mention the entire staff of British Estates that now walked the halls of their home with pride, pleased with their latest acquisition and frowning whenever a member of Tally's family came into view before closing time. I'll also be avoiding Simon, she thought, annoyed at the mere thought of him happily trundling his wheelbarrow around, having forced Grampy to also have nothing to do.

'I'll go if you come with me,' she said, willing to compromise.

Grampy started. 'You want me to go to a mum and baby club?'

'If you want me to go so much, then you better come with me, because I'm not going alone.'

'I doubt I'll even be allowed in.'

'Of course you will, come on, please.' Then, smiling wryly, she added, 'What else will you be doing next Tuesday, anyway?'

Grampy laughed and dunked a biscuit. 'Okay,' he conceded, pausing. 'You've got me cornered there.' The biscuit fell apart and sploshed into the bottom of his tea cup.

'I've missed this!' Leila laughed, as they pulled up, their horses still eager to run despite the long gallop. They enjoyed racing as much as their riders did, and it had been a week since they had been out together. Even Peter, who was officially semi-retired, had reverted back to a youngster at the sight of the unending green track disappearing into the horizon.

Tally wheezed, realising she probably shouldn't be doing such strenuous exercise so soon after giving birth. She was probably doing irreparable damage to her pelvic floor. Although she had always said she preferred Match, she was delighted with the way Peter had powered along, with the right mixture of speed and sensibility to let her really enjoy herself on top of him without fearing things might go awry. Michael had been a fool to give up riding this beautiful horse, she mused, stroking his neck as he took a moment to catch his breath now the tempo had slowed.

To her foolish brother, the draw of girls and partying that accompanied puberty had been too strong to resist, and poor Peter had been shoved on the back burner. The silver lining was that Tally and Leila could now ride together, rather than one after another, which they had been forced to do until Michael had lost interest. Match had been relieved, too, since he no longer had to put up with them both. Match needed a companion and Tally was never going to let Helena sell the horse, so it had worked out rather well for the girls, especially now Tally was home unexpectedly.

'Me too,' Tally sighed as they made an about turn so they could amble back to the stables at a much slower gait, down the sloping gradient. Although she had sorely missed horse riding, it was impossible to ignore the circumstances that had caused her to end up back here, riding, when she should still be in the middle of her autumn term of her second year at university.

It was already approaching dusk and Tally couldn't leave Edith for long. She looked at the trees to either side and was sad to think they no longer belonged to the family; they were owned by British Estates. I should have appreciated these trees a bit more, she thought. She glanced around, aware the same applied for every square foot of their estate. From here, the house and stables were visible in the distance and Tally instinctively squinted to see if she could make out Simon in his horrible maroon jacket.

'Have you spoken to Andrew yet?' Leila asked.

Tally tensed up, wondering when this question would come from Leila. She had jumped to the same conclusion as everybody else. 'Not yet, he's in Scotland, anyway.' If he was still in the village he would have visited by now, word would have got out. Andrew had gone off to university, too, and they had agreed to stay friends, accepting that a long-distance relationship was not going to last forever. It wasn't as if theirs had got very far, anyway. Andrew was probably busy spending time with girls who actually liked him back, which was what he deserved.

'Don't you think you should call him?' Leila asked gently.

Tally shook her head, 'Edith isn't his.'

'Oh. Really?' Leila was thrown by the revelation. 'But I thought that you... at the party...'

'We didn't. He didn't have a condom.'

'Right.' Leila coughed, because the irony was hard to avoid. Tally had still somehow managed to get pregnant, even if she had – allegedly – sensibly abstained from unprotected sex with Andrew.

'It was just some random guy from uni,' Tally answered the unspoken question, the one on everyone's lips. 'A silly, drunken mistake. I don't even remember his name.' She looked away, to the sinking sun, wondering if she had sounded convincing enough. She had decided it would be easier to make him an invisible stranger, less susceptible to cross-examination. She wished it really had happened like that.

'You never told me,' Leila said quietly. They had spoken together on the phone regularly and kept in touch over text message daily, and yet Tally had never mentioned a random guy who she had lost her virginity to.

'I guess I was just embarrassed. It was such a cliché way to do it.'

'But, your first time, I thought I'd be the first to know – after you and him, of course.' Leila didn't care about the cliché, she was just disappointed to have been left out of the loop. Best friends were supposed to be for sharing embarrassing stories with, especially when they involved the opposite sex. 'You don't ever have to be embarrassed in front of me, we can tell each other everything.'

'I'm sorry. I know, I should have told you,' Tally nodded, swallowing the thought that perhaps she really should tell Leila everything, perhaps she should tell her *the truth.* I can't, she quickly followed up with. I just can't. 'You still are the first to know, actually.'

'You kept this to yourself all these months?'

'I didn't know I was pregnant,' Tally clarified, 'At least, I didn't *think* I was pregnant.' She gazed down at Peter's ears, and thought about all the things that had made her pause. Perhaps she had known all along. Perhaps she had been lying to herself about it, too. Had it all been denial?

'Was there anyone else?' Leila asked, not wanting to dwell on whether or not Tally had really known about the pregnancy. It wasn't exactly going to change anything now.

Tally laughed, unable to help herself, and then she felt guilty. 'Only Doug,' she said, 'we're just friends. It was another one-off, a silly, drunken mistake. He's such a dweeb. He was with me, though, when Edith was born.' She swallowed, realising she should give him the respect he deserved. 'I don't know what I would have done without him, Leila.' She looked at her friend with wide eyes, remembering how scared she had been.

'Don't think about that, because he was there and you didn't have to do it alone.'

'I miss him. He's wasn't you – obviously – but he was my only real friend there. You were right about university not being all that. I don't know what I was looking for there.'

She beheld the landscape all around them and could see no reason to have left her home, except to run away from that night. She had missed out on the last year of their freedom, of enjoying these acres without a curfew, or having to share, and there was no way she would be able to get that last chance back. It hadn't been worth it. Running away had only led her back home, exactly where she had started.

'I should call him,' Tally said after a few minutes of walking in silence, listening to the rhythmic breathing of the horses and the wind rustling the trees. 'I should let Doug know we're both doing alright.'

'Are you? Are you both doing alright?' Leila probed, wondering how Tally could be coping, without even knowing the full extent of it. Leila had seen the stress and the fatigue Tally carried around. Even if Tally had looked content it didn't take a genius to guess such a young mum might be floundering. That was before you considered Tally was single and wholly unprepared, luckily her mother was around to help with the strain.

Tally shrugged, unable to know for sure, 'Edith is coping. Sometimes I just can't seem to settle her, but that's just babies, I think.'

'And you?' Leila persisted. 'You're so young to be doing all of this.' *Alone,* she added silently, although Tally could hear it as if she had shouted.

'I'm a baby myself, right?' Tally laughed. 'I feel too young, but I just have to muddle on with it. Mum's a big help and it's such a game changer that I think perhaps no one is ever really ready to become a Mother, no matter how old they are or how much help they get.' She shrugged at the sunset. Even if she had a stable partner, she imagined it would still be full of hurdles.

'I'd like to have a baby one day,' Leila said dreamily. Tally hadn't actually answered the question, which meant she probably wasn't alright, but Leila knew when to stop pursuing.

'What? You? I thought you hated kids – and men, too. I thought you were saving yourself for a millionaire before you commit to anything serious.' Tally laughed, remembering all the declarations Leila had made over the years.

'I guess I've changed my mind on all of that,' Leila smiled shyly, 'I might want to settle down with someone for something other than money and fame.'

'Grampy is coming with me to a baby group in the village tomorrow.' Tally offered after they spent a few moments walking side by side in silence, enjoying the gentle rocking of the steady horses below them. She cringed again at the idea of introducing herself to a load of strangers on the premise that just because they had all produced offspring they might get along with one another.

'Oh dear,' Leila smiled. She pushed Match into a trot, and Peter picked it up without Tally even asking.

Tally tiptoed across the hallway, with her towel wrapped tightly around her. She enjoyed the way her bare toes dug into the thick carpet, and longed to be back in this part of the house, where living was a luxury. Sneaking around what used to be her domain was bizarre. She cursed British Estates once more as she made it safely to her old bathroom and locked the door, dropping her towel now that she was in her secret sanctuary. She turned on the hot water and took a deep breath, already relaxing at the prospect of indulgence. Edith had just fallen asleep so she would be guaranteed at least twenty minutes to pamper herself while Helena kept an eye on her. A hot shower should make her feel better.

As she stood under the water, washing what she could of her tension away, she reflected on the village baby group she had visited yesterday. As much as she had protested about it on the walk there, with Grampy hobbling alongside, it hadn't been as awful as she had anticipated. If the mums had judged her for being young, single and completely unprepared, then they hadn't shown it. From the zombie-like state of them, they seemed to be too focused on their own tiny little bundles of terror to have the energy to think anything derogatory about Tally. There were three other mums there and they had appeared delighted to be joined by someone new. There hadn't really been a structure to the meet up, just a circle of chairs, endless refills of coffee and a table full of cakes, which was all they really needed. There were toys laid out on the floor at their feet but the babies were still too young to even lift their heads up and notice the offering, let alone be set down to play.

 The kindly old lady who ran the group had welcomed them in, taking two pounds for the coffee and cake as she did so, which seemed financially unsustainable considering the sheer amount of baked goods they had on offer. The host, who explained that her own babies had grown up over thirty years ago and were now producing offspring of their own, had been delighted to greet them. Her name was Angie and she had almost immediately dragged Grampy off to one side, leaving Tally to fend for herself. A man of over eighty was, apparently, unheard of at the baby group, and it was unclear whether or not the age or sex of Grampy had interested Angie the most as she plied him with a giant slice of chocolate cake and batted her eyelashes.

 Tally edged her way towards the others and then lowered herself awkwardly into a chair, leaving a napping Edith in her pram, wishing she would wake up and save her. From the odd encouraging glance the lady threw over, Tally wondered if Grampy had been removed on purpose, to force Tally to interact with the other mums.

'Welcome,' a particularly bleary-eyed mum said, taking a large swig of coffee. 'I used to love gin, but this is my new drug of choice.'

Tally laughed politely, and used the opportunity to pour herself a cup. 'Refill?' she offered, flinching at the immediate chorus of 'Yes!'

'Okay, I'll introduce us all and you don't need to worry about immediately forgetting our names, because you can blame practically *everything* on baby brain,' the first mum said, rejuvenated after a gulp of caffeine. She then took a deep breath and pointed everyone out, alternating between each mother and their respective child, starting with herself. 'I'm Katherine, this is Eva, that's Gwen with Bobby, and Susan with Clem.'

'Natalie with Edith,' Tally said, pointing between her and her baby, deciding not to reveal her nickname just yet because she felt that Natalie sounded a little more grown up.

'Oh, she's gorgeous,' Katherine said, peeking into the pram, her eyes lighting up as if she really meant it.

'Thanks,' Tally said, and then as an afterthought, 'yours too.' Tally looked at Eva, and although she tried it was hard for her to muster up any real interest. I'm just not ready for kids, she thought, panicking once again at the idea of being a mum, as if someone had just tapped her on the shoulder and reminded her that she was now responsible for a small and defenceless human being. The inescapability of it was terrifying, but it was also the reason she had to keep her head and soldier on, because she couldn't exactly take Edith back to the hospital and tell them she had made a terrible mistake.

She looked down at her sleeping child. Although she wasn't ready, or entirely sure how she felt about her, giving her up was not an option. Helena wouldn't allow it, but that wasn't the only reason Tally couldn't consider it. She just wouldn't be able to live with herself if she let Edith go somewhere new, without her. She was already having to live with enough without that hanging over her. It was hard enough facing the world and explaining she was now a mum, however the prospect of explaining she had become a mum and then decided to opt back out was something else; it was unbearable.

'Thanks,' Katherine beamed, acknowledging her compliment with a wide grin, as if Tally had just given the magic password to their exclusive mummy club. 'Are you new to the village?'

'No.' Tally was cautious about revealing where she lived, and which family she belonged to. She was reminded of her early school days, before Leila had saved her from exile, and a sickly dread swept over her. She didn't want to be pushed out, not when they had hinted at letting her into their circle already. Her concern swung from one extreme to another. At first she was worried they would think her not good enough for them - a trashy teenage mum - and now she was worried they would think she was too privileged. She supposed she could always explain that they didn't have any real money to speak of. She could point out how British Estates owned the family home now, because they had been on the cusp of losing everything and Helena had been forced into a corner, and signing over the house to a business had been the only way for them to continue living there.

Tally ran her hands through her hair, enjoying the immersion of both body and mind below the thundering hot water. She wished they had been allowed just a little more space, just this one bathroom, because surely British Estates didn't need this room, and the visitors surely couldn't be all that interested in looking at it. The pull of Edith, who would be waking any moment now, forced her to turn off the shower. She missed the heat and the noise immediately, because now her limited time was over and she had to go back to being a parent. If only she had the time to shower all over again. She wrapped her towel around her, then unwound it, cursing that she had forgotten to bring the head towel. She rough dried her hair with the big towel so it would not be sopping wet and then re-adjusted her towel, getting the corner tucked in to secure it under her armpit one second before the door was flung open and she was confronted with Simon.

Her heart hammered in her chest as she immediately thought the worst. Realising it was Simon quelled her fears, because surely he wasn't *like that*. He jumped almost as much as she did, and the only thing Tally could be thankful for was the security of her wrapped towel, which only slipped slightly, and she was quick enough to grab it before it ended up around her ankles. Simon was wearing a smart suit, looking nothing like the handyman she had met previously, except for the dark red hue of his tie, which was why for a moment she hadn't even recognised him. She mused that she probably looked quite different to him, too, with long wet hair and bare skin on show.

She opened her mouth to tell him to bugger off, because he was just standing there and gawping at her, but then he did the opposite from what she was expecting and ducked into the room, quickly pulling the door shut behind him. He locked the door. Tally immediately started to panic, thinking perhaps he was *like that* after all, and shouldn't she have learned by now that you never really know what people are capable of. But then the door handle rattled, and she realised Simon had not been alone.

'That's funny,' she heard a voice say, attempting to laugh off the unexpected locked door it had been presented with, 'Security must have shut this one by accident. It's just a bathroom, pretty modern so not of much interest. Let's show you a few of the bedrooms. There are some delightful period features in the master suite.'

There was a murmuring of agreement, signalling a large party of visitors, and then a shuffling of feet as they continued down the hallway. Tally should have been grateful, she supposed, because Simon had just saved her from a really embarrassing situation. But now she had to deal with him standing there in a suit while she was wearing just a towel, and the steam was curling around them both, making them fluster. She detested the idea of a bunch of strangers making their way to the master bedroom to ogle at the 'delightful' period features her family were no longer allowed to enjoy. He was sweating from the heat, still staring at her through lingering mist, apparently just as mortified.

They stood in silence as they waited for the footsteps to disappear, with every passing second making the situation more awkward.

'What on earth are you doing in here?' he finally hissed, when they were safe to talk. 'That's the *owner* of British Estates and his entourage visiting his newest acquisition.'

'I'm the owner of this house,' Tally hissed back, outraged that Simon considered some random person to have more claim over this bathroom than she did, when she had been showering in here for years. The way he had coldly referred to the snatching away of their family home as an 'acquisition' outraged her further, and if he thought the owner of a greedy company was going to intimidate her then he was sorely mistaken. She would tell them to their face that she should have every right to use this bathroom.

'You can't be in here,' Simon continued, 'they'll go mad if they find you.' Simon was managing to somehow ignore how she was only wearing a towel, and how his shirt was sticking to his back. 'They didn't even want you to stay on site, your mum negotiated hard and the terms agreed excluded you from using this bathroom.'

'What do you know about that? Aren't you just some lowly employee?' Tally shot back, eyeballing the suit and recognising quality when she saw it. He must just have it for special occasions, she decided. The nasty tie was definitely pure silk.

'I hear stuff,' he shrugged, glancing away.

'I need this bathroom,' Tally argued, deciding he was just a busybody snoop 'Why keep it out of bounds? No one wants to see it – you heard her say it's not of much interest.'

'They want to see some other rooms in this segment of the house. You can hardly just totter past excusing yourself, wearing *that*.' He brought their attention back to her lack of clothing, making her realise just how much he had noticed the towel.

She was glad of the warmth, because it helped to disguise her flushing cheeks. His face was just as red and, like her, it wasn't really all because of the heat.

'What's wrong with your bathroom, you don't want to trek all the way over here.'

'Are you serious?' Tally scoffed, 'the entire *segment*,' she used her fingers as inverted commas around his stupid terminology for her house, 'is in ruins. You've forced us to live in the dilapidated quarter, I've had to move my baby's cot three times because the roof in my bedroom keeps leaking for goodness sake.' That was a white lie, because they had not had to move the cot, but it was a moot point because the bucket was still there and the mention of the baby having to survive sub-standard conditions had the intended effect. I need to get back to her, Tally remembered.

'Oh, I didn't realise it was that bad. I'm sorry.' Simon frowned. 'I'll take a look at it.'

'I need this bathroom,' Tally stepped towards the door, closing the gap between them, and he flinched and automatically stepped aside. 'I need to get back to Edith.'

'Edith,' he said, 'what a beautiful name.'

Tally paused with her hand on the doorknob. The way he had said her name shot an odd feeling through her. She thought about responding, but couldn't think of a suitable reply. He didn't deserve her to be nice to him, she couldn't let him use compliments to weed his way into her good books after everything his company had done to disrupt her life. She was annoyed she had shared that piece of information with him, and concerned he had misconstrued her response as an olive branch. She pulled open the door, beyond caring whether or not the party of intruders was standing outside and ready to gawp at her. She walked calmly and confidently along the corridor, with water still trickling down her limbs, just to show Simon she wasn't planning on making his job any easier. There was no way she was going to allow him to become her friend, even if he did think her daughter had a beautiful name.

'I spoke to Simon earlier,' Helena said as she buttered her piece of bread. They were having soup for dinner which added to the sense of poverty as they sat cramped around the table, breathing in a fog of cooked onions.

'Who's Simon?' Michael asked, giving Tally a moment to compose herself. He made a point of never remembering any of the names of British Estates employees even though by now even Michael *had* to know who Simon was.

She bit her lip, ready for the stern telling off. She should have known Simon would have grassed her up as soon as possible. She endured Helena reminding Michael who Simon was, and then adding that she had already told him this and he should really pay more attention. Michael shrugged and finished his beer, emphasising how he really didn't care about retaining information on the new staff. Michael hated them as much as Tally did. Charles simply ignored them all, because he was beyond hate and in a whiskey-induced stage of denial.

'He's changed around the visiting hours, so the stables aren't open for viewing during the regular tours.'

'What does that mean?' Tally asked, taken aback that she wasn't being berated for sneaking half way across the house to take a shower in front of the owner of British Estates. Then it dawned on her that Simon hadn't told on her. He was probably too embarrassed to explain that he had walked in on Helena's daughter in just a towel. Tally felt her cheeks darkening as she replayed the moment.

'It means you can ride during the day,' Helena beamed, 'He'll do a short guided tour at eleven and two every day, but otherwise the yard is out of bounds for visitors.'

Tally was initially pleased, but then she thought of Edith, who was currently strapped into her bouncy chair, staring up at the garish toy dangling down from the toy bar. 'I can't exactly skip down there whenever I fancy a ride.'

She wondered why Simon had done that. It was probably out of his hands, or something to do with low visitor interest. The stables were period, but the atmosphere was spoiled by all their modern equipment lying around, not to mention the strong whiff of horse that would put off most people. Except in the hope of catching a glimpse of the horses in the paddocks beyond, she didn't consider the yard as a particularly interesting place to visit for the type of person who was spending time on a British Estates property. Other than nice brickwork, visitors weren't going to get much out of it. So that must be why Simon had relaxed the out of hours rule. She wasn't going to thank him for it; it would be illogical to be grateful for a stranger to give you a little bit of your own home back.

'Should have kept your legs closed then,' Michael quipped, earning himself a slap on the wrist from his Mother, which made Tally glad the small table put them within hitting reach of each other. 'I'm just saying, it's a bit too late to regret having her,' he protested, digging himself a hole.

'No one regrets her,' Helena scolded, deciding she could speak for everyone on the matter. 'Edith is the best thing that's happened to this family.'

'She's not too bad,' Michael conceded gruffly, 'Obviously I'll change my mind when she starts crying in a minute.' He glanced down at his niece.

Tally watched his features melt as he looked at her. Oh God, she thought, he loves her more than I do.

'It was just a joke.' He shrugged, meeting Tally's eye to check she hadn't taken it too badly, yet refusing to apologise properly, because he was her big brother and had a reputation to uphold.

'I can help out, Tally, so you can have time to yourself every day, to ride or otherwise.' Helena said, being overly nice to make up for Michael's hurtful comment.

'Thanks,' Tally mumbled, trying to concentrate on not crying into her soup at the assumption made by Michael that she had any choice in whether or not she got to keep her legs closed that night, and how it had messed up how she felt about the resulting baby.

'Oh, another thing,' Helena beamed, 'I can't believe I nearly forgot.'

'They're buggering off and giving us back our house?' Michael asked, one eyebrow raised, because unless that was what she had to tell them he disagreed with her perky tone.

'They're fixing the leaky roof.' She ignored her son.

'How charitable,' Charles muttered, finally contributing to the conversation. The rest of them were surprised he had even been listening, they had assumed he was too drunk to keep up as he sat there, gazing unseeing into his soup. He scraped back his chair, fed up of having to hear his wife talk about their oppressors as if they were heroes. He went to his hideout to get another drink.

Tally noticed how once again her dad hadn't acknowledged Edith. He didn't seem to agree when his wife said she was the best thing that had ever happened to them. Tally had told Simon about the leaky roof. Helena was trying too hard to put a positive spin on their dire situation, because she felt guilty and defensive about being the one to have forced them all to move into the leaky wing of their house. Michael was acting like a child, with mood swings to rival those of a teenage girl, and Edith was fidgeting, on the cusp of demanding milk. Tally was exhausted, and the people around her were not exactly helping. Even Anna, who was making a concentrated effort to appear as if she wasn't listening as she wiped down the kitchen counters, was frazzling Tally's brain with her persistent cooking and cleaning.

'I'll ride tomorrow morning, if that's okay?' Tally got to her feet. She unclipped Edith from her harness and lifted her gently into her arms.

'That's fine, darling, do you want some help getting her into her cot?'

'No,' Tally said, probably a bit too sharply. She could do with the help, she always needed help, but she also needed to be left alone, and whilst she had no choice but to stay with Edith, she could at least get a breath of fresh air away from the rest of her insane family.

※

Tally almost staggered to the yard. Her eyes were blurry and her limbs ached, but she was determined to ride Match, no matter how much easier it would have been to follow Helena's suggestion and spend her baby-free time in bed. I must be mad, she thought, as she rounded the corner. Then she saw Match's sweet face over his stable door and knew she had made the best decision. She couldn't use her me time to sleep, it was such a waste. She would sleep later – nap when the baby naps – that was what they had suggested at baby group. They were always full of helpful yet annoying suggestions that only appeared to work in the perfect world. Who is able to nap on demand, under pressure and in the middle of the day? She would see them all again today, and despite her cynicism she was actually looking forward to it. It was humbling to have to admit to Grampy, who had practically forced her to go that first week, but she needed these new friends, and they seemed to need her too, for some unknown reason. Even though she still hadn't been able to contribute one single piece of advice on parenting.

'You're already horse riding?' Katherine had asked, astounded, 'I'm still using recent birth as an excuse to sit on the sofa and binge-watch Netflix.'

'Did you need stitches?' Gwen asked, 'Because I had four and there is no way I'm straddling anything for a long time – horse or otherwise.'

The rest of them laughed dirtily, and Tally was both mortified and elated at the way no topic was out of bounds with these women, even though she had only just met them.

'At least you don't have to live with a scar forever,' Susan lamented, lifting her jumper to show the evidence of her emergency C-section, as if it was socially acceptable to flash your stomach to relative strangers, 'Although, on the plus side, my midwife said she knew I had a lady surgeon because of the precision she used to stitch me back up.'

'It is rather neat, albeit very purple,' Katherine observed.

'Bio-oil,' Gwen said, prompting a murmur of agreement before they turned their attention back, remembering they had asked Tally questions.

'I'm okay to ride,' she said tactfully, hoping they weren't expecting her to go into similar detail on the state of her private parts, 'My mum is a massive help. She loves taking Edith for an hour or two every day.'

'Bet your midwife wouldn't be too happy about you riding so soon,' Gwen remarked.

'I don't have a midwife.'

'Yeah, I mean, if she had known before they signed you off,' Gwen corrected, thinking Tally had misunderstood, and was referring to her discharge at six weeks.

'No, I mean, I never had a midwife.' Tally wondered why she hadn't just left them to assume.

The three Mothers looked at her, and all of the babies fell eerily silent, as if to punctuate the confusion. Everyone had a midwife, right?

'I, err, I didn't know I was pregnant.' Tally thought she might as well just get on with it, so she wouldn't have to spend the rest of their friendship dancing around the subject and waiting to slip up. With the speed news travelled around the village, she was surprised they didn't know already. They didn't seem to know where she lived yet, or which prestigious family she belonged to, so she guessed times had changed. There were a lot of new faces in the village and not everyone was as cruel as her old classmates. She was about to find out if they were as judgemental, though.

'Oh,' Susan managed, speaking up for the rest of them, yet struggling to find anything constructive to say.

'Well, you didn't miss out on much, my midwife was bloody awful,' Katherine shrugged.

'Mine was lovely, you were just unlucky,' Gwen said, shaking her head.

'Natalie was the unlucky one, she missed out on all that time spent in waiting rooms, needing a wee,' Susan countered, getting over the initial shock and catching up with the others.

'What about all the time wasted on making a birth plan, for it to then go completely out the window,' Katherine added.

'Don't forget the late nights spent googling all of the things that could go wrong with pregnancy and birth,' Gwen said, snorting with laughter. 'And, anyway, your birth went completely to plan, Katherine, so don't give us that!'

'I bet you got to eat loads of goat's cheese, didn't you?' Susan was clearly jealous.

'Yeah, I had plenty of pate and alcohol, too,' Tally winced, thinking about all those nights out she'd enjoyed, at Edith's expense.

'Yeah well, so did I.' Katherine waved her hand dismissively. 'The babies are fine.'

They all paused to survey the babies, checking for evidence that they were not permanently damaged by alcohol poisoning from the womb. With the way they were all dribbling and sucking their fingers, it really was impossible to tell. Tally glowed inside, her guilt easing despite her suspicions that Katherine was only trying to make her feel better. Katherine would have been careful with her alcohol intake, certainly more careful than someone at university with no idea they were growing a baby, but Tally was still touched by the sentiment. The way they were all laughing about it already, offered her a huge sense of relief. It looked like they were not going to ask her any awkward questions or shun her for being an atypical Mother, as in a completely oblivious one. Tally was grateful she had met these people, because they knew what she was going through with the sleepless nights and the constant cycle of feeding and changing and soothing. They weren't in the same boat exactly, because they all had loving, long-term life partners who had knowingly impregnated them, and now helped them out, but at least they were fellow new mummies with shoulders to cry on. They still had no idea what they were doing half of the time.

'Hang on,' Tally called, her memory of baby group broken by shrill horse whinnies. She stirred the feed bowls and when she went back outside to deliver breakfast. It was nice to see Peter's head also over his half door. Both horses whinnied again, telling her to hurry the heck up, and she smiled, despite pretending to curse their impatience. Although in the old days Grampy would have done most of the chores, Tally had always enjoyed coming out early to feed the horses in the crisp morning light. She wished once again that things hadn't changed, and Grampy was still here, about to arrive in his little old car, but things had changed. Everything was different now. The only consistent thing in her life was the demands made by the two horses and the insults thrown around by her brother.

Tally opened each stable door and slid a feed bowl in, chuckling as the horses attacked them as if they had been starved for months. 'You look disgusting when you eat,' she told Peter, who blew out contentedly, spraying bits of grain across his bowl, ignoring his human now that she had delivered the feed. She decided to muck out around them, figuring she would still have time for a quick ride after doing a few more chores, and that Match would need some time to digest his breakfast before his morning workout. She didn't much like the way their stables had been prepared, so she decided to drag out the beds, making them bigger so the horses were not restricted in where they could lay down. She also added more bedding, seeing that the current depth was not enough. She simmered at why the beds were substandard; it was because Grampy wasn't doing them.

'You know, Helena put up a big fight to secure our help with horse care,' a voice said from the other side of the door, making Tally jump as she was scraping out bedding with her fork. He watched her swap utensils and round off the corner to

Match's bed with a broom, unfazed that the horse would kick it all over the place within minutes.

'That's because you were about to leave her in the lurch by firing Grampy,' Tally finally said, wishing Simon would stop randomly appearing, before lamenting that it was not 'random', it was just that he now practically lived here along with a load of other unwelcome staff from British Estates. He should also stop trying to use Helena's quest for half decent terms as leverage over Tally; it was an underhanded tactic. She let herself out of the stable and propped up the equipment so she could finish perfecting their beds after her ride, without being hassled.

'Mum's allergic to horses, Dad is too busy sulking and Michael would have refused to help on account of his busy social life.' She regretted responding in so much detail. Simon didn't deserve to know anything about their family.

'We let Anna stay.'

'She's got enough on her plate in the house,' Tally snapped, resenting his use of 'we' and 'let', 'besides she isn't exactly horsey.' She lifted Match's headcollar from a hook and went back into the stable to retrieve her horse. She supposed he was also going to lord over her the way he had 'let' her ride on a more flexible basis in a minute and expect her to be thankful. I'll never be beholden to him, she thought with gritty determination as she secured Match and led him outside, hoping he would swing his hindquarters into Simon as she turned him towards a tie point.

'What about you? You're clearly into horses.' Simon stepped aside, and from the way he reached out to Match to say hello, Tally could see Simon knew his way around a horse.

'She didn't know I'd be home,' she sighed, wishing her mother had confided in her about the takeover. Tally was not naive enough to think she could have prevented it. The finances were too far gone, from what she could gather, to enable any kind of alternative rescue plan. If someone had forewarned her though, she might have had a chance to help. Helena was cracking under so much stress and guilt, and she didn't deserve the blame. Tally could have been at least one person on her mum's side, when the others all seemed to think it was all Helena's fault that they had been forced to give up their house, as if she had made a flippant decision one day and that she had not actually been backed into a corner. Helena didn't deserve the treatment she received from the rest of the family. Even if Michael did secretly agree that Helena had no choice, he wasn't making that clear to his Mother, because he was too angry about it to be nice to anyone.

Tally was sympathetic because Helena had decided to support her and embrace Edith. Her mum had rushed to her side with no thoughts to lecture her for getting herself pregnant and then not even realise it, and ruining her expensive education – her whole life, potentially. Helena had surprised Tally with her attitude, so Tally wanted to do the same right back. She supposed that in both situations, looking back was not going to help anyone, they just had to get on with it and accept what had happened, which was easier said than done. Tally wondered if she was maturing, or just getting used to dealing with horrible situations, so used to dealing with them that it was now easy to just take them in her stride. Or I'm just shell-shocked, she thought as she lifted Match's feet to scrape out the muck, and nothing could ever exceed the hell I went through. She shuddered, and then scolded herself for letting that thought weave its way in. It never happened, remember? That wasn't you, in that room.

'With a baby,' Simon added, and his curious tone gave away all his prejudices.

'Don't you dare,' Tally snapped upright, making Match snort in surprise at her sudden movement. She placed a calming hand on his neck, to show him that it was nothing to do with him. 'Don't think you know me.'

'I don't know you.' Simon raised his palms apologetically.

'You don't know me at all.' Tally left to grab the tack, hoping he would be gone when she returned. Unfortunately, he wasn't. She paused when she saw him, because he was rubbing the spot between Match's eyes, laughing at the way the horse responded. Match was practically purring with appreciation at the groom. Tally felt something stir inside her and she had to quickly re-build the barrier of hatred and remind herself who he was and what he represented.

'You're good with horses,' Tally retorted as she lifted the saddle onto Match. She was relieved when he stepped away and left her horse alone. She tried not to be annoyed at Match for enjoying a scratch from the enemy.

'I rode a little, growing up, don't most kids?' Simon shrugged. 'I should get to work.'

No, most kids don't, Tally thought, her suspicions now raised. She watched him walk away. Something about his response was guarded, and it had made him scarper. She supposed she didn't know him either; she was almost convinced she wanted to keep it that way.

❄

'I can't believe I agreed to this,' Michael muttered, as the horde of women approached pushing their prams.

'Gwen is about to become single,' Tally said, feeling instantly guilty for making light of it. Gwen had only recently revealed that things between her and her husband were not peachy, and how it was becoming increasingly apparent that the baby bandage was not working. Gwen had revealed that her marriage had been on the rocks for a while, and that although never spoken out loud, the baby had been their last ditch attempt to stitch their relationship back together. It had been a high stakes gamble and had failed to work. Tally didn't relish in other people's woes, but she did glean some small comfort when Gwen confided in her because it made her feel a little more normal, a little less pathetic.

'Which one is Gwen?' Michael asked, wondering if he could even deal with inheriting a baby with a relationship, and deciding that he probably couldn't. He wasn't ready for any baggage or unnecessary complications.

It was too late for Tally to reply, because they were within hearing distance. 'Hey, this is my brother,' she said, not needing to tell them his name because she had whinged about him so much to them already. Their faces lit up with delight upon learning that the handsome man in front of them was the brother Tally had often complained about, and she could tell they were surprised by his good looks, wondering why she had left them out of her damning descriptions of him. Obviously it was because he was her *brother* and she had never really noticed that he was attractive. She hoped this wouldn't tempt them to sympathise with him from now on, whenever she needed to moan. Gwen appeared to have especially perked up, and stepped forward to shake his hand with her free arm. Tally could see she was tempted to announce her almost single status.

'I am so excited about this,' Katherine said, 'I've never been to see a baby friendly movie before.'

'Me neither,' Michael said through gritted teeth. He had been cornered into playing chaperone today because Tally couldn't drive and the cinema was in the next town. Helena had loaned Michael her more practical car. The others had suggested they go to the movies and Tally was keen to demonstrate her willingness to join in. Meeting outside of the official baby group signified a proper relationship with the other mums. When Tally had asked for a lift at dinner the night before, Helena had told

Michael that he had to do it, being an uncle now, and he had reluctantly agreed in the hope he could cash in on the favour at a later date. Helena had dropped her car keys into his lap, to sweeten the deal. Right now, though, as they filed into the darkened room to find their seats amid the fidgeting and crying of infants, he couldn't see it paying off. The way Gwen squeezed her way past Tally so she could sit next to Michael didn't even make him feel better, because even though Gwen was pretty hot, she had a wriggling baby on her lap.

'Where are you going?' Tally asked Michael as he got up to leave half way through the opening scene.

'I need the loo,' he said.

Tally watched him walk out, taking his coat with him, and she just knew that he wasn't coming back. 'I told you he was a knobhead,' she told Gwen, who shrugged and moved over one, filling in the gap he had left.

'At least he tried,' Gwen said, 'my brother would sooner jump off a bridge than hang out with four women and four babies.'

'Yeah,' Susan whispered from the other side, 'I was impressed he got this far.'

Tally settled in to the film, glad the others were okay with his abrupt departure, and tried not to worry about the infrequency of buses between this town and her village.

❄

'Just my bloody luck,' Tally cursed the storm clouds as they started spitting, wondering where they had even come from. She had turned down the offer of a lift from the other three to be polite, and because the sky had been bright and clear, but now it was sodding raining and the bus stop was at least a mile from her house. She then remembered that the rain cover for the pram was stuffed in a drawer at home, and that poor Edith was wearing a cotton jumper with no waterproof coat to speak of. She was being a negligent mum. She had the hood of the pram pulled up, but the slant of the rain meant that most of Edith was still getting wet. She pulled off her own bobble hat and tucked it over Edith's legs, making a secondary layer to absorb the water, exposing her own hair to the elements as the rain began to worsen. Luckily Edith had her own miniature bobble hat, complete with button detailing, freshly knitted by Helena and pretty impressive for a first attempt at homemade baby clothes.

Tally picked up the pace, power walking to try and get home quicker, although it was only making the rain hit them both harder. She was tempted to cry but it wasn't going to help and would just make her face even wetter. She shivered as cold slivers worked their way down the back of her light jacket and cursed her foolishness for thinking she could rely on the British weather, or her brother. Just as Edith started crying and Tally considered joining her a tempting option, a car pulled up beside her. She wondered if it was Michael, but he was too self-absorbed to even notice it was raining, and certainly wouldn't have thought about how abandoning her could have resulted in her being stuck in bad weather, having to trudge home.

Someone jumped out of the car, carrying a big coat. She jerked away as he wrapped it around her, with no idea who her saviour was, but then relaxed because the giant hood was offering her warmth and protection. 'The baby,' she said, wanting Edith to be protected from the sheets of water first, but he was already reacting, leaning over the pram to take Edith out. Tally had worked out who it was, so she knew her baby was safe in his hands, but she still didn't like it all that much. It was Simon. 'Your car doesn't have a car seat,' she said, as he shouted for her to get in. She clambered in anyway, hoisting herself up into the passenger seat of his giant vehicle, ignoring the offensive logo of British Estates printed on the side.

'Do you really care in this?' he replied, lifting Edith onto her lap. She snuggled her baby to her chest, opening her wet layers to let her press against her warm, dry jumper, and decided that she didn't care. It was now less than a mile to home and she was going to trust that Simon would get them back there warm, dry and safe. She pushed her sodden hair out of her face as she watched him struggle with the pram, wondering if she should open the door to shout instructions on the way you had to release the latch, but then he worked it out on his own and was able to collapse it and throw it into the back.

He threw himself into the car, and shook away the water droplets with a flick of his head, spraying her with them. She could hardly complain, because it was because of her that he was soaked, and if it wasn't for him then she would still be out in the downpour. He turned on the ignition and glanced at her, then realised her arms were full, so he reached across her and secured the seatbelt carefully over them both, taking his time so as not to wrap the belt over Edith. Tally tried to look away, but he was taking forever, so she couldn't help but peek back. His grey eyes locked onto hers and her cheeks immediately flushed. She took a sharp intake of breath, and then the seatbelt clicked in and he moved away, to crank up the heater and find first gear. Tally was left wondering if Simon had noticed the colour of her eyes.

'Go slow,' she warned, knowing that she didn't need to say it, but unable to help herself.

'I know. I am.' He kept his eyes diligently on the road ahead. Even without the baby he would have been forced to crawl along, because it was almost a monsoon out there. 'Good job I spotted you,' he said, whistling as he flicked the windscreen wipers to maximum, and could still barely see through the windshield.

Tally didn't reply, because she didn't want to have to be thankful, but she knew she would have been screwed without him. There hadn't been another car in ages, and by now she would have been forced to stop pushing and huddle over the pram to protect Edith from the worst of it.

'How is she?' he asked, daring a glance at Tally's chest, where Edith was whimpering.

'She'll be okay,' Tally said, not sure if that was true but unwilling to let herself panic. 'I'm going to kill Michael for letting this happen,' she said, gritting her teeth.

'Next time you get stuck, call me,' Simon said.

'I don't have your number.'

'It's on the side of the car in giant letters,' Simon said without thinking.

'Your number is on the side of the car? Aren't you, like, some lowly employee?' she raised an eyebrow at him.

'Lowly employee with decent car benefits,' Simon shrugged.

'With personalised telephone numbers on each car?' Tally tilted her head.

'Sure, why not? We're here.' He turned into the drive, not needing to announce that they were there, because Tally recognised the entrance to her own house, but needing to change the subject.

Tally wanted to ask him another question about the supposed perks of working for British Estates, because something about them was not adding up, but then she spotted Helena's car parked in front of the house, the car her brother had been loaned in exchange for transporting his sister and niece safely to the cinema and back, and she was now too preoccupied with all the scathing things she was going to shout at him to even worry about Simon.

'He feels *amazing*,' Tally commented, as she took Match around the corner and asked quietly for a canter. The horse flowed into a gorgeous smooth gait, and Tally remembered how he used to jump into a canter, throwing his head and swishing his tail in protest at having to school nicely on the flat. 'You guys have really been doing your homework.'

'I'm aiming for a dressage competition next month; I've entered a prelim class.'

'You're going to win,' Tally grinned as she changed the rein across the centre of the school, asking for a few strides of trot and then the opposite bend before moving effortlessly into canter on the other leg. She was jealous, *insanely jealous,* but she was also proud of her horse – and her best friend – for the improvements they had made since Tally had been away.

'How did I not notice how good he's become?' Tally mused. She halted and dismounted, so Leila could take her place in the saddle. She watched Leila take Match around a few times, showcasing his moves, and he looked even better under Leila than he had felt to Tally.

'Because you only ever want to go galloping or jumping,' Leila pointed out, sticking out her tongue at Tally cheekily as she pulled up by the fence. 'And you were too busy off gallivanting at university to notice.'

'Fair point,' Tally replied. She looked down at Edith who was asleep in her pram. I should be at university right now, she thought, gallivanting. Instead I'm standing here with nothing to do with myself except wait on this baby, and ride occasionally, with help or when I can blag a free babysitter for an hour. 'I didn't do much gallivanting,' she said mournfully, thinking she should have perhaps done a little more. There was that time with Doug, obviously, but that had been a pretty big mistake.

'I disagree,' Leila said, kicking her feet free of the stirrups. 'I mean, what about the random guy?' Leila made eyes at Edith, the supposed result of that fictional encounter.

'What random guy?' Tally asked, completely forgetting what she had told her before.

'Edith's father? What was it, a drunken one-night-stand with a complete stranger, or did you know him, if only just a little?'

Tally felt her cheeks darkening. Leila dismounted and pulled up her stirrups. 'Come on, you can tell me, we tell each other everything, don't we?' Leila grinned.

'No we don't,' Tally snapped, 'You didn't tell me about Michael.'

'What?' Leila started, taken aback at the sudden attack. 'What are you talking about?'

'The last Christmas party we had here. You and Michael?' She didn't want to talk about it, to *know* about it, but she had to get the heat off of her, and this argument was going to happen one way or another, one day. She had kept it bottled up until now, because something else much worse had always been on her mind. Now that Leila was pressurising her to talk about Edith's father, she had found herself blurting it out as a distraction. It had happened on the same night, after all, and from the reaction it prompted, it had definitely worked.

'Oh.' It was Leila's turn to blush. She led Match out of the arena, towards the stables.

Tally pushed the pram behind, giving her friend a minute to think about her next sentence. Part of her had hoped that Leila would be clueless, unable to understand the question, because perhaps Brad had been lying, but her reaction confirmed something had happened between Leila and Michael. She watched as Leila took her time fastening Match's headcollar, and then released the girth.

'It was just a silly mistake, a one-time thing.' Leila turned towards Tally with big, fearful eyes. She had hoped Tally would never find out about it, because they had agreed she never needed to know. The girth swung below Match's sweaty stomach.

'Why didn't you tell me? He is *my brother*.'

'That's exactly why I didn't tell you,' Leila said, 'I knew you would be upset and it didn't mean anything, so we thought it would be best not to say anything. It's ancient history.'

'You agreed that between you, did you?' Tally narrowed her eyes, hating the idea of a conspiracy between the two people she loved the most.

Leila approached, arms open, leaving Match abandoned in his tack. The released girth swung below his belly, leaving a visible sweaty stripe behind. 'I'm *so* sorry,' she pleaded, 'we were both drunk and...'

'And?' Tally crossed her arms.

'You don't want to hear the gory details, do you?' Leila hesitated.

'Yes, I do.' Tally threw her hands in the air. 'No, actually, I don't. I don't know. Did you sleep with him?'

Leila paused, wondering how to answer.

'Oh my God, you did! You had sex with my brother!' Tally had been hoping it was just a kiss, or a fumble at most.

'It was an accident.'

'How do you accidentally have sex with someone?' Tally asked, and then she thought back to the bathroom floor, to Brad, and the way she had not intended for it to happen. At least Leila had been able to make a choice. She turned away, thrown by the memory, and swallowed down the bile. What had happened between Leila and Michael didn't matter anymore, because all she could think of was his rank breath and the weight of his body on top of hers. Leila continued to grovel, trying to explain, but Tally couldn't hear her.

'Please, please don't hate me,' Leila said at the end of her outpour, as she wrapped her arms around Tally, thinking she had turned away from her because she couldn't bear to look at her best friend. She pressed her chin onto Tally's shoulder, terrified the damage she had inflicted was irreparable.

Tally took a deep breath, needing the hug, wishing she was able to talk to Leila about what had happened to her. I could tell her right now, she thought, half tempted to do so. Then it would be out in the open, we would be even. But then Simon walked around the corner, into her view, like a bad penny. He hesitated when he saw them, his eyes meeting Tally's for a moment, before he sharply turned and retraced his steps. Leila dropped her arms, as startled by the intrusion as Tally. Match whinnied, requesting attention, and the removal of his tack. Leila hoisted the saddle from his back.

Tally watched her work for a minute while she considered what to say next.

'I forgive you, not that you need to be forgiven. Just because he's my brother it doesn't mean I own him, and just because you're my friend it doesn't mean I own you, either. You're both free to sleep with whoever you want to.' Her friendship with Leila was more important than a childish ban. She was still hurting, and it was going to be difficult to accept, but she would save the argument for Michael because Leila was too precious. Michael would withstand the fight and still be her big brother when the dust settled.

'I'm still sorry, and it won't ever happen again,' Leila promised, visibly relieved to have been forgiven, and probably to have also shed the secret from her shoulders. She dumped the saddle over the stable door and returned to Tally for another hug, this time facing each other.

Tally squeezed her back tightly.

'I'll never keep another secret from you again,' Leila promised, 'That one was torture.'

'I'll bet,' Tally smiled sadly over her friend's shoulder, far too aware of what it was like to carry around a silent burden. I can't tell her, she realised as the seconds slipped by and her window of opportunity rapidly closed, because I don't want this hug to change. She tried to blame Simon's interruption earlier, because that could have been the perfect moment to explain about Edith and about that night, but she knew it wasn't his fault she had kept quiet, she could hardly blame him for the past year of silence. There was never going to be a perfect time, because she didn't want Leila's pity. She didn't want to have to watch her expression change to horror, or to second guess her glances from now on. She didn't want Leila to take it upon herself to inform someone. She just wanted her best friend, and the history with Michael was already one complication too many.

'You ready?' Michael asked, nudging Tally in the ribs.

'Ow, yes.' She wondered if this was a good idea now that they were standing on the entrance steps to their own house, wearing ridiculous disguises.

They had raided their parents' wardrobes and had to admit that they had gone a little overboard. Why exactly they had felt the need to dress so exuberantly when they were just trying to pass for normal members of the public, completely eluded her. Then she remembered that they had shared a bottle of wine during the dress up phase and allowed themselves to go overboard, because it was fun and ironic and they wanted to prove a point. Right now, though, as the house loomed above them like a stern relative asking what on earth it was that they thought they were doing, the plan seemed ridiculous. Michael was standing there in a tweed waistcoat with a pocket watch chain and she wore a massive string of pearls and a fur shrug. They were about to get into so much trouble.

'Here,' Michael nudged her again, but this time to draw her attention to the hip flask he was wielding, top already unscrewed.

She gulped down half of it and then handed it back, wiped her mouth, and clonked up the steps in borrowed heeled boots that were slightly too big. Michael laughed and, upon glugging the rest of the drink down, followed her, adjusting his flat cap as he went.

'Two adults, please,' Tally said in her best worst posh accent, tittering, because for some reason they had decided to put on silly voices to match their clothes, even though they could have just gone in speaking normally. None of the staff would even recognise them as the former occupants, since they never had to mix with them because of the way the visitor parts had been set up, allowing maximum privacy for the family. They had agreed on the theatrics just to make things more interesting, because after a few drinks it seemed like a good idea.

The lady on the desk stifled her bemused reaction and nodded, deciding to humour them. 'That'll be thirty six pounds, please,' she said, bemused as Tally opened and shut her giant purse.

'Good gracious, that's an awful lot of money to have a snoop around this house. Darling, do you have money? You know I only ever carry enough for an emergency gin and tonic.'

'It includes the gardens,' the desk clerk said to justify the cost. She watched with one eyebrow raised as Michael patted all his various pockets, making a show of scratching together enough for the extortionate entrance fee.

'In that case, it's a bargain.' Tally covered her mouth with a gloved hand in mock amazement.

'Do you take poker chips?' Michael asked, to which the lady shook her head, wondering if he was being serious and whether she should call security. He finally produced the money and Tally held out an elbow for him to take. They pottered down the corridor, making a show of gasping at the paintings. They suppressed giggles as the desk clerk stared after them.

'Welcome,' said the next person working for British Estates, a small elderly man, as he invited them into the front room with an elaborate wave of his arm, as if it was a palace.

It almost *was* a palace, Tally thought, looking around with fresh eyes. She had become used to luxury and only now it had been taken away did she really appreciate it. She could now only enjoy it if she paid the entrance fee. The room she stood in now, with little pine cones balanced on expensive chairs to remind visitors not to sit, had just been her ordinary front room, and she could finally understand why she had been disliked by the rest of the school. This sort of wealth was not normal.

'Please,' he continued, choosing to ignore their outlandish outfits, 'just ask if you would like to know anything about this room.'

'Darling, what would you like to know?' Michael asked Tally, wiggling his eyebrows, egging her on. He lifted up then reset a priceless vase on the mantelpiece, causing the man to gasp and mutter a request that they refrain from touching anything.

'The people who lived here, were they fantastic?' Tally asked, getting into the swing of it now that she was over her initial nerves. With Michael's encouragement and alcohol coursing through her veins, she was able to swallow the bitter sweet swirl of nostalgia and despair.

'The family has been here for generations,' the man replied tactfully, wondering what on earth she meant by 'fantastic'.

'The posh bastards aren't here anymore though, eh? You lot put an end to that!' Michael said, pointing at the man, as if it was exclusively his fault, laughing cruelly, and letting Tally join in, pretending they found it brilliantly funny.

'They got into a spot of financial difficulty.' He stepped from one foot to the other, deciding it would be unprofessional to convey any humour.

'Oh, you talk about that with the visitors, do you?' Tally asked, also turning on him, her smile twisting, 'You tell everyone about this spot of *financial difficulty* the posh bastards got themselves into?'

'It was bloody stupid of them, really, to let things get so bad that they lost their house!' Michael quipped.

'Especially when it was a house that has been in the family for generations!' Tally added.

'Well,' the man coughed awkwardly, cowering slightly under their piercing stares, and then declined to expand. He couldn't think of an appropriate response that was guaranteed to diffuse the situation.

Tally watched him expectantly, waiting for him to answer, so he continued cautiously, slowly selecting his words 'people often ask why, you see.'

Michael immediately pounced. 'People want to know how the posh bastards were bloody stupid enough to give up the home that had been in the family for generations,' he summarised, before eyeballing the man, seeking further clarification.

'It's a matter of public interest,' he nodded, wishing he had refused to expand, feeling cornered. His eyes darted nervously from one to the other, and he wondered what was up with these two strangely dressed, aggressive visitors. Something told him, besides their ridiculous clothes and accents, that they were not *just* visitors. He had the unnerving sense he was under attack and he couldn't fathom why.

'Tell me, John,' Tally asked, stepping closer, squinting at his name badge, making him sweat, 'Do you think it's okay, then, to just blab about this financial difficulty to whoever might poke their nose around here?' She could feel herself growing angrier by the second, and that same anger was mirrored in her brother. This was not as fun as it was meant to be. They were getting out of control and were probably going to regret ever deciding to visit. It was supposed to be a silly game, a way to have a look at what was happening in the wings of their house that they were now barred from entering. It was turning into a confrontation, and their unwitting victim was an elderly man. But they couldn't help it, because they had lost their family home, and it was being openly stated that it was all their bloody stupid fault. Although they *knew* the public would learn they had sold out to British Estates, and it was easy to reach the conclusion that they had not had any other choice because no one in their right mind would happily give up such a beautiful home, they hadn't anticipated that broadcasting the family's financial difficulty would be a part of the official tour.

'Madam, are you drunk?' he asked, smelling the alcohol on her breath, finding a sense of resolve, deciding that as a willing volunteer he hadn't signed up for this kind of abuse from the visitors.

'Possibly,' Tally replied, just as a firm hand grasped her shoulder. She was wrenched around to be confronted by Simon. He just couldn't leave her alone, it seemed. 'Get off me,' she cried. Another man had detained Michael.

'What on earth are you doing here, Natalie?' he asked, exasperated, ignoring her clothing and nodding to the old man to show that he would take it from there.

'What are *you* doing here, Simon?' she growled back, hating the way he used her proper name as if he was somehow in charge of her. 'What are all of you doing here?' She pointed at the other people in the room. 'This is *our home.*'

'Come with me.' Simon tried to guide her away, before another guest saw the commotion, but she pushed him off.

'It's alright, we're leaving. Come on, Michael.' She hurried out, and heard Michael running behind her, having also shaken off his captor.

'That was crazy,' he chortled when they reached the bottom of the steps, ignoring the odd looks they were receiving from the people milling around who were wondering why they were in fancy dress.

'It was a bad idea,' Tally shook her head, still reeling from the way Simon had clamped a hand onto her shoulder. She wanted to sit down on the last step and cry, to hug her knees into her chest and sob, because it should still be their home; it should be Edith's home. She should have spent her baby-free hour horse riding, not doing this and torturing herself. Their mother was going to go mental when it got back to her - when Simon told her.

'Hey, it was fun.' Michael was already over it. He had that carefree manner that enabled him to get over everything. He had this ability to waltz through life and let nothing affect him, not even this.

'Are you ever planning on growing up?' She put her hands on her hips, cutting through his laughter, ignoring how ironic that sounded coming from a lady who was drunk and wearing fancy dress in this middle of the day, having just been forcibly ejected from a stately home for aggressive behaviour towards an old, defenceless man.

He straightened, surprised by how she was now turning on him, when today they were supposed to be allies. 'No, I don't think so,' he said finally, as if it was a reasonable decision.

'Nothing bothers you, does it? You didn't even care that Leila was my friend.'

A wave of confusion, followed closely by realisation, swept over his face. 'She told you?' he asked tentatively, tilting his head to one side.

'Why didn't you?'

He shrugged, recovering quickly, because nothing fazed Michael, 'It wasn't important, just a drunken screw. You would know the sort.' He smiled at her thinly, returning the stones with twice the force, making her wince and wish she had never asked. He was so good at twisting the knife that she often asked herself why she ever went up against him. Because he was her big brother, she concluded, and they were hardwired to argue, even if he was always going to win.

'Get lost,' she said coldly, trying not to let her knees give way after he had insinuated how Edith had been conceived. Everyone had the wrong idea. Everyone thought it was all down to her careless promiscuity, and that was supposedly what she wanted them all to believe. But it still hurt like hell, and although she tried to live with it, it was impossible to let them believe their own story without the truth following on behind, like a snide whisper for her ears only.

'With pleasure,' he nodded back, tipping his hat, before striding off, whistling, glad he had upset her, refusing to let her tears get under his skin.

Tally sat down, right there on the step, and cried. A couple walked past, and glimpsed at her briefly, before ascending the steps ready to pay thirty-six pounds to stare at her home. Tally lowered her eyes to the floor. Another pair of feet walked past, and she recognised them, surprised it was possible to tell it was him from only his shoes. Or perhaps it was his smell as he passed at such close quarters, or his distinctive gait. It was Simon, and he didn't stop to check she was alright, he just kept walking, to get back to whatever it was he had been doing before their little pantomime had interrupted his busy schedule.

❆

Tally sat at the table and watched Anna bake. She wanted to ask her what she thought of all of this house drama, but Anna had never been a talker beyond the transactional and had stuck staunchly to her role as an employee for all these years. The thought of a personal conversation that went beyond niceties made Tally anxious, and perhaps did for Anna, too. Tally mused that perhaps Anna longed for someone to actually ask her something sincere, especially after all these long years of employment, but that task was going to have to fall to Helena or Michael or someone who had the energy to make the effort.

'Oh, look,' Anna said as she turned away from the oven after putting her latest creation in to bake.

Tally looked down, aware that Anna was referring to Edith, and was expecting to see baby vomit all over her lap, but then she noticed Anna sounded overjoyed as opposed to disgusted. It took her a moment to realise what was being pointed out, but when she did, her heart overruled her head and skipped a beat. Edith was gazing up at Tally, staring right into her eyes, as if only just seeing her for the first time. She was beaming.

'Her first smile?' Anna asked, captivated. She crept forwards as if Edith was a wild animal and might scurry off at any moment.

'Yeah, I think so,' Tally said carefully, experiencing something close to unease at the way Edith was looking back at her as if she worshipped her. Tally didn't deserve to be worshipped. If Edith had heard some of her Mother's dark thoughts, then she would not be smiling up at her. Tally didn't know how to react. She thought that she didn't care much for this child. The way she had arrived unexpectedly had meant Tally had not had any time to emotionally prepare for her. She had been unable to see past the sleepless nights, the unending cycle of feed, change, rock to sleep, and the unescapable memories of her creation. She often forgot it was an actual human she was caring for, rather than just a thing. Being a mother was a reluctant job Tally had been forced to take. But when she looked down at her little gummy smile the world stopped rotating for a second.

'She loves you,' Anna said, her voice cracking. She was no longer the robot employee Tally had always assumed her to be, she had morphed into a close family friend. She lowered herself into the chair opposite, acting completely out of character all because of a simple baby smile.

'It's probably just wind,' Tally challenged, echoing something Susan had said at baby group. She knew it wasn't wind. If she dared to believe this baby loved her, then she would need to decide if she loved her back, and she didn't know if that was possible. Edith deserved to be loved, but she was half Brad's baby. She was an unending reminder and evidence of that awful, unspeakable night. Tally was forced to spend every moment, waking and sleeping, with her and sometimes she sensed she was with Brad, or a portion of him at least. Although the smile stirred up an astonishing feeling of joy she had never experienced before, it also pulled her in two, and she had never felt so conflicted.

Edith's love for her mother was driven by instinct, but also experience. She hadn't noticed the sideways glances or heard Tally's destructive thoughts. Edith didn't know who her father was, or how she had come to exist. She had only ever experienced warm arms around her, and a comforting feed at her Mother's breast. She woke up and knew her mother would tend to her, and her crying would prompt a swift response. She had never known real hunger, abandonment, pain, or the cold. She was content in her little world, now able to react to the regular faces and voices, and she felt loved. She smiled because she was happy, and wanted to communicate that to her Mother, to reward her for all the hard work. Tally knew she would have to face this dilemma eventually, but today was way too soon, even if it meant that, in a moment, all those teary, sleepless nights suddenly felt worth it.

'It's definitely a smile.' Anna rejected the claim that it could be trapped gas. 'Look at her, she adores you.'

Stop saying that, Tally wanted to shout. At the same time, she also wanted to smile right back at her baby. 'Where's mum, we should show her,' Tally said, to distract Anna so she could wipe away a conflicted tear from her cheek, and to distract herself so she wouldn't be forced to decide how much this moment had affected her.

'I'll get her.' Anna hurried off.

'I don't know if I can do this,' Tally whispered to Edith, warning her off, hoping she might be able to make her daughter understand her predicament, just in case Tally had to let her down and could not come through for her. 'I'm not who you think I am.'

Edith gazed right back at her and wondered what her mother was saying to her. She smiled again, trusting it was something good, and that her mother could never decide not to hold her anymore, and would never consider giving her away.

Tally swallowed hard, because she knew she had to keep going. How could she let Edith down? She was just an innocent baby and she hadn't asked to be here; it wasn't her fault her mother had been raped.

❄

'You're here!' Tally ran down the steps, opening her arms to receive Doug. He dropped his bag at his feet and grinned that floppy grin of his, then scooped her into his arms and twirled her around as if she was as light as a feather. Tally hit his back, pretending to protest at the dramatic show of affection.

Michael did a wheel spin as he drove away, splattering them with gravel. He had reluctantly collected Tally's friend from the train station, knowing he owed her one for the time he left her to take the bus and then get soaked. He also owed Simon one, for rescuing her and Edith, but was less likely to allow that favour to be cashed in.

When Tally saw Doug, she stopped worrying it would be weird, what with the drunken sex and then him helping her deliver a baby. It was just Doug – good old Doug – her only real friend from university. He was visiting for Christmas, and up until this moment she was worried that inviting him had been a mistake.

'I can't believe you live *here*.' He stepped back to appraise the house one more time. It was adorned with twinkly lights and bits of tinsel, artfully placed by the British Estates team, which had a nice effect and made Tally wonder why they had never bothered to put Christmas decorations outside the house.

'Well, technically we only live in a very small part of it.' Tally shot a glance at Simon, who was walking towards them, no doubt to tell her off for receiving a friend at the front entrance, which should be exclusively for visitors. She could hardly have Doug traipsing around the back of the house, getting lost.

'I thought that might be the case when I saw that,' Doug nodded towards Simon's huge car, branded with the British Estates logo, 'My parents love going to these places, I actually renewed their membership as a Christmas present.' He made an apologetic grimace, and Tally waved it away.

'Tell them not to bother visiting this one,' Tally sighed, her bubble already burst. It seemed she could not escape reality for very long anymore. 'Let's not talk about it, it's a long story.' She didn't want Simon to overhear her venting anyway, and he was only a few steps away.

'It was just a one-off thing,' Tally said, pre-empting his lecture.

Simon opened his mouth as if to respond, but then closed it again, deciding it was not worth making a scene. He looked pointedly at Doug.

'Oh no,' Tally said, shaking her head at him, wrapping an arm around Doug's waist, which she knew she shouldn't do in case it encouraged him to think they were anything beyond friends who had once had sex. 'He's none of your business.' She led Doug away, who smiled triumphantly at Simon, and muttered 'Let's go and get a drink,' into Doug's ear. He laughed and agreed, giving the desired reaction. Tally knew that Simon could see them embracing and she wanted him to be curious, perhaps even jealous, although she didn't really know why.

'Who is he?' Doug hissed.

'No one,' Tally replied curtly.

'He just looked at you like he was someone.'

'What is that supposed to mean?' Tally paused, tempted to turn back to look at Simon to see if she could work it out. She fought the urge and then continued to drag Doug away.

'I don't know,' Doug said, deciding he didn't want to draw too much attention to it. 'He just seemed to be walking up to you like he really knew you or something.'

'He doesn't know me,' Tally laughed a little uneasily, 'he just works here.'

Tally led him around the side of the house and through the back door into their cramped quarters. Here, there was less to be impressed by.

'Where's the little lady?' Doug asked as soon as they were out of the cold winter air, not that it was much warmer inside.

'Mum has her.'

Helena entered the kitchen singing a silly song to the baby. Anna was cooking, so there was residual heat which made it the room of choice for the family, especially since the living room was so dark and dreary.

'She's trying to get her to smile again,' Tally commented, reaching for some wine glasses and rolling her eyes at the baby talk.

'Remember that you are breast feeding, dear,' Helena said after giving Doug a big hug, having got to know quite a bit about him during her time spent with Tally in hospital. She was indebted to him for everything he had done for Tally during her time of need, and had been delighted to hear he would be visiting. She eyeballed the size of the glass Tally was pouring.

'I'll pump and dump and we'll give her some formula,' Tally said coolly, damned if she was going to be denied a nice glass of wine whilst she caught up with her friend and pretended to be normal for an hour.

'I thought we could go into the lounge?' she asked Doug as he plonked himself on the other side of Edith, and after reacquainting himself with her mum, started cooing at the baby.

'Not a chance, I want to see this one,' he said, tickling Edith's chin and eliciting the much sought after smile, much to everyone's delight.

'Fine,' Tally said flatly as she carried over the glasses and lowered herself into a chair, allowing her mother to respond to the almost unending 'Hasn't she grown?' and 'Isn't she gorgeous?' questions that weren't really questions that Tally couldn't be bothered to deal with. She had hoped Doug would bring her a sense of freedom away from being a Mother, but almost immediately all of the attention was on Edith, as if the old, child-free Tally and all of her individual hopes and dreams didn't matter anymore. Tally stared into her wine glass and realised bringing Doug into her home would not enable her to transport back to the life they had shared at university. As he tickled Edith under the chin and listened avidly to everything Helena had to tell him about how wonderful she was, she started to doubt that he was going to be the fun distraction she thought he would be. If anything, his focus being on Edith instead of her was just making her feel worse.

❄

Tally was losing at cards and it frustrated her. Michael always beat her – always – and she was hoping this year she would be able to turn the tables. She deserved a streak of good luck at some point, right? Anna was actually sitting with them, around their family table, because Helena had insisted. She had been scheduled to leave an hour ago, but the game had sucked her in, and she had declared that her cat would be more than happy to wait for its dinner. Edith was asleep in her cot and – most shockingly – Charles was with them. Tally had tried to convince Doug to sneak off with her so that they could avoid the traditional night of family card games and catch up instead, but he was having none of it and was too keen to embrace the spirit of Christmas and insert himself into family life. It was probably because Helena treated him like the son-in-law that she wished Tally had gifted her with *before* presenting a grandchild.

Charles barely said a word, and was constantly topping up his glass with whiskey to the extent that Tally wondered why he didn't cut out the middle man and simply raise the bottle to his lips directly, but he was there at least, in body if not in mind.

They had pulled their crackers a day early – as was their Christmas Eve family tradition, and so they were all wearing brightly coloured paper hats.

    Tally looked at her father over the top of her cards, when she should have been making a strategic decision about her hand. She was distracted from the game by his being there. She sighed internally when he didn't even twitch at her gaze on the side of his face. He was too drunk to properly consider his daughter, sitting there, asking herself if he was ever going to warm to his new granddaughter. She kept telling herself this wasn't going to play out like a movie. Her dad wasn't going to come around and become a better person, but she still half expected it to happen, because surely any normal father would come around. He had always been distant and aloof, yet now he had folded in on himself, taking his bottle of whiskey with him. If Helena couldn't reach him, then the rest of them didn't stand much of a chance. The house and its heritage were his identity, and without it he had lost his purpose. He was still barely speaking to his wife; it was amazing that he had even agreed to sit across from her and play cards. He was probably going to drink himself to death before Edith's first birthday, and if he did have a poignant change of heart it would probably be too little too late.

There was a knock at the door. They all looked at each other blankly. No one was expecting company, especially not on Christmas Eve. Anna rose from her chair, sensing it was her duty to answer the door, even though she had technically finished her shift and was currently there in the capacity of extended family rather than employee. From her stilted greeting, Tally guessed the visitor was unwelcome. As Simon stepped over the threshold, carrying a giant hamper tied with a burgundy bow, Tally took a sharp intake of breath and glanced back at her father, concerned about what might happen next. She wasn't disappointed. Doug buried his nose further into his cards, pretending Simon didn't exist.

'Let me guess, you want this part of the house now and we're to move into the stables?' Charles bellowed, standing up suddenly with such force that Tally flinched and dropped a couple of cards.

Michael grinned when he saw what she had in her hand, so she kicked him under the table for still thinking about that when Charles was potentially about to commit murder, or simply drop dead from a heart attack.

'I'm sorry for interrupting,' Simon said, 'I saw your light was on and wanted to drop this by.' He placed the gigantic hamper down onto the nearest worktop, politely ignoring Charles's outburst. He was used to abuse by now.

'We don't need your charity,' Charles said, waving his hand of cards around like a weapon.

'Charles, it's a gift,' Helena warned, standing up to thank Simon and wish him a Merry Christmas, making a vain attempt to make up for her husband's rudeness. 'Would you like to stay for a drink?' she asked, feeling obliged to offer, since it was Christmas.

'Mum?' Michael challenged, at the same moment Charles flung his cards down and walked out in a huff, still wearing his paper hat.

Michael didn't leave, but he did glare at Simon as he dared to sit in Charles's empty seat. Tally was a tad impressed with his bravery, even if she sided with Michael. As Simon gathered up the dropped cards scattered around his seat, she raised an eyebrow at her Mother, asking her silently what the heck she was playing at, inviting the enemy to sit down at their table.

Helena shrugged, as if to say 'It's Christmas.'

'Coffee?' Anna offered hesitatingly, unsure if she should ask.

'Yes, thank you.' Simon was clearly on a mission to pretend everyone else in the room didn't despise him in some capacity.

'Don't you have somewhere to be on Christmas Eve? Like your own home – one you didn't steal from someone else?' Michael asked.

'I'm driving back to London tonight, hence why coffee is a good idea.' Simon ignored the sarcasm.

Tally frowned. She had no idea he lived in London; she had thought he was just some local boy. Travelling over a hundred miles from London to work each day was impossible, which meant he must lodge somewhere in the village during the week. The cost of his travel and accommodation versus the wage of a handyman didn't stack up.

'You didn't have to buy us a gift,' Helena said, rising from her seat to inspect the contents of the hamper. Tally couldn't imagine they were going to eat or drink anything from it.

'Unless you wanted to give us our house back?' Michael added, determined to keep poking Simon with a verbal stick.

Helena recoiled at the contents of the hamper, and Tally guessed it contained a selection of branded goodies from the on-site shop, probably all bearing twee pictures of their house and grounds. Simon had settled on an insensitive gift and Tally hoped it was ignorance and not malice that had steered his selection.

'Do you want to take some of this with you, Anna?' Helena offered, hoping she would be able to palm most of it off before Charles saw it.

'No, thank you,' Anna said, not keen to have any of it either. She placed Simon's mug in front of him then reached for her coat. 'I'll see you all tomorrow.'

'She works on Christmas Day?' Simon asked after Anna had left.

'She joins us for Christmas day,' Helena corrected.

'Although, she does do all the cooking, still,' Michael pointed out.

'She won't let me help!' Helena protested.

'Because your cooking is dire,' Tally said, and as Simon joined in with the laughter that followed she looked at him curiously, because he was somehow shoehorning himself into the family evening when they were all supposed to hate him.

Simon paused, as if sensing her thoughts, and got to his feet. 'I should probably hit the road, otherwise I won't even get home until Christmas morning.' The way he said it suggested that wouldn't be such a bad thing.

'You haven't finished your coffee,' Helena said.

'You haven't even had one sip,' Tally pointed out, finally saying something to him.

'I know, sorry.' He looked at her, as if he had been waiting for an excuse to do so. 'I just wanted to drop off the gift.'

'Then why come and sit down and accept coffee?' Michael asked, trying to make him feel awkward.

'I don't know.' Simon continued to look at Tally and it made her nervous, as if she was something to do with his decision to come inside and sit down when really he should already be in his car, winding his way through the country roads until he hit the dual carriageway. 'I also wanted to say that I changed the access route around the house, so you can now get to your old bathroom, the main one on the second floor.'

'Really?' Helena asked, taken aback by the random adjustment.

'Really. Feel free to use it at your will.'

'You're too kind.' Michael remained sarcastic, and Simon took it as his cue to leave before someone was punched in the face. He wished them a Merry Christmas, as if they were all friends. Tally stared at her cards, refusing to dwell on the idea that he had changed the access route just for her, and even less on how the handyman was somehow responsible for authorising access routes. Something didn't add up.

It was Edith's first Christmas, and she was three months old. She wasn't old enough to unwrap any presents, or understand what was going on, but that hadn't stopped everyone from spoiling her. Tally stared at the mountain of gifts.

'You don't really have much for her,' Helena explained.

'That's probably because she didn't even know she was pregnant,' Michael reminded the room, earning himself a cold stare from his sister. He flashed her a humourless grin and then took a swig from the branded British Estates bottle of beer he had fished out of the hamper. He had childishly ripped off the label in an attempt to scorn the company, but the protest was half-hearted because he wasn't going to let beer go to waste.

'This one is from Simon,' Helena said, doing her best to keep her voice neutral as she tossed a gift at Tally.

'I assume you didn't need to read the label to work that one out,' Michael said, noting the dark red wrapping paper. 'Does he scrounge *everything* from the company?'

Even Tally ignored him as she opened the present, pushing down a wave of excitement. She could feel Doug's eyes burning into her but ignored him, refusing to let him spoil the moment. She pulled out two matching hat and scarf sets, one for her and one for her daughter. They looked expensive.

'They're not maroon,' Michael exclaimed, earning himself a glare from his Mother. It was clear that they weren't from the gift shop, either. They screamed expensive London boutique but everyone refrained from saying as much.

'Beautiful,' Helena smiled.

'Practical,' Tally corrected, pushing them into her lap so she could finger the soft fabric and admire them in secret.

'Someone has to help me open these.' Tally flung a parcel at Michael's head and hoped it wasn't breakable. She was eager to distract the family from Simon's gift, wary of the unspoken thoughts bouncing around the room. He hadn't snuck a Christmas present under the tree for anyone else.

Michael eagerly ripped the wrapping paper, revealing a teething toy, delighted to open something else since his pile of socks and chocolate was depressingly small. The only money they had left to splurge on gifts had gone towards Edith. 'It's what I've always wanted,' he said flatly.

Tally smiled as he turned to dangle the toy over Edith's head. She was lying on the mat between them, thinking about rolling over, and was delighted when her uncle presented her with a new toy. Tally rotated the next present in her hand, wondering what else they could possibly need for the smallest person in the family. She had already unwrapped countless clothes, toys and other baby paraphernalia; there couldn't be much left to buy. She ripped off the paper to be presented with a garish face. She jumped, as if it had burned her hands, and dropped the Santa figuring onto her lap, contaminating her new scarf. She then shot to her feet, unable to bear it touching her. It tumbled to the floor, narrowly missing Edith where it fell. Michael scooped it up in a flash, concerned it would bounce onto his niece. Everyone stared at it.

'That shouldn't have been wrapped up,' Anna laughed, 'I found it in the old bathroom cupboard and put it to one side. It must have got accidentally mixed in with the presents.'

'Thank God we don't have to use that shitty bathroom anymore,' Michael said, having ambled to the old, plush bathroom for his Christmas morning shower. He placed the Santa figurine onto the coffee table, no longer concerned with it. The entire family moved on, already forgetting Tally's disproportionate reaction.

'Thank Simon, don't you mean,' Helena added.

'Why would I thank him for anything? He's a jumped-up little minion sent here to spy on us by the soulless corporation that snatched away our house.'

'Michael will you get over it? You're beginning to sound like Charles,' Helena sighed. Charles grunted, but didn't especially resent the comparison.

'Why do we get that bathroom back, but nothing else?' Charles asked forlornly, for once expressing grief rather than anger, having made a mental note not to ruin Christmas for the family with his signature outbursts. He was also starting to accept that shouting at his wife every day was not going to get them their house back.

'It's a bit random,' Helena admitted, 'I mean, it's a rather long walk in your towel. I imagine it's something to do with the dodgy plumbing in the old bathroom.'

'Or it's because one of us used to sneak to that bathroom regardless of the access route.' Michael smiled wryly. The rest of them followed his gaze to Tally.

Tally was still staring at the Santa, however, unable to shake the shock of holding it. It took her back to that night, and she could almost feel Brad touching her. She had no idea it was still there, in that bathroom. She had managed to never set foot in there once since Brad had cornered her inside, even though it was supposed to be their main bathroom up until yesterday evening when Simon had given them their old one back.

'Is that true?' Helena asked, 'Were you sneaking back to the old bathroom?'

'Yes.' She finally tore her eyes away from the Santa that had walked her nightmares for nearly a year and was now perched merrily on the coffee table, seemingly invited to join them for the remainder of Christmas.

'Maybe if you start sleeping in your old bed Simon will just give it back to you,' Michael suggested.

'Why would he do that?' Tally asked, somehow managing to hold herself together.

'You tell me.' Michael shrugged nonchalantly, but his eyes glinted.

Simon leaned back in his chair, exasperated. The bar chart projected onto the office wall told unwelcome yet not unexpected news. He braced himself for what was coming.

'I told you,' his father said, almost satisfied with the poor results because it helped him to make his point, 'Taking on that place was a bad idea. We should have sat back and consolidated rather than added another asset to our portfolio.'

'We needed a new house, we haven't got many in that county,' Simon argued, not about to give up yet. His dad had been against the acquisition all along, despite it being a perfect fit for their portfolio, filling in East Anglia, a gap on their map, quite nicely. Simon had found the house, negotiated the deal and then offered to run it hands on, and he guessed this was the reason his dad had been disinterested. Even if the figures were good he imagined his dad would have twisted it somehow and found a fault in some aspect of the management of the property. Simon hadn't expected warm encouragement because his dad was not that kind of person, but the level of disdain he possessed had been sobering. It was the first time Simon had questioned if inheriting the company was something he even wanted to do; something his dad would ever sanction.

'That's because no one wants to go there – it's out in the sticks!'

'It's nestled in the Fenland countryside,' Simon corrected. He stared into his coffee, wishing he had asked the secretary to bring him a double espresso instead of a flat white.

He was knackered from the past few days of exhausting and enforced Christmas festivities. He wished he had bailed on his friends and family from London and stayed on his own in Fenson. Perhaps he could have somehow wangled a way in to watch Tally open his gift. He hoped Doug hadn't bought her something similar.

He was disappointed at being fought on every aspect of this latest project, even though he was not overly surprised by it. He tried to resist the idea that his father disliked this particular house purely because it was his son's brainchild. His father had pledged to begin handing control of the family business over, and Simon had been shadowing him diligently for five years now, but so far, he had kept a death-grip on everything. This project was Simon's baby, his first find, and his father was dead against it, for unknown reasons. It met all of their criteria. It was a gorgeous period home with lavish gardens and rolling grounds – plenty to occupy visitors for the day. That it was located in the deep fenland countryside, with no other British Estates property for fifty miles in every direction, was a pro, not a con, because it should attract new guests who would not want to travel further afield. A house in East Anglia supported their claim of being nationwide, and of being accessible for families everywhere, even in the Fens.

They had only had the house on the books for one quarter and even his father should know they had not given it enough time for them to be able to start making bold statements or hard decisions about its future. Simon suspected he resisted change, and perhaps harboured a fear of letting go. His dad didn't do much except from work, so perhaps the idea of retiring and leaving the business to his capable son terrified him. It couldn't just be about *this* house. As Simon had become more confident and knowledgeable on the day to day running of the business, he had also been increasingly exposed to the high-level strategy, and that's where they had started to clash. They disagreed on where the company was going, and how they planned to get there. His father wasn't used to being challenged on his ideas and decisions. He wanted to sit still and let the world change around him, never having the courage to keep up. Simon was young and could offer a fresh perspective. It should have been welcomed, but his father only saw him as a threat; about to undo years and years of hard work. Time and power had caused him to grow rigid and complacent.

'Christmas should have been booming, the visitor numbers barely peaked,' his dad said, tapping his pen on the table, frowning at the page of statistics on his lap.

'People don't know about it yet.' Simon had been disappointed with the turn out, but he wasn't going to share in his father's perspective. He had worked too hard to lose faith.

'We spent a chunk of the advertising budget on it. We gave it a four page spread in our magazine. People should have known.'

'People don't read the magazine, Dad,' Simon sighed, having already told him this more than once. Printing and circulating a quarterly magazine to the members was expensive and time-consuming – not to mention damaging to the environment. 'The internet is your best tool to spread the word. The magazine needs ditching, so let's do that and focus on utilising social media, it'll save money and enhance our environmental credentials. We need to make an App.'

'I won't ditch the magazine,' his dad said sternly, having made his decision clear on that more than once. 'The older members don't use the internet.' His father had no idea what an App was.

'I beg to differ, Dad, everyone is online. Everyone has a smart phone, even old people. The small minority that don't are worth the sacrifice when you consider all the younger members we would attract with a revamped marketing strategy.'

'We need to recuperate from fixing that bloody roof. That was not in this year's budget.' His father was losing the battle over advertising mediums, so he was going to attack from a different angle. He shot his son an accusing glance, wishing he hadn't gone behind his back to arrange for the repair work to be carried out.

'We couldn't leave it in that condition over winter, it was a health and safety nightmare.' Simon knew he would be wasting energy by explaining that there was a new-born baby living under that leaky roof, because his dad wouldn't care.

'For whom? Certainly not the guests, from the condition report I can see it was the back quarter of the house that needed the major repairs, and guests don't go into that section.' His father narrowed his eyes, reinforcing Simon's decision to keep quiet about the baby.

'Do you think a dead resident would help boost our visitor numbers?' Simon spat back. He was being dramatic, although the leaky roof was in dire need of repair it was still a long way off collapsing.

'This was exactly why I didn't want to let them stay. It's led to unexpected risk, expense and unforeseen situations. We should have forced them to leave. We only have residents in ten percent of our houses, and it's always a hassle when compared to the empty properties. There's just so much more work – and resistance.'

'They never would have agreed to a deal otherwise,' Simon said. Charles would have chained himself to the fireplace.

'They wouldn't have had a choice; they were flat broke. Maybe you should have been a better negotiator.'

'It's been their family home for generations.' Simon tried not to flare up as his father almost laughed at the family's struggle, as if such devastation was a trivial problem, as if it would be ethical to monopolise on their desperation. 'They didn't want to leave.'

'That's never bothered you before.' His dad scrutinised his son, wondering why this house was different. They had kicked out their fair share of families over the years. He asked himself if his son was too soft to be an exceptional businessman. It hadn't occurred to him that the best businessmen were also those who listened to their hearts. 'You convinced me to let them stay and agreed to take on extra duties there, why?'

'Mrs Hampton was distraught, you saw that.'

'She was reckless, they all were. They got themselves into that situation in the first place. They were living it up, refusing to work, and then the cash ran out earlier than anticipated. It was inevitable and they were fools for not spotting it sooner. Besides, their mistakes mean a few more people can enjoy their house.' His father sat back, dropping the pen on the desk. He had always resented the owners of these wonderful properties for keeping them all to themselves and considered himself as some kind of Robin Hood character, taking from the rich to give to the poor. It had been his motivation all along. The irony that this task had made him a millionaire with his own big country house was completely lost on him.

'I just wanted to help.' Simon shrugged. Helena had struck a chord with Simon. She was exasperated with her husband, practically abandoned by his refusal to face the facts alongside her, which reminded Simon of his overbearing father, who had pushed away his own mother – far too distracted by work to think about her - until she had been forced to leave. Simon wasn't going to explain the parallel to his dad, because he wouldn't understand the emotional baggage that Simon still carried around. Simon had immersed himself in the business in an attempt to get over losing his mum. He wondered if she feared he had turned into his father. *I should reach out to her*, he thought. He was fourteen when she left, and he hadn't seen her in ten years. Meeting Helena had forged a connection with his mother within his thoughts. When he was in Fenson he could reconnect to a forgotten aspect of his life. He could imagine her influence, and it had prompted a change within him, a positive change his father disliked. For some reason, Fenson reminded him of her.

Simon blinked away thoughts of his mum, and Helena, to find that his dad was still ranting.

'And now I can't get hold of you half the time because you're standing in the middle of a flower bed somewhere, or worse – knee deep in dirty straw!'

'The horses aren't kept on straw,' Simon clarified, knowing his dad didn't really care about accuracy when he was stating that his son was failing to run a company from the grounds of Hampton House. He paused and touched his tie. He looked down at it, taking the tip in his fingers, and examined the familiar logo stitched into a burgundy background. He didn't even particularly like burgundy. 'I just wanted to get a feeling for how things are really going out there.' He pointed at the bar chart. 'That isn't atypical, all of our houses are losing visitors. We need to understand the problem better. It's a global issue.'

'Do you think you'll achieve that whilst wearing wellies?' his dad sneered, refusing to relinquish Fenson as the scapegoat.

'I don't know.' Simon stood up, deciding he was wasting his time trying to talk sense to his dad.

'Son, we're hardly on the brink of failure, look at us.' His dad gestured to the world around them in general.

They were still multi-millionaires with a rich portfolio of stately homes, but he didn't want the houses to lose money just because they had decided to stop trying. What was he supposed to do with his time if it wasn't this? He couldn't just play at being a socialite, it simply wasn't his scene. He needed this business to keep him from going insane. Otherwise, what exactly had he wasted the last five years of his life for? He walked towards the door, unwilling to be bullied by his father over this, 'We need to try something different.' If they didn't act, then they could eventually find themselves in the same situation as the Hampton family; in way over their head and out of time to correct their errors. There must have been a point when the Hampton family had thought themselves to be invincible, and Simon was aware of the outrageous expenses maintaining a lavish lifestyle – and a multitude of houses – required. Simon was trying to stay ahead of the curve, since his father was seemingly oblivious to the downward trend they were following. Hampton House was not an anomaly.

'Where are you going?' his dad asked sharply.

'Back to work.' He let the door slam behind him and despite the bad news, that their profits were down for the third quarter running, Simon couldn't help but smile at the way he had stood up for himself in front of his relic of a father. Christmas duties were now well and truly over.

❄

'Are you sure about this?' Doug asked, with one foot suspended in Peter's stirrup.

'You'll be fine, Peter is a good boy.' Tally grabbed his shin. 'Now, on three like we practiced. One, Two, Three.' She strained but Doug hadn't jumped up as high as rehearsed, nowhere near enough to get him over Peter's back. She nearly toppled over as his weight came crashing back down on her. 'You bounce, bounce, jump,' she reminded him after straightening up, exasperated. Peter's ear was rotating, as he stood there lazily and wondered what was taking them so long. Tally was glad he was such a good-natured horse and willing to put up with Doug's incompetence. Match would have thrown a tantrum by now, whilst Peter was much more steadfast when it came to novice riders.

'I'm not sure about this,' Doug chortled.

'Come on Doug, if I can squeeze out a baby, then you can bloody get on that horse,' Tally laughed, grabbing hold of his knee and not letting him wriggle out of it.

'Fine, fine.' Doug accepted he wasn't going to get out of going for a horse ride that easily. 'Although, I do remember one point where you declared that you definitely could not squeeze out a baby.' He turned back to face the saddle obediently, adding, 'In fact, there was a moment where you were convinced you were going back to the dorm.'

'Come on, we agreed never to talk of the details,' Tally cringed, remembering the part where she had gone into a panic and tried to leave, before Doug and the midwife had gently restrained her and informed her that leaving was not an option, and she certainly could squeeze out a baby, because there was nowhere else for it to go. 'Bounce, bounce, jump, okay?' Simon might show up at any minute and she didn't want him overhearing anything, especially intimate birth talk. He was due back from London soon and Tally couldn't understand whether her stomach squelched with anticipation or dread.

This time on the count of three Doug managed to get up and on to the horse, with a bit of pushing and yanking from Tally. She wedged his toes into the stirrups and showed him how to hold the reins before releasing Match from his headcollar and mounting him as well, making Doug scoff at how elegantly she hopped on in comparison to him. She beamed at him, eager to show him some of her favourite tracks.

'We'll ride around the perimeter of the estate first,' she said, 'then we can head into the forest next door.'

'You have a forest next door,' Doug exclaimed, shaking his head in disbelief, 'You know, I have a supermarket on one side and a dodgy underpass on the other.'

'Yes but you also have transport links and reliable Wi-Fi.' Tally pouted.

'Fair point.' Doug gave Peter a click and, although he didn't usually respond to vocal cues like that, the horse got the general gist and ambled off, almost visibly sighing at the clueless person he was being forced to lug around.

Tally led the way out of the yard and followed the fence line. The edges of the gardens were left to wide bark beds, overrun with tall grasses and interspersed with spindly wildflowers, so the horses could traipse through without causing an uproar. She peered down at the mixture of pastel and brightly coloured flowers poking up through the grass, competing for the light, and wondered if Simon would notice the hoof prints. Although he was still away in London, she felt like checking over her shoulder because she was so used to seeing him around and certain he listed keeping a beady eye on her activities as one of his daily chores. She should be enjoying his absence, glad the crushed flowers were not going to invite any underhand comments about her damaging the property for the visitors, however every time she found herself waiting for him to return and anticipating his presence, all because of the confusing comment Doug had made, that Simon had looked at her like he was someone. All those times he had been watching out for her breaking his rules, had he just been simply *watching* her?

All those unwelcome glances and random appearances had played on her mind and, now he was absent, she almost missed them. I hope he's okay, she found herself thinking. She worried her reckless antics had led to him being fired. Maybe someone powerful had found out about her sneaking into her old bathroom, or terrorising a member of staff whilst pretending to be a visitor. Maybe the boss had summoned him to his office and asked him to tender his resignation. He was only the gardener slash stable hand, how much trouble could he realistically get into? She remembered the time he had erupted into the bathroom wearing a smart suit. When he had thrown her out of the house after her silly game with Michael had got out of hand, he had also been wearing a suit. He looked good in a suit, despite the awful tie, almost as good as he looked in wellies and that hideous maroon jumper. She shook her head free of these images. He must just be a jack of all trades, stepping in to help on house duties when they were short staffed. He looked awful in a suit, and even worse in that maroon jumper.

'Come on,' she put Match into a trot, even though it was a bit soon for Doug to be trying out a faster pace, but she wanted to get out into the cold winter morning and try to stop her mind from wandering back to Simon. She heard Peter trotting behind and assumed that Doug was still in control from the lack of screaming. The wind picked up and she was lifted by the sensation of being out in the elements, on top of her horse and away from everything else in the world. She had decided to ignore Doug and pretend she was alone. She wanted to go faster and run away from her problems. At the end of this track, is my old home and my old life. Would Edith still be in it? Would it be possible to keep her baby if everything else could be reversed or erased?

'Come on,' she repeated, asking Match for a canter. Match complied and then they were flying. She listened to the regular hoof beats, oblivious to Doug shouting from behind, pleading for her to slow down. She didn't care about Doug in this moment; besides, she knew Peter would look after him as he followed in his rocking horse gait. *I want to go even faster*, was all she could think, so she threw away the reins and let Match gallop. Peter wouldn't even be able to keep up. They shot ahead and Tally smiled, her face muscles unused to the expression of pure happiness.

Match was blowing, but she didn't want him to slow down, because then the wind would stop smothering her and she would have to face reality again. She kicked him on, ignoring the way he struggled, having lost any sense of compassion. She was the only person here, and even the vehicle for this sense of freedom was unimportant to her as she remained submersed in her fantasy, in which nothing else existed except this sensation of flying. She gave Match another big kick and he protested, begrudging her selfishness. He threw up his head and then bucked, dipping his head as his quarters raised into the air, dislodging her. She tumbled forward over his shoulder and as she hit the ground she knew she had been wrong to push him.

Doug was still far behind her; Peter had given up long ago and was still panting, managing a slow trot. Doug had been a passenger so was grateful for Peter's lack of fitness. He had seen Tally fall and he was no longer angry with her. He urged Peter forward, but the horse would not pick up the pace. I don't blame you, Doug thought as he too gasped for breath at the unexpected exertion.

Tally pushed herself into a sitting position. Match had stopped as soon as he had forced her dismount. He munched the grass by her feet defiantly, daring her to tell him off when the nasty buck had been so well deserved. She had come to her senses the moment she had seen the ground rush towards her.

'I'm sorry,' she said, 'I deserved that.'

Match snorted in agreement.

'Have you lost your mind?' Doug shouted as soon as he was within shouting distance. He could see she was still breathing so his immediate concern was promptly replaced by a simmering outrage.

'Quite possibly,' Tally replied weakly. She flexed her limbs and found nothing was badly hurt – although she was going to pay for it over the next few days, especially since she would be picking up a baby.

Doug didn't need to pull Peter up; as soon as he reached Match, he also lowered his head to the grass, rewarding himself for making it to his friend. Tally bit her lip as she examined the three of them, all sweaty and out of breath, all of them angry with her.

'Are you hurt?' Doug asked, concerned about her even though she had shown no care for his safety. 'You know I can't ride, right?' he added.

'I just…' she slowly got to her feet, staggering as she realised that she had hit her head and it hurt.

'You just lost your bloody mind,' Doug finished, not unkindly. He jumped off Peter, eager to be back on firm ground. 'Let's walk them back, we could all do with a breather and, quite frankly, I'm never sitting on a horse again.' He took Peter's reins in one hand and Tally's hand in the other, and side by side the four of them walked back towards the stables, grateful to be alive. Except Tally, who in a twisted way, wished she had hurt herself a bit more.

Simon arrived at Hampton House to find an ambulance parked at the bottom of the steps. He immediately thought a visitor had hurt themselves, and how much his dad would perversely relish in the bad news. There was a special bar chart for visitor accidents which his dad would make a point of updating and then forwarding on to every employee. He rushed up to the stationary vehicle and found Tally sitting in the back, being attended to by paramedics. His heart began to hammer, but from a quick visual sweep she was conscious, there was no visible damage.

'Sorry, we need to get going,' a paramedic said, flashing Simon a brief apologetic smile before reaching to close the door and blocking Tally from his view. She looked at him for a second but her eyes were glazed, and it was as if she didn't really register him standing there. He stepped back without question as the door was shut in his face. He didn't want to slow things down if she needed urgent medical care. Tally was wearing jodhpurs, so the answer was pretty obvious. It was some kind of injury after a fall from Match.

'What happened?' he asked Doug. He only just noticed as the ambulance drove away that Tally's friend was standing there.

'She had a mental breakdown, that's what happened,' Doug huffed, still mad at her for letting it nearly be Doug in the back of the ambulance, yet also angry because she had scared him, and he was going to remain concerned until she was discharged and returned home, then he could concentrate on being angry.

'Tell me something new,' Simon whistled, remembering all the meltdowns he had witnessed. 'Did she fall?'

'She was thrown.'

'Thrown? By Match?' Simon was startled. From what he had seen Match would never maliciously unseat his owner.

'She had it coming, she just took off suddenly at gallop up that bloody hill, and I was completely out of control behind her. She knows I haven't ridden a horse before! She just lost it. She nearly drove him into the ground and eventually he had just had enough.'

'You sure he didn't just spook at something and bolt?'

'She wanted to gallop; she was the one who bolted. Eventually he bucked her off. We dismounted and started walking back but then she started talking gibberish, just kept repeating the same things over and over again. I called the ambulance.'

'What was she repeating?' Simon asked, trying not to sound too intrigued. He wasn't fooling anyone. Doug looked at him pointedly.

'Something about it never happening yet it not being her fault,' Doug shrugged, not wanting to give away too much. He had barely been able to understand Tally's nonsensical talking so he was safe there.

'Tally's fault?'

'No that's the weird thing, I think she was referring to Edith.'

'Your baby?' Simon frowned, thrown at the idea of something being a baby's fault.

'My baby?' Doug blinked.

'Isn't it your baby?' Simon asked. He had assumed Doug was the father from the way they had embraced.

Doug let out a half laugh and shook his head ruefully. 'No, she's not mine. I don't know who the father is.'

'You don't? Aren't you friends?'

'You ask a lot of questions.' Doug clenched his jaw. It hurt him that Tally hadn't told him about the pregnancy. He couldn't believe she hadn't known, despite the midwife and Tally's mother agreeing that it was possible when they were in hospital after the birth. She could have told him. Simon was hitting a raw nerve now, it was bad enough having to admit he wasn't the father, let alone acknowledging he wasn't even privy to her deepest secrets.

'I'm just confused. I thought you two were an item, or something.'

'Yeah,' Doug scoffed, running a hand through his hair, 'that would be nice, but she's not interested in me – she's not interested in anyone.' He eyeballed Simon, hoping he got the message to stop pursuing her, if that was what he was doing. 'Why do you care?'

'It would just make my life easier if she was, I don't know, a little easier to read.' Simon didn't know why he cared, and he wasn't about to reveal anything to this random guy, not only because he felt like competition, but also because Simon was too confused about how Tally made him feel to even begin to be able to explain it.

Tally made his life difficult at Hampton House, there was no doubt about that, and she mostly did it on purpose. She was usually getting in his way or disrupting the smooth running of the house with her horse in her hand or baby on her hip, however, whilst being away in London he had missed her. It hadn't felt like the well-deserved break he had envisioned. Muttering under his breath as he found all the stable equipment left dumped in the yard and rolling his eyes whenever she laid her blanket and her baby out on the lawn and boldly ate her sandwiches whilst the tourists picked their way around her had been such a familiar sight that he had almost stopped finding it irksome. Going up to her to warn her off had started to become just a reason for him to talk to someone he knew. Although they were pitted firmly against each other, she had morphed from an inconvenience into a companion, and considering how lonely he imagined life was for her now that she was a young mother trapped on her estate and surrounded by strangers, he wondered if perhaps she had started to feel the same way about him. Had she missed him, too? He was worried she was hurt, and glad Doug wasn't Edith's father. Everything else; Match throwing her off and her cryptic comments as a result of the concussion were just confusing him further.

'I can't figure her out either,' Doug said, offering his condolences because he wasn't the only confused man in Tally's life. 'That girl is a mystery. Good luck to anyone who even tries.' He nodded at Simon, punctuating the end of his sentence and the end of their conversation. He wasn't prepared to share anything more with him in case it constituted going behind Tally's back. He recognised the look on Simon's face, and it wasn't just envy that caused him to warn him off. He genuinely thought Simon deserved to know what he was up against with Tally. *She's never going to fall in love with me*, Doug thought to himself resignedly, *so I might as well accept that it could be this guy.*

❄

'I'm fine,' Tally said flatly as soon as she saw Michael at the entrance to the hospital, pre-empting a barrage of abuse. She was sort of glad it was him and not her worrisome mother picking her up. She assumed Helena had volunteered to look after Edith instead.

'Should you be out galloping when you've got a dependant?' Michael asked, steering her towards his car.

'Blimey, did Mum tell you to say that?' She blinked at him, surprised he would even come up with something like that. Since when did Michael care? She figured he was just mindlessly echoing something someone else had said.

'What would happen if Edith lost you?' he continued, opening the passenger door for her like a gentleman before walking around to his side.

'I must have hit my head harder than I thought,' Tally muttered as she slid into her seat, wondering what had got into her brother. That second question seemed too heartfelt to simply be stolen from someone else's lips. He sounded like he had actually pondered that scenario. He should be making stupid jokes – asking her if the fall had knocked some sense into her.

'That's not funny,' Michael snapped, 'you really worried us.'

'Us?' She wasn't used to her brother making their family sound like a cohesive unit.

'Yeah, me, Mum, err, Dad.'

'Dad? Yeah right, you should have just said Anna instead of Dad.' Tally raised an eyebrow. She was certain that her dad hadn't even been informed of her trip to hospital. Even if he could grasp the idea of her having a riding accident and being whisked off in an ambulance whilst in his usual alcohol-induced state, she doubted he would be overly concerned. He had always been a tough love kind of father. To him, falling and hurting yourself was a sign of weakness and even as children they were lucky to receive a reserved pat on the head from him over anything sad or painful. Sometimes Tally wondered if her dad even realised that she was home from university, or had brought home an infant to live with him, under his leaky roof.

'Your annoying friend Doug has been moping around all afternoon, I can't seem to shake him. He's been following me around like a lost puppy.'

'I suppose there are some perks to having an impractical two-seater.' Tally made a point of looking behind them at the non-existent back seats. She was quite glad it was just Michael. She felt rather sheepish and was not looking forward to having to face Doug now her brain was functioning again. She had to apologise for being reckless, but she hoped he wasn't after a detailed explanation because she had no idea why she had acted so wildly. In the heat of the moment, it had been for freedom – escape – but now she saw how ridiculous that was. Michael was right, she had to stop thinking about herself and start considering Edith. She had to consider that it was not just her anymore. Edith needed her to make sensible decisions for them both. Any one of them – human or horse - could have been hurt as a result of her silly, selfish stunt.

'He's in love with you, you know that, right?' Michael put the car into reverse and carefully backed out of the parking bay. 'He loves Edith too, as if she was his own.'

'Yeah, I know,' Tally sighed, 'and it would be easier if I was in love with him, but I'm not. I tried.' She thought back to the night they had slept together and cringed. It was odd that Edith had been born the very next morning, in the early hours, when Tally should have been enduring a lecture and nursing a hangover along with one-night-stand regrets.

'He would take on Edith in a heartbeat,' Michael nodded, sighing because it was a shame Tally didn't feel the same way. He wasn't surprised though; Doug didn't strike him as his sister's type. He was too straight-laced and dependable for her liking. There was nothing exciting about him. If she said the magic word, Doug would give her everything. He would finish university and then find a great job, and make the perfect family home for his sister and her daughter, but there wasn't much point in dwelling on those possibilities if she didn't love him back. Although he was a meat head, he still knew how important it was to fall in love, and how futile it was to hope Tally might choose Doug if her heart was not in it.

'Are you going to ask me if Edith is his baby?' Tally was surprised he hadn't made *that* joke yet. She had been bracing herself for it since her friend had come to visit. It was weird enough that Michael was talking about love. She sniffed the air between them, but there was no evidence of alcohol. Perhaps he was just having one of those rare, caring moments. Either that, or her head injury had really scared them all. It made her realise how serious it must have been.

'No, I'm not.' Michael cleared his throat and Tally got the distinct impression he was going to say something else, something even more serious, but then he changed his mind and turned up the radio.

❄

'Watch this.' Tally lowered Edith down onto the play mat, and then stepped back triumphantly. 'Ta-da!' she waved her hands at her sitting child, to add emphasis to the way she remained on her bum, self-supporting with ease.

Edith looked around Gwen's living room in confusion, wondering why she had been plopped onto centre stage and then abandoned. Tally swiftly scooped her back up, catching her just before she screwed up her face and cried. She didn't like being separated from Tally at the moment, which was a nightmare. Poor Helena was trying her best not to take it personally, since Edith was even protesting when being handed over to her grandmother for a cuddle.

'Fantastic!' Gwen clapped, eyeballing her own baby who was still lazily lying on his half of the padded mat. 'Bobby is far too content with me doing everything for him to even think about sitting up unaided.'

'He'll get there.' Tally smiled at Bobby who really was the most chilled out child she had ever met, not that she had met too many small babies. If it wasn't for the baby group she would only have Edith's development to go by, and it certainly helped to be able to share and compare with other new mummies and their similar aged babies. She checked her watch and wondered what was taking the other two so long, concluding it was probably some kind of baby-related disaster. The four of them had decided to meet up for coffee at each other's houses halfway through the week, as well as continuing with the baby group in the village hall. Tally was nervous because it would be her turn to host next week, and she was going to have to invite them all to her crumbling mansion, and ask them to drive around the back so they didn't upset British Estates.

'What about the tummy roll?' Gwen asked, 'Because Bobby actually went from front to back yesterday. Just once, mind, and I'm sure he was annoyed that I saw him do it in case he thought I might give him some chores or something.'

'She can flip both ways, she's pretty mobile. I can't believe it wasn't too long ago they couldn't lift up their own heads.'

'The time just flies. I know everyone warned us, but they really do grow up so fast!'

Tally nodded in agreement. Time was flying. She placed Edith back into a sitting position. Edith had progressed from helpless to almost mobile and her personality was starting to emerge, including her likes and dislikes. She had developed a penchant for a little stuffed rabbit Michael had bought her and decided she didn't much like being dressed. As she grew, Tally feared she might start to look like Brad, which would make it even harder to forget, but so far no one had spotted the resemblance. Every morning Tally was overcome with a gripping panic that she would peer over the cot and Brad's eyes would gaze right back at her, but so far it had only ever been Edith smiling up at her. Tally tried to console herself that it would only ever be Edith, because her baby would never replicate that greedy expression on Brad's face that still lingered around her mind.

'Did you text Michael?' Tally asked, making the most of their time alone, without the other mums in earshot.

'Yeah, but he wasn't exactly forthcoming.'

'I'm sorry,' Tally grimaced, deciding it was probably for the best if her brother didn't date her newfound friend. 'I was under the impression he wanted to settle down but perhaps not.' She looked at Bobby, and wondered if it was the baby that had put her brother off.

'It's not that,' Gwen said, reading her thoughts, 'he hinted that he's seeing someone else.'

'Michael? No, definitely not. He would have mentioned it.' Tally shook her head.

'I saw him out with someone the other day, a really pretty dark-haired girl.'

'Really?' Tally frowned, 'Where was that? What were they doing?'

'She was getting into his car on the high street. She was wearing riding boots actually, so I wonder if you know her from the horsey world.'

Tally froze. Dark-haired and wearing riding boots suggested one person in particular. Yes, she bloody well knew her. Perhaps Michael was just giving Leila a lift. It wouldn't be something he would care to mention to Tally, although it would have most likely cropped up in conversation with at least one of them, if it really was just a casual lift back to the stables. She stared at Edith as she folded forward, face-planting the mat, before wriggling around to free her legs and lie on her tummy. Tally tried to decide how much she was going to read into this piece of news. She couldn't believe they were serious. Had something been going on this entire time? Had they been together since that awful party? Leila had promised it was a one-off mistake. Surely, that hadn't been a lie?

'They're here!' Gwen hopped up and went to the door to greet the others, leaving Tally with the two babies and her thoughts.

❊ Before Edith ❊

Brad grunted and then rolled away. It was over. Tally remained frozen where she lay, terrified that he wasn't finished with her yet. He got to his feet and pulled up his trousers, signifying that he was spent. That didn't mean he wasn't going to hurt Tally any further. She focused on keeping her breathing steady and discreet, in the hope he would forget she was there. It must have worked because he left the room, not even glancing down at her where she remained sprawled across the dusty floor. The hem of her dress was still rucked up over her hips. She stared up at the ceiling, listening carefully for any hint he might return, but he was gone, heading back to the party as if nothing had happened. Gently Tally moved, wincing at the pain. There was blood and semen smeared on the inside of her thighs. She bit back a sob and reached for toilet roll to wipe her legs. It crossed her mind that she should preserve the evidence, but she quickly discounted that, because she had already decided she would never tell anyone about this. The thought of going into detail about what had just happened to her made her physically sick. She threw up down the toilet, on top of the scrunched up toilet roll, and resented the way her bodily fluid was mixing with Brad's. She asked herself if somehow this was all her fault.

I need to get away from here, she thought, in case he comes back for more. The idea of him returning motivated her to get up and smooth down her clothes. She used the blurry mirror to wipe away the smeared mascara and combed her fingers through her hair. She grabbed the garish Santa and threw him into the bin, wishing he had not witnessed the attack. She walked back to the party, finding herself sober despite all the drinking that had gone before. She tried not to look for him, instead she searched out Leila, but her best friend was nowhere to be found, and neither was her brother, for that matter.

❈ After Edith ❈

Tally spotted Michael's car on the drive as she negotiated her way outside with the pram, preparing to amble around the grounds and rock Edith into an afternoon nap. She saw him walking towards the stables with Leila. He was carrying her saddle, and from their trajectory it looked as if they had been in the car together. They were firm friends these days, it seemed, despite neither one of them having ever mentioned it to Tally. They had never exchanged more than a few words during the entire time Tally and Leila had grown up, despite all the time Leila had spent at Tally's house. He must have just given her another lift, Tally guessed. She aimed the buggy towards them and as she hurried to catch up she swallowed down her irritation at being left out of the loop. Perhaps he had spotted her in town and seen her struggling with the saddle. Although she usually drove her own car to the yard, so why she might be wandering around town carrying a saddle without any transport eluded Tally. Still, she was willing to give them the benefit of the doubt.

She watched them walking together as she followed at a distance. They were engaged in a friendly chat. It was nothing outwardly suspicious, but Tally kept her mouth shut because her instinct told her to observe for a little longer before making her presence known. Leila touched Michael's arm as she said something, but in itself it didn't look overly familiar. They rounded the corner into the stable block. Tally picked up the pace, keen not to miss anything, even though curiosity had progressed quickly from following into spying. When she turned the same corner only half a minute later she was confronted with a saddle dumped onto the floor and Michael holding Leila in his arms, pressing her against a closed stable door as he kissed her and ran his hands through her hair. Things had progressed to something much more than friendship.

Tally tried to speak, but she was motionless, utterly shocked by the discovery. Although Gwen had suggested something could be going on, Tally had not been mentally prepared to see her brother and her best friend kissing. She had just about convinced herself the attachment was harmless, nothing but an acquaintance, and up until today that story had sat well with her. Perhaps it had been another case of Tally staying in denial and ignoring all the clues.

It was Edith who gave them up, with an innocent babble. Michael and Leila broke away in surprise and blushed profusely when they saw Tally standing there, both hands still on the pram handle for support in case she keeled over.

'Can you please pick my jumping saddle up off the floor,' was all Tally could manage after a pregnant pause. It was relatively new and extremely expensive. If the leather was scuffed, then she was going to be even more upset. She didn't need a memento to remember that kiss by, it was already seared into her eyelids. The way they had simply cast the saddle aside, as if it was Tally herself, symbolised their selfishness.

Michael complied, glad to do something other than standing there like a lemon under her stare, for once having nothing clever or spiteful to say to his sister. For the first time in his life he appeared sheepish. Leila tried to approach Tally to explain. 'I'm sorry you had to find out like this,' she started, revealing it had been going on for months, this wasn't the first kiss.

Tally blinked, and all she could see was the sea of bodies in their front room, pushed together in the dark, dancing and laughing and enjoying themselves. The music pulsated through her ribcage. She was searching frantically for Leila or Michael, for someone to rescue her, but she couldn't find them, because they were pressed together like that, hidden away from Tally in their secret world of mutual consent.

'I needed you two, and I couldn't find you.' She was overcome by the memory of stumbling from room to room, pushing past strangers, sure she would find them at any moment because she wouldn't trust what Brad had said to her, because she couldn't even contemplate it happening.

'Why what's wrong?' Michael asked, misinterpreting her need as right now and not on that snowy winter evening.

'I looked everywhere for you.'

Edith picked up on her Mother's distress and started to cry.

'We're here,' Leila said, 'we can help, is it your dad again?'

'Where were you? How could you leave me?' Tally broke into an uncontrollable sob, and Michael went to Edith, to pick her up and try to soothe her, since Tally didn't appear to have even heard her cry. Leila was just standing there, stunned by the disproportionate way Tally was reacting to the discovery, afraid that her actions were unforgivable to Tally. Was it so wrong to fall in love with her best friend's brother?

Simon emerged from behind Tally, just as she fell down to her knees. She was still holding onto the pram and it tipped back. Simon moved like lightning. He wrapped one arm around Tally to cushion her fall onto the hard concrete and caught the pram with the other, managing to right it before it toppled. He then realised Edith was safe in Michael's arms and had not been lying in the pram, about to be catapulted out. Tally clung onto him as she cried, unable to pull back the drawbridge she had let fall open. Discovering Michael and Leila's relationship had triggered the overflow because ever since Brad had mentioned their attachment it had been locked away into the same sealed box pushed into a corner of her mind, forever tangled up with the other unspeakable events of that night.

Simon looked to Michael and Leila for guidance, but they were both blank, unable to process why their secret had hit her so hard. Tally discovering their relationship should not have caused this much grief. 'Hey, it's okay,' Simon murmured into Tally's ear. Michael was busy calming Edith and Leila was shaking slightly, staring at her friend in confusion. He tried to ignore Tally's warmth and inviting smell. Her hair tickled his cheek. Her fingernails dug into his wrist, but he didn't mind.

'It's not okay,' Tally managed, 'I can't forget it. I've tried. I can't forgive her.'

'I'm sorry, please, let me just explain,' Leila began, her voice cracking.

'Not you.' Tally looked at the tearful baby in Michael's arms. 'I can see his face now, when she looks at me. I saw it this morning. She's got his eyes.'

Leila glanced to Michael for help, but his face had clouded over.

Michael rocked Edith, shushing her, trying to focus on not imploding with rage. He gazed down at her little face, into her eyes, and saw no one but Edith gazing back. But he knew who Edith must remind his little sister of, and the conflict she caused. His hands began to shake. His worst fears were realised as he appraised the little girl and questioned who her father really was. Up until now he had allowed himself to believe he had been mistaken, that Edith was the result of a one-night-stand with someone at university, a drunken tumble or split protection, but Tally's admission had just crystallised the truth. His instinct had been right, and for once in his life he wasn't going to feel smug and boast about guessing correctly.

'Here.' he thrust Edith into Leila's arms and bolted, knowing as he ran that he was making a mistake to leave but unable to stop himself from fleeing, just when Tally needed him the most. He stopped at the corner of the house and leaned into the ancient brickwork for support. He doubled over, clinging on to the wall, and couldn't stop the tears from surfacing. *I let it happen*, was all he could think, *and I didn't save her. I wasn't even there to comfort her afterwards – I was off somewhere with Leila.*

'I am no good with babies,' Leila said to Simon, wide-eyed, as she held a wriggling Edith, who screamed even louder now she had been rudely shoved into a new set of hands.

'Take her to Helena,' Simon instructed. 'Go now,' he urged when Leila didn't move. His stern instruction worked and she jogged off, holding the baby awkwardly. Simon raised his eyes to the heavens, praying Leila would not trip over on her way to find Edith's grandmother.

Simon remained crouched, with Tally in his arms, her back pressed against his chest. He waited patiently for her to calm. His legs were cramped and hurting, but he didn't rush her. Eventually, he felt her breath steady as she fell into step with the rise and fall of his chest. He felt her pause as she considered how close they were, and he hoped she wouldn't notice the way his heartbeat accelerated as her ear brushed against his lips. He was supposed to be a gentleman.

She released his arm, breaking the spell. She offered to help him up, but he declined and stood up unaided, stretching his legs and wincing as shooting pains travelled up and down them. He flexed his toes, waiting for the pins and needles to abate. He hoped she would speak first. From his experience with Tally, he had learned it was best to let her lead any conversation. She blew too hot and cold for him to second guess. She might be about the thank him, but equally she might be about to bite his head off.

'I should get back to work,' he mumbled, when it became apparent that she wasn't going to say anything at all. He turned with stooped shoulders, half expecting her to stop him – to grab his arm – but she did nothing, and then he wished he hadn't left but it was too late to retrace his steps. She had to get back to her daughter anyway, and to Michael and Leila and the demons that lingered.

❄ Before Edith ❄

'This has got to be one of your best so far,' Howard said, cracking another beer and raising it to congratulate some random girl as she proudly burst into the room wearing only her underwear, as if to punctuate his point.

'You say that every time,' Michael laughed, catching Leila's eye across the room.

She was talking to someone but kept glancing over their shoulder to lock eyes with Michael. He watched her, trying to work out her intent. This was the first party he had not made a big deal about Tally and her best friend attending, because he couldn't really say they were too young anymore, and so Leila now stood there on a level playing field. It stirred something unexpected yet welcome in him.

He put on his best inviting half smile and was pleased with the results. She continued to glance over – increasingly so - and her interest in him was now unmistakable, as she questioned whether or not he was staring at her. It made the hairs on the back of his neck stand up, and it made him want to know if she had always been curious about him or if the prospect had only occurred to her right now, as he smiled at her.

She had always caught his attention, it was impossible not to notice Tally's pretty little friend who practically lived at their house, but it was only really tonight that he had dared to let his mind wander. Tally was now away at university – back tonight but soon to be off again for the new term – so what was stopping him? Leila had grown up, too, and he was now able to see past the gangly teenager stage and notice that somewhere along the way she had morphed into a full grown woman, with a small yet perfectly formed chest and slender legs to prove it.

'Look who it is,' Howard said.

Michael flicked his eyes over to the new arrival. He clenched his jaw when he saw him, even though he could not put his finger on what had turned him off one of his closest friends.

'Great night,' Brad said, holding out a hand to Michael.

Rather than shake his hand, Michael thrust a cold beer into his palm and nodded in greeting. He looked back to Leila, but she had slipped away.

'Is your sister here?' Brad asked after taking a gulp from his beer can.

'Why?' Michael asked, head snapping away from the Leila-shaped hole and back to Brad.

'Just wondering, because you usually tell them not to come and they sneak in anyway.' He shrugged, playing down his interest in Michael's sister.

'I said they could come to this one,' Michael said, still suspicious but accepting of Brad's reasoning. Brad had seen the arguments around each and every party Michael had hosted over the last couple of years, so it made sense that he would enquire. But Michael still watched him carefully as he lifted the drink to his lips, because something was amiss.

'Isn't that the other one?' Howard asked, gesturing across the room.

Michael turned to see Leila leaning against the doorway, watching him. He swallowed. She was undoubtedly interested, he could see that now from the way she boldly smiled at him, daring him to approach. 'Don't say anything to Tally about this,' Michael hissed at Howard, as he placed his empty can down and made his way over to Leila, with all protective thoughts for his sister pushed firmly to one side.

❋ After Edith ❋

Tally stared at the padded wall. It was covered in psychedelic colours and she was almost hypnotised by it. She couldn't work out what it was depicting, but there was definitely a dancing lion in there. Edith let out a half cry and Tally snapped out of her trance. She checked on her baby, who was now tentatively crawling, and saw that all was well. Edith had slipped with one hand and face-planted the floor, but since they were in a soft play area, the surface she had landed on was well cushioned. Only her pride had been dented and she was swift to recover when she realised no one had noticed except her Mother. Edith righted herself, checked for injuries, and then merrily continued her adventure – having already forgotten the incident. Tally took a long swig of coffee, relaxing after the pause Edith had enforced as she debated whether or not the accident was worth a tantrum. Tally appraised the other mums. They were in varied states. Today, it was Susan's turn to look totally dishevelled. Katherine seemed rather well groomed, and Gwen was middling. The way they looked tended to reflect the last twenty-four hours they had endured. Tally was on the struggling end of the spectrum.

Each week, they would vote on who looked the sanest, and that lucky person – who had been blessed with the most sleep – had to pay for the coffee. It was more than fair. Today, Katherine had paid, and looked smug whilst doing so, because Eva had slept for eleven hours straight the night before. Edith, on the other hand, had been up every three hours complaining. Tally had used almost an entire tube of teething gel on her gums, and was praying for this next phase of baby torture to be over.

'Just when you think you've nailed it,' Tally said, to no one in general but any mother in the vicinity who was listening, 'they go and throw another developmental stage or growth spurt at you.'

'Tell me about it,' Susan said, 'Clem has decided she doesn't like nappy changes anymore. It's like a wrestling match that I nearly lose every time. Once I suppose I did technically lose because poo ended up all over my arm and the carpet.'

'How hygienic are these places?' Gwen asked, voicing a thought they'd all had, after watching Bobby dribble into the ball pit.

'I guess it's better if we never find out.' Tally glanced around at the brightly coloured cushions and toys, and decided she shouldn't examine anything too closely. Before Edith, she would have never set foot in a place like this without wearing gloves, but now she had more important things than germs to channel her limited energy into, like the fact her daughter was currently attempting to climb up some plastic steps, and Tally could see her sock slipping and her chin crashing onto the corner of them before Edith even thought about lifting her little foot.

She rushed over and scooped Edith into her arms, ignoring her complaint, and then reset her trajectory towards somewhere safer. Despite the initial outburst, Edith soon forgot all about the steps once she had been put back down, and trundled towards the ball pit, deciding that out of all the multi-coloured balls she wanted the one Bobby was sucking.

'I should get going,' Susan sighed, checking her watch.

'Yeah, me too,' Katherine said.

Gwen made her excuses too, and they all herded their respective babies out, leaving just Tally and Edith in the under five-year-old section of the play barn. Edith didn't seem to mind that her friends had gone. She continued to play whilst Tally sipped her coffee and wondered how this had become her life. It was a shame they all had to leave, but they had proper lives to get back to. Tally was at the soft play place to get away from being stuck at home and she had no intention of rushing back.

It was heart-warming to watch her daughter enjoying herself, but Tally still couldn't shake the truth; that she was sitting in a dodgy warehouse on an old industrial estate. She had just seen another mum hurry past in pursuit of a child who looked about three. Tally groaned internally when it hit her that she would probably be coming to this grimy warehouse for at least the next three years. My life could be so much better, she thought. Then Edith paused; her back was turned to Tally, and she must have suddenly panicked at the idea she could be all alone. She swivelled her head, looking for her Mother, and a huge gummy smile spread across her face when she saw Tally was nearby, watching over her. Okay, it's not too awful, Tally conceded, as her daughter beamed at her as if she was the most important person in the world.

'Have you had enough fun? Shall we head home?' Tally asked Edith when her coffee was gone, and her baby was starting to run out of steam. She didn't expect a reply, or any response in fact, but it was necessary to ask, for Edith's exposure to conversation as well as Tally's own sanity. To the other parents milling around it wasn't odd at all to hear a one way conversation playing out.

Tally took Edith into her arms and headed for the door. Edith wriggled in protest, wanting to stay for longer, but she was getting tired and Tally knew from bitter experience that it was better to quit whilst they were ahead. Edith was rubbing her eyes as Tally clipped her into the buggy and from the gigantic yawn that followed, Tally decided heading home now was the best idea. Within a few hundred yards of the play barn Edith had fallen fast asleep, having exhausted herself with all the crawling and stimulation. Tally did an invisible jump for joy. The novelty of getting her baby to sleep without a fight had not yet worn off, and was unlikely to do so for a long time.

Tally paused to zip up her coat, and then checked Edith's blanket was securely tucked in. It was bitterly cold. The sky was cloudless, which was beautiful but also meant the temperature was arctic. The low February sun shone deceptively. The rays emitted no warmth for Tally as she trundled home, with her chin tucked into the scarf Simon had bought her. A big off-roader vehicle slowed down alongside her and, since she didn't recognise it, her initial instinct was to ignore it and continue walking. It beeped its horn, forcing her to acknowledge the driver. Her terror vanished when she saw her brother was behind the wheel, grinning at her. He wound down the passenger window.

'Fancy a lift?'

She glanced behind him. This car had seats in the back and, astoundingly it also had a sturdy-looking baby car seat that had been fitted in already. Michael jumped out and attended to the baby and the pram, assuming that Tally's response in the harsh weather would be affirmative. She gawped at him as he negotiated the buckles of the pushchair and then those of the car seat, all the while Edith happily gazed at him, completely trusting to be in his hands, not even annoyed to be woken up by the uncle who in her naïve eyes could do no wrong. Michael opened the boot with the press of a button on his car keys and stowed the buggy away with such a flourish that Tally wondered if she should applaud him.

'Are you getting in or not?' he asked her before hopping back behind the wheel.

Tally scrambled in, before he decided to drive off without her for a joke. 'What happened to the sports car?' she asked, glancing around to see that Edith was thawing out nicely inside the warm car.

'I figured it was impractical,' Michael said casually, as if trading in his prize and joy had been easy.

'You traded it in for this?' Tally eyeballed the interior and guessed it was top of the range. Yet, Michael had dearly loved that impractical sports car.

'This is my company car, perk of the new job.' His eyes flickered to the rear-view mirror and she realised he had fitted a baby mirror onto the back headrest so he could keep an eye on Edith.

'You got a job?' Tally gawped. Her brother working was a novel concept.

'Don't laugh, but I'm a Trainee.' He grimaced at the idea.

'Everyone has to start somewhere,' Tally said, suppressing a snort, because she knew he had done it for them, to bring some money back into the family.

'I'll be running it in a few years, just you wait and see.' Michael gripped the steering wheel, and from his look of determination, Tally believed him.

'What are you doing?'

'Selling these.' Michael nodded at his new car, 'I went to trade in my car and left with a new job, as well as a car. They said they'd never seen anyone negotiate harder and they would prefer it if I worked for them rather than against them.'

'Now that, I certainly can believe,' Tally chortled, feeling sorry for all his future customers, who may not have been certain they had wanted a new car and would then find themselves driving one. 'So, you just decided there and then to accept?'

'I was heading to the job centre after that, so yeah, I immediately accepted.' He glanced down at the bag stowed in the foot well near Tally's feet.

She grabbed it, and Michael tried to stop her, but the precious cargo in the back restrained him from taking his left hand off the wheel for more than a fraction of a second. Tally pulled out copies of his CV. 'Wow, I just can't believe this.' She laughed, 'My big brother has finally decided to grow up.' *I wonder if that means it's now my turn?* she added silently.

'I didn't really have a choice, did I? I've just got to earn enough to cover the bills and Dad's whiskey and we'll be okay.'

'Should I sell Match and Peter?' Tally asked, her face clouding over. Her brother had just given up his favourite possession and she felt obliged to contribute.

'No, of course not, they're family. You need to keep riding or you'll go insane.'

'Gee thanks,' Tally rolled her eyes, but she was smiling, because Michael had never been this nice to her in her entire life. He had never ever referred to the horses as family before. She wondered what had turned him so soft. It was either Edith working her magic, or major guilt about Leila. Their father had become useless, so Michael had probably decided it was time for him to become the man of the family. Just on cue, he cleared his throat, and Tally prepared herself for what was coming.

'Listen, Tally,' he began meekly, unclear exactly what to say but keen to get something said before they reached their driveway.

'Hmm?' Tally replied, unsure if she wanted to hear the next bit.

'The thing with Leila, it was an accident.'

'Yeah, that's what she said.'

'Did she?' He sounded slightly put out at that.

'She said it was a one-off drunk thing.' She was blunt in the hope it would hurt him, which was unfair.

'Well, I guess it was, the first time,' Michael said carefully. 'We never meant for anything to develop, and we certainly never meant to hurt you.'

'You could have just told me.' Tally looked out of her window and stared at the white wind turbines rotating in the distance, standing proud on the flat fields all around them. They looked so small from over here, as if she could pluck them out of the ground with her fingertips, yet they were giants. It was hard to judge him for withholding secrets from her, since she was just as guilty. He was as entitled to his privacy just the same as she was to hers. Brad was his best friend and Leila was hers; the irony had already smacked her hard in the face and was perhaps what made the situation so difficult to accept. Their secret was so much better than hers.

'We were going to, I promise, we just hadn't found the right time yet. You've been, well, busy.' He glanced purposefully into his mirror again.

'Okay.' Tally looked down at her lap and twiddled her fingers. She could hardly argue against that. Her head had been all over the place for the last few months, and finding out about her brother and her best friend before might just have sent her over the edge.

'Okay?'

'Do you love each other?'

'Yes, we do.' He didn't even have to think about it. 'I know that's probably hard to believe.'

'She's my best friend – you've got to promise not to hurt her.'

'I promise. I wouldn't have got involved if it wasn't serious, you know I wouldn't just mess around with your best friend.'

Tally raised an eyebrow at him, because the old Michael certainly *would* have messed around with her best friend, and there was no way he had been contemplating a long-term relationship the first time he had approached her.

'I've changed,' he said, reading her thoughts. 'I know it sounds cliché, but I really have.'

'Let me guess,' Tally rolled her eyes, 'She's changed you.'

'No,' Michael shook his head, 'You have.'

'Me?' Tally scoffed, 'What, you decided you didn't want to become a complete screw up like your sister?'

'I actually liked that you screwed up,' Michael admitted. 'I was pretty bored of holding that title the whole time we grew up. You made me look bad with your perfection, and then you came home with a baby and Mum started to treat me differently.'

'I think she started to take some eggs out of my basket and spread them around a bit more,' Tally laughed, understanding how he felt now she had experienced what it was like to disappoint her family.

'Besides, you're not a *complete* screw up, Tal, look at you, you're an amazing mum. Look at Edith, she's so happy. Watching you made me want to grow up, too.'

'You have no idea,' Tally mumbled. She tried to argue it, but he was right. She had been forced to grow up so quickly that her head was still spinning. She still felt like a child most of the time, but it seemed that to the rest of the world she appeared as grown up as any other Mother. As much as she tried to brush off his words, they warmed her. Someone had noticed how hard it had been, and even more surreal – had been inspired by it. Someone else had spotted that Tally made Edith happy. Perhaps she made Tally happy, too.

'I do, I have every idea.' Michael indicated and pulled over, even though he really shouldn't be stopping in a bus stop. They were only minutes from home. Tally looked at him questioningly, and was afraid by his grave expression at what he might say next. He took a couple of deep breaths and then, without looking Tally in the face, said, 'It's Brad, isn't it? Brad is Edith's father.'

Tally gulped. It was hard to hear someone say it out loud, but it was also a massive relief, as if a giant weight had just slid off her shoulders. She nodded, not able to say yes. Michael slammed both hands on the wheel, honking the horn inadvertently. Edith yelped, shaken out of the doze she had slipped into. 'Sorry,' Michael whispered, and Tally was unsure if he was directing it at her or her baby.

'You knew,' Tally whispered back.

'I suspected something had happened. If I'd known it was *that*...' his voice wobbled and it made Tally grateful he hadn't known for sure, as much as she had wished harm on Brad for what he had done to her, she couldn't bear to risk losing her brother over it. He would have killed him with his bare hands if he had the chance, she could see it in his clenched jaw.

'I wasn't there for you, because I was with Leila, that's what you meant when you caught us together, wasn't it?'

'It was stupid to blame you for what happened to me.' Tally shook her head, regretting the outburst. She blinked away the memory of her squeezing through the cramped and darkened rooms, searching for help, unable to find either her brother or her friend because they had disappeared together. She could still remember how Simon had held her as they knelt on the concrete, and just thinking about it made her spine tingle. She had been avoiding him since, too embarrassed to face him.

'I shouldn't have held all those parties,' Michael groaned, wishing he hadn't exposed Tally to any of his sleazy so-called friends.

'We crashed your parties, you never invited us.'

'I invited you to that one, remember. Jesus, I even used the fact you were older to justify looking at Leila twice.' He put his head into his hands.

'Don't even think you're anything like Brad,' Tally snapped, 'you asked her permission, and she loves you back.'

Michael nodded slowly, allowing Tally to convince him that he was not the same as the man who had attacked her. 'I...' he started, but Tally cut across him.

'I love Edith,' she said, with a force that almost exploded from her chest. She had never even said it out loud before, because it had taken the last eight months to fall in love with her baby. 'I was scared I didn't – that I couldn't – because of how she had come to be, but I've made peace with it now.' She swallowed, unable to believe she was admitting all of this to her brother. 'I can't blame her for what he did, even if she does have his eyes. She deserves to be loved and we can't link the two of them together.'

'I love her too,' Michael said resolutely. 'And she doesn't have *his* eyes because that's impossible. She has Edith's eyes.'

Tally reached across to his hand and squeezed it.

'Shouldn't I be comforting you?' Michael wiped his cheek.

'Comfort me?' Tally scoffed, 'Come on, you can't have changed *that* much.' She punched him lightly on the arm and he boxed her back, instantly falling back into the routine of sparring siblings. 'Ow!' Tally screeched, ready to launch into another round when a loud honk startled all three of them, causing Edith to complain loudly this time, from the cusp of sleep.

'We should get rolling.' Michael put an apologetic hand up to the bus driver on his tail.

'Michael?' Tally asked as they rolled to a stop on their driveway.

'No, I haven't got twenty quid you can borrow,' Michael said, back to his usual annoying self.

'You didn't get rid of your car for me, did you? Or the new job? I don't want to make you unhappy.'

'No, not completely,' he replied, waving through the windscreen as Leila approached. She hesitated when she saw Tally in the car with him, her loyalties split. 'I really did need to grow up, and who knows, we might need that baby seat one day.'

Tally laughed, thinking she had now heard it all, 'I better go and make the peace, can you watch your niece?' She got out of the car to approach Leila, not waiting for him to reply because she knew he would watch Edith, especially if she was going to make it up with the woman he so clearly wanted to marry and have lots of babies with.

Helena was in her favourite spot by the window, knitting. Her skills had developed and her creations had progressed from simple scarves to more complicated items of clothing. Edith was crawling around in a homemade purple cardigan, and Helena was currently working on a fetching mustard coloured one in the next size up.

'You never knitted before,' Tally commented as she stirred the coffees. Anna was away on holiday, a treat Michael had insisted on buying her for sticking around when times had been tough, and they were having to fend for themselves. Now that some money was coming in they could afford to pay their house keeper's wages. Tally was still getting used to the idea that her brother had grown a beating heart.

'I used to just buy anything I wanted,' Helena said, pausing her work to accept the hot drink, 'It was meaningless, really, all the shopping. I'm almost glad I've been forced to economise.'

'Although, you've only made clothes for the baby so far,' Tally pointed out.

'Hopefully I will be good enough to move on to adult clothing before the first holes appear in our jumpers.' Helena sipped her coffee while Tally admired her Mother's latest project, amazed that someone could make a cardigan out of a ball of wool. Tally never had more than one hand free to even contemplate knitting.

There was a tap at the door.

'Come in,' Helena called.

Tally bit her lip because she just *knew* it would be Simon. He glanced at her as he stepped over the threshold, pausing as if he might say something directly to her, and then looked at Helena. 'I've got that paperwork for you to take a look at,' he said, formally.

'Oh, come on in, join us for a coffee and I'll give it the once over.' Helena jumped up, thrusting her precious knitting to the side as if it hadn't taken her hours and hours of work, and hurried over to the kettle. Tally wished she hadn't invited him in or, if she had, that Tally had been able to busy herself with making him a coffee instead of making eye contact.

Simon shuffled towards the table, unable to refuse the offer for a drink when Helena was already pouring it out for him. Luckily, the baby was there for them to concentrate on. 'Already trying to stand,' Simon commented.

'She's worked out how to pull herself up on practically anything,' Tally sighed, because now her life was changed forever. Edith was almost completely mobile which meant Tally couldn't leave her unsupervised for more than ten seconds without the risk of injury.

'She's grown so much,' he said with affection, as if he was proud that he had witnessed it.

Tally nodded but reflected that it sounded weird to hear him say that, because he was there watching her baby grow as an uninvited guest. He must have seen Edith nearly every day since she had come home, either in the yard or the garden or just playing in the kitchen when he popped over to see Helena. It was hard to hate someone who acted like they cared about your baby.

'What is the paperwork for?' She wanted to direct the conversation away from Edith, so she might stop feeling disarmed by him. He was bound to say it was about British Estates so then she could detest him just as much as usual.

'Just some stats to keep me in the loop.' Helena plonked his coffee cup on the table and fished up the paperwork.

'Why would British Estates want to keep us in the loop?' Tally asked Simon, scathingly.

'Because I care about you,' he replied, and then amended, after an awkward cough, 'I mean we – British Estates – care about your family.'

Tally sipped her drink, trying not to read into his slip up. The liquid burned her tongue but she was able to ignore the sharp pain. It's just mumbo jumbo corporate bullshit, she reassured herself, he's just a brainwashed employee taught to pretend he cares about the family from whichever home he is sent to invade.

'Do you mind if I go riding now?' Tally said to her Mother, refusing to stay sitting opposite him for any longer.

'Of course,' Helena said, although her tone suggested – for once – that she was not keen on the idea. 'I'll watch Edith.'

Tally knelt to kiss Edith on the head, then grabbed her scarf from the back of her chair. It was the one Simon had brought her, the one she wore constantly. She avoided his eye contact as she wound it around her neck, hoping it would hide the blush developing in her cheeks. She left him with a whole cup of coffee to get through, which guaranteed her at least ten minutes of peace before he had a chance to follow her to the stables. She marched to the yard, relieved to put some distance between her and Simon, because she wasn't ready to let someone make her feel like that yet. She buried her chin into the scarf, aware that she wasn't just wearing it for warmth.

※

Tally groaned as she heard the pole knock beneath Match. She pulled him back into a trot and then swivelled in the saddle to appraise the carnage. 'I don't get it,' she said, shaking her head.

Leila opened her mouth to respond, but then Simon beat her to it.

'You're pushing too much the stride before – you're firing him at it and it's making him go flat.'

Leila and Tally shared wide-eyed glances. Simon had crept up on them from somewhere unknown, and was hanging his arms over the arena fence, looking far too comfortable where he stood, as if he owned the place. Tally bristled, but she knew he was right. She was sitting too sharply over the ground line set down a stride before the take-off, and clamping her legs on before the fence, anticipating the jump with too much energy. It was sending Match forward too fast. He was swiping the pole out with his front feet, and she should have known instantly what her problem was. I wish I'd just kept my mouth shut, she cursed. Why did Simon have to be watching, and why did he have to be *right?*

'What do you know about jumping?' she shouted back as Leila re-set the pole.

Leila was choosing to ignore the way Simon kept randomly turning up and irritating her best friend. She was going to stay well out of whatever was going on between them, because as much as they both were in obvious denial about it – *something* was happening.

Tally didn't hear his answer, if he even gave one, because she pushed Match back into a canter and then rounded the corner again, ensuring to sit quieter and wait. This time, her horse used his energy to propel them up and over instead of straight ahead. His back rounded over the straight bar beautifully, and they sailed the fence clear. When they hit the ground her elation at finally getting it right was snubbed by her irritation that it was only because she had listened to Simon's unwelcome opinion. She knew what she had done wrong already, anyway, she had just stupidly forgotten. It had been so long since she had jumped that she had lost her fine-tuned skills, and her mind was too scrambled these days to think straight and dig up the dormant knowledge from where it lay hiding.

She praised Match, and as she patted his neck, she peeked a look at Simon from below the rim of her riding hat and he was clapping, smiling that smug gorgeous smile of his, the one she was increasingly struggling to resent. The way he lifted one side of his mouth more than the other drove her insane and she was still working out if it was lust or loathing that made her afraid to even look at those lips of his.

'You cleared it,' Leila pointed out needlessly, in a vain attempt to break the tension between the other two.

Simon shrugged, clearly pleased with himself, then turned away from the fence to resume whatever duties he had been doing before choosing to spy on Tally's practice session.

'Wait a minute,' Tally said, enraged at the way he had just decided to walk away after invading her afternoon, just like he always did, and confusing her with that smile. She didn't consider how she had repeatedly done exactly the same thing to him, as if it was some kind of game. She threw her reins away and kicked out her stirrups then jumped off Match in one smooth movement. She ran across the surface of the arena and vaulted the fence, leaving both Match and Leila staring after her in shock and awe. Simon paused and turned, pivoting on the spot, to be confronted by Tally waving her riding whip in his face. 'Who the hell do you think you are?'

'I assume that's a rhetorical question?' He tilted his head to one side, and the way he mocked her only made her angrier.

'No, it's not.' She whipped him on the arm, and he grabbed it, surprising her with his lightning speed. He tugged the whip out of her hand and dropped it on the floor, disarming her in one quick movement. She stared at her empty hand, suddenly lost. A tiny part of her worried she had hurt him with the smack, even though he hadn't flinched. He probably hadn't even felt it below all that muscle, she thought, before quickly stopping herself from picturing his bare arms. The emotion drained away, as if it had been supplied by the whip and not her confused heart and clouded head.

'What do you want to know?' he asked calmly.

Tally hesitated, unsure now she had run all the way over. 'You ride?'

'Yeah, I ride,' Simon shrugged.

'You never mentioned it.'

'You never asked.' He looked at her, right into her eyes, and she squirmed. She had avoided him ever since she had returned home.

'You live in London?'

'Yes, at the weekends.' He bit his lip and she could see this question had put him on edge a little.

'You're not just a handyman at British Estates, are you?' She was now fully clarifying that in her own head, just as she asked it, piecing together all the clues.

He let out a long whistle of breath, deciding how best to answer, and then settled for the simple truth. 'No, I'm the son of the CEO. I'll be the CEO, one day.' He frowned, as if only just realising he would acquire the company one day, when his father finally retired.

Tally raised her eyebrows. 'Right, well that's everything, thanks.' She turned and walked back to Match, surprised her numb legs could even carry her after hearing the news. He wasn't just one of the enemies; he was their leader, and he had been masquerading as a minion all this time. She was half expecting him to follow, but he didn't.

'What the hell was that?' Leila asked as she stood out of earshot, holding a bemused horse.

'Nothing.' Tally didn't feel prepared to share her jumbled thoughts about Simon with Leila, and part of her knew it was not just because she would struggle to explain how she felt. Leila still felt somewhat estranged, and Tally was reluctant to share as much as she might have done before she had discovered the secret relationship between Leila and Michael. Or perhaps it was the secret about Brad that had taught Tally she didn't always need to confide in her best friend. Maybe choosing to keep some things to herself was another sign she had grown up. Whatever it was, there was something between them that prevented Tally from speaking as frankly as she used to.

'Remind me to never talk to that prick again, okay?' Tally took the reins and prepared to remount.

'Yeah, sure.' Leila rolled her eyes, because she was definitely not getting involved with them two, at all.

Tally strolled back from a refreshing ride with a rare spring in her step. Match had worked his magic and showed her life wasn't really that bad because no matter what else, she could still horse ride, and wasn't that all that mattered? She passed a Laurel bush and paused, wondering why it was grunting. Then she heard the unmistakable bounce of a high-speed tennis ball and, before she could worry it might be heading right for her, about to explode out of the leaves, there was a satisfying twang of it being intercepted by a racket and returned with just as much ferocity.

Immediately, she was three years younger, excited to scurry around to the opening in the hedge and peek at Brad who would be playing tennis with her brother. His toned thighs would mesmerise her and she would eagerly watch, hoping the point stretched on because as soon as the ball left play her brother would order her away. It was jarring to imagine a time when she had felt excited to spy on Brad, when a glimpse of his body parts would enthral her.

Michael was one end as expected, but Brad was replaced with Simon. His bare thighs hypnotised her, more so than Brad's ever had. Perhaps it was a tennis shorts thing. She thought the court had been abandoned, but the net was a new one and the lines had been repainted. The once scruffy hedge was now neatly clipped and two plastic chairs were positioned along one edge, either side of an invisible umpire's chair.

The men had noticed her; they appeared to up their game in the presence of a spectator. The shots increased in speed and tempo and Tally started to wonder if it was safe to be standing so close. Then it was all over, with Michael's shot not quite skimming the top of the net. Rather than swipe at a ghost ball in frustration, he simply laughed as if all the effort he had expended was irrelevant. Simon wiped his brow with a sweat band on his wrist and approached the net to collect the ball for his serve. It had rolled close to Tally's feet which obliged her to scoop it up for him. She turned it around in her palm, it was also new.

Tally held it out politely when she could have bounced it, saving Simon the walk. He didn't seem to mind. Neither did Michael who should have been complaining but had used the opportunity to nip back to his towel and retrieve his phone to text Leila. Simon swivelled his racket loosely from one hand to the other and on just a flick of his wrist Tally could tell he was well practiced at the sport. Did he have *any* flaws? He planted his feet in front of her, not intending to grab the ball and continue, willing to disrupt his flow for a moment with her. He glanced over at Michael, as if checking it was safe to talk, as if them just standing opposite each other was a risk. Was it a risk? Tally hadn't decided.

'You play tennis, with my brother?' Tally tilted her head to one side. It seemed like a safe question; a conversation that would appear innocent should Michael overhear. Was this another secret relationship to have completely eluded her? Were they going to reveal they were best friends? Was this why Michael had stopped attacking Simon so vehemently whenever Helena mentioned his name?

'I mentioned I played, and he mentioned he needed to get fit for the wedding, so we reached a deal.' Simon was catching his breath and Tally was trying not to let it have an odd effect on her.

'The wedding,' she said darkly, dragging the notion out of her 'still to be processed' box.

'Michael and Leila's wedding,' Simon clarified.

Tally didn't need it clarifying, she knew damn well who had announced an upcoming marriage. It was less than one month away. She just hadn't accepted it yet, despite immediately accepting the position of Maid of Honour because she didn't have much choice, and although she was imperfect, she wasn't a monster. She had dutifully screeched congratulations along with the rest of them.

'He was starting to get porky,' she managed, choosing to push her conflicting position on the happy news to one side. It was difficult to simmer about weddings when Simon was standing there in his sweaty short shorts.

'He's still making me work for it,' Simon laughed, which came out as a half gasp as he struggled to right his breath.

'I noticed.' Tally hoped her response didn't sound flirty, but Simon paused, suddenly perfectly able to breathe, and Tally could see him wondering why she had said it quite like that.

'Your serve,' Michael prompted. He had resumed his position at the back of the court, ready to respond to the next ball.

'Your ball,' Tally reminded Simon. He had left in a fluster, forgetting to collect the neon yellow object Tally had been diligently holding out.

'Of course,' Simon whipped around to grab it, and she wondered if his cheeks had been quite as flushed before she had mentioned her observation.

❄

'Have you seen the state of him?' Michael was shouting across the kitchen when Tally entered the room, having just finished tending to the horses.

'What's going on?' She rushed to her mother's side, acting confused at the sight of her irate brother when in reality she knew what it would be about. Michael was just back from work, and she was still struggling to adjust to seeing him in a smart work suit complete with gaudy company tie – something he said he would ban the moment he was promoted to a position of power within the car dealership. He had made notably fewer quips about Simon's tie since acquiring his own.

'They're cheesy,' Michael had declared upon fingering the tie with disdain, 'and employees will feel more empowered if they're given the freedom to dress how they choose – within limits. Customers are sophisticated people, they don't need to see a uniform to understand who they are talking to, this tie isn't going to sell cars – I am. A car sales man in a bad suit is such a cliché. We should be wearing jumpers or be able to roll our sleeves up.' As unnatural as it was to agree with him, Tally had seen his point, but until that day when Michael was promoted, he would be forced to comply and wear the awful tie.

'He's fucking pissed his pants this time,' Michael shouted at Tally, diverting her attention firmly away from the slip of material hanging around his neck.

She flinched at his language and the ferocity in his voice, even though it was not directed at her. The way it scared her made her instantly think about Edith, and how she would be reacting if she was able to hear this exchange.

'It's okay, she's asleep in her cot,' Helena said, her voice cracked. She had been crying.

'Oh, Mum.' Tally wrapped her arms around her, then made eyes at her brother.

'Sorry.' Michael followed Tally's lead and lowered his voice, 'I just don't know what else we're supposed to do.'

'If in doubt, shout?' Tally replied curtly, raising an eyebrow at him when she knew he was just as hurt and disappointed as she was about who their father had become. It was always so much easier to be angry with her brother. Judging their father was relatively new territory for them both. They were still struggling with his fall from head of the family, his transition to the liability – to becoming more work than Edith.

'It's my fault,' Helena cried into Tally's shoulder, 'I drove him to it.'

'No, you didn't, Mum,' Tally soothed. 'If it wasn't for you, we'd have been forced to leave. We would be living in some hole.'

'We *are* living in a hole,' Helena sobbed, gesturing at the peeling walls and stained ceiling.

'We're still in our family home,' Michael agreed with Tally, which was still a rarity these days, despite his development into maturity.

'It hasn't done your father much good though, has it? Perhaps a clean break would have been better for him. Maybe he wouldn't feel the need to drink himself into a stupor every day if he didn't have to confront everything he's lost.'

'We couldn't leave this place, Mum, you know that.' Tally patted her back.

'I think he would have turned out this way regardless,' Michael scoffed.

Tally wasn't so sure, but it seemed like a moot point to argue. She flashed Michael a glare, telling him to pipe down with his pointless theory. It was true, their father had been a disappointment. Tally had been waiting for some kind of light bulb moment, at least a glint of hope, but he had remained closed off ever since she had returned home. He had never really had any time for Edith, and barely acknowledged the child. It was something she would never be able to forgive him for, even if he did now turn a corner and decide to come back to them. He was never going to be able to reclaim the first year of his granddaughter's life.

'What?' Michael challenged her, 'You didn't see him during your first year of uni, Tally, he was already on the slippery slope.'

'Was he?' Tally detangled herself from her Mother's arms. She had assumed it had all started with the acquisition by British Estates, but that had not happened until the start of her second year at university, just before she had unexpectedly returned home with Edith.

'Tell her, Mum.' Michael sat down at the kitchen table and loosened his tie.

'Well,' Helena coughed nervously, 'it turned out he had been gambling, as well as drinking, for a few years. I had no idea at first, and after I found out he downplayed it. It was just a few drinks, just a few hundred quid, but then it spiralled, and one fuelled the other – although I'm not sure which. He's the reason our finances fell off a cliff. We lost a lot of money.' She stared at the floor, still feeling responsible for not noticing the danger they were in before it was too late. She had been too busy shopping and socialising with friends that had now abandoned her, seemingly mortified to be associated with someone who had lost all of their money – even their house.

'Dad lost it *all* through gambling and drinking?' Tally had assumed it had been a gradual decline over a number of years, a slow and irresponsible tumble they had all been jointly responsible for as a result of their flamboyant lifestyle choices. She thought it had been the horses and the parties, the flash cars and the clothes. Now things were making a bit more sense.

'He just kept putting more money in, hoping he would be able to bail us out. When he lost he drank to feel better; when he was drunk, he gambled harder and when he lost, he drank more. It was a vicious cycle and when I found out how serious it was, it was too late.' Helena started crying again.

'When Mum put a stop to it, he thought he was going to win the next time,' Michael said, shaking his head at the ludicrousness of their father's drunken logic. 'That's the real reason he blames her, because he thinks that if she hadn't stepped in then he would have made us millionaires and we would have bounced back. He thought he would eventually win.'

'Where is he now?' Tally asked, blinking back tears because someone had to hold it together in case Edith woke up. She seemed to remember her brother blaming his Mother, too, although from the way he was supporting her now, she realised he had just been wounded and bitter. By his own admission, he had done some growing up since then.

'Lying in his own piss on the bathroom floor,' Michael said, his top lip curling up in revulsion.

Tally shuddered. She never entered that bathroom. She only ever used the one in the main house. Her father was now lying where Tally had been lying all that time ago. She was hit with a vivid flash back and had to work hard to remove it. There was no way she was going to be able to tend to him in that bathroom, not that she would know what to do with him, anyway. 'Is he safe? Could he choke on his own vomit?'

'Michael put him into the recovery position.'

'Yeah, and that's when he bloody wet himself.' Michael shuddered.

'So what, we just leave him there?'

'That's what I usually do,' Helena said quietly.

Tally put her head in her hands, unable to believe that their family life could get so grim.

❄

Tally twirled the empty champagne glass around her fingers as she watched her brother twirl his new bride around the make-shift dance floor. Everyone was drunk and elated whilst Tally remained sober and glum, no matter how much she tried to enjoy herself. She was starting to suspect someone wearing burgundy had watered down the wine. Edith was tucked up in bed after having worn herself out with all the excitement of a family wedding, and the monitor on the table confirmed she was still sleeping soundly, snoring gently. At least if she cried Tally would have an excuse to leave. Pretending to be merry for her brother's sake was starting to grind her down, after a long day of fake smiles and forced conversation. She checked her watch to see if it was an acceptable time to go to bed, but it was still too early. The Maid of Honour had duties to maintain until at least midnight. She reached for the bottle of lukewarm fizz and re-filled her glass with a sigh.

Doug had been her plus one, and it had been distracting fun for a while. It was refreshing when he visited, it revived an old part of herself and reminded her of the carefree confident girl who had been going somewhere with her life. They had laughed and drank and danced, but Doug had been keeping his eye out for single ladies who may be interested, now finally accepting that he and Tally would only ever be friends, and the inevitable had happened and now he was off with someone eligible and enjoying the attention he deserved. Tally was relieved there hadn't been any confusion between them because she didn't want to break his heart again, or worse, get drunk and do something regrettable. A tiny part of her smarted when she watched him wrap his arms around another girl, showing her what she was missing out on as she sat alone at the edge of the dance floor, trying to convince herself this was what she wanted. *Maybe I should have compromised,* she thought.

      Charles had dragged himself out of his hole and put on a convincing act today. He had pretended to know his granddaughter, pretended to be on speaking terms with his wife, pretended to be delighted with the lowly social status of his new daughter-in-law. He had said a few clipped false, but not unforgivable, words at the wedding breakfast, much to Michael's horror. He had started the day slurry and was now completely sloshed, but nobody batted an eyelid because daytime drinking was acceptable at a wedding. He had performed a half-convincing duty of entertaining the guests, many of whom had wormed their way out of the woodwork despite having abandoned the family months ago, when their support and reassurance had been most needed. They were tempted back by a party, by sheer curiosity, and the unfortunate situation was not discussed, it was barely even hinted at.

It was as if someone had dropped a note in with the invitation requesting that British Estates was not to be mentioned. Tally appreciated the stoic manner in which everyone acted as if this was just another epic event orchestrated by Helena, as if she still freely roamed the rooms of the manor house serving as the backdrop to the special day, as if strangers didn't walk the lawn below their feet every other day of the week. British Estates did not exist today, even if they were hovering in the background, their employees topping up glasses and clearing away plates. Helena had forgiven her ex-friends for the cold shoulders, even if it was only for a brief interlude. Today, they had their old home back, but not really, not even today, because it was a show trial wedding for Simon, a dress rehearsal, and British Estates had only allowed it to happen to serve his requirements. There was something in it for them and as usual he was there, scrutinising a personal, magical day as if watching a documentary as part of a school project. There was no reason he shouldn't be leaving before midnight.

Michael lifted his new wife into the air, and she screeched, her laughter inaudible over the noise of the band and the cries of the other guests. Ties had been loosened and once perfectly pinned hair was now sticking out in all directions. The guests were becoming undone, at first gradually and now rapidly, and Tally was jealous because she couldn't let herself be swept up with the joviality. Michael had allowed British Estates to organise his wedding, he hadn't even really minded because he was too in love to be outraged. He had shrugged and said, it's free, it's still going to be the wedding of Leila's dreams. Tally couldn't refute either point. Michael wasn't yet in charge of the car sales company and a wedding usually carried a price tag of thousands. This was the best he could offer, and selflessly, surprisingly, with a staggering change of heart, Michael was swallowing his pride and accepting the family's fate.

Tally was outraged. A thought niggled at her, that she should probably do the same, but she was resisting it, refusing to allow acceptance to take hold. Acceptance signified the end game. She had now lost her ally in the fight against British Estates. Leila had stolen his attention and his priorities. Leila didn't mind living in the old wing of the house, her cup was still half full and now Michael shared her optimism, as if it was futile to fight it, as if they hadn't been at war. Tally was cornered, and Simon was stationed in the back of the marquee, clutching his iPad, openly dissecting the day for his own benefit. Tally grabbed the neck of the bottle, to give her free hand a weapon to wield, and marched towards him.

He sensed her approach and braced for impact. Clutching the IPad with both hands, he reluctantly raised his eyes to assess how emotional the exchange would be. She was drunk and her face already showed a scowl before even opening her mouth. He was used to that expression; it was set to default. Whenever he occasionally caught a smile, her beauty astounded him. He assumed the weapon was just for show.

Tally opened her mouth to accuse him of something, of stealing her brother's wedding day, of profiting from it, of not leaving at a respectable hour to grant them the dignity of celebrating in private. Exhaustion hit her like a tidal wave. It was difficult to fight a war on your own. The laughter and frivolity surrounding her had drained her anger. It was impossible to disrespect love and companionship on a wedding day. Simon remained impassive, watching her wearily, because he was also tired, a day of matrimony had also left him depleted. For some reason, the war between a family and a company had become a personal battle between just the two of them, as if they had been nominated – sacrificed – by their respective sides. They were both a little miffed at being abandoned by their own team. If Simon asked his dad for help then he would have to endure the smug I told you so, and there was no guarantee it would be followed by good advice. His dad would push to sell, and then Tally would really have something to be upset about, a real reason to hate him; for losing her home entirely.

Simon shoved the folder off the chair next to him, his movement sharp and unexpected, as if he hadn't been in control of his hand and was now annoyed at its decision to offer a truce. His precious notes hit the sticky floor with a slap. The act was small, but a step towards reconciliation. It was a white flag requesting an interlude. Tally was tempted to refuse to sit down, to throw his kindness back into his face. She was afraid she would look weak otherwise or would miss an opportunity for victory. But then she remembered how tired she was, how much her feet ached from a day in shoes picked out by someone else, how rarely she was able to just sit down. It would be satisfying, but short lived. It would be childish to reject the truce, and it was only for tonight, for maybe a few minutes. She could break the truce if she needed to. She still had the bottle in her hand.

Tally took her place next to Simon, instantly awkward to be by his side because it suggested some kind of alliance. She scanned the room to check no one had seen, but they were too absorbed with drinking and dancing and shouting at each other to notice two drop-outs tucked into the corner of the tent. Simon had at least had the decency to swap his tell-tale fleece for a suit, so if quizzed he could pretend that he was a distant relative. They looked like an item, probably, from a distance, but Tally didn't readjust her position. She didn't move her chair away or cross her arms or punch him in the arm. Instead, she kicked off her shoes, sending them further away than intended. Simon looked down at her painted toenails and flinched. It reminded him of finding her in the bathroom, of seeing her bare feet, her wet hair, a towel wrapped tightly around her body, tucked under her arms and skimming her thighs. He looked away from her toes. She drained her glass and dropped it onto the floor, uncaring about whether or not it smashed. British Estates would have to pay for it if it did. She took a swig from the bottle. Simon pulled it away from her. She started. He looked at the bottle, considering his next move. He was planning to put it down, to lecture her about being drunk, but that was what the son of the CEO of British Estates would do. Instead, he took a gulp. The bubbles fizzled reluctantly on his tongue, lazy with the heat.

'It's flat,' he said, swallowing with effort.

'It's cheap,' Tally commented, because she wasn't going to completely relax around him, she refused to.

'It's standard issue,' Simon fired back, because he had a sheet to balance, and supplying the sort of champagne her family were used to just didn't make the numbers work.

Tally didn't mention that she preferred prosecco to champagne, and that nearly everyone did. She didn't want his numbers to work. She eyeballed the folder, wondering why he hadn't moved to collect the escaped sheets, his precious notes.

'What's your verdict?' she asked, finally.

'It's a no brainer,' Simon nodded, 'we need to make this a wedding venue.'

'Need?' Tally frowned, wondering why it was a need and not a bonus. She saw it as a silly hobby of his, not a serious business venture. She thought he wanted to erect a giant marquee on their lawn every other Sunday just to annoy her further.

'How else will I pay for the double glazing in your wing?' Simon found himself taking another gulp of disgusting wine. He probably shouldn't have said anything, he hadn't received approval from his dad about the new windows yet.

'You're replacing the windows?' Tally latched on, because she had just endured a winter of rattling, leaking single-pane window misery. Edith was always worryingly cold, piled under too many blankets.

'And hopefully the carpets,' Simon decided on the spot, as if Tally had taken over control of his decision-making facility.

'The carpets are really scratchy,' Tally conceded, and it was probably the least hostile thing she'd ever said to him, the first time she had ever agreed with him.

'I'm thinking grey,' Simon nodded.

'It's the new cream,' Tally agreed.

There was a pregnant pause, as they both recognised the exchange as the closest they had managed in the way of an actual conversation. It was also the most banal topic, but it was almost platonic.

'Your friend is waiting for you,' Tally nodded towards a timid girl hovering in the distance, attempting to catch Simon's eye. Simon flicked her a thumbs up, and her cheeks flushed before she scampered away, to inform the rest of the team they had been relieved from duty.

'They're not my friends.'

'Sure.' Tally rolled her eyes.

'My dad owns the company. One day I'll own the company. People are too nervous to like me, I'm too *different*.'

'Oh.' Tally knew exactly how it felt to be cut out of social groups for being too different. Despite personal experience, she had gone and fallen into the same trap of thinking Simon had it all. Peering at him now, she recognised loneliness. She tried to tell herself he deserved it, to be stuck in Fenson with no friends and no life outside of British Estates, having to drive back and forth to London, but the part of her that still smarted for being rejected by her peers stepped up and raised a hand. The raised hand within her whispered, perhaps you could be his Leila. She shook it away, forcing the hand back down. Calling a momentary truce was one thing, volunteering friendship and offering sympathy was quite another.

'You'll have to clear this away on your own now.' Tally gazed at the chaos. The floor was strewn with glasses, dropped napkins, wonky furniture, parcels of debris and suspicious wet patches.

'I'll come in early tomorrow.' Simon loosened his tie, theatrically, to denote the end of his shift.

Tally found herself wondering where he stayed when in Fenson, when he wasn't travelling back to his shiny penthouse on the Thames. It must be somewhere in the village, and it wasn't exactly a big village.

'Talking of friends, yours seems to be getting a bit cosy with that bridesmaid.' Simon gestured at Doug who was starting to embarrass himself now. Luckily, the bridesmaid was just as drunk and interested. She was Leila's colleague from the café and Tally had tried really hard to not be jealous of her. Learning to share Leila with her brother had been tough enough.

'God he better not try to bring her back to the sleeping bag on my floor,' Tally groaned, imagining them crashing through the door in a few hours, waking both her and Edith.

'He's sleeping in your room?'

'Yes, is that allowed?' Tally snapped, wondering why he was so interested, and if there was a hint of envy in his voice. 'Where else can he sleep, his car?'

'Michael and Leila have his old room in the house tonight, he could move into Michael's room.'

'Michael wouldn't have allowed it, anyway, it's not something you need to worry about. He probably won't even make it back to bed.'

She was alerted to a flash in the distance, and immediately recognised the baby monitor. Although she couldn't hear the cry from where she sat, the tempo of the flashes suggested it was an urgent one.

'I need to get that.' She jumped to her feet, slightly disappointed when only a few minutes ago she had been eyeballing the monitor, hopeful for a reason to slip away.

'Shall I come?' Simon offered, standing up dutifully, as if it was half his responsibility.

'No,' Tally said automatically. She watched his face fall, despite his request being unorthodox. 'Unless you need to look at the carpets?' Tally added, modifying her tone, providing him an alibi.

'It does need to be done,' Simon agreed. They picked their way through the crowd and over the dark lawn, towards the house. No-one saw them leave together, and neither of them acknowledged the elephant at their side, the one pointing out that nothing really did need to be done about the carpets, not tonight anyway.

❄

'He had a sister?' Susan asked the following weekend, latching on to the Simon aspect of Tally's recount of Leila and Michael's wedding day, skipping the standard questions about the dress, the food, and the drunken antics.

Tally had expected them to be more interested in hearing about Simon's unexpected interaction with Edith than the blissful unity of marriage, and it made her glow with pride when they did just that. They were *her* friends and wanted to hear *her* story. They were abrupt and to the point, too short of time and patience to be anything but straight shooting. They were too jealous of child-free couples to spend much time dwelling on the wedding itself. Leila had probably had great sex followed by a deep durable sleep, and the mums were far too sex and sleep-deprived to want to consider how wonderful Leila's magical day might have been. Weddings bored them, they wanted to talk about Tally.

They eased Tally's guilt of enjoying the last hour of Leila's wedding day the most, whilst away from her Maid of Honour duties. She had preferred being tucked away in her damp bedroom, watching Simon bounce Edith gently. He had help to soothe her toddler back to sleep while she watched, resisting the urge to feel awe at how gently he cradled her in his arms, as if she was his. His offer to help, to pick her up, had felt genuine and Tally had accepted before thinking it through. She had never seen him like this, his strong arms were usually sweeping or digging, or at least carrying important looking documents or reaching out for a formal handshake. She had only ever seen work Simon, and this was a glimpse of home Simon – the real Simon.

Michael was always so rough with Edith, making it his duty to be the missing strong male influence in Edith's life, to counteract the caution Tally emitted and the experienced yet soft femininity oozing from Helena. Michael found it necessary to hurl Edith into the air or tickle her until she screamed. Tally hoped for Leila's sake they had a little boy of their own when it was their turn to be parents. Simon appeared to approach Edith differently, which was surprising especially in contrast with his burly disposition. He also knew exactly what he was doing, causing a familiar flash of resentment to flare within Tally. Did he have to beat her at *everything?*

Tally took her time to process Susan's question. She dipped a bread stick into the humus, overloading it because it was rare to have two hands free for eating, and she enjoyed the novel feeling of female friendship outside of just Leila. It was perfect timing, because with the joy of watching her best friend find love came the fear of losing their closeness, and the envy of having to share. She had met some nice girls at university, being no longer constrained by the cold-shouldering social bubble of her village peers, able to reinvent herself – able to be proud of her unique life as it became an interesting draw and no longer a badge of shame. University had given her a second chance, but she had wasted it, none of her alliances had stretched far beyond chatting during lectures and around the communal kitchen in halls. The accidental pregnancy and forced resignation from university had swiftly quashed any hope of making life-long friends she might stay in touch with, apart from Doug. Doug hag swiftly replaced Leila, and before now, Tally had thought she was a one-friend kind of girl.

Motherhood had introduced her to a group of girls who completely understood the largest aspect of Tally's life, and even if they had different backgrounds and personalities, their bond of shared baby experience anchored them together, and their differences kept them interested in each other rather than pushing them apart. It thrilled her to feel not only wanted, but essential, as if the group hadn't functioned correctly beforehand. She suspected this had been Grampy's plan all along. It had worked, and she smiled when he reminded her of it every

Wednesday, of this third chance of friendship he had orchestrated. She allowed him to boast about his achievement, to bask in the glory that he deserved. These four new mums *needed* each other, and part of that need was to openly share what was either boring or taboo to the other people in their lives. Their baby-free friends quickly became bored of talking endlessly about the next wonder week or the latest weird behaviour, a worrying new freckle or bizarre sleep patterns of their newly toddling child.

'Bobby, put that *down,*' Gwen snapped at her toddler, before turning shining eyes back to Tally. They all ignored the interjection, of Bobby nearly ingesting a piece of rabbit poo, because there was always a second conversation going on with the children, snuggled closely behind the adult conversation they were attempting to maintain, interrupting them almost constantly and trying to take over. They refused to let their dialogue fall apart, because otherwise they might as well give up ever speaking and sit there staring at their toddlers.

'I think he still *has* a sister,' Katherine corrected Susan, 'unless you're about to drop another bomb-shell about a dead sister?' They continued to gaze at Tally expectantly, sort of hoping for a tragic yet interested back story, if only for their entertainment.

'She's still breathing,' Tally said through a mouthful of humus, sorry to disappoint. Simon's sister was still alive, and that had been the interesting part. Simon didn't have a sister anymore, but his sister was presumably still alive to be had. She was lost somehow. They continued to stare at her, keen for more details, sacrificing the rare chance of eating without a toddler interfering for Tally's gossip. Tally shook her head, almost unable to believe it herself. Edith had just fallen over, tripping over a dropped branch from the tree they were picnicking below. She got back to her feet without a second thought, keen to continue chasing a butterfly that had long ago vanished, and Tally was grateful she had chosen not to make a big deal of it. Tally had finally invited them over to her house, and despite reassurances they would only bring a few bits of food, nothing fancy, they had enough to feed an army of mums. The draw of a sunny day outside, of no need to clean up dropped crumbs and spilt yoghurt was appealing to all of them. Tally had spread her patchwork blanket below a large tree positioned near the back of the property, as far away from guests and frowning British Estates staff as she could get. She had managed to steer them unnoticed around the house and past watchful eyes. She hoped Simon wouldn't think she was taking liberties, just because they had started to almost get along. She possibly *was* taking liberties. Tally tried to remember his exact words, and she was transported back to the memory of him standing in her bedroom and rocking a simpering Edith:

'Mum used to do it like this,' he explained, his faraway voice immersed in a dusty memory, and Tally got the distinct impression he was recounting something he had witnessed first-hand, and not simply passing on something his mother had told him when he was much older. She waited for him to continue, 'I used to ask for a go but she never let me, because I would wake her.'

'You can't blame her for denying you a cuddle, it is too precious to risk.' Tally nodded knowingly. He had struck her as an only child, so to hear of a sibling threw her slightly.

'I used to sulk, but I get it now. I had too much fun with her when she was awake to hold a grudge about it, anyway.' His eyes misted over, and he was suddenly sad, grieving.

'I'm so sorry for your loss,' Tally breathed, stunned.

Simon was quick to shake his head, 'I didn't lose her, not like that, anyway.' He continued to bounce on the spot, even though Edith was sound asleep. Tally enjoyed watching him, biting back a smile because humans just couldn't help jigging when they held a child, driven by instinct. Simon was going to lower Edith into her cot just as soon as he had finished enjoying his cuddle.

'What happened?' Tally asked after he had finally straightened from tucking the toddler back into her rightful place, taking care to push the edge of the blanket under her chin.

Simon stood up straight, his arms now empty. Instead of tending to a distressed child, he was now just standing in Tally's draughty back bedroom, revealing secrets from his past. Tally watched his face close, disappointed as he visibly decided it would be unprofessional to continue talking.

'I should get back.' He stuffed his hands into his pocket.

'What about the carpet?' Tally asked, scratching around to find an excuse for him to say. Surprise flashed across his face, because neither of them had ever really cared about carpets. She had just gone and admitted she wanted him to stay, with her, in her draughty bedroom. She told herself she was just being polite because his ability to hypnotise her child back to sleep had been a massive favour.

They attempted small talk for a short while, both hoping to stretch out their time together. Simon made a show of examining the almost thread-bare floor. 'You definitely need new carpet,' he concluded. 'In grey, because it is the new cream.'

'Thanks,' Tally smiled, accepting he was about to make his excuses and leave. She wasn't going to ask him to stay. She wasn't going to *beg*. She was tired, he was tired, and it was only ever supposed to be a short truce.

'What happened to her?' Susan asked, 'How do you lose a sister anyway?'

'You lost Clem last weekend in the farm shop, remember?' Katherine shot, wiggling her eyebrows before ducking below the strawberry Susan launched at her head.

'I misplaced her, for just a minute,' Susan snorted, resisting the tug of a smile as it battled with the memory of ice shooting through her veins, and of her stomach dropping as she realised Clem was out of sight. 'She tried to go outside to see the chickens,' she qualified, earning sympathetic nods. Now they were walking and curious, they were impossible to keep still, and their quests rarely made much sense.

'He's never mentioned his mum or sister before now, just his arsehole CEO of a Dad.' Tally stabbed her bread stick back into the humus.

'Does Simon consider his dad an arsehole?'

'He thinks he's outdated,' Tally shrugged. 'He doesn't tell me much.' *He doesn't tell me anything*, she added with a silent sigh. 'Mum said he makes all the decisions on this property, it's his little project.' She stabbed the humus again, putting it off limits for anyone else as little bits of bread stick crumbed into what was left.

'Then it was his decision to replace the windows, carpets and broken roof tiles?' Gwen winked.

'He's such a saint,' Tally rolled her eyes, deciding she would fight the urge to be grateful. He had still decided to keep them out of the rest of the house, *their home*. Tally was thrilled by how easily the girls had accepted her bizarre home life. No one had even blinked as she had tentatively described the situation during a routine coffee and cake session in the local cafe. They were probably all too tired to blink, or their brains too murky to fully understand when Tally admitted to being a vast landowner but also to no longer owning any land, to living in a mansion but also living in squalor. They had all just continued to clutch their coffee cups as their children sat in identical highchairs and worked in isolation yet also in complete unity, pushing stubby fingers into muffins and squeezing once fluffy, edible morsels into questionable pieces of sticky sludge with a level of dedication that suggested it was a really important task. The mums were avoiding eye contact with Leila's friend who stood at the till and watched them horrified, wondering how long it would take her to clean up the ocean of crumbs. No one had even asked a question, they just accepted the bizarre abridged, when-Tally-met-Simon, chapter of her life. Except for being raped, Tally had told them everything.

'It doesn't make sense,' Katherine remarked. She nudged her sunglasses off the top of her head and onto the bridge of her nose so she could peer at the house, which gleamed joyously in the sunlight.

Tally glared at it as it sat smiling at her. It enjoyed the guests walking its floors and peering around its walls. It was showing off, no longer underappreciated by a family who had failed to future plan or maintain their own assets. It blamed them for letting this happen, and delighted in the way it was now the centre of attention, argued over, cried over. *I've really gone mad if I've personified the house,* Tally thought to herself. She brought her attention back to Katherine, who was counting elaborately along her fingers.

'He buys it to expand the portfolio, it's a flop, so he spends his investment pot on the bit no one even gets to see, just to make the old occupants more comfortable. Yes, you are stakeholders – you're still an interested party – but your influence is minimal. Except for kicking up a fuss and causing management a headache, you're no real threat. You're less important than the guests. The money should be invested on the tourists. He should have converted the stable block into a tea room or something. That might boost interest, sales, create cash. You don't have any shares, or any financial involvement. It doesn't make sense that he would replace the windows, carpets and broken roof tiles.'

'Thanks for sugar coating it,' Susan said, glancing anxiously at Tally.

'I'm just saying,' Katherine shrugged, her smile slightly sly, 'but what do I know.'

'Just because you're a financial director when you're not giving birth or raising a child, it doesn't mean you know what Simon should be doing. You work in a completely different sector,' Gwen said, even though her tone was doubtful. It really didn't make much sense when Katherine put it like that.

'Supply and demand is universal,' Katherine said, refusing to take the hint. 'Simon has supplied to the people who have no demand.'

'I was pretty demanding,' Tally interjected.

'Yes, but from a *business* point of view, Simon really should have spent the money on his paying guests. He's closed the deal with your family, why bother sweetening it now?'

Tally's mouth turned down at the corners.

'Sorry,' Katherine winced, 'you know I didn't mean it like that.'

'It's just her *business* point of view,' Susan laughed, hoping it might defuse the situation. 'Her *personal* point of view is much more tactful.'

'Do you want to hear my *personal* point of view, then?' Katherine added, her eyes dancing deviously, taking a risk on something cheeky to get herself out of the dog house.

Tally braced herself. She could hardly say no.

'He fancies you.'

'Don't be ridiculous,' Tally said, immediately pushing the words away. She turned her face back towards the house, hoping they wouldn't see her cheeks flush. She watched as shadows moved inside, passing the windows like ghosts. People were poking around their bedrooms, peering up at paintings and admiring furniture. Many of the rooms had been locked up when Tally was growing up, and only now did she wish she had been granted more access to explore. She hadn't even asked, what a wasted opportunity. The house leered at her, taunting her mistake as it basked in a new glory. She pursed her lips into a thin line of acceptance. She had lost her house; Simon had taken it from her. Yet he was making all the wrong decisions. She didn't suspect him to be someone who is naive, he had proven himself as a capable businessman, even if this was his first major project. There must be another reason he was diverting limited resources into all the wrong pots. If he was risking his reputation – possibly even his career – she didn't want it to be because of her. She didn't want to owe him anything. She wanted Katherine to be wrong, but everyone sitting on the picnic blanket under the tree knew that Katherine wasn't being ridiculous.

❄

Tally breathed in deeply, enjoying the sway of her hips as Match rocked below her. The clip clop of hooves bounced off the row of brick houses they were making their slow way past on the outskirts of the village. Leila was behind her, urging Peter to keep pace and Tally was glad it was her turn to ride Match. Now her riding mojo had returned, it was increasingly difficult to share. Edith was no longer breast feeding, providing Tally with more opportunities to ride, but Leila was always there, and compromise was usually required. Today, Tally had insisted on Match, and Leila had no choice but to graciously concede. Peter had to be persuaded into action whilst Match literally took the bit between his teeth and marched ahead, his ears swivelling as he took in his surroundings, excited for the road trip. Match just arrogantly assumed Peter was following. They hadn't ridden this route for ages, since the village was situated a good couple of miles away, and lack of any off road riding routes forced them onto the twisty sixty limit road, the only route in by horse or car, which was occasionally used by idiot drivers with no imagination. They were spoilt by car-free farming tracks and routes around the property at home, so very rarely did someone suggest they follow signs into Fenson.

It was turning into a promisingly warm day, and Tally was baby free, so they had decided to brave the traffic and ride over to the pub for lunch. Michael was working the weekend shift at the car sales place, which meant Tally had her best friend all to herself. *I wonder if I'm still her best friend or if Michael has succeeded me?* She immediately pushed away the childish thought. It was petty to get jealous. Leila didn't appear to be jealous of Doug, she was probably relieved. Tally didn't like the idea that Leila pitied her now that she was happily married, and worried about her social well-being. Doug took the pressure off Leila to be a dedicated best friend and also a present wife. Tally wished Leila was jealous of Doug, but instead she sensed that Leila was simply relieved that Tally had another close friend now that Leila was busy making a new life with her husband. Tally was equally grateful for Doug, but he didn't completely make up for losing Leila to someone else.

She would rather a lot of things, she sighed, as she turned her attention outward, to enjoy the emerging delights on offer. She peered into front gardens and through gaps in curtains, able to catch a glimpse of the goings on from a higher vantage point and slower pace than usual. She wondered why no one rushed to the window to look at the horses as they passed, alerted by their hooves on the tarmac. That's what she would have done if she was living in one of these houses. She would have burst from her bed and yanked at the curtains and shouted 'Horse!' to the rest of the household. The idea that not everyone was fascinated by horses, drawn to the sight and the smell and the warm touch of them, still fascinated her. If she had driven to the pub, she would have missed out on the little things, things that now made her smile, such as the pair of courting pigeons dancing between fences on her right, the female switching between interested and offended as the male persisted in wooing her. She laughed at the familiar stuffed fox standing on a window sill, recognising it from previous rides spread over many years. She couldn't understand the appeal of taxidermy, but the owner of the poor russet creature clearly possessed a sense of humour. The fox was regularly adorned with seasonal attire, such as antlers in December and bunny ears at Easter. If the fox could see himself now, she hoped he would find it in his removed heart to forgive. She hoped he had died a quick, peaceful death from natural causes, and hadn't been killed specifically so he could be stuffed, placed on a window sill and dressed up for human entertainment.

Tally dragged her attention away from the blank eyes and pointy yellow teeth, and took her chances on the next front garden. She observed the newly painted door and tried to remember what colour it had been previously, surprised by the bright cobalt blue enough to suspect it had been a nondescript colour much in need of a refresh, because it had never caught her attention before. It opened and Simon stepped outside.

'Oh,' she said, as shocked as he was at the chance meeting. Her eyes instinctively went behind him to the slim terraced house with its bricks aged and crumbly at the corners and its courtyard garden slabbed with mismatched tiles and decorated with low maintenance pots. 'You live here?' she asked, not that it needed to be clarified. Unless a girl lived here, a girl he had hooked up with last night. He looked slightly dishevelled, as if he could be creeping away before she woke.

'Yes,' he said, squishing her flash of imagination and envy with one word. 'I'm out of milk,' he explained.

'We can counter offer beer,' Leila called, as Peter finally caught up. 'We're headed to the pub for lunch.'

'It's ten thirty,' Simon raised an eyebrow.

'Brunch,' Leila modified, with a wink. 'Whatever you'd like to call it, we're having a pint. She's baby free and I'm husband free, so there's cause to celebrate.'

Tally eyeballed Leila offended that she had just invited someone on their exclusive girls-only brunch, and not just anyone; she had invited *Simon*. Leila didn't notice Tally's death stare, or if she had then she was doing her best to ignore it. Tally wondered if the reason Leila could extend the invite so flippantly was because she didn't value their friendship as highly. Tally had probably done irreparable damage by choosing to leave Leila and move to university. Tally had probably become boring now all she talked about was her baby, her restricted living conditions and how much she blamed Simon. She looked down at Match's withers. The saddle cloth was pinching the end of his mane, so she tweaked it free, clutching at the coarse grey hair and anchoring herself inwards. *My life is so boring,* she thought, *Leila is bored of me.*

'Is this some kind of a girlie brunch?' Simon asked, worried he might be interrupting by joining them, picking up on the cold shoulder from Tally.

'Yes,' Tally said, at the exact moment Leila said 'No,' and her voice drowned out Tally's. Match and Peter continued to mooch along the road, and so Tally was now adjacent to the garden two doors along from Simon, her neck craned back at him. Simon peered at her, because perhaps he had still heard her protest, but then he yelled he would meet them there.

Tally was angry with Leila for inviting someone else to their brunch, it *was* supposed to be a girlie brunch, just them, and now Simon was going to ruin it. She wasn't yet ready to let Leila see how her defences had slightly dropped around Simon, and adding him into the mix was just going to complicate what should have been a simple afternoon catching up with Leila. Leila seemed completely oblivious to how Tally felt, which made Tally worry Leila didn't treasure their time together quite as much as Tally did. Leila mistook Tally's quietness for companionable silence, which only made Tally seethe more.

'I'm going for the full English,' Leila decided as she ran her stirrups up. The horses were secured on dedicated posts at the back of the car park. There was a trough and a salt lick provided by a thoughtful publican who had made the pub rider friendly.

'Isn't that the only option?' Tally's frosty edge was intentional.

'Last time I only had eggs on toast,' Leila said, a tad offended, and Tally wondered if it was because she was hurt Tally had forgotten her last breakfast choice, or if she had finally picked up on her mood.

They settled at their usual table, before Tally pointed out it was a little snug for three people.

'He can squeeze on the end,' Leila dismissed with a wave of her hand as she went to the bar to place their orders. Tally folded her arms and decided not to grab another chair, descending into full sulk mode as she glared at Leila's back.

'Match got free,' Simon's voice made her jump. 'It's fine,' he added, as Tally placed her hands flat on the table ready to launch into action, 'I tied him back up.'

'Thanks,' Tally mumbled. She begrudgingly settled back down, her reason for escaping squashed, and watched Simon as he swiped a chair from a nearby table and positioned himself right next to her. His knees were almost touching hers, but she resisted airing the suggestion that they relocate to somewhere with more space. He looked at her, his face calm and his eyes clear, his thoughts clearly not jumbled with the same complicated resentment she carried for him. Her tongue had suddenly gone dry and her gut twisted, and she couldn't explain why. He simply looked at her, his eyes not even flickering, and it was like he had sent a wave of relief crashing over her shoulders, soaking her from top to bottom. She pulled in a deep breath, her diaphragm stretched down, and her lungs almost burst. Oxygen swarmed through her blood stream and drowned the fear, confusion, the hurt, and she was simply Tally sitting in a corner of the pub she had known forever.

'I assumed lager,' Leila said, breaking the spell as she returned clutching three pints, her eyes on the froth as she concentrated on not wasting any and not getting sticky fingers.

'You girls drink lager?' Simon raised his eyebrows.

'I'd be offended if you thought us hard-core horse girls only ever sipped white wine,' Leila shot back.

'Although, we do also like white wine,' Tally clarified, choosing to join in rather than sulk and reinforce her self-perpetuated fear that she was in fact boring.

'Horse girls really are hard-core,' Simon chuckled, thinking of the way they were always tripping him up on the yard, in all weathers, at all times of day, content in mud-splattered clothes and comfortable in wellies. 'You'd cringe if you saw the girls I know.'

'Girls *you know?*' Leila's ears perked up. She said it with such relish that Simon instantly went pink.

'Just friends, and stuff,' he mumbled into his beer.

'And stuff?' Leila persisted.

'The girls back home care more about nail bars and cocktails.' He tried to find a way to end the conversation, but Leila was having too much fun. Tally watched quizzically. It was confusing to hear him refer to a different place to Fenson as his home, when he was always here, in her home, living in a little terraced cottage just down the road, eating breakfast in the local pub.

'We don't have a nail bar,' Leila said, a little sadly.

'Or cocktails,' the landlord snorted from over Simon's shoulder as he approached. He lowered three plates of breakfast in front of them and Simon was saved by the draw of hot food.

'We wouldn't go to a nail bar even if we had one,' Tally agreed, noting her nails were chipped and short, up against it with both a horse and a toddler to contend with. 'Although we did used to try our hand at making homemade cocktails.'

'I remember!' Leila squeaked, cutting into her egg and shaking her head with laughter, 'the Bloody Mary was by far the worst attempt we made.'

'I don't think it's great even when a professional attempts it. Tomato juice and alcohol is just wrong.' Tally grimaced, remembering the incident.

And just like that, she was dangling her feet into the pool. She admired her newly painted neon toenails, how the colour set off her sun kissed skin quite nicely, and wondered if Brad would notice. She was still naïve, still untouched, still fantasising about being kissed by Brad. Her whole life still lay ahead of her, full of education and opportunity. She tilted her face towards the sun. She breathed in innocence and breathed out hope. She was truly happy. She lifted her latest creation to her lips, dubious of how vodka would taste when combined with tomato juice.

'Have you lost your appetite, Tal?' Leila asked, noticing her friend hadn't touched her breakfast, and bringing Tally out of the memory.

'No, course not,' Tally snapped, annoyed at how a simple drink had evoked such a strong memory. She stuffed a whole piece of French toast into her mouth, just to punctuate her point. She was ashamed to carry memories from times before Brad attacked her, when she had actively fancied him, perhaps even actively pursued him. She worried it eroded his responsibility somehow. She worried it meant she should carry the blame, be it some of it or all of it. She was embarrassed to have old thoughts in her head, and if anyone saw her thinking them, she worried they might learn the truth too, that she had potentially been, as they say, *asking for it*.

'I'm starving,' Tally managed after forcefully swallowing such a large chunk of toast she had nearly choked on it. It scratched her throat all the way down yet all she could taste was the curdling tomato and vodka. She wasn't starving anymore; she wasn't even sure she could take another bite of her food. So, she turned to her drink instead.

❄

'You *can't* do this to me,' Tally hissed as Leila fluttered her fingers through the top of the closing window, narrowly missing the glass as it slid shut on the passenger side of her mum's car. 'You're not sick,' Tally continued to tell the departing vehicle as it crawled out of the pub car park. 'You're just cruel.' Tally sighed as they rounded the bend, leaving her all alone with two horses. *I wish I was alone,* she sighed again, turning and bracing herself for the sight of her new riding companion. He was already sitting on top of Peter, grinning at her, as keen as a goofy riding school kid. Peter looked as placid as ever, accepting his passenger with more grace than Tally would have liked. *Traitor.*

'I can't believe it,' she muttered as she approached Match.

'She's a lightweight, huh?' Simon stroked Peter, unable to smother his glee at agreeing to stoically assist when Leila declared herself too sick to possibly ride Peter back home. He hadn't felt the warmth of a horse below him in so long, too long, and he had been daydreaming about getting back into the saddle since first finding himself in Fenson, face to face with two horses. It was a dream come true. He was selfishly glad that Leila had drunk too much. He was also glad he had been brave enough to walk out of his cottage and declare himself out of milk just as they were riding past. He had heard the hooves from a distance, and ran to the window excitedly, his younger self lifting him from the sofa, unable to resist the urge of rushing to take a look at the approaching horses.

'I've seen that girl do ten shots of tequila in a row,' Tally said as she swung her leg over Match's waiting back. 'There is no way two pints of weak lager are going to make her sick.' She urged Match forward, not bothering to check if Simon was ready, and sighed again as Peter stepped into action, his hooves crunching a little too closely behind her on the gravel driveway. He was a little too keen for her liking, as if he was actually going to keep pace all the way home just when she would have preferred for him to trail behind.

'Maybe she's pregnant and doesn't know it yet,' Simon shrugged, somehow managing to steer Peter alongside her as they navigated the high street, placing himself on the offside as if sheltering her from danger.

'I don't think so.' Tally looked away, pretending to study the house they were passing, focusing as hard as possible on the flowerbed as if she liked the colours or the species or something.

His words slapped her in the face. She hadn't given a thought to Leila and Michael having a baby. Not yet, it was far too soon, and she was far too bruised to have the capacity to be happy for them for getting to want to make a baby together, for sharing the joy of being parents, for having *a choice.*

'Michael is besotted with Leila, besotted with Edith, maybe he's ready for a baby of his own,' Simon mused aloud, having somehow caught up. Peter now walked shoulder to shoulder with Match.

'That's ridiculous,' Tally snapped, 'Michael can't even brew his own tea.'

'He seems capable to me. He's changed.' Simon shrugged, 'People change.'

Tally bit her tongue. She didn't like his comment that 'people change' it seemed loaded; almost as if to carry a meaning she didn't understand. Did people really change? Would Brad ever be trustworthy or kind? Would Michael ever grow up? Would she ever heal? Simon had started as her mortal enemy yet now he was riding alongside her, and had eaten breakfast in the pub with her, as if they were now friends. Had their relationship changed? She didn't think so. Circumstance kept pushing them together, but he was still her adversary. He was still the easiest person to blame. A flash of guilt clutched at her, because she knew not everything was Simon's fault, but it was just so much more convenient to blame him. That way, she didn't have to think about Brad, about her father's condition, about her parent's spending and inability to future plan, about the slow decline into rack and ruin herself and Michael had witnessed but never paid attention to, leaving protecting their family name to someone else. It was simpler if Simon was the architect of her unhappiness.

'People don't change due to having a choice,' she said, 'they are forced to adapt to survive.'

'That's deep,' Simon laughed, 'Very dramatic.'

'Look at me, I had to adapt to take care of Edith. Parenting wasn't exactly something I knew anything about. I was just thrown into the situation and had to learn on the job.'

'I don't think anyone knows anything about parenting until they have their own children. I think Michael changed out of choice. He fell in love with Leila, and he became an uncle overnight. He decided to grow up.'

'Yeah, because he *had no choice,*' Tally argued.

'He could have stayed lazy, then lost Leila, and never got to know his niece or be close to his sister. I'm certain he decided to change because he didn't want to lose all the good things in his life.'

'I'm certain it's none of your business.' The hurtful words tumbled out of Tally's mouth before she could stop them. His declaration that Tally and Edith equated to *good things* didn't miss her attention. She presumed he was just thinking from Michael's perspective, putting himself fleetingly into her brother's shoes. Michael might well have changed out of choice, but the ability to choose who you fall in love with, who you have children with, and who gets to own your house was missing from Tally's life. She preferred to consider Michael as being forced to adapt, just like she had been, because that made her less jealous. And now she had been spiteful towards Simon for saying something positive about her brother. Now she had changed his mind about being good for anything. She wanted to apologise but her injured pride didn't let her; it never did.

I'm a horrible person, she told herself as the ponies plodded on, she stalled at saying sorry and Simon kept his eyes glued ahead, visibly dampened by her words when he should be enjoying the horse ride he had longed for since moving to a strange village miles away from any friends or family of his own.

'You're right, none of my business,' Simon eventually nodded, deciding to be the bigger person and clear the air, swallowing his hurt and offering the olive branch to avoid the afternoon falling into total ruin. They both knew it was Tally who should have apologised but Simon spoke first, as usual.

I'm a horrible person, and he's too good for me.

❄

'Pour me a glass,' Tally pleaded as she dropped onto the worn sofa and winced as a rogue spring dug into her left bum cheek. The room was slowly transforming from drab to cheerful, mainly through the constant dusting and hoovering done by Anna and addition of flowers and clever lighting by Helena, but overall, it was still threadbare and grimy since what it really needed was re-carpeting and all the old furniture to be taken to the tip. Michael had painted one end wall during an uncharacteristic splurge of enthusiasm, and then became distracted, so they had a crisp cream feature wall and the rest remained peeling wallpaper. It almost hurt Tally's eyes to look at the new wall, it was in such stark contrast to the rest of the room it felt like it was standing in another dimension, waving at her through a portal. Helena was crouching in front of the ancient oak drinks cabinet, wrestling with a giant lock around the handles.

'What is that?' Tally watched Helena work her fingers on the numbers and wriggle the lock until it reluctantly clicked free.

'Your dad,' Helena huffed, wrenching the door open as if it was her and not Tally's father who had the alcohol problem.

'You have to lock away the booze now?' Tally asked, exasperated with the new low her father must have hit, wondering if she had been shielded from another episode of him being unconscious, lying in his own bodily fluids on the bathroom floor.

'No, no, this was actually his idea.' Helena waved away the accusation, apologising for her shortness. It was a great idea when she didn't want an innocent drink and had to mess about with remembering whose birthday they had selected for the code to get one. She selected a bottle containing a dark and sinister liquid, and holding the heavy glassware instantly calmed her down. 'I guess I just need a drink more than usual and the barrier is a bit inconvenient. I shouldn't criticise really; he's made good progress this week.'

'What are you talking about?' Tally said accepting her glass and sniffing the contents so she could make a decision on whether to neck it without it touching her tongue or sip and savour it. It was whisky, so she went for the former and winced, immediately cloaked by the haze.

'The counselling, he's had two sessions now. Didn't someone tell you? He had a phone consultation last Tuesday and a face to face today.' Helena started leafing through a magazine.

'Well, you certainly didn't.' Tally crossed her arms, miffed her mother hadn't kept her in the loop over something so important, and had just relied on the grapevine to keep her informed. 'Who else could've told me? Michael?'

'Yeah, but I guess he's busy being happily married,' Helena chuckled to herself; the pinch of disbelief mixed with sheer unbridled joy that her unruly, no hoper, eldest son would settle down first made Tally wince.

'Anna?'

'Anna's on holiday.'

'Holiday? Anna? Michael already gave her a holiday.'

'She fancied another break; she deserves two holidays after putting up with us for all these years. Besides, I quite like taking the reins every once in a while.'

'Isn't she as broke as we are on account of us being unable to pay her up until only recently, when Michael found work?' Tally asked. She had noticed her mother become more hands on since she had returned home, and not just with Edith. She had found her hoovering and cleaning, generally mucking in alongside Anna with the housework. She still avoided cooking, which was a relief to them all; especially Anna. The old Helena would not have dreamed of getting her hands dirty, and Tally decided it was a combination of many things. Helena was more easily bored; she had less spending and socialising to keep her occupied, and she also probably felt more responsibility towards the household and perhaps even Anna, who was more of a companion than an employee now. Since Charles had become unhinged and her friends had all left her, Anna had become Helena's only source of friendship outside of her two children. Helena wanted to edge her way back into everyone's good books, and helping to keep their accommodation clean and tidy eased her guilt a tad.

'She had some help, just like your dad.' Helena glanced sideways, giving it all away.

'I get it.' Tally rolled her eyes, 'And I get why you decided to hide it, too.'

Helena finally put down her magazine, but she let her eyes linger over her article as if the conversation wasn't very important, as if Tally was somehow falling short and Helena didn't hold her in such high regard anymore. Tally hadn't noticed it before, but her mother looked a little pissed off with her, as if Tally had worn her out. *This must be how it feels to no longer be the golden child*, she thought, *this must have been how Michael felt for all of those years.*

'What do you get?' Helena asked, one eyebrow slightly raised, suggesting she was not impressed at being accused of hiding facts.

'Simon did it, didn't he? Simon stumped up the cash to pay for counselling for dad, and a holiday for Anna, and let's not forget Michael's flash wedding.'

'Yes, he did,' Helena nodded. 'The counselling is an employee benefit, and he managed to get a special extension for your dad so he would be covered under the company policy. As for Anna, he's been propping up her wages for a while now, she wasn't going to mop our floors for free. And you know why he paid for Michael's wedding, it was a test wedding for the company, so it was of mutual benefit really.'

'That doesn't make you suspicious at all? He doesn't even know us. Why would he help us? Why go through all the bother?' Tally didn't like how Helena kept defending Simon, as if he was just doing something nice and normal when he must have spent thousands on the family as if they were his personal pity project, as if he *owned them.*

Helena gazed at Tally, to see if she had anything more to add, which prompted her to plough on.

'He can't just buy our compliance to make up for taking away our home. He can't just throw money at us to ease his guilt. He can't make us like him!'

Helena pursed her lips together but waited patiently for Tally to finish.

'What about me? He didn't give me anything.' Tally slammed her empty glass down with a flourish, aware she was starting to sound childish, aware she had just got to the crutch of her annoyance. She could do with counselling or a holiday or a big fancy party held in her honour.

'That's not true.' Helena picked up her magazine, clearly deciding Tally was not even worth her attention whilst in full rant mode. 'He sorted out your bedroom, he let you ride more often and he's fine with you and Edith playing in the grounds all day. Quite frankly, he...'

Tally stared in disbelief as Helena paused and seemingly made her way through a whole paragraph of her article. She could see Helena chewing on her next words, choosing then modifying them with great care.

'He what?' Tally finally prompted, going crazy with the anticipation as she waited for her mum to spit out whatever was rolling around her mouth.

'He'd give you everything, if you would only let him,' Helena finally said, and then flicked over the page so casually that Tally thought perhaps she had misheard her.

The phone jolted Tally awake. She grabbed it and answered with lightning speed, before the noise had a chance to wake Edith. The number was unknown, and for a split-second Tally was terrified it was Brad, calling to confront her about having his child.

'Hello?' she croaked.

'Tally, it's Ned, from the pub.' His voice was apologetic, and Tally knew Michael had previously received phone calls like this. Michael was probably still too busy being happily married to go and scrape their father up from the pub floor. It was as if someone had swapped their lives, and she didn't much like being Michael. She had never considered how her brother had felt when she had escaped to university, leaving him behind to avoid their father and upset their mother whilst she enjoyed herself.

'Oh no, how many did he have?' Tally groaned, pushing herself into a sitting position and readying herself to crawl out of bed.

'It's not your dad,' Ned said, 'not this time. He's tucked up in bed as far as I'm aware.'

'Michael?' Tally asked, immediately guilty because perhaps married life was not so peachy.

'No, your new friend, the one you had breakfast with the other day.'

'Simon? Are you sure?' Tally asked, shocked, unsure what she was even asking. Was she asking if Ned was sure it was the same Simon? If he was sure Simon was her new friend?

'Yep, it's him, he ain't never been drinking in here before and then boom he's on it then collapsed in a heap. I don't think he's from around here, I reckon you're the only person he knows.'

'He's from London,' Tally confirmed, and she could *hear* the knowing nod from Ned, as he scorned Londoners and their reckless behaviour and weak drinking capabilities.

'Well, right now he's a nuisance. People are having to step over him to get to the loo. Come and collect him please, before I have to call last orders - or a paramedic.'

'Does he need a paramedic, Ned?' Tally asked, scrambling for nearby clothes and trying to slide her legs into jeans with the phone pressed to her shoulder, all without stirring Edith who was snoring gently in her cot. She rolled her eyes at the shuffly patrons who probably really were just ignoring Simon and sipping their own drinks in silence. Despite all the dark thoughts she'd had about Simon, she didn't want him to die or anything, the idea scared her a little.

'We rolled him onto his side.' Ned said, proud of himself for at least ensuring his drunkard wouldn't choke on his own vomit.

'I'm on my way.' Tally debated whether or not to call 999 immediately. She leaned over the cot and gave Edith a peck on the forehead, then jogged down the hallway to Helena's room. She pushed open the door and was thankful to find Helena still up, reading a book. Her father was rolled over, his back facing her, and it was comforting to see Ned had been right. Maybe her father really was newly committed to changing his ways? Helena looked at Tally, unsurprised to see her at the door, it wasn't the first time she had searched her out in the middle of the night to ask for help with the baby.

'I need to go out,' Tally said.

'Oh, you do?' Helena frowned.

'Edith's fast asleep, but here's the monitor just in case.' Tally put the speaker onto a nearby dresser. 'I won't be long, I hope.'

'Okay darling, take care.' Helena smiled, and Tally was grateful she wasn't being quizzed about why and who and where. She also wasn't being asked how she thought she was going to get anywhere on account of not owning a car.

Tally grabbed her Mother's keys and hurried out of the house, into the car, along the road to the village, and into the pub. She found Ned straining under the weight of Simon, half lifting and half dragging him towards the doorway, clearly hopeful that Tally would soon rid him of his problem. Ned dropped him by the door and wiped his brow. Tally leant down to see Simon was still breathing, his eyes half open, silently muttering something. His front was completely soaked.

'It's just beer, thankfully, I'm hoping he'll save chucking up for your car,' Ned said, turning back to serve another customer, one who could still stand and spend money.

'Hang on a minute, there's no way I can lift him on my own.' Tally crossed her arms and ten minutes later three tipsy blokes had been roped in to hoisting Simon into the passenger seat of Helena's car. Tally knew unloading him outside his cottage in a few minutes time was going to be nigh on impossible, although it looked as if he was starting to come round which made her hopeful that he might regain the ability to walk. She also worried Ned might be right about him being sick all over the interior. Helena would no doubt order Tally to deep clean her car if that happened and whilst she was used to baby milk sick by now, fully grown man beer sick turned her stomach. And she *didn't even like* Simon.

'We're nearly there,' Tally huffed, more to herself than the half unconscious man propped up on her shoulder. She was staggering to his front door, praying the neighbours weren't tweaking at the curtains. She held him against the door with one hand, aware she was pushing his face into it but struggling logistically, and patted down his pockets with her free hand to search out the key. Eventually she found it and then had to squeeze two fingers down the tight front pocket of his jeans, feeling her cheeks flush as she did so, to ease out the key. When she turned the lock, they both fell inside and she hoped he hadn't smashed out any front teeth. She rolled him over with force and was horrified to see the fall had already bruised his cheek. She muttered angrily at him, blaming him for bashing his head on the tiled entrance way, then shoved his legs away from the door so she could close it. They were now in a darkened hallway and she had to untangle herself from his non-compliant limbs and search out a light. Simon groaned when the bulb turned on directly above his head and lifted a heavy arm to shield his eyes. Tally took the movement as a positive sign, he appeared to be coming to. She had been here so many times before with their father, too many times, and she knew the drill.

'Come on, up we get.' She clapped her hands together, going for cheery but firm. There were so many ways to play it, and if she really had to then she would cycle through being sympathetic, angry and disappointed until it produced a result. Luckily, Simon responded to her request, as if now he was back in the room, he wanted to compensate for being a sack of potatoes previously and prove he wasn't really that drunk, there had been no need for everyone to make a big deal out of it. She recognised his attitude, her father had also played this role, and of all the options Simon could have selected, this was probably the easiest on her. She was grateful he hadn't gone for angry or depressed or hysterical; she could cope with denial just fine.

Simon pushed himself up and staggered towards the kitchen. Tally followed, ready to catch him although it was clear if she tried to, that they would just both hit the floor again. Simon was stocky and muscly and that translated to a lot of weight. He grabbed a glass from the drainer and filled it with water then gulped it down with such desperation that it overflowed his mouth and dripped onto his t-shirt. He didn't notice or care, and Tally just waited. He finished the glass in just a few big gulps and then gasped for air.

'You feeling okay?' Tally asked cautiously, hoping they weren't both about to see the water reappear almost as quickly as he had sucked it in.

'Not really.' Simon rubbed his eyes, willing himself to sober up so he would only see one Tally standing nervously in his kitchen. 'I'm sorry he called you.'

'He didn't know who else to call.'

Simon slumped back against the counter. 'No, I suppose he didn't.'

'He doesn't have any of your work friends' numbers,' Tally hastened to elaborate.

'Friends? I don't have any friends here.' Simon turned towards the sink and ran the tap. He splashed cold water onto his face and was instantly refreshed, almost jolted back to sobriety.

'Well, me neither. I mean, I've got Leila of course, but she's with Michael now. Doug is miles away, so I'll probably never see much of him. Then there are the three mums, I suppose,' she trailed off, because listing out friends probably wasn't helping. She was going to add something about Gwen being single, and that Simon might have a chance but then decided not to mention it. *He doesn't want to be lumbered with a baby,* she thought.

'You should get back to Edith,' Simon said, turning off the tap but keeping his back turned. He was embarrassed Tally had seen him like this.

'She's fine, she's fast asleep and Helena's watching her. I can stay for a while and make sure you don't fall unconscious then never wake up.' Tally prised him away from the sink and steered him towards a chair. 'You sit down, and I'll make us some toast. A bit of dry toast is great for mopping up alcohol.'

'Do you think I'm barred?' Simon asked weakly after watching Tally search for bread then plates without thinking to provide any prompts.

'Nah, course not. In fact, I would have preferred if Ned had minded a little bit more. He shouldn't have let you get so drunk.'

'I am a grown man.'

'Well, exactly,' she smiled coyly, 'I've had a grown man for a brother for long enough to know that doesn't equate to sensible or measured.'

'I'm usually sensible and measured.' Simon stared into his lap.

'What was the special occasion then, for the idiocy?'

The toast jumped into the air and Simon didn't answer until Tally had settled down at the kitchen table with him and pushed one slice towards him. Despite a cupboard full of condiments, she kept to dry toast for herself, too.

'My mum died today,' Simon said, before taking a bite of toast.

※

Tally was not woken up by a baby crying, or gurgling, or any other noisy bodily function. She woke up naturally, far later than usual, and enjoyed a rare and gentle ascent into morning. She allowed herself to slowly flow into consciousness as opposed to being reluctantly dragged or jolted by some external factor such as an arguing family or a demanding child. She had not felt this content and refreshed for months. Warm sunlight danced over her cheeks and a fresh breeze toyed with her hair. Slowly she opened her eyes, and they met a room she didn't recognise. She moved and her limbs were weighed down by a wool blanket. Someone had tucked her in on the sofa, so precisely that it couldn't have been her own doing because her arms were by her sides and the blanket went right under her chin. She recognised the pastel pattern as one from the British Estates gift shop. She then remembered. Simon's mum had died, and she had been the one to rescue him in his hour of need. Although she had a lot to unpack, her immediate concern was Edith, and how desperate she suddenly was to get back to her.

'He invited you to his Mother's funeral?' Katherine asked in disbelief, staggered by Tally's latest Simon news. It was impressive she had managed to say anything at all since Eva was climbing up her chest, smothering her with rogue limbs and slobber as if launching an unprovoked toddler attack.

'Like, as his date?' Susan asked, eyes rounding at the concept. She had a wailing Clem tucked under her arm for an enforced time out. Clem had refused to stop attempting to shove an entire conker into her mouth and was now having a meltdown after Susan had hurled it half-way across the lawn, well out of choking distance. They were gathered for another picnic below the trees, it was developing into a firm tradition falling somewhere within the first weekend of every month. It had been Susan's turn to bring the prosecco.

'More like a friend,' Tally corrected, horrified at the idea of attending a funeral in any kind of romantic capacity.

'A shoulder to cry on?' Gwen smiled. She was smug because Bobby was still asleep in his pushchair, and had been since the moment they had arrived, even with all the screaming.

'I couldn't exactly refuse, could I?'

'You could have said no,' Katherine disagreed, 'I mean, it's in London, you could have used Edith as your excuse.'

'I used Bobby to get out of a birthday party I didn't want to go to last weekend,' Gwen agreed. 'Total white lie.'

'What will you wear?' Susan asked.

'Black, duh!' Katherine laughed.

'But sexy black? Casual black? Black lace?' Susan added, winking.

'Not black lace!' Tally cried.

'You can't just wear black jeans either, you've got to show some respect to the dead lady you've never even met,' Gwen said.

'Your, would-have-been mother-in-law,' Katherine dared to add with a wry smile.

'You're just being ridiculous now!' Tally screeched, her cheeks flushing. She mentally searched her mind for something black to wear. There must be an old simple dress in there somewhere. If not, Helena was sure to have something suitable. She couldn't exactly turn up with her legs on show. She didn't want Simon to think she thought it was some kind of date. What was she thinking accepting an invitation to go to a stranger's funeral with a man she was supposed to dislike? Had she accepted out of pity? Or did she wish the dead woman had been her mother-in-law?

'Are you going to stay at his place?' Susan asked, 'London is a long drive.'

The three girls exchanged gleeful looks, knowing Tally was cornered into admitting the full truth.

'On the sofa, obviously,' Tally said.

'Oh, I'm sure he'll offer his bed and he'll take the sofa,' Katherine grinned.

'Gallantly,' Gwen added.

'Like the hot guy always does in the movies,' Susan nodded.

'I wish I hadn't told you all.' Tally put her face in her hands, even more worried about the whole thing now that she had seen their faces and had been tortured by their suggestive questioning. How was she going to be able to sleep in Simon's flashy London apartment bed, knowing he was just a door or two away on his sofa? Surely nothing else would be on his mind on the night after his Mother's funeral? Was it sick that something had flashed into her mind? She swallowed, convincing herself the girls had just planted the idea, and it was all their fault she was now imagining some kind of steamy movie scene involving sofas or beds with more than one occupant.

'We're just jealous you have something other than a toddler to think about. We want to be able to think about it too. Please don't stop sharing your interesting life,' Susan pleaded, 'we promise to be more helpful from now on.'

'I think telling her not to wear black jeans was helpful,' Gwen piped in.

'It was, it was.' Tally had briefly considered black jeans, and at least now she wouldn't be making that mistake. She looked across the lawn. There were a few families milling around, one making use of the lawn games Simon had thoughtfully planted. The eldest child appeared to be attacking his younger sibling with a giant chess piece whilst the parents were looking the other way.

'I think I said yes for the break,' she admitted. 'Sounds awful, doesn't it?'

'Not to another mum with a toddler. I'd willingly go to the dentist for a filling if it guaranteed me some alone time,' Susan nodded.

'I'd offer some community service, cleaning park bins or scrubbing graffiti,' Gwen agreed.

'I'd definitely watch a hot guy bury his mum,' Katherine finished, popping open the prosecco to punctuate her cheekiness.

Tally shook her head, speechless, but smiled all the same. They knew how to cheer her up. They had no censor, and Tally sometimes wondered if they had always been like that or if being new mums had destroyed their filter. The four of them had been through so much together and could share literally anything without it causing so much as a flinch, that it felt like a privilege to be party to the outlandish conversations, where no one thought twice about speaking their mind or teasing the other. They were real friends who held each other's children when they cried and offered to change nappies or wipe noses. Tally was going to report back on the bizarre funeral, and they would listen eagerly, cracking jokes and making sly comments, and then one of the kids would wet themselves or fall over and then life would move on. They made Tally feel safe. She still couldn't bring herself to tell them about Brad, but perhaps some things were never meant to be shared. Perhaps there were limits to what could be told, and Tally didn't want to risk tarnishing the close friendships she had fostered. She couldn't risk Brad ruining this one good constant, not when her circle of mum friends had only come to exist after what Brad had done to her. They were her silver lining, after Edith, of course.

※

Everyone paused when Charles strolled casually into the room, as if he joined his family for dinner every night without fail.

'I'll grab another chair.' Anna disappeared before she could get flustered, worried Charles might demote her to eating dinner on her own in another room like the old days, before the family had truly welcomed her into the fold. The house disaster had changed their perspective, if anything they worshipped Anna now, their one remaining constant. Despite Anna being called family for years, it was only since they had lost the house and been crammed together in one derelict corner of it that she had been truly treated like family. Everyone noticed it, and felt a little bit guilty. Helena was extra nice, offering to help with the chores she paid Anna to do, just to try and make up for past oversights such as never inviting Anna to eat with them in full knowledge she was scraping her portion out of the dishes in the kitchen, on her own.

'Shepherd's pie,' Charles announced as he tucked himself into a gap around the tiny table, his tone not giving away whether this was a good or bad discovery.

'Home grown mash,' Helena said.

'They let us keep the vegetable patch?' Charles asked, causing everyone to flinch. Mentioning anything about British Estates was a risky topic with Charles, but it inevitably came up. Every conversation inevitably led back to losing the house.

Anna dropped the chair she had just carried in with a clatter.

'Mm,' Helena murmured cautiously through a mouthful of the now difficult to swallow mash.

'That Simon chap isn't too awful, is he?' Charles said as he helped himself. Anna was just in time to slide a clean plate in front of him.

Michael and Tally exchanged wide-eyed glances.

'He's lovely,' Leila replied, slightly unaware of the impact Charles had on the rest of them. Despite the stories, since the wedding he had been nothing but pleasant to her, albeit a little odd.

'Is he drunk?' Michael mouthed to Tally.

'I don't think so,' she mouthed back after taking a discreet sniff. She caught her Mother's scolding eyes and dropped her attention swiftly to her dinner.

'It's good you're here, Dad,' Michael cleared his throat and wrenched up his glass in readiness to make a speech. Everyone obediently paused, observing his slightly nervous yet eager expression with curiosity.

'Leila and I have some exciting news,' he turned his eyes upon Leila and just looking at her caused a surge of calm to spread across his face, as if she was an elixir.

Despite accepting and then blessing their relationship, witnessing the transformation still made Tally flinch. The betrayal of a brother who had once vowed to stay away from Tally's best friend with a scowl, as if the very idea of fancying Leila disgusted him, and the way Leila had always agreed Michael was awful, still made this new sight of two people so clearly in love difficult to process. Had they lied to her, or had they changed? It was difficult to say and Tally suspected the truth was a little bit of both. They were young back then, and life was simple; now it was complicated, even the good stuff.

'Get on with it lad, mash is getting tacky,' Charles said, digging his fork in to prepare for another bite after Michael had spat out his exciting news.

'We're having a baby.'

'You are?' Helena cried, launching at him from the side, wrapping arms around him in joy.

'We are,' Leila placed a hand stereotypically onto her belly, even though it looked completely flat still. 'I'm twelve weeks today, we went for the first scan.'

'Did you get a photo?' Anna asked, eyes brimming with tears at the cast iron proof Michael, the tear away child, had finally grown up and become a man who did things right, in the right order. She had as much right as Helena to feel proud and partly responsible, and at times, when Michael had been a brat, she had also questioned what she had done wrong in raising him.

Tally clenched her jaw. She was the one who had messed things up. There had been no reason for people to cheer and cry happy tears about her conception of Edith, no one had even had a chance to experience any kind of emotion other than belated shock at the news of a new-born baby. She felt like a thief who had robbed them of this moment for Edith. Michael was giving them a second proper go at it and they were grateful, almost determined to set things straight. Her world turned dark green; a surge of pure jealousy enveloped her. She wasn't even going to pretend it was simple envy. She couldn't even look at them as they fawned over a little black and white photo of a kidney bean shaped blob, her niece or nephew, Edith's cousin, the new golden child. How was Edith ever going to compete with this? How was she ever going to compete with Leila? Michael was going to get to be a father a full nine months before Tally had even known she was a mum and the head start seemed grossly unfair. Even Charles got to his remarkably steady feet and clasped a hand onto his son's shoulder. Charles hadn't even been able to look at Edith at first, and now he was pointing out blurry marks and agreeing they were definitely tiny wonderful toes.

After a few minutes of fawning people started to notice Tally sitting statue like in her chair, her hackles almost visibly raised.

'You okay, Tal?' Michael ventured and only then did it dawn on him that perhaps it had been a little insensitive to spring this on his sister without warning. Only he knew the full extent of Edith's beginning, only he had the power to approach the situation with caution.

'Fine.' Tally mentally put herself back together. 'I'm delighted for you both,' she managed. She reached over to squeeze her best friend's hand and then did her best coo over the photo. She listened politely with a smile plastered onto her face as cute little questions were asked over the rest of dinner. Her shepherd's pie went cold.

※

'What about this one?' Tally asked, desperation starting to creep into her voice. It was the fifth black garment she had tried on today and from the raised eyebrow on Helena's face it was probably going to be the fifth dress she would throw onto the reject pile. She was certain she was now clean out of black dresses. The only one left in her wardrobe was a throwback from one of Michael's old parties; short, sparkly and probably a size or two too small since it had not left much room for the imagination. Her back was getting sweaty and her hair was all flat and she probably should have decided what to wear the night before - not the morning of - the funeral. Simon would be picking her up in less than thirty minutes and so far, she had only settled on a pair of subtly sheer but not too transparent tights. Getting the balance right between respectful and not frumpy was almost impossible. If Simon's relatives and closest friends were going to wonder who the hell she thought she was then she simply *had* to look half decent. She hadn't even allowed herself to panic about shoes yet.

'It's the best so far,' Helena said, as optimistically as she could muster.

Edith let out what Tally could only describe as a scowl at the sight of this particular outfit from where she sat playing with a plastic tractor by the foot of the bed.

'But it's still not quite right?' Tally smoothed down the edges, tugging the skirt a little in the hope it would grow a respectable inch longer.

'It looks like you bought it for a party,' Helena said, glancing at the reject pile because she had similar opinions about those dresses too and needed to double check she hadn't accidentally missed a gem. Unfortunately, none appeared to have dramatically transformed.

'That's because I did buy it for a party, I bought all of them for parties.' Tally flopped down onto the bed and flung her arms above her head dramatically. 'I didn't buy any of them for a 'just in case' funeral.'

'I've been to a few funerals in my time,' Helena meandered over to her wardrobe, 'there must be something here you can try.'

'Mum you're so much taller and thinner than me,' Tally groaned, rolling onto her stomach and burying her face into the luxurious throw draped across the foot of her parent's bed. She was probably rubbing off her face powder but was starting to not care anymore. At this rate she was going to have to fake a stomach bug and cancel. Helena was hardly going to allow her to cancel though.

'Try this one.'

Tally peeked up to see what her mother was holding out and was grateful her initial reaction was not to squirm. It wasn't *awful*. 'It's blue,' she said, finally putting her finger on with was wrong with the dark lace dress, complete with modest capped sleeves, high slash neck and a thin shiny waist belt. The length was going to be longer than intended on Tally, what with Helena sporting the physique of a gazelle, but it could still work, it wouldn't go past Tally's knees and would allow her to get away with a pair of high heels. She even had a pair of stilettos in midnight blue somewhere. It could work.

'Blue is fine, it's still dark. Black might look cliché, anyway, think about how brides never wear pure white at their weddings these days, it's all oyster and ivory.'

'Isn't that something to do with brides not being virgins on their wedding day anymore?'

'Well, you're not a virgin at this funeral, are you? So maybe the same thing applies here.'

They glanced at Edith who was now running the tractor up the pile of abandoned dresses, getting bits of fabric snagged on the wheels.

'Hmm.' Tally decided not to continue that weird conversation and instead wriggled out of the inappropriate black dress and tried on the blue lace dress. Admiring herself in the full-length mirror, she had to concede it sort of worked. It was the best she could have hoped for at such short notice.

'Hair?' Helena steered her towards her vanity mirror and Tally obediently sat. She had been expecting to sort out her own hair but clearly her mother was on some kind of crisis management mission. 'He'll be here in fifteen minutes,' she said as she started grabbing twists of Tally's hair and clipping them artfully into place, creating a messy yet also somehow stylish up-do. It was almost like wedding day hair.

'He's always early, too,' Tally said, eyes wide. She reached towards her Mother's powder to try and repair the smudged makeup. It was too late to wash it off and start again.

'You know him so well,' Helena smiled, then avoided Tally's piercing eyes in the mirror.

'We didn't really have a choice but to get to know him.'

'No, we didn't,' Helena clenched her jaw, grateful Tally still acknowledged that Helena also never really had a choice. She had invited him in, but what alternative had she had?

'You still look flustered.' Helena said, when Tally was completely ready, looking gorgeous. 'What is it?'

'I've never been to a funeral before.'

'Okay, what is it really, Tally?' Helena rolled her eyes.

Tally looked at Edith who unfortunately didn't appear to require any assistance or attention. Helena was hopefully going to have a really easy breezy time of babysitting and Tally was hopefully not going to miss her baby so much it would be a constant distracting pain in her heart. She hadn't left her before, except the night she had fallen asleep on Simon's sofa, she had hoped it would sound plausible that imminently leaving for the night would cause her such dismay.

'It's Leila, isn't it?' Helena encouraged.

Tally wasn't going to be able to blame her anxiety on the prospect of leaving Edith, Helena wasn't about to buy it.

'Not so much Leila...' Tally trailed off, wishing her mum hadn't read her mind so easily. Leila hadn't even told Tally about the pregnancy. She and Michael had kept it as their special little secret, and as a former best friend, the person who used to keep Leila's secrets, Tally felt cheated. She had had to find out with the rest of the family, with Anna, she hadn't even been granted the privilege of finding out second. Not even Michael had confided in her. She knew Michael had gained a special status, far above and beyond best friend, and the couple had every right to treasure the news of their unborn baby between them for as long as they wanted, but Tally was still envious, still grieving the passing of the baton and the changing of the tides.

'Leila struggled with you leaving,' Helena said, guessing her thoughts after watching the wave of emotion engulf Tally. 'She stayed in her home town to work as a waitress and ride your horses, stuck in your old ways yet this time alone, and you left to study at university in a big city. Leila's heart broke first, she was devastated when you left. Although you might think she was always so sure of what she wanted from life, your leaving made her wobble, it made her worry she had not aimed high enough and would forever be left behind.'

'I hadn't thought about it like that.' Tally bit her lip. She had, of course she had. She had felt guilty about leaving, she had tried not to act superior for continuing her education, for striving for aspirations and improving herself. She was glad she had been modest about their difference in life choices and never made fun of Leila for dreaming so small, although internally she had secretly felt some kind of triumph over her, sure that she was making better life choices. Keeping her thoughts to herself meant she did not have so far to fall when her life made an abrupt turn and she returned home, tail between her legs and baby in her arms. Leila had not flinched, no hint of a smirk had crossed her open face, even if her own internal thoughts had been smug. It wasn't some kind of twisted revenge to take Michael and have a happy consensual baby, to even consider it would be egotistic. Tally was just jealous, because Leila's life was playing out better, more conventional, more *normal*. Tally was trying to find something solid to blame.

'I know it means I'm evil, but I resent Leila's unborn baby.'

'You're not evil, you're just human. I understand why it's hard. You know you don't resent the baby itself, just the idea of an unborn baby. You didn't get to enjoy your pregnancy. It is okay to feel this way, Tally, it's something you need to work your way through.'

'I didn't even realise it until last night when they told us, because I had never had a reason to think about it before, but I now feel robbed of my pregnancy. All those weeks Edith was growing inside me and I didn't even notice. I didn't get the opportunity to enjoy it, to worry about it, to bond. I was so woefully unprepared.' Tally gazed at Edith and wondered what her little twelve week scan photo would have looked like. She wanted her very own flimsy kidney bean blob print. She might have been able to make out a head and a bum, and little limbs, maybe even tiny clenched fists.

Helena sat down heavily on the bed and combed a nervous hand through her perfectly coiffed hair. She was debating over whether to say something.

'What is it, Mum?' Tally sat gingerly next to her and reached across to her slightly shaking hand.

'It's for the best, the way Edith surprised you. It meant you didn't have a chance to do anything stupid. Look at her. Imagine if we had decided it would be best to end her life before she could even live.'

Tally gulped, her mind blown by the prospect, because Helena was right, because if she had known about Edith before it was too late then she would have ended it. She would have never been blessed with giving birth to Edith. She would have decided it would be for the best to end it then and there. The fresh memory of Brad crawling over her would have terrified her into cleansing her body of all evidence.

'I did something stupid once,' Helena continued, 'I didn't realise it was stupid until I met Edith. Sometimes, realisation takes a while to dawn. Sometimes we need time to truly understand what we've done or been through.'

'What did you do?' Tally asked. She almost couldn't bring herself to ask; she had already guessed the answer.

'I was young, too young, and so was he, he wasn't your father, he was before your father. Your father wouldn't have touched me if he had known. It would have ruined everything.' She looked around the room, picturing how differently her life would have turned out.

'You and Michael might never have existed if I hadn't gone through with it. It was just an accident, and my mother insisted, and I just agreed to do it.' She swallowed and placed a hand on an empty stomach. 'She was so small when she went, I never got to feel her kick. There was no evidence of her, except for what I flushed down the toilet. I was stupid.'

'Oh, Mum.' Tally wrapped an arm around Helena and clenched her hand tightly. She had never known; Helena would have never shared a story like this with her before. 'You weren't stupid. You were scared. At the time, it was the best thing to do. You can't second guess your decision now.'

'It wasn't the best thing to do though, was it? Keeping Edith was the best thing to do, even if once, a long time ago, ending the pregnancy might have felt like the best thing to do.'

'You know it's impossible to make the decision retrospectively, Mum. That's not fair on anyone.'

'I'm not sure it was even my decision. My mum made it for me.'

'She was trying to help you, don't blame her, not now, it doesn't help.'

Helena nodded. 'Sometimes, when I look at Edith, when I see everything you went through, the bad timing, the inconvenience, the hell. I see how happy she is, how happy she makes you, heck how happy she makes me, and I'm certain that keeping my baby would have been the right thing to do.'

'If keeping the baby had meant never marrying Dad or having me or Michael, then there would have never been an Edith. Maybe Edith is that baby, maybe she came back to us.'

Helena squeezed Tally's hand. She had always been a practical woman, but she would indulge in this poetry. 'We've got to trust the timing of our life,' Helena reaffirmed, building herself back up to full strength, pulling the curtain closed and transforming back to her usual aloof Helena. 'Now say your goodbyes to Edith, because by my reckoning reliable Simon will be here in two minutes.'

'Gee what a nickname, reliable Simon,' Tally laughed. The intensity of their previous conversation vanished, and Tally felt lighter. She hoped she had been able to help lighten her Mother's load, too. Tally knew better than anyone what it was like to carry a secret, what a burden it represented, how it gnawed at every aspect of your life and never completely went away.

'Well, what would *you* call him?' Helena asked, lifting a probing eyebrow.

Tally was saved from having to answer, because her phone lit up with reliable Simon calling to tell her he was here, on the driveway, five minutes early.

✷

'We could have stayed at your Dad's, he seemed upset to hear you wanted to head back home,' Tally said as Simon let her into his apartment. She glanced around and nothing in there made her think of Simon. It was as if he had rented a room for the night. Simon wore wellies and an old fleece, but this apartment appeared to belong to a plush city banker. She was glad they hadn't stayed; the day had been awkward enough and it was obvious from seeing their interactions that Simon and his dad were not very close. All they appeared to be able to talk about was their business, and since Tally was not keen to hear about the success of scooping up homes from families in need and filling them with tourists, she had made a conscious effort to zone out and concentrate on working her way through the buffet. She had made a conscious effort to not get drunk throughout the day and so nodded when Simon gestured towards a bottle of red wine. One more glass before bed couldn't hurt. Her shoes were pinching her toes and she wanted nothing more than to kick them off, but she didn't feel at home enough in a penthouse walled with glass to do it just yet.

Instead, she edged her way towards the walls and dared to peek down, towards the empty grey streets below.

'He didn't want us to stay,' Simon scoffed as he busied himself in the open plan kitchen. 'He was drunk and a little nostalgic. If he found us there in the morning then he'd have been disappointed, and unable to hide it.'

'Your sister is lovely; did you know she lived on the other side of London?'

'No, I didn't know mum was so close, either. Tragic really. I could have walked past either of them and I wouldn't have even noticed.'

Tally wanted to ask so many more questions about their history, about why they had broken off all contact, about whether or not he had tried to track them down, but she could see Simon was exhausted, and knew there would always be time for more conversation. She was suddenly fascinated by him, starkly aware that whilst he knew her inside out, he was still very much a mystery to her, almost a stranger.

Simon let his mind wander as he poured the wine, silently answering all the unspoken questions Tally was desperate to ask. He hadn't seen his younger sister since she was a baby, since his mum packed her bags and left, choosing her favourite child to take with her. He had spent most of his younger years harbouring jealous thoughts of the sister he could barely remember, questioning what she had that he lacked, and what he had done wrong. Why had his mum chosen her and left him behind? Had he associated himself too closely to his father, the man his mum had desperately wanted to leave? Had she looked at her son with disappointment, seeing him as a lost cause, a carbon copy of the man she hated? Simon hadn't been given the opportunity to pick sides and as life tumbled onwards - he became more convinced that if he had been given the choice, he would have gone with his mum. Meeting Siobhan, Simon had not felt the anger or resentment he had expected. She had been timid, probably harbouring her own theories and worries over Simon. She was like a deer caught in headlights when facing her father, and Simon had stayed stoically by her side, pushing aside any of his own demons to ensure their father didn't try to divide and conquer.

Simon didn't have a large family, Tally had helped make up the numbers at the funeral which had been a short, impersonal service followed by a cremation. Simon had agreed to take the ashes because his dad seemed incapable of deciding what to do with them. Tally wondered if Simon had even known his mother well enough to have a good idea of where to sprinkle them.

'Our family isn't very close, either,' Tally offered. She stepped back from the glass, deciding she didn't like standing by the edge. One nudge and she might be free-falling. Simon was stretching out on the sofa putting her in a dilemma on whether to join him or opt for the single chair. Simon made her choice for her by placing her glass of wine next to his.

'It doesn't look that way to me. Even your dad seems to have come around a bit lately.'

Simon kicked off his shoes, compelling Tally to take a deep breath and do the same. She dug her aching toes into the thick rug below the coffee table and took a gulp of wine to numb the pain.

'You mean, he's recently been sober enough to find his way to the kitchen table.' She noticed a slight run in her tights and lamented, wondering when it would be acceptable to swap into her jogging bottoms. She was used to sleepovers with Leila; a sleepover with a boy was a complete minefield. She was discounting her drunken one-night-stand with Doug, there had been no lessons to learn from that except gratefulness that he had been with her when the labour had started.

'He's making the effort to change.'

'For Edith,' Tally said into her glass.

'She's glued you back together.'

'After you ripped us apart,' Tally said dryly, realising the joke wasn't at all funny as soon as it left her lips. In truth she hadn't tried to be funny, it was just an automatic attack she launched into whenever she was around Simon. 'Sorry,' she added, a little too late. Simon shifted uncomfortably in his seat but didn't say anything. What could he say? His silence was an admission of sorts, and Tally realised what he had done could not be undone, and it hadn't even been his doing in the first place. He wasn't going to sink down to her level and say it was all Helena's work, that in an unorthodox way he had saved them, saved their family home. Tally bit her lip. She should have given it a rest at least for today, it *was* his Mother's funeral day, and she *was* supposed to be here with another white flag, as a friend.

Simon put his empty glass down, alerting Tally to how quickly he had finished a large volume of red wine. He paced around the room making her nervous. She started to worry whether or not he was going to do something crazy like tell her to get out of his swanky apartment and make her own way home. It had been a difficult day for him, so she wouldn't even be able to resent him for it. She wouldn't know how to arrange a taxi because she had never had to hail one. She would have to call Michael, an idea which momentarily warmed her heart because she knew he would be there in a heartbeat, the brother who used to communicate with her almost exclusively through punches and insults.

Perhaps her family had become close. Perhaps it was Edith. Despite her awful choice of wording which now threatened to result in her ejection from the city, some of it was also due to losing their home. They had been forced to band together, living almost on top of each other, and the sense of shared loss had pushed them to stand together in solitude and keep each other sane. The undercurrents of blame towards Helena had eased over recent months, as the family accepted their situation and began to accept that the acquisition had not been a direct result of Helena making the wrong choices. They had all accepted some part in the gradual decline of the house, and that perhaps it had been unavoidable. Simon caused less of a rift, he had been begrudgingly accepted, and no one could deny his professionalism towards the family when they hadn't especially deserved it. He had been flexible and accommodating; he had been kind. They understood now that he wasn't really the bad guy, he never had been; he had been the scapegoat.

'Dad wants to sell.' Simon didn't even dare to turn around as he said it.

'The business?' Tally asked, hoping he would say yes.

'The house.' Simon swivelled around to lean against the glass and Tally bit back the urge to warn him against it, in case the glass gave way and he fell. She knew it would sound silly if she warned him against leaning against it, as if she was an uneducated country girl who didn't understand how high rise buildings were built, as if this wasn't his home and he hadn't leant against that pane of glass a thousand times. If she expressed concern Simon would only laugh, and then perhaps he would thump the glass to show her that falling was impossible, and then perhaps he would push too hard and fall.

'Our house?' Tally sat up, keeping her sanity in check. She nearly slopped red wine onto the gorgeous rug that was healing her toes.

'Yes,' Simon confirmed, polite enough to not remind her it wasn't her house anymore.

Tally remembered. She didn't tell him he couldn't sell what was hers, although her heart burned with injustice, because it was still hers, it was still their family home. If they sold it, everything would end. They would be left with nothing at all. What about Edith? Where would her roots lie then?

'Why?' Tally whispered, 'you've been doing great, it's popular, it's busy.'

'Not enough, not nearly enough. He was right. He warned me all along.' Simon sighed, hating the idea of having to give up and admit defeat, hating the thought of having to ask Tally and her daughter, her entire family, to pack their bags and leave. His dad had been on his case for months and nothing he came up with seemed to be good enough to prove to his father that he had the capability of stepping into his shoes. Making the house a success wasn't going to be good enough. His father would just find a way to measure success differently and move the goal posts. He wasn't going to share this with Tally because he didn't want to take away her last ounce of hope. Where would Tally live if he asked her to leave? Where would Edith live?

'What can we do to change his mind?' Tally asked, aghast. How much time did they have? From what she had seen of his father, he was a dominating man who knew his own mind. If he had already made the decision, they were unlikely to be able to convince him otherwise. He probably had the viewings booked already.

'Attract more visitors, make more money, all the things I've been trying to do for months.' Simon loosened his tie. He pulled it free from his neck and slung it at the empty armchair. 'He keeps extending my deadline to turn it around and refuses to see how the wedding venue plan will pay off in the long run, once we get ourselves on the map.'

'Can you show me?' Tally's eyes darted around the room in search of a laptop or some files.

'Show you?'

'How the business works. What decisions you've been making. Show me your business model for the company, and then specifically our house.'

'It's been a long day, you probably don't really want to get into that now.' Simon glanced at his wristwatch. They should be thinking about going to bed, it had been an exhausting day already without a detailed analysis of his accounts. He wasn't sure if it would be ethical to show Tally anything, he couldn't be completely clear of her motives.

'I want to help, I'm sure I can help.'

'I thought the last thing you wanted to do was help British Estates.'

'The last thing I want to do is to lose the house completely. Besides, I'm not offering to help British Estates, I just want to help you.'

Simon pursed his lips, debating what to do next.

'Please, I'm starting to go mad with nothing to do all day, and I was studying for a business degree. I know I didn't get very far but I aced Business at A-level and I've read all my university books. I'm going to continue my course online this September so I can complete my degree.'

'Really?' Simon raised his eyebrows.

'I'm not just giving up on my dreams, Simon, and neither should you.' Tally got up and started sniffing around the flat, searching for his work paraphernalia.

'I'll get it, you open another bottle of wine.' Simon relented. It couldn't hurt to run through some ideas with her, a second pair of eyes might help and she had such a unique perspective on the property and the local area that she might actually be able to assist.

Simon placed a ring binder onto the coffee table. Tally flinched at the impersonal scribble on the spine, declaring the contents to relate to her family home. She pulled the folder onto her lap, intrigued to know what lay within.

'It's just figures,' Simon reassured her as he topped up their wine glasses.

'It's just business,' Tally chuckled, shaking her head, 'There's your first mistake.'

'What?' Simon paused, glass half way to his lips.

'It's a *home* Simon, you need to treat it like one, like it's *your* home.'

'And you need to remember it's now also a business.'

'Your business?'

'I'm open to collaboration.' Simon smiled cautiously, wondering if he had just entered into one of the most dangerous business partnerships possible.

'Especially if all the meetings involve wine,' Tally smiled, allowing herself to relax for the first time all day, despite the first graph on the first page declaring a crippling amount of overhead costs just for the daily running of the house. Although she didn't even have her business degree yet, Simon had been genuinely impressed, and she knew if she put enough work in then she would be able to help him turn the business around. She wasn't going to let his dad win. For the first time since meeting Simon, she finally felt like his equal, rather than some spoilt brat who had gone and got herself knocked up and then ran home crying to her Mother. She was wearing a nice dress and drinking wine in a posh flat; she didn't feel like a failure anymore, and she wasn't going to let Simon fail. Besides, she thought, as she sipped her glass and peeked sideways at Simon, he couldn't leave them now, she was only just starting to get used to him.

Tally had her books sprawled out across her bedroom floor. She was trying to decide where to start. Her eyes rested on Business for Dummies for a moment, because that was the logical choice. Edith had been so over excited to have her mum back home that she had barely slept a wink last night, and so now that it was mid-morning, Edith had finally crashed and Tally was walking around like a zombie.

'She needs her own room,' Tally said to whoever it was who opened the door, no doubt to complain about all the noise last night.

'We don't have a spare room and you know it, not one we're allowed to use, anyway.' Michael slumped onto her bed.

'I suppose you need to get used to sleepless nights anyway, Edith's helping you train.' Tally disregarded Business for Dummies and selected a glossy fat blue book, mainly drawn by the enticing cover illustration rather than any persuasion made by the blurb.

'What are you doing?' Michael asked, unable to feign disinterest in the carpet of books any longer.

'Saving the house.' Tally flicked through the book, noticing some highlighted bits she couldn't even remember adding. University seemed like a distant memory now, it was almost as if she had dreamed about sitting in lecture theatres and hanging around the dorm with Doug. Perhaps Doug would be able to help her, he was a lot further into the degree now. He had probably bought some more books.

'A tad late for that, isn't it?' Michael scoffed.

'Apparently not. Simon's dad wants to sell it, which would mean we all get kicked out.' After no immediate response, Tally looked over her shoulder at Michael. His mouth was literally hanging open like a cartoon character. 'Before you overreact, I'd like to remind you that there is a sleeping toddler in the room and if you dare to wake her it will be your personal duty to get her back to sleep again.'

'I don't think shouting and screaming would be considered an overreaction. Where would we go? I have an unborn child on the way.' Michael swept his hands over his face in disbelief. 'I thought things couldn't get any worse.'

'You weren't going to stay here though, were you, all three of you? There's no room.'

'Yet there's room for you two, is there?' Michael balked, 'I was here first, remember, you weren't even supposed to be coming back home.'

'You've got a job now; you could afford to rent a small place in the village.'

'Now you want me to leave whether or not they sell the house?'

'I just think you'd be happier with your own space.'

'You'd be happier, you mean, with us out of your sight?'

'Of course not, you're my brother and Leila's my best friend.'

'And you're insanely jealous that we did everything the right way, better than you have,' Michael snapped.

Tally raised her eyebrows. Yes, she was jealous, for all the reasons her mother had teased out of her. She was jealous Michael had beaten her to the normal grown up lifestyle since he had spent his youth messing around and Tally had been dedicated to building herself a future. She was jealous of the baby because it was going to have a father, and no one was going to question whether or not they loved it. She was jealous of Leila just for being so damn happy. Michael should have known not to go there. He knew everything had unravelled in Tally's life because of Brad.

'I also think you're the only ones with a decent chance of getting out of here and staying happy. The rest of us will have to find a council flat somewhere. You three could stay in Fenson.' Tally blinked away tears at the idea of bringing Edith up away from the village, somewhere she would never truly be able to call home. Edith was too young to be able to remember Fenson if they were to leave anytime soon, she would never believe they had once lived on a grand estate with stables, gardens, a tennis court and a swimming pool. She'd laugh at the idea of them once having a housekeeper called Anna. 'I suppose we could still visit,' Tally said, fingering a pie chart on one of the pages of her book, wondering if the answer lay somewhere within.

'I'm not leaving, not yet anyway, and neither are you.' Michael snatched up a book from the floor. 'You think your old books can help?'

For once he wasn't sneering, he was genuinely hoping she might be able to go up against an experienced CEO from a nationwide corporation with a slightly out of date textbook aimed at university students, full of utopian theories and irrelevant case studies. He was hoping he could move the conversation quickly on and be forgiven for his sharp tongue. He could understand why Tally was jealous, and it wasn't something he was used to. He had spent his childhood feeling jealous towards his perfect academic sister, who, until Leila had come along, seemed perfectly confident in her own skin, following her own path. He had been so worried about being left out that he had sacrificed everything to stay popular, including any prospects of ever going to university. Now the shoe was on the other foot and somehow, he had landed on his feet and Tally had fallen; it was his duty to try and pull her back up again, and references to the rape and her failed life plans were not supposed to be made. He was still working on not being an arsehole; it was a hard habit to break.

'I think they can help more than doing nothing.'

Michael started reading a chapter, wondering if he was going to be of any use at all. He soon decided he should leave clever thinking to his sister. 'I should probably just try and sell some more cars,' he volunteered, checking his watch to find he was running late for work.

Tally had grown tired of reading. Her brain was frazzled. Although it had been the most fun she'd had in ages. 'I'm such a nerd,' she told Match. He mumbled something in response, most likely a 'yes' and then continued to plod on at the sedate pace Tally had allowed him to set. They weren't in a hurry, Tally was out riding for the sole purpose of taking a break from reading, note taking and thinking. She had one hand on the reins and another on Peter's lead rope, who was loping alongside, more than happy to join them without the added weight of a rider. Leila had elected to stop horse riding due to her pregnancy, so Tally was keeping both Peter and Match as fit as possible, although there wasn't really any reason to do so, she didn't have any aspirations other than ambling through the village and around the estate. It was enough to simply be on a horse, to ground her. She was transported back to a carefree teenager whenever she was in the saddle. I used to be so competitive, she mused, remembering the days when she would get up with the dawn to prepare for a show jumping class, now I'm just a fair-weather rider, with no expectations.

'What about pony rides, would you let the tourists get on you?' she asked Match, still unable to leave the puzzle of how to save their home from being sold. He snorted, which was a most definite 'no'. 'I thought not,' she sighed, 'I'm not sure even sweet Peter would be thrilled.' She wouldn't want a bunch of novices mounting her horses anyway, and there was probably a really expensive insurance premium to pay and all sorts of rules and regulations they would have to explore. Two horses weren't able to provide a sustainable arm of the business, and there was no way they could afford to buy any more. Pony rides was going to have to join the other rubbish ideas she had already thrown in the bin.

Match stopped unexpectedly, causing Peter to also pull up abruptly, nearly yanking Tally's arm out of the socket. She stayed relaxed, secretly prepared for a bolt if that was what Match was about to do next. She would just have to drop Peter and concentrate on getting Match under control, and hope Peter didn't get the loose rope tangled up in his front legs. She aimed her gaze between Match's pointing ears and laughed at the object of their snorting and trembling.

'It's just Grampy, you silly sausage,' she chuckled, placing her palm onto Match's neck to calm him down.

He was on the other side of the fence, in the orchard, tending to the apple tree they had planted together, years ago.

As she watched Grampy work she allowed her mind to slip back to the memory of the day they had first pushed the apple tree into the ground. She had been about three and her brother was around six, Grampy had declared they were off on an adventure and they were instantly captivated, following him and his wheelbarrow containing the quivering apple tree, carrying their plastic buckets and spades to find the perfect place to plant their tree. Grampy had done the real digging, naturally, whilst they had become distracted by new games invented in the orchard, mainly involving Michael chasing Tally around the other trees. After it was planted, they had stood back to admire their work. The sapling looked vulnerable in the middle of the orchard, surrounded by the much larger well established fruits trees, as if the next Fenland breeze might strip it of its delicate leaves and snap the trunk in half.

'You'll grow up with this tree, it'll still be here after I'm long gone, looking out for you, bearing you fruit.' Grampy said to the children, hoping they weren't too young for him to pitch the idea of him ever leaving them.

'We don't want you to go, Grampy,' Tally said, shocked at the idea of Grampy ever leaving them.

'I won't go, I'll stay here, with this tree, to keep an eye on things.' Grampy patted her on the head and Michael rolled his eyes, less gullible than his younger sister. But he still bought into the story, because it sounded better than reality, and perhaps Grampy was right; he always seemed to know more than they did about life.

Match snorted again, pulling Tally back to the present. 'Grampy!' she shouted. Tally stood up in the stirrups and waved, but Grampy didn't look up. He was patting the earth down at the base of the tree, as if he was planting it all over again. The earth at the base was not bare and newly dug like all those years ago, it was now thick with grass and fragments of shed leaves and old apples.

'He can't hear me,' Tally said to the horses, 'the wind is blowing the wrong way.'

Peter started tugging, urging them to turn back. Tally complied, she would come back after the horses were turned out and collect some windfall apples for their feed bowls. If she hurried Grampy would still be there. Realising they were leaving, Match broke into an eager trot, causing Peter to explode, resulting in a few metres of utter chaos while Tally fought to regain control.

'Woah, what's got into you two?' Tally snapped after forcing them both into a walk. Despite complying, she had never known them to walk so fast, both threatening to jog. 'This was supposed to be relaxing,' she muttered crossly, deciding at this rate they would only be getting half an apple each as their evening treat.

Despite the horses' best efforts, and Tally rushing to get them sorted, when she hurried back to find Grampy he was gone. She let herself into the orchard, realising it had been forever since she had been inside the fence – she hadn't visited since she had moved back home. As she weaved her way around the trees to locate their apple tree, she decided she would bring Edith back here tomorrow and tell her all about the day Grampy, Tally and Michel had planted the baby tree. She would tell Edith the tree would be here, long after she had gone and Edith would gaze up at her with those big inky eyes and not understand. Edith thought Tally would always be there, because she was still at that tender age where nothing changed and bad things never happened.

Looking at the sturdy tree now, she could barely believe it had once been so small. Now it owned its spot, no longer intimated by its older, taller neighbours. It was confident in its own bark, unbothered to remain relatively the smallest tree in the orchard. It had the best apples, the healthiest sap; the perfect place. It was planted with love and hope and that spurred it on. 'I hope I can be like you one day, safe and secure, happy with my place,' she said to the tree, touching its bark, half expecting it to answer.

She looked around, searching for evidence of Grampy, but there were no footsteps indenting the grass except her own, no crushed or eaten apple cores. She wondered if Michael still visited him once a week or if Leila had been too much of a distraction. She had been unable to go for a few weeks because something had always cropped up. I will go tomorrow, she promised, and see how he's getting on taming that ridiculously overgrown garden of his.

Michael was waiting for her at the yard. She waved and then threw him a shiny apple, picking the biggest one she had plucked from the tree. Tally had filled an entire bucket with fruit and planned to take those she wouldn't feed to the horses back to the house so she could bake an apple pie with Anna.

'What is it?' she asked Michael when he stuffed the apple into his pocket without taking a big bite out of it first. She paused, thrown by his twisted expression, and then she knew. She *knew.*

'It's Grampy,' he said, unable to stop the tears from rolling down his face, despite willing himself to stay strong for his little sister. 'He died last night.'

※

Leila sat down on the edge of the bed with a sigh.

'You alright?' Michael asked, rushing to her side as if she had just fainted.

'Yeah fine, I just need to sit down for a minute,' Leila rubbed her tummy subconsciously.

Tally rolled her eyes but refused to comment. Michael was flapping around his wife enough for the both of them. She wondered why he had bothered bringing Leila with him today, she wasn't much help considering they were there to pack up Grampy's stuff and she wasn't able to lift anything heavy or even walk up the stairs without making a fuss. You're just jealous because you never got to be dramatic and pregnant, Tally scolded herself. Edith was busy chewing on something she shouldn't be, finding the task of rooting around Grampy's things rather entertaining, as if they were all engaged in a massive game. She kept untidying tidied boxes and so Michael was having to remove each box as soon as it was filled and labelled. Helena had given them strict instructions to bring everything back to the house for sorting between keepsakes, charity shop and – if they really had to – rubbish. Tally wasn't sure where they were going to store all of the keepsakes, because looking around at all Grampy's precious things it was hard to picture any of them having the will-power to part with any of it. She wondered if they were still allowed access to the loft, otherwise she could imagine they'd have a portion of it crammed into each room.

'I'll get you a glass of water,' Tally said to combat her dark thoughts, because she was determined to not transform into a green-eyed monster every time she saw Leila's neat little baby bump, and also because it was a legitimate reason to escape the two of them so she would feel less like a gooseberry.

She plodded downstairs, leaving Edith in their capable parents-to-be hands, and fished a glass out of an already packed box from the kitchen. Tally and Michael were lagging behind schedule, mainly because they had stumbled across old photo albums and spent a good hour reminiscing, pointing out memories from their youth and bickering over who had the most accurate recollection of the day in question. Leila had joined in a little, but she had soon grown tired because the memories were not hers and so the stories were less interesting, and Tally had enjoyed having her brother to herself for a little while. Tally looked forward to taking the photos back home and repeating the exercise all over again with Helena. She flicked on the tap and gazed out of the kitchen window, imagining Grampy sitting just behind her, in his usual spot.

Heartbreakingly, the garden was perfect. Slowly, Grampy had wrestled it back under control and now it was destined to unravel all over again, to be reclaimed by wilderness. Despite the resentment he must have felt for being retired from his day job against his will, Grampy had simply picked up his tools and redirected his efforts into his own garden, a place he had neglected for all those years when he was too busy perfecting someone else's outside space. Tally wondered if the garden had forgiven him for pushing it to the back burner for so many years, and if transforming his own plot of land into an outside haven had granted Grampy some kind of closure, and given him a renewed purpose. He had probably discovered his priorities had been all wrong, Tally mused, hoping it hadn't resulted in him resenting her family for pulling him in the wrong direction.

'Don't be ridiculous, I could never resent you,' she pictured him saying from over her shoulder. She squinted outside at something near the back of his garden that caught her eye. It was a white label fluttering in the wind. She pushed open the backdoor to investigate, and there in the middle of the furthest circle of neat grass surrounded by beds stood a proud sapling, its little curved leaves reaching for the sunlight and resisting the force of the wind as it swirled around the garden, determined to dislodge a thin branch if it could. Tally stooped down and turned the label over in her fingertips. *For Edith, after I'm gone*. Tally cried, she dug her fingernails down into the freshly turned over earth at the base of the tree, where Grampy must have pressed down his own fingertips only a day before.

※

Tally had given up on trying to keep the children under control. There was no way of asking toddlers to play respectfully. They were running around people's legs and giggling, and despite her initial fears, there were plenty of encouraging smiles cast upon them. People were enjoying the comic relief, the joy of youth was a lifting reminder of why life was worth living, and why sad days were bearable. Grampy would have liked to have them at his wake, he wouldn't want them to have been muzzled on his account. There were also few outfits made for toddlers that were appropriate for wearing to a wake. Edith was in a dark grey cardigan and navy leggings; her bright pink socks could be forgiven since it was impossible to buy muted colours and Tally had forgotten to even consider suitable funeral socks. She was wearing the same dress she had worn to Simon's mum's funeral, and since he was in the same dark suit she assumed he wouldn't mind.

She wandered towards a bay window and peeked out at the sunshine. She couldn't decide if she was delighted or offended by the amazing weather. Was it taunting their sadness

– emphasising the simple pleasures Grampy was missing - or celebrating his long and fruitful life? The answer was not set; it depended on her perspective and whether she chose to be all-consumed with grief or whether she chose to rejoice in his memory. She swilled the end of her champagne around the glass. A break down would be satisfying, she could indulge in a bout of self-pity. She could cry and scream and make a big scene, let it all out. But she was supposed to be the host, she was supposed to keep it all together for the rest of them. She had a daughter to keep an eye on, she had to set a good example. She chose to hold it all in, save it for another time, a time when she was alone and she could have another good cry and tell the world it was unfair for taking Grampy now, when they all still needed him, before Edith would be able to really remember him.

Tally turned to observe the room. People were playing their parts well, mingling and chatting, taking care to keep their voices in check, no one wanted to be seen to be having too much fun on a day like today. Most of the village had turned out, the church had been packed and the vicar had done his best to hide his glee at replacing the pub, if only momentarily, as the hub of the community. There had been heartfelt speeches and loud songs and then the large group had split into a procession of cars and a much slower crowd of walkers all weaving their way out of the village and towards the house. Even the vicar had joined them for the after party, his white gown billowing behind him as he faced into the strong wind. Simon had closed the estate to visitors, declaring it a private event, and thrown open the doors once more, allowing the guests to remember the rooms Grampy used to frequent, usually still in his boots, and usually being chastised by Anna for leaving flecks of mud on the carpets.

There was a donation pot near the door, which Tally had insisted on setting up despite Simon's protests, and it was overflowing despite all the generous donations people had already given to the church. Tally was taken aback by Grampy's popularity. To her, he was simple Grampy, and he was rarely seen with anyone else. It was usually just her, Michael and Grampy traipsing the grounds, playing and working and enjoying the fresh air. From all the faces and stories that she had heard today, she realised just how naïve it is to be young. She had thought his world revolved around her, and of course, in way it had, but he still enjoyed a life outside of her small world, and with it he had seemingly touched numerous souls. His most recent companion was Angie from the baby group who had spent the entire day sobbing, and had clearly struck up a very close relationship with Grampy since first meeting him. It was comforting to learn that he had not been lonely.

'He was a dark horse,' Michael said, sidling up to her, pointing at Angie as she continued to dab a tissue under her eyes.

'Heartbreaker,' Tally agreed, swallowing back a wave of fresh tears as she fought to keep the promise that she had just made to herself to stay strong. Michael had a way of melting her resolve, probably because he was the only person who was as devastated as her at losing their Grampy. It felt like they had been abandoned, almost orphaned, and it was now just the two of them against the world. She was so proud of him for speaking for them both, his voice wavering but not cracking as he addressed the hushed congregation. She had stood by his side, her knees trembling, and held his hand so tightly it had turned his fingers white. It had been a rare moment of pure solidarity, and through her grief, Tally could see her mother was beaming with pride for her two children, and relief that despite all the squabbling and hiccups, they were destined to stay firm friends forever. It had not been lost on Helena that this was Grampy's doing, his legacy. Tally had let her eyes sweep over Simon, and he was watching her intently, willing her to get through the day, providing the same unspoken support she had so recently provided for him. He pursed his lips together into nearly a smile, and she took a deep quivering breath, allowing his message of calm to enshroud her body. She squeezed Michael's hand tighter still, and he too appeared anchored by the unspoken message.

Now the serious duties were over, the pressure was off. Ties were loosened and food and drink were being consumed. Slowly, people were shedding their masks and relaxing, telling themselves Grampy would have wanted it that way. The atmosphere was starting to lighten as the afternoon wore on and Tally wondered if it would develop into a full blown party. She was worried they didn't have enough wine.

'How's Leila doing?' she asked Michael, turning towards him.

His face was an uncanny shade of grey.

'Michael?' she asked, grasping his arm, petrified for a moment he was about to drop to his knees and die.

'Don't look,' Michael hissed.

Immediately Tally looked. She followed his hard gaze to the door, searching for the source of his distress. She wondered if it was Grampy, if perhaps he hadn't really died and was here to ask what was going on and why he hadn't been invited. When she saw him standing at the door, her heart stopped, and it was her turn to nearly collapse on the floor. She hadn't seen him since the night that was still haunting her, but his face was just the same, the dark eyes and shadowy beard, no longer handsome because she had seen the way he could leer and set this jaw. He was on the other side of the room, but she knew his features in such detail from how close he had been, and how often he haunted her. She could smell him breathing over her and feel the dead weight of his body on top of her, suffocating her. She relived the pain and confusion, as if someone had just stripped her naked. Once more her dignity was chopped into pieces and was falling to the floor, like those tiny snowflakes. He was standing in the doorway to the ballroom, being offered a flute of champagne by a British Estates waiter as if he was a long-standing family friend. As she shrunk into the curtains behind her, Michael did the opposite.

He released his glass causing it to shatter and splatter liquid up Tally's ankles, grabbing the attention of everyone nearby. Then the focus on him rippled outwards as he ran towards Brad, elbowing his way through the crowd, shouting at him to get out of their house. Brad paused and the people standing near him stepped back and stared, leaving him isolated, like a sitting duck for Michael to lunge at. He tried to look surprised and innocent, but his act barely lasted a moment. The second of confusion at being attacked by his best friend who he had not seen in months was shortly replaced by understanding. Michael *knew*. Brad was not going to be able to defend himself, too shocked Tally had told someone, especially her big brother, to be able to mount a defence. He had thought it would stay their little secret. He had expected to be able to wield power over Tally, to be protected by her humiliation. He had been looking forward to giving her a knowing look, to put his arms around her and drag her close and chuckle at the way she would be forced to play along in front of the others. He had been too proud to even consider that today might go badly for him, and that Tally might have had the courage to speak out. So he set his face into a cold smile, because the punch was coming and he was compelled to feed Michael's rage, to appear remorseless. He thought he was being clever, when really it was the only self-defence strategy he could adopt. If he acted like he deserved everything he had taken from Tally, then he would be able to live with himself for what he had done.

All Tally could remember from the event was her mother screaming, whether at Brad or Michael she couldn't tell. It was a display of general distress at the sight of her son and his friend rolling around on the floor in the middle of Grampy's wake. Simon and a couple of other men mucked in to drag them apart, almost physically unable to rip Michael off. By the time they did, Brad was almost unconscious, his face already swollen, blood dripping down his once white shirt. Most of the donation pot was going to have to go towards the carpet cleaning bill.

'I'm going to the police,' Brad stammered as he was dragged out of the room, to be dumped on the front steps under

Michael's order. Some of the people carrying Brad were friends of them both, but they had chosen their side, out of respect for Grampy and a suspicion that Michael must have had good cause to beat the hell out of Brad.

'Fine, us too,' Michael spat, causing Brad to promptly look away. He couldn't afford to go to the police, not if doing so galvanised Tally to do the same.

Tally quivered at the idea of having to tell the police. What use was it, two years after the attack? There wouldn't be any evidence, it would just be her word against his, and statistically only half of the village would believe her. It would get out within hours and by the end of the day everyone would know. She couldn't bear her dad finding out, he would be outraged at the smear against their reputation. Michael shouldn't have said that, it was her decision to make, her threat to throw. Michael was just making everything worse. She wished he didn't know. She was also glad Brad had been forcibly removed from the wake. She wouldn't have been able to face him, or to cope with him enjoying himself whilst in the same room as her, in her home. He would have found a way to talk to her and she wouldn't have been able to find a means of escape. Hiding behind the curtain wasn't a long term solution. Whilst the room was preoccupied in gossiping about the fight and speculating about its origin, Tally slipped out of a side door and weaved her way towards the kitchen to splash cold water over her face.

Simon had beat her to it, he was running the tap and washing blood from his hands. Tally was tempted to back out of the room slowly before he noticed her, but he was already turning, aware of her presence before she even had a chance to retreat.

'Did you get splattered too?' he asked, wiping his clean hands before removing a stained tie. 'This is silk,' he lamented, wondering if he should just chuck it.

'Anna can sort it out, she can get anything clean, trust me,' Tally said, thankful for a distraction. Simon obviously hadn't noticed Tally hiding inside a pair of curtains, far away from the drama. 'I know some of her tricks.' She held out her hand for the tie and joined Simon at the sink. She changed the tap to run cold water and fished out some salt. Simon watched bemused as she lay his ruined tie onto the worktop and carefully dabbed it with her saline solution.

'You really are a mum if you know stuff like that,' he chuckled.

'It's module three on the course,' Tally smiled, wishing there had been a course. Anna had been there for laundering assistance, and Helena had been a personal tutor of sorts on all things motherhood. The other new mums had helped her stay sane, and were always at the end of a phone to provide automatic advice, educated guesses or much needed sympathy.

'I won't have a clue when I have kids,' Simon said, staring off into the distance.

'You want kids?'

'Sure I want kids, doesn't everyone?'

'Not really, not these days. Especially not free and single men.' Tally bit her lip. She had just made the outward assumption he was free and single and now hoped she wasn't about to be bitterly disappointed.

'I guess I need to work on *not* being free and single before I can consider the kids.'

'Shouldn't be difficult for you,' Tally said as breezily as possible, trying to conceal the joy at her assumption being confirmed, not that she *wanted* him to be lonely. She just didn't need to hear about another happy couple right now, not tonight.

'There aren't too many eligible ladies in Fenson,' Simon laughed, 'going from the demographic in the pub, if old farmers were my thing my chances would be much improved.'

'My friend Gwen is single,' Tally said, instantly wishing she hadn't mentioned it. 'She has a baby though, so lots of baggage I'm afraid,' she added.

'Babies are bonuses, not baggage, like a readymade family.'

'Are you joking?' Tally scoffed, abandoning the tie. It looked like the stain wasn't going to come out. She eyeballed him, wondering if he was making fun of her and Gwen's situation as single Mothers.

'No, I'm not joking. If I fell in love with someone then I wouldn't then discount them because they already had a baby.' Simon held her gaze, and Tally felt all wobbly hearing him talk about love, like a grown up.

'Wouldn't you be a bit jealous of the dad, of not getting there first?' Tally asked.

'Life isn't a fairy tale, as we both know. I can handle complicated.'

There was a long pause as they both looked at each other, trying to figure out what was really going on.

'I'll tell Gwen,' Tally swallowed.

'How's the tie?' Simon sighed, giving Tally the impression that her reply had caused him some dismay. What was she supposed to say? Take me, I'm complicated with *plenty* of baggage? She would be doing Simon a favour by aiming him at Gwen. She would be doing Gwen a favour, too.

'You should probably throw it in the bin.'

❄

'You slept in his bed?' Katherine shrieked.

'Alone, obviously,' Tally snapped. They were all wrapped in giant coats for their picnic, realising it was a tradition that they probably couldn't continue much further into winter. The kids were running around completely unaffected by the cold, keeping themselves warm with their constant playing. Despite being together for the funeral and wake, Tally had banned any Simon talk until he was not standing in the same house as them. The long wait had meant they pounced on her almost as soon as she had sat down and set Edith down like a little wind-up toy ready to chase the other toddlers around the tree.

'Obviously,' Susan echoed, rolling her eyes, because she didn't think it was obvious at all.

'I don't know why you guys keep making these little suggestive comments, we're *just friends*.'

'Of course you are,' Gwen smiled sweetly, pouring out four cups of mulled cider from a flask.

'He actually wants to go on a date with *you*, Gwen,' Tally said, despite promising herself she wouldn't mention the conversation she had had with Simon in the kitchen. Being cornered had made it pop out of her mouth.

'Me?' Gwen was startled, 'Why on earth would he want to go on a date with me?'

'He wants to settle down, says pre-existing kids aren't an issue.'

'Tell me, did he look directly at Edith when he said this to you?' Katherine tilted her head to one side questioningly.

'No,' Tally cried, 'we were alone.' But she understood the line of questioning. Perhaps he had been trying to make a point about Edith.

'Just to clarify. You slept *alone* in his bed?' Susan chipped in.

Tally opened her mouth to say something in outrage, but then found it was impossible not to laugh. They had tied her up in knots and made her blush despite the cold, just like they always did. A tiny part of her had wondered if Simon had been giving her some kind of cryptic clue, but then she had brushed it off as fantasy, because why would he ever be interested in a big fat failure like her? Gwen was much more sophisticated, older, more his type. Gwen had her own house. 'I'm going to stop inviting you guys over,' she muttered into her cup, enjoying the hot tangy liquid as it warmed her from the inside out.

'Thank God for that, it's bloody freezing on your lawn. When can we come inside your actual house?' Katherine asked, complaining at how long it was taking to gain house guest privileges. They all looked forlornly towards the dilapidated wing Tally lived in, as if it wasn't on the verge of falling down.

'You came inside for the wake,' Tally reminded them.

'Your real house, that bit,' Katherine pointed, 'not the fancy tourist bit. I can just buy a ticket if I want to see the ballroom again.'

'Our real house is a shambles,' Tally said as she shook her head. There wouldn't even be enough chairs in the dark and dingy sitting room. The kids were more likely to catch something inside than out here rolling around in the mud.

'You've seen mine, right?' Gwen arched her eyebrows, 'Even after Ian took all of his crap, there's junk and mess everywhere. I literally can't find my hoover.'

'I just prefer it out here.' Tally looked up to see Simon strolling past. He offered the group a wave, now used to seeing their regular congregations on the lawn. It was really bad timing, and Tally flushed an even deeper shade of crimson as the three girls flashed her a knowing look. *Of course, you do,* their smiles told her.

'Because of the fresh air, not *him*,' Tally protested, although it was pointless trying to convince them when they were ganging up on her and in full teasing mode.

'Will you go on the date with him?' Tally asked Gwen after their picnic, as the toddlers started to get tired and cranky and everyone decided it would be best to leave before someone started bawling.

'No bloody way,' Gwen shook her head.

'Why not?' Tally wondered if she found Simon ugly, or otherwise unappealing in some way. It suddenly distressed her to think he was not as attractive to anyone else as he was to her.

'Because I'm your friend, Tally, and friends don't date each other's future husbands.'

Tally laughed, but it was a forced laugh. She looked at the other two to see if they had heard, and rather than looking surprised at Gwen's comments, they were nodding in agreement, as if Gwen had just made a sacred vow.

'He's not my future husband,' Tally managed.

'I guess one day we'll see.' Gwen scooped up Bobby on his way past before he made another loop around the tree.

Tally decided she needed to sit back down on the blanket to process Gwen's ridiculous comment, which to the others had seemed to be completely sensible. Edith crawled into her lap, sad to see her friends go but also not protesting, because she was weary and wanted to indulge in some one-on-one time with her Mother.

'I wish you could tell me what to think,' Tally said, gazing into her daughter's brown eyes.

Edith stared at Tally for such a long time that Tally wondered if she was going to actually give some valuable advice. 'I need a wee wee,' she eventually said.

'Helpful,' Tally muttered, hurrying to her feet so she could pop Edith onto the potty before she wet herself.

❄

'Will he go to the police?' Tally asked Michael. They were waiting outside the GP's office for Leila to have her midwife appointment. Tally had hitched a lift because she needed some bits from the village shop, and a chance to escape in a car was a luxury. She had probably walked a million miles with the pushchair since being home and her legs were the most toned they had ever been, even though she had spent most of her childhood horse riding and swimming. Being a mother to a small child was another level of all body workout.

'No, he wouldn't dare.' Michael stared into the rear-view mirror, as if keeping an eye out for Brad so he could deck him again. The fat lip Brad had inflicted upon him had only recently healed.

'Mum was mortified.'

'She still is. Apparently I ruined the wake and Grampy would have been ashamed of me.'

'Grampy would have loved the drama. I think you spiced it up for most people.'

'Not for you though, I imagine?'

'I'm conflicted. I didn't like to watch you fight, but I'm glad you got him out. I'm not ready to face him, I don't think I ever will be.'

'You shouldn't have to see him ever again. I just lost my head, Tal, I am sorry if it added to your distress. He's just a monster. What was he thinking, showing up like that? Arrogant prick.'

'Okay, enough of that,' Tally gestured towards Edith who was playing with a pretend mobile phone, smashing buttons and then holding it upside down to her ear.

'I could have killed him,' Michael continued, ignoring the language warning, 'Did he really think we were going to let him into our home?'

'He didn't think you would know. He thought I'd have kept quiet. He doesn't know that we get on now.'

'I suppose,' Michael said. He then turned in his seat. 'We do get on now, don't we?'

'Yes, of course,' Tally frowned, wondering why he had phrased it like a tentative question.

'I did marry your best friend.'

'And go out with her behind my back,' Tally added.

'And rib you endlessly about getting knocked up.'

'And break the leg of my favourite toy horse.'

'You have no good reason to like me.'

'Yeah, but then you beat the shit out of Brad.'

'Enough of that,' Michael gasped, pointing at Edith.

Tally rolled her eyes but smiled all the same. Michael was the most annoying and wonderful big brother ever, and he was going to make such an incredible dad. Finally, Tally had stopped feeling jealous and realised happiness for both her best friend and brother was all she could have ever wished for. Their baby was going to be her two favourite people rolled into one. Edith was going to be lucky enough to have a cousin and a best friend all in one.

'What's he doing here?' Tally asked, glancing out of the window, afraid she might see him. The thought of bumping into him had nearly made her decide not to come today, but then she had decided she couldn't let him win. Avoiding visits to their village wasn't a practical plan.

'Apparently he's visiting family, he'll be gone soon. He might be gone already.'

'I hope so.' Tally watched Leila walk towards them, smiling from another smooth appointment.

'Hey, Michael, do you think Gwen is Simon's type?'

'Gwen?' Michael laughed, and then added cryptically, 'No, Tally, she's really isn't his type at all.'

Tally knocked on Simon's office door eagerly. She was too impatient to wait for a response, so she went straight in. He was just hanging up the phone, saying a stilted goodbye. He dropped the phone onto the table, seemingly frustrated at the call. Tally could tell it was his father, she recognised the frown line he saved specifically for any frank conversations with him.

'I have some proposals ready for you.' She skipped inside and dropped her paperwork onto his desk, convinced he was going to love her ideas and implement them all, immediately. They were going to gradually turn the profits around and save the house, she was certain of it. Then he would hire her, and they would end up becoming long term business partners. She had even gone through the extensive list of outgoings and cut items they could wait for, new carpets in their dire sitting room for a start. She had been willing to make some short-term concessions, for the greater good. With her business hat on, she was able to see why throwing money at updating the old part of the house that's closed to paying tourists, for the benefit of the tenants, was a low priority. It was probably Simon's selfless upgrades of their wing that had fast tracked them to the situation they were now facing.

Simon didn't even look at the paperwork, he didn't make a move to acknowledge Tally or her hard work. He simply stared at the phone, as if his dad was still on the other end, lecturing him. Despite the strain of working with his awful father, she thought Simon was being a bit rude.

'Shall I take you through them?' She picked up the first page and wafted it under his nose. He shoved her hand away and turned to the window. 'What's up with you?' Tally fumed, 'Are you not even going to give me a chance to help you? I've put a lot of work into these plans, I think they could really help.' She had been up most of the night finalising them, and then bribed Anna into swinging by the newsagents on the way to work to print them all out for her. He could act just a tiny bit grateful for her efforts.

'Trust me, they can't.' Simon leaned back in his chair and stared at the high ceiling. He didn't want to repeat to Tally what his dad had just told him. He didn't want her to be as devastated as he was. He wondered if he should keep it from her for a little while longer, until the first viewing at least. He could indulge and show enthusiasm for her plans, it was obvious she had worked hard on them, one glance at the first page showed that.

'I don't understand.' Tally crossed her arms. Simon wasn't going to be able to avoid explaining the situation because Tally had just planted herself on his office carpet.

'Dad's selling. He won't wait. He doesn't want to give us another chance.'

'What? Why not? He can't sell. We deserve another chance.'

'I can't reason with him. He wants this property off our books.'

'What's wrong with it?' Tally was affronted. British Estates should be proud to have their home on their portfolio. They had swindled Helena out of it and now they were dropping it just as rashly.

'He just doesn't think we can ever make the numbers work.'

'He's wrong.' Tally picked up her papers, 'This will work. We just need to show him.'

'I'm sorry, Tally, but he's made his decision. I've tried to convince him.'

'You haven't tried hard enough,' Tally snapped, 'Phone him back, right now, let me speak to him.'

'If he's not going to listen to me then he's certainly not going to listen to you.'

'What's that supposed to mean?'

'I'm his partner, you're just, well, the ex-homeowner's daughter.'

Tally threw the paperwork at him. Half of the pages hit him in the face and the rest fluttered all around. Hours of her life had been wasted writing them, and she had actually been excited about using her brain again, being on a mission that might just work. She had poured over textbooks and searched the internet like an excited school girl and it had all been in vain. Simon's dad had just squashed her hope before giving them a chance, and Simon was just letting him get away with it.

'I'm just a nobody then? A stupid little girl?'

'I didn't say that,' Simon said, ignoring the papercut she had just inflicted on his cheek. 'You've met my father, he's tricky.'

'Stand up to him, you coward, you're more than just his partner, this business is going to be yours one day soon. He just doesn't want to let you make the decisions, he's afraid of letting go.' Tally was doing her best not to cry. Her heart was hammering in her chest, because soon she and Edith would be homeless, and Simon would be leaving, going back to London to pick up the old glamourous life he had put on hold. He would be able to turn away and move on and her family would have to suffer the consequences. Anna would lose her job, Helena and Charles would be completely torn apart. Charles was simply not going to move into a dinky house somewhere, he would rather die than leave this house, like the captain of a sinking ship. He would decline back into alcoholism. This decision could be his death sentence.

'I've tried to stand up to him, but he still has the final say. Until he literally hands power over to me, he gets to make the big decisions. He's the CEO.'

'Then I'm wasting my time being here,' she sneered, keen to get out before Simon saw her cry.

'Wait, Tally, don't leave like that.' Simon jumped up, his feet crunching on her words as he sprinted around the desk to catch her before she stormed out of the room.

'I have nothing further to say to you.' Tally put her hand on the door handle, but Simon wrenched it off. She flung her arm out, hitting him hard in the ribs, hurting her knuckles. He staggered back slightly, surprised by her strength. Tally stared, also surprised she had fought back. To be touched unexpectedly triggered a deep fear within her, and she was suddenly back in that grimy bathroom, shut in by Brad. She could hear the clicking of the lock and she was cornered, like prey. She started to struggle to breathe.

'Tally, are you okay?' Simon asked, as she clutched her chest.

'I can't breathe,' she gasped, clutching at her chest as the room began to spin.

'You're having a panic attack,' Simon said, grasping her arms so he could guide her into a nearby chair.

'Don't touch me,' she managed, dark images flashing through her mind. She could imagine Brad looming over her, she remembered hitting her head on the toilet basin, and the sharp pain echoed through her again, making her vision blur. The room went in and out of focus and all the while her lungs were struggling to drag in the oxygen they craved.

'Listen to me Tally, you need to slow your breathing down, count with me.' Simon knelt on the floor in front of her and placed one hand on each of her knees. Tally tried to push him off but she was so weak, too scared of what was happening, that she couldn't resist. She thought it was Brad clawing at her legs, trying to get to the top of her jeans.

'Get off me, Brad, get off me,' she managed, flailing around, when she should have been trying to keep calm, to recover her breath. Fighting was doing the opposite, making it impossible to replenish her body with clean air.

'I'm not Brad,' Simon urged, 'I'm Simon, just Simon. Count with me now, one, two, three.'

Tally finally understood; it wasn't Brad. It was just Simon. She was safe. The numbers weaved their way into her brain and she tried to match the rise and fall of her chest with his steady words, holding onto them like a hand in the dark. Slowly she regained control of her body, and the room came back into focus. Simon appeared before her like a guardian angel. There was a line of blood on his cheek. She reached out a finger and wiped it off.

'I'm sorry,' she whispered.

'Who knew research could be so dangerous,' Simon smiled, surprised she had touched his face. In all the time he had known her, she had never offered intimacy. Tally tried to move but he gently pushed her back into the chair, careful not to seem rough and prompt another episode. 'You need to rest for a moment, let's stay here.' He wanted to ask about Brad, what had happened with Brad? Was this linked to the fight with Michael? But he couldn't.

He didn't want the moment to end, because when they got to their feet the home would be up for sale and their argument might restart, then they would be ripped apart. He would have to return to London with his tail between his legs, to his soulless flat and his empty life. His venture had not failed, his cruel father had simply decided to put a stop to it, just because he was taking the business in a direction he didn't agree with. His father refused to diversify or adapt with the times. He was acting like a relic, sticking his nose up to using the house for one off functions or themed days, blocking Simon's every move. Simon was exasperated with his father for believing that the houses should take care of themselves with very little input from management to immerse families into an experience. Simon understood it was no longer enough for visitors to simply roam the rooms of a stately home or admire well-kept gardens. They wanted to interact with the history of the house and become involved, they wanted to attend exhibitions and themed days – anything to convince their children to peel their eyes away from their phones. Simon worried that if his dad wasn't proactive, if he continued to simply sit back and expect people to keep coming, then he would accidentally run his business into the ground before Simon even got the chance to take it on. If Simon inherited the business with too many houses in jeopardy then he might be forced to sell them all.

'Really, I'm fine,' Tally said after a few more deep breaths. She looked at her papers sprawled all over the floor and was embarrassed by how much effort she had wasted, feeling foolish for thinking she might be able to help. She was humiliated by having a panic attack just because Simon had touched her hand. She was just a stupid little girl after all, destined to be a stay-at-home mum with no real future career prospects. Simon was looking at her with puppy dog eyes and she really didn't want his pity, all she had wanted was to feel like she mattered and could contribute, like she was part of a team.

'I'll call him again in the morning, I promise.' Simon was reluctant to let her go, and the hollow smile she returned suggested she didn't hold much hope that he was going to be able to exert any further influence. Simon stared out of the window, waiting for her to descend the front steps and as he watched her signature saunter, always so much bouncier when she didn't have Edith hoisted on her hip, he was flooded with an overwhelming sensation of shame, because he had just gone and let her whole family down and yet there she was, still pausing to admire the view she had grown up with and the view that she would soon lose forever.

※

It was Edith's second birthday, and everyone was jolly. Simon had opened up the old living room, once again closing the house for a private function when there was only a dozen or so people attending – the family plus Tally's baby group – and Tally was enjoying the feeling of the plush carpet on her knees as she crawled around playing with Edith and her new toys. There was a Christmas vibe in the air as people stepped over scrunched up wrapping paper to top up their glasses and children screeched in joy and weaved in and out of the grown-up's legs. There was a modest buffet set up at one end of the room and the television was set to silent cartoons whilst Michael shuffled through his phone's playlist and beamed it across to the sound system, a function that Charles had taken much interest in learning all about. Tally tried to forget that this would be the last birthday party in her home, but Simon's nervous glances kept reminding her.

'Can you quit the forlorn looks?' she hissed at him after finally cornering him on his own in the hallway.

'Sorry, I didn't mean to, I guess I just feel guilty,' Simon winced, wishing he hadn't been so transparent.

'It's not your fault is it, it's your knobhead father.' Tally wondered if he would take offence, but he simply nodded. He took a big gulp of his drink, deciding today counted as a day off even though he had justified his invite as being for business purposes. He didn't realise they had wanted him there anyway, somehow, he had become a part of their family, even Michael was chatty with him. Charles had stopped the filthy looks and as long as no one mentioned fudge he was now welcome. Anna usually set a place for him at the breakfast table on a Monday, because he would always swing by on his rounds and end up staying.

'Gwen keeps avoiding me, what's with that?' Simon asked, deciding they deserved a change of topic. 'Did you try and set us up?'

'Ah,' Tally decided to drink some more wine. 'I may have mentioned you were single.'

'She clearly wasn't interested then,' Simon sighed, glad she hadn't been but still slightly dismayed.

'Oh, she was, it's just...' Tally trailed off.

'What?'

'Well she said she didn't want to tread on my toes.'

Simon stared at Tally. Tally stared at Simon.

'And would it be treading on your toes if she was interested in me?' Simon finally asked tentatively, wishing he'd topped up his glass before this conversation.

The hallway was shadowy and the noise of the music was filtering in from the next room. At any moment someone was bound to burst through the door, heading towards the kitchen for a refill or the cake or something to mop up a spilt toddler drink. Simon was frustrated that the seconds were ticking past on this potentially crucial conversation and they were holding it in a corridor, the day before the first scheduled house viewing.

Tally imagined having the conversation she wanted to have. She could start by admitting to Simon what everyone else claimed to already know, even before she had truly known, and telling him that he meant something to her, and that she desperately wanted him to stay. She could hand over her delicate heart with both hands. But what would he do with the news? What time did he have left to change anything? Did he even feel the same way? If she exposed her true feelings, regardless of how he might react, she would still have to watch him show the future owners around her family home. As much as she wanted him to be in charge of the house, his father had the final say and was immovable on his decision to sell. Tally pouring her heart out to Simon in a dingy hallway was not going to influence the next step, it would only make life harder. The house was going to sell regardless, and then she would have to pack up her little box room and try to find a suitable way to explain to Edith why they wouldn't be able to go back home, to try to convince her that somewhere sterile and strange was their future, all the while not believing it herself. Simon had no choice but to leave, no matter what conversation they might have, and she was destined to cry herself to sleep every night while he visited swanky wine bars with someone else on his arm, a hundred miles away.

It didn't seem worth the heartache to tell him how she really felt today, on Edith's birthday, when she was supposed to be thinking about her daughter and planning a way to give her a half decent childhood, even though it could never be a patch on her own now that their history was being ripped away from them. Watching on the side-lines had been painful, but losing sight of their past completely was unthinkable. Yet they would be forced to think about it tomorrow if the prospective owners looked interested.

'I don't think it matters, for me or Gwen, you'll be going home soon.'

'This is my home, Tally.' Simon wished she had said something different.

'It's neither of our homes, that's the problem,' Tally shook her head, and then the door flew open as expected and

Anna rushed out, announcing it was time to light the candles on the cake.

※

'What a total dick head,' Michael spat as they watched the man and woman uncurl themselves from a sports car, as if they had to show up looking like they could afford to buy the place. The man tweaked his hat and the woman smoothed down her skirt and they both looked about them as if they expected to be pestered by swooning fans.

'I was expecting someone old.' Tally was disappointed; the potential buyers looked about Michael's age.

'Perhaps they're window shopping, people do that, bored couples pretend they want to buy a house just so they can spend their weekends snooping around places they could never afford.'

'They would have been thoroughly vetted to view this place,' Tally shook her head, 'Simon has dealt with this as sensitively as possible.'

'Do you think they're famous?'

'Why would anyone famous want to live here?'

'It's the middle of nowhere, so it's probably *exactly* where a famous person would live for some peace and quiet. Perhaps this will just be their weekend getaway.'

'Oh gosh, I never considered that the house might not even be lived in, not even properly loved.' Tally stuck out her bottom lip.

'That famous showjumper lives nearby doesn't he, Ryan whatshisname.'

'Ryan Winters.' Tally had swooned over him when she was a teenager, and followed his progress avidly. She had bumped into him in the village a few times and forgotten how to talk. 'Show jumpers don't earn enough money for this place, this is footballer or movie star territory.'

'He isn't good looking enough to be a movie star,' Michael commented.

'Neither is she,' Tally said, feeling bad for making cheap shots. They both needed to be nasty to stop themselves from feeling distraught.

'Did Mum go out?' Michael asked.

'She took Charles, Anna, Edith, everyone. She didn't want anyone to stumble across this.' Even though Charles was now fully sober, they both struggled to refer to him as 'Dad'. He was still winning them over, proving his newfound sobriety wasn't just a phase.

'We probably should have gone too.'

They fell silent as Simon hurried down the steps, making his apologies for leaving them waiting, even though they had been outside of their car for less than ten seconds.

'He could try and be a little less nice,' Michael sniffed. 'He's supposed to be on our team.'

'I think Simon always plays for his own side,' Tally said darkly, trying to justify her inability to talk to him truthfully at Edith's birthday party, for letting something slip through her fingers that probably would have never worked, but just might had been something good. If these people bought the house then she could rest assured that she had done the right thing, and choosing to stay quiet in front of Simon had been a good idea and not just cowardice. If the plan went well for Simon's father, then she could be certain she had not just made the gravest mistake of her life.

'They're going inside,' Michael said needlessly; Tally could see just as clearly as him, as the party turned towards the entrance and made their way into the house, to scrutinise and value.

'He'll do the reception rooms first,' Tally whispered, scooting out from the tree they were hiding behind to scamper to a ground floor window.

They peered into their old home from a flower bed, taking care not to crush any plants even though they soon wouldn't be theirs. As Tally watched Simon talk, unable to understand a word he said as he gestured around, no doubt reeling off facts about the history and the architecture, something inside her stirred. It was a growing sensation that she was less and less able to suppress. In the early days, she had been able to link it with hate, but over time as the hate eroded, her body had continued to react to his presence, and only now as their final weeks passed was she now realising it was quite the opposite to hate.

'Tally, I went to the solicitor's office yesterday morning, before Edith's party.'

'Oh?' Tally enquired absentmindedly as she gazed at Simon and wondered what he would have done if she had told him Gwen would have most definitely stomped on her toes by agreeing to go on a date with him.

'Grampy left us his house.'

'That's nice,' Tally said without truly listening, taking a few moments to register Michael's words. 'What?' she exclaimed, so loudly they both had to duck below the window sill in case someone inside had heard.

'What?' she repeated in a whisper, crouching in the mud next to Michael.

'In his will, Grampy left you and I his house in the village, equal ownership,' Michael clarified.

'I can't believe it.'

'Well, I can. He didn't have any heirs, no family, no one except from us.'

'We can just have it?'

'Yes, the will was straightforward, there aren't any issues at all. No challenges, paperwork trail is legit, he wrote his will with the village solicitor so everything is straightforward, they knew him, and they knew he loved us.'

'What an amazing thing to do for us.'

'I guess my weekly visits helped,' Michael joked, earning himself an elbow in the ribs. They fell quiet as the voices inside moved towards the window, both petrified they would be visible if the man or woman looked out and then down.

'We should move in, when we get kicked out of here,' Michael continued when they felt safe to talk.

'Don't be silly, you and Leila need it for your new family.'

'Don't you be silly, there are three bedrooms. You can have one and the two girls can share.'

Tally looked at Michael. 'You're having a girl?'

'Shit, I wasn't meant to tell you, Leila wanted it to be a surprise.'

Tally lunged at him for a hug, delighted to hear she would have a niece. Edith was sure to be best friends with another girl. Michael protested as he fell into the mud, but he hugged her back, relieved to have let the news slip out. Keeping secrets from Tally used to be a strong point, but since they had both grown up she was his confidant on most things.

'Leila doesn't mind us moving in?' Tally continued, unsure if this was a good idea.

'Of course not, she could do with the help and company anyway, I'll be back at work after two weeks. Anyway, where else will you live?'

'What about the rest? Where will Mum and Dad go?'

Michael's face turned dark. 'I don't know,' he whispered, just as worried as Tally at the predicament they were facing. If they had to, they would live in Grampy's living room. Michael wasn't about to see them go homeless.

Tally was working on her trot to canter transitions, pushing away the niggling thought that seeking to improve her riding relationship with Match was a complete waste of time. If the house was selling, then so was he. She should be able to rehome Match, he was still in his prime as a polished riding horse, but creaky Peter was going to prove more of a challenge. Ideally, she would insist on them staying together and sell as a pair, but they didn't have the luxury of time and Tally knew it would be unlikely to find them a good home together. The market was flooded with field companions too old or injured for ridden work, and horses were not a luxury commodity people could justify the effort and expense for if there was going to be no return. Peter was destined to end up in the rescue centre, a realisation Tally had to keep forcibly shoving away so she didn't get too upset.

The horrible rich young couple with the tasteless sports car had made an offer. Simon had told her this morning. He had seemed disappointed, but not overly upset. To him, it was a reluctant business offer – a cutting of losses – whereas to her and her family it was a devastating blow. He said his dad was considering the offer, but it was well below asking and therefore he might not accept, but he didn't seem optimistic on this scenario because his dad badly wanted rid of the house, and they all knew there wasn't going to be an endless stream of offers. She didn't like to see the pity in his eyes as Simon avoided asking her the obvious question of 'What are you all going to do now?'

She could have answered him. She and Edith would move into Grampy's old house along with Michael and Leila, and the soon to be born baby. Anna would take in Helena and Charles because they had nowhere else to go. Tally had heard Anna offer it in a moment of weakness. She couldn't see how that could work when her parents had no money to contribute towards bills, and weren't even properly paying Anna for the help she still offered. Anna had probably realised as soon as she had suggested the solution that she had made a dire mistake. She had picked up some extra cleaning jobs in the village to prop up the sudden lack of salary after the acquisition, and Tally wondered if she would recruit Helena and teach her how to wield a pair of marigolds. If it wasn't so tragic it would be comical, imagining Helena working as a cleaner after spending her entire life too privileged to tidy up, even after herself.

Tally had been walking past the sitting room only a week ago, the day after the viewing, to hear Helena sobbing. She peeked through the gap in the door to see Anna sitting next to her, patting her arm and making impromptu offers she was probably now going to have to uphold. Or perhaps she had put some thought into it, Anna rattled about her house in the village all alone, and she was practically family, so perhaps she would enjoy the company. But equally, there would be some difficult conversations to be had about the new power balance between them. Anna would go from housekeeper to landlord overnight, and Helena and Charles would be living under her roof and her rules. Charles would probably forget that and still demand his breakfast with two fried eggs. It was likely to go horribly wrong.

Tally eased Match to a halt and praised him for acing the last few transitions. If he did have to be sold, then she was going to ensure he impressed the best type of horse rider out there. She was out of breath from the workout, regretting wearing an extra layer. She unzipped her fleece and let the reins slip before nudging Match into a gentle walk around the perimeter of the school. His neck was damp with sweat and she would need to sponge him off before bedtime. She knew she should really be focusing on her own forthcoming household dynamics instead of worrying about her parents and Anna surviving.

Living only a few doors down on the same street, she and Michael would be equal home-owners, but Michael was still going to assume the position of man of the house. He would have a new baby and an expectant wife to keep happy and he would wield the older sibling authority over Tally. She could see them falling out, even with the best of intentions. She was going to end up as a gooseberry, too awkward to join them on the sofa as they snuggled up to watch a movie. She would probably spend most of her life exactly as she did now, cooped up in her small room, just her and Edith playing together. She loved Edith with all her heart, but it was a bit lame, and not quite the future she had imagined for herself. She could imagine the walls were paper thin and the last thing she wanted to hear at night was the noise of her brother and her best friend making love as she sat there alone trying to get to sleep or force her way through a novel designed to grant escapism.

She would end up clashing with Michael, their disagreements descending into silly sibling arguments, and then Leila would have to pick sides. Unfortunately, Tally knew Leila would ultimately choose her husband over her oldest friend. As a new mother she would be right to put her family first. It would tear a young marriage apart, having to live with a third person, and the last thing Tally wanted was for anyone in her beaten-up family to suffer another heartbreak. Tally and Edith would ultimately feel unwelcome in their own home, and even when things went well, they would be woken up by a screaming baby at various intervals throughout the night. Edith had inflicted it enough times on Michael, so Tally wouldn't even be in a position to complain, she would just have to suffer from the lack of sleep along with the rest of them, and then deal with Edith who would be grouchy and tired after another night of disturbed sleep.

Although the mortgage was paid off on the house, they were going to have to earn money to pay the bills, and if Tally had a hope in hell of keeping both Match and Peter at the local livery yard then she needed to find a job immediately and start saving. She should be looking now instead of riding Match. She had no qualifications beyond A-levels, and she would probably leave out the fact she had gone to university then promptly quit, to prospective employers. She wasn't going to have a chance of a decent starting salary, and probably no career ladder. Working in the village limited her opportunities, but with Edith to take care of, there was no hope of aiming higher. Helena might offer free childcare for core hours, if she wasn't working for Anna, but Tally was hardly going to be able to negotiate the extra time required to commute to a big city, like Cambridge or London. Besides, without a degree it would be a waste of time choosing a job in a city because she wouldn't be able to justify the commuting cost.

Perhaps if she had curtailed her dreams in the first place should could have worked her way up to café manager by now. Perhaps if she had been a little less selfish and stayed at home, she would have spotted the dire situation just in time to save the house, she could have at least negotiated something better with Simon. Would it have been possible to tie them into a no future sale clause? Or some other kind of guarantee? Probably not. Perhaps they would all just drive themselves mad with hindsight.

Tally had reluctantly asked Leila if there were any vacancies at the café and Leila had grinned, delighted at the prospect of them working together, as if everything was about to work out exactly how she had always hoped it would. It stung Tally, as if she had been taught a cruel lesson, because deep down she had always looked down on Leila for being unambitious, and now she was going to end up living the exact same life as her, except without the fairy tale wedding and the stable relationship. A waitress wage wouldn't cover two horses. Leila promised to buy in, but that would put the cost of two horses onto their already strained family household. Michael was due another promotion at the car sales company, but it would already need to stretch to feed three adults and two children. Feeding two horses was probably too much of a push for him, even if they were his childhood ponies. Unfortunately, Tally couldn't see his nostalgia winning out over the simple crushing calculations.

And during all of this, the new horrible couple would be rattling around their wonderful estate, deciding which parts of history and which special memories they were going to carve up and redecorate next, and Simon would be in London focusing on his next big project, making a mental note to not screw it up like he did in Fenson.

'I'll try my best to keep you both,' she promised Match. 'If I can't, I'll try my best to find you a good home.' She wished she hadn't said that last bit, because it was the admission that she didn't have faith that she could keep them. Match's ears flicked back as if he had perfectly understood, and now she was crying all over again, hating the way she was having to face up to the reality of the situation when all she wanted to do was steal an hour to herself to ride her horse and pretend nothing was ever going to change.

※

There was a tentative knocking on Tally's bedroom door. She glanced at Edith, who was still fast asleep, then crept to the door. For a breath-taking moment she wondered if it could be Simon working late, stopping by to let her know the house was no longer for sale because his dad had a sudden change of heart, so when she discovered Leila clutching a tablet anxiously to her chest, she was a little disappointed.

'Are you free?' Leila asked, her voice hushed because she had long since learned it was best to talk quietly when there was a chance Edith might be sleeping.

'Yes, I'm free,' Tally stifled a laugh, because although it was extremely polite to ask there really wasn't much Tally could possibly be doing that meant she would be far too busy to speak to Leila.

'Could you help me? Michael's useless.' Leila held out the tablet to show Tally what she had been researching online. 'I've been making a list of everything we need and started looking, but it's a bit overwhelming. I keep getting distracted by how cute and pastel-coloured it all is.'

'Michael would definitely be useless at this kind of thing,' Tally agreed, honoured at the privilege of being asked. For the first time in a long time, she was going to be able to offer Leila something Michael couldn't. She ignored the idea it may be all done out of pity, and instead accepted the olive branch of a recently dwindling friendship. Nothing in particular had happened to cause them to fall out, Leila had just been justifiably preoccupied with the pregnancy glow and Tally had been busy trying and then failing to help Simon save the house. Leila had probably been sensitive to the green-eyed monster Tally had to beat into submission following the pregnancy announcement and was a little guilty for not confiding in Tally before announcing it to the rest of the family. There were some unspoken conversations to be had, but tonight they would tread carefully and browse nursery furniture and baby essentials.

'I can give you a load of stuff, don't waste money until you check what I have.'

'Are you sure?' Leila glanced around the room to see if there was anything she liked.

'Even the cot, Edith is too big for it now really, as soon as we move into the house I'll get her into a single bed.' Tally hesitated, wondering if Michael had even told her about the decision to all live together as one big happy family. She watched her face to gauge the reaction.

'That's if Michael can remember how to re-build that cot after the misery that he experienced the first time around,' Leila smiled, clearly set on building bridges no matter what her secret concerns might entail. After all, it was a free house gifted to Tally and Michael; Leila didn't have a say. If they weren't going to all move in together, they would have to sell to split the asset, and neither of them could afford to put down a deposit on a house on their own.

'It's lucky she's a girl, you can have *all* the clothes. Some were worn only a few times before she grew out of them, they haven't got a single mark on them.' Tally dragged the stuffed boxes out from under her bed, starting to get excited about the idea of being able to spread her possessions over an entire house. She was going to have to ensure she didn't let Michael and Leila take control of the décor, she was determined to make her mark on every room and not let her older brother convince her she was just a lodger.

'I was going to sell them as a bundle on eBay,' Tally commented as Leila excitedly dug through the stash of clothes, admiring all the adorable outfits yet unable to imagine dressing her own baby in them.

'Let me pay you for them,' Leila said, pausing as she misinterpreted Tally's words as a hint.

'Oh no, I don't want anything, what I mean is you're helping me out. I wanted rid of them, and selling then posting them was just going to be a hassle I don't have time for right now. I'd much rather recycle them with your baby and get to see them worn again. Just put the ones you don't want into a charity shop bag,' Tally added after she saw Leila hesitate over a baby grow that was a bit stained around the neck.

'Hey, did you know Simon's house is up for sale?' Leila asked.

'What? No.'

'We saw the for-sale sign in front of it when Michael took me to have a look at the house.'

'Gosh, it's really happening, isn't it?' Tally put her head into her hands. 'Every day there's another step towards losing this place. Even interviewing for the café job; I felt like I was giving up, making it all real.'

'It's tough on Michael, too. He's taking double shifts at work to try and build up our savings because I'll have to stop work.'

'Do you think I'll get the job?'

'Definitely, it's yours. The rest of the applicants are fresh out of school.'

'Of course, they are.' Tally put her head back into her hands, wishing Leila hadn't informed them of how over-qualified she should have been to take a local waitress job.

'Sorry.' Leila bit her lip.

'I'm the one who should be sorry. I'm such a snob, just like my Mother. I don't know why you ever made friends with me.'

'Well, it was for the swimming pool and the horses, as I'm sure you recall. I guess you're just lucky that over the years you grew on me, so I'll still want to be friends after you move out of here.'

Tally swatted her playfully on the leg. 'The horses, what will we do about the horses?'

Leila fell quiet, and Tally could tell this segment of the conversation had already been rehearsed, with Michael no doubt. 'I don't think we can afford them,' Leila whispered.

'No, don't say that.' Tally grimaced, 'We can't let them go.'

'Is Simon interested? He loves them to pieces.'

'He's moving back to London; I've seen his flat and it does not have space for a stable.'

'Yeah, you never did tell me about that night,' Leila grinned, keen to move the conversation on because she also couldn't bear to face the idea of selling Match and Peter.

'There's nothing to tell. We drank some wine, looked over his business accounts, I got naively excited about the idea of saving this place, then we went to bed – separately.'

'Separately,' Leila echoed, nodding.

'Don't look so disappointed. You know I hated him.'

'Past tense, I notice?'

'I still kind of hate him for screwing up his business plan and failing to sort out his Dad,' Tally confirmed.

'But you don't really *hate* him, do you? You kind of love him, really.'

'Love? Don't be ridiculous Leila!' Tally exclaimed. They both glanced at Edith to check the exclamation hadn't woken her.

'I've seen the way you look at him, and the way he looks right back at you,' Leila replied, overcompensating for the outburst with a whisper, just in case Edith was on the cusp of waking.

'You're seeing things.' Tally thrust the tablet back at Leila. 'Write your wish list and I'll tick off what I - or the other mums - can give you.'

'Thank you, you're fantastic,' Leila said, tiptoeing out of the room. 'Also,' she turned at the door, 'I'm not seeing anything that isn't real. You should do something about it before it's too late.'

After the door closed Tally lay down on her bed and stared up at the peeling ceiling. What should she do? Should she really do something? Wasn't it already too late? Simon had given her some heavy hints, but he hadn't made himself clear, meaning Tally would have to take a terrifying plunge, and she didn't think she had the courage to do it. Besides, he had already put his house up for sale, he was moving back to London, there didn't seem to be any hope left.

※

Tally decided to do something about it. She hitched a lift with Michael into the village under the pretence of going to the shop, and as he drove off towards work, she made an about turn and walked back up the high street. The sale board Leila had claimed to have seen had already been swapped with a sold sign. Simon was definitely moving away. He probably isn't even home, she told herself as she approached the house. Then a flash car pulled up against the kerb and a tall blonde got out, stretching toned legs first, careful where she placed the end of her high heels. Tally quickly ducked into the gateway of a nearby house and hid behind the overgrown tree in their front garden. She didn't recognise the lady who was smoothing down her sheer shirt and re-tucking it back into the top of her skirt. Just as Tally wondered if Simon would answer the front door to the mystery blonde, Simon got out of the passenger side of her car. He said something friendly to the girl, indicating they knew each other quite well, then they made their way into the house.

Tally was startled, she hadn't been expecting that. She was then startled again as the home-owner of the garden she was hiding in knocked angrily on the window before making gestures for her to leave. Tally mouthed sorry and rushed back onto the pavement. She snuck into Simon's front garden and peered through the window, once again finding herself spying although this time anyone walking or driving past the house was going to see her. She couldn't quite see into the kitchen, but she glimpsed them as they walked past the door leading from the hallway into the living room.

Tally sighed. Simon had a girlfriend, and probably had all along. She was from London no doubt, and from his affluent circle of friends. She had probably been in his life far longer than Tally and was here to rescue him and take him back home. Simon clearly hadn't been dropping any hints, Tally had just misinterpreted him. Or, worse, he was considering cheating on his gorgeous girlfriend and having a quick fling with Tally before breaking it off and forgetting all about her, just so he could at least say he had achieved something in Fenson. Tally was a fool to think someone like Simon would be interested in someone like Tally. Perhaps before, when she lived in a different world, she would have had a chance because they would have been on an even keel.

'At least I won't have to put up with the father-in-law from hell,' she muttered as she let herself out of his garden, humiliated she had decided to act on Leila's advice and visit, and was now going to have to walk all the way home with nothing but disappointment to keep her company. She glared at the car as she passed, refraining from doing something childish like scratching it or ripping off a windscreen wiper because she didn't need another reason to feel stupid. She noticed the number plate was personalised and decided it was incredibly crass. Stop being so jealous, she lectured herself.

'Tally?' Simon called, causing her to freeze. She shrunk on the spot, wondering if she had misheard and was going to be able to continue walking. The last thing she wanted was to turn around and look at Simon, or worse, meet his girlfriend. She might be a fiancée, she thought, or even a *wife.* In truth, Tally knew absolutely nothing about Simon, especially not the life he had led before moving to Fenson, the life he was about to resume living. Fenson would just be a hiccup for him, soon forgotten along with her.

'Tally,' Simon called again, giving her the benefit of the doubt and deciding she just hadn't heard him.

Tally slowly pivoted, her mind whirring as she searched for an excuse. She should have bought something from the shop as an alibi. 'Oh, hi,' she feigned complete surprise at seeing him, as if she had completely forgotten he lived there. She was glad to see the lady was not in sight so she would be spared the torture of a polite introduction. It looked like Simon had been nipping back to the car to grab something when he had seen her retreating. He clicked the key to open the doors and she wondered if perhaps it was his car, or even their *family* car. He reached in and grabbed a briefcase. It was clearly not his, far too feminine.

'Do you need a lift back home?' he asked.

'No,' Tally lied, 'I'd like to walk, clear my head.'

'Come on, it's cold, let me take you. I'll just run this in to Camilla, hold on a second.'

He rushed back into the house and Tally briefly considered her options. If she ran towards home he would be able to see her because the typical Fenland road was long and straight, devoid of trees or anything to duck behind, and she would look ridiculous. She could go and hide in the neighbour's garden again, but he was probably keeping a wary eye out for more intrusions. She was trying to forget the name Camilla. It was a lovely name, really classy. Simon and Camilla had a sickeningly nice ring to it. She was going to have to endure the drive, she realised, and trudged her way to the passenger side. She slid into the car and cast her eyes around, searching for more proof of their relationship. At least there wasn't a booster seat in the back revealing an entire secret family. She nosed through the centre console and found some tissues, a red lipstick (of course) and a wedge of business cards. Peering at one, she saw Camilla had a different surname, so at least they weren't married yet, and worked as a solicitor. As Simon reappeared, she stuffed a card into her coat pocket and scrunched it up between her fingers.

'How are you?' Simon asked as they set off, sparing a moment to look her over, wondering why she appeared so fidgety.

'Fine,' she replied robotically. Had she ever been fine? Not in the last couple of years. How British of her to swallow down all her complaints, bury the desire to tell Simon that she had been about to tell him she loved him and he and his bit of fancy stuff and this car had just gone and ruined it – or saved her from further embarrassment. Instead, she was just sitting there saying she was 'Fine' as if someone wasn't about to buy their family estate against their will, she wasn't about to be forced to sell on her forever horses, and the only person she had ever loved was about to move back to London.

'You?' she felt obliged to ask. She gazed out at the poplars in the distance, standing sturdy despite the relentless winds. She caught the sight of a family of deer bouncing across a distant stubble field and then disappearing down into a ditch and it lifted her soul for a moment. Simon was a fool to give up this countryside for an urban jungle of concrete and wine bars and people in expensive suits. His wall of glass could never match these open plan views of half sky and half land, each a different colour every day.

'Yeah, also fine, I guess.' Simon didn't sound quite as convincing. He sounded like he had just walked up a hill carrying a giant sack of potatoes above his head, only to discover it was merely the first peak of many, and they stretched off into the distance, ascending further into the clouds. He sounded like he was tired, worried, and lying. Perhaps he was also afraid he would miss the view.

'Good.' Tally was ashamed to brush it off, when a decent person would have dug deeper, instantly realising he was certainly *not* fine and needed someone to ask him how he was *really* feeling. Camilla could ask him later.

Before she had shrugged off the sulk, they were back, tyres crunching over the gravel, and Simon had stopped the car at the base of the steps. She gazed up towards her front door. It was so familiar, and it broke her heart to imagine the sand slipping through the hour glass, seemingly speeding up as it reached the last few hundred grains. She wanted to grasp it with both hands and spin it over and let it count down all over again. Perhaps then she would get the chance to do things properly, in the right order, at the right time.

'I'll miss you,' Simon said to the steering wheel as she unbuckled her seat belt. 'I'm sorry things didn't work out.'

Tally had been reaching for the door handle. She paused, but then rested her hand on the cold plastic, determined to get out of the car. She was too afraid to become embroiled in an emotional goodbye, besides, a goodbye today made tomorrow seem closer. He should wait until the last possible moment, just in case something or someone swooped in to save the day. It made her realise Simon didn't have a secret back up plan. Only upon hearing his deflated tone did she realise just how much she had been holding on to that outside possibility. She had been counting on him to save them all.

'Me too.' Tally looked at him, wondering if he was referring to the business, or to them. They had tried to work at the business, they hadn't really put much work into them. They had been too busy living their own lives to really think about them and it was as if the moment they had noticed each other time had already expired, and it was too little too late. He might have noticed you earlier, Tally thought, and perhaps you secretly noticed him too.

'You know what they say,' Simon shrugged, visibly picking himself up from the floor.

'What do they say?' Tally asked, indulging, a speck of hope revived as he reinstalled his tough veneer.

'It's not over until it's over.'

'It's not over yet,' Tally echoed, wanting to believe in the notion that perhaps the situation could be recovered and the impending doom deflected. Leila walked around the corner of the house, saw them and after gauging she wasn't interrupting anything passionate, smiled and waved. Tally jumped out of the car before Simon said anything to deter the flutter of a dream that whispered the end might not be as close as they feared.

'Well?' Leila asked, hooking her arm into Tally's and flicking an interested glance over her shoulder at Simon, who raised a hand to them both as he crawled away, catching Tally's eye as he passed.

'I tried, I promise, but we must have got our wires crossed. He's with someone else.'

'What? No. You're sure?' Leila couldn't believe it. Simon had never mentioned another person. 'He told you he was single, didn't he?'

'I guess he moved on fast. That's her car.' Tally shrugged, not wanting to think about it anymore.

'It's so tacky.' Leila squeezed her arm, transferring her condolences through the soft grip of her fingertips. 'Help me finish the horses would you, my bump is slowing me down.'

Tally struggled with another box, her brow starting to shine. Leila was too busy directing Michael with his gigantic box to spot Tally taking a break half-way up the stairs to catch her breath. Tally lifted the cardboard flap to find her box half filled with books.

'Typical,' she muttered, wondering why Michael even had all these books since she had never seen him read anything thicker than a magazine.

'Did you declutter *before* we decided to lug all your stuff across Fenson?' she snapped at Michael as he walked past, heading towards the horse trailer to reload.

'I threw out the cookbooks because I figured we can just get our recipes online,' he said.

'Yet you kept the Guinness Book of World Records?' she held up the thick hardback.

'That's a classic, it's probably worth thousands.'

'I've seen at least four copies at every car boot sale I've ever visited.'

'Give it time, it'll be priceless,' Michael winked, before disappearing outside.

'Can I help?' Simon asked, poking his head through the front door. 'Michael told me you're huffing and puffing over a box of books.'

'In more ways than one,' Tally said, secretly glad Simon had showed up because she wasn't sure she was going to be able to lift the box of books after placing it on the stairs.

'Here.' Simon joined her on the tenth step, 'let me.' He lifted the box easily, putting her to shame, and headed upstairs.

'Left door,' Tally called. She waited on the landing for him. She glanced around their new modest terrace and wondered once again how on earth they were all going to live here. Three adults and two kids was going to be a squeeze with only one upstairs bathroom and a downstairs loo. The homely smell of Grampy had disappeared, taking his presence with it. She tried to picture him but the more they cleaned and painted and filled his old home with their possessions, the less he seemed to be there. She was hoping he would keep her company whilst she was living here and give her some of his valued advice. It was hard not having him to talk to, he was the only person who ever truly listened. She sometimes didn't even have to talk for him to understand what she was thinking or feeling. He would have probably made her do something about Simon sooner.

'Can I see your room?' Simon asked, joining her on the upstairs landing.

Her skin prickled at the request. She pushed open the door on the right and let him enter. There was a double bed, an upgrade from her single, and Edith had her old single pressed against the other wall. There was only a narrow strip between them, wedged open by a shared bedside table.

'A big girl bed,' Simon smiled.

'Are you talking about me or Edith?' Tally laughed, using the opportunity to open the curtains wider. She at least got the garden view, so she could check on the tiny apple tree. She had already decided that gardening would be her new passion, a way to try to stay sane. Michael would find it too much hard work and Leila would have her hands full, so it made sense that Tally would keep their wild-flower garden in order. There was a cluster of birds at the newly filled bird feeder, hopping and squabbling to get their fair share of seeds.

Tally heard the click of the bedroom door. Her pulse began to race. Calm down, she urged, he isn't Brad, it isn't happening again. Snow isn't falling. She gripped onto the window sill, frozen rigid by a combination of exhilaration and utter fear. What was he doing, closing the door like that, why had he shut her in? Michael was near this time, he would be able to hear her scream. He could rescue her if she needed it. She started to breathe so heavily that her breath bounced off the glass and hit her, clouding her vision of the apple tree as if forming a protective barrier, ensuring the innocent tree didn't witness anything to shake its tender faith in humankind.

Simon was standing right behind her now, not touching, but she could sense his body close and hear the steady rise and fall of his chest as his breath ruffled her hair. Whatever this is, she thought, good or bad, I'm simply not prepared. I don't want him to hurt me or tell me goodbye or sorry. She didn't want him to touch or kiss her either, because it would only make her heart ache worse when it was time for him to leave. She had been hoping things could end quietly, without ceremony. She shouldn't have accepted his help on the stairs.

'Natalie,' he said softly, using her real name. It sounded alien but also like the most intimate word he had ever uttered.

She squeezed her eyes shut, unsure if she wanted to will this moment away or pause time so it could last forever. She tried to quieten the thoughts shouting at her, demanding she ask what the hell he thought he was doing when he had a glossy girlfriend with a red sports car.

He pressed his fingertips gingerly to her arms, and upon no reaction, he wrapped his palms around them, as if grasping onto her, not for control or to inflict pain – not like Brad – but as if he needed her to anchor him to the ground, to keep him there in Fenson. It was like he was searching for a reason not to leave. She blinked and a tear dropped onto the window sill. She stared at it, wondering what it meant. Her body seemed to accept things were over before her mind had. What does he want from me? What am I supposed to say or do next? What do *I want to do?*

She turned, causing him to release her and step back. He didn't know what she was going to do either. She was like a wild horse, unpredictable, with the potential to fight or flee. He'd been spending all this time just trying to earn her trust, her affection, and now he had gone and touched her, and it might have been too soon and he might have just spoiled it.

'We can't do this,' she whispered, wiping another tear from her cheek. 'I can't let you in and then watch you go.'

He nodded, agreeing, it would be too hard, too reckless, he shouldn't have asked to come into her bedroom, and he shouldn't have closed the door. But then he couldn't stop himself either, so he stepped forward and kissed her, and the ledge dug into her back. It was everything Tally had anticipated it would be when she allowed herself to indulge in the what ifs, and now it was happening and so unexpected it was like an out of body experience. Months of miscommunication and frustration, the growing spark of potential, all culminated with this kiss shared in a cluttered back bedroom filled with boxes and a new future not intended to include Simon.

She was supposed to push him away, to mention Camilla and remind him how kissing her was going to lead to broken hearts, but she was overpowered by the urge to let him in for a moment, ignoring the price they would ultimately pay, and embraced the novelty of wanting everything that was happening to her to be done, of actively participating, of experiencing a man doing something to her that was welcome. It wasn't Brad, who had forced himself, or Doug, who had worn her down, but it was Simon, someone she had somehow, against her will, fallen utterly in love with.

The kiss healed her, banishing the demons that had hovered around her since the attack, suggesting she might never be able to be touched by another man, might never be able to let someone lie on top of her, telling her she was destined to stay scared. She didn't feel scared, she felt empowered, as if Simon had just restored her faith in herself, and love, and the ability to trust another human to get this close. Even if it was the last kiss, even if her heart shattered into a hundred pieces and she never saw him again, he had just gifted her something so precious, she wasn't going to be able to resent him anymore.

He finally broke away and rested his forehead against hers while they regained their breath. There were so many things to say, too many things, that it was best not to start, not to ruin the moment. So, he cupped her face in his hand and then left, leaving her staring after him, wondering if that really would be the last time that she'd ever see him.

'See you,' Simon nodded to Michael and Leila at the foot of the stairs. Michael went to ascend, to find Tally and ask her why she was slacking, but Leila gently restrained him and suggested they put the kettle on. Michael looked at her, taken aback by her sudden change of heart since she had been the bossy pregnant one directing her two workers, and then he saw the tender expression on her face, and realised Simon had looked on the verge of tears as he had said goodbye as casually as he could muster. Michael nodded and followed her into the kitchen, praying his sister would eventually be okay.

It was midnight, but Tally was tossing and turning, unable to get comfortable or switch off her whirring mind. There was a slit of moonlight poking through the curtains and no matter how much she adjusted them to try and close it off, it found its way through and cut her bedroom in half. She could hear Edith snoring gently and tried to focus on the steady rhythm, remembering how when she was a tiny baby she would listen intently for the reassurance she was still there, terrified it might just suddenly stop. She hadn't slept well since they had moved, despite it being an upgrade in living conditions. The walls had been painted and the boxes unpacked and the room assembled tastefully. The baby paraphernalia clutter that had clogged up her old room had been crammed into the spare box room, which Michael had promised to transform into a nursery. Every time she nearly fell asleep she sensed Simon was back in the room, standing near the window. When she realised it was just a trick of her mind, and that Simon had already packed and left for London, she felt disappointed and then struggled to fall asleep. A new couple had moved into his old house, she had spotted the moving van and then seen the estate agent remove the sold sign with relish. She hadn't noticed Simon leave, although he probably didn't own much in Fenson and might have left the house furnished since the new residents looked like first time buyers; fresh faced and ridiculously in love.

Her parents were still stationed at the old house, waiting until the final shove to leave. No one had told them to go, so they carried on as if there might be some second chance. Helena often visited, usually to get away from Charles rather than to actually see her children and grandchild. Tally was still going back to the house daily to sort the horses, which put a strain on Michael who had to drop her over on his way to work. She would then rely on Helena to take her home. She had discounted buying a cheap car because soon they would need to draft up an advert for the horses, and then she wouldn't need it anyway. She could be a village hermit living between the house, shop and pub, never experiencing anything new. She turned over again, failing to push the misery from her mind.

The bathroom door opened, signalling Tally was not the only person awake. It would be Leila needing another wee, experiencing the discomfort of third trimester pregnancy that had somehow completely eluded Tally. She lay waiting for the toilet to flush but instead heard Leila suddenly start to shout for Michael. She sat bolt upright in bed and then hurried to the door. Michael was stumbling out of the bedroom, his bleary eyes wide.

'My waters have broken, I thought I'd wet myself in bed, but now my plug has come out.'

Tally and Michael glanced at each other, neither of them understanding what a 'plug' was and neither particularly wanting to learn.

'But you're only thirty-two weeks.' Michael stared at the bump, horrified. He hadn't even sorted the cluttered nursery out yet. He glanced towards it, as if magically it might be ready, but the room was still stacked with unpacked boxes.

'I know,' Leila whispered fearfully. They both looked at Tally as if she was some kind of premature birth expert.

'Phone the hospital,' Tally suggested, which was something they could have worked out without her. She didn't have any other advice to offer, other than it helps if you didn't even know you were pregnant. 'I'll pack your bag while Michael phones. You sit and watch Edith,' Tally added, not really needing Leila to watch her two-year-old sleep, but it would give her a purpose as she waited nervously for the next direction. Tally whizzed around her bedroom, grabbing clean clothes and various bits the new-born baby might need, all the while praying there would be a happy and healthy baby for Leila to meet soon. She met the couple at the front door. Michael gave her a big hug; he was trembling slightly. 'Are you okay to drive?' Tally asked, 'Take it steady.'

'I'm fine. We will call you as soon as there is news.'

'Please do, I'll let Mum and Dad know what's happening first thing in the morning. Tally put the kettle on once they had left; there was no chance she was going to get back to sleep now. She dialled her mum as soon as the sky began to tinge pink with dawn, aware her mother would rather miss the last hour or two of sleep than be excluded from the news. Besides, Helena was used to middle of the night 'you're a new grandmother' phone calls. It was a shame this one had to come with more worry, Michael's baby was supposed to be the nice, normal one with no concerns or surprises along the way.

'It'll be okay, I learned a lot when waiting with you on the neonatal ward, thirty-two weeks is fine, the baby will be fine,' Helena reassured Tally, or perhaps herself, 'I'll go to the hospital and wait for news there, I can't hang around here. I won't get in the way,' she promised, knowing Tally was about to warn her against going. 'You'll need to sort out the horses and take Edith to the yard. You could leave her with your father but, well, you know.'

'Don't worry about us.'

'It's just such a long way to walk, and on the side of a busy road,' Helena lamented.

'Well, it won't be for much longer.'

There was a pause before Helena said goodbye. It sounded like she had hesitated, as if she had opened her mouth and was about to say something, but then she moved on and said goodbye, refusing to acknowledge the comment as if Tally hadn't said anything. She still had her head buried in the sand over her upcoming eviction. Tally put the phone down and stared forlornly at her computer to re-read the two internet sale adverts she had drafted whilst waiting for a more sociable hour to call her mother.

There was one advert for Match and one for Peter, and she had selected some suitable photographs to upload from her phone, too. They were still so handsome it made her heart ache to look at their perky ears and sweet faces. She sighed as she completed her registration for the online horse sales website, forcing herself to fill in the correct contact details. After the horses and her parents had moved out there would be no reason to visit her old home, regardless of whether the new people moved in straight away it would be trespassing to just turn up and have a sniff around. It would probably be easier if she didn't ever go back, a little trip down memory lane would only depress her.

It would be unwise to hold off selling the horses any longer. The leaving date would be confirmed imminently and the swish couple who had purchased the estate would not appreciate two old nags hanging around. They probably had a yard full of expensive thoroughbred types waiting to move in or worse, they would convert the stables into something hideous or knock them down all together. After living in the new house for a month with Michael and Leila it was obvious there wasn't going to be enough spare cash to keep two horses on a livery yard, even after Tally had got the job at the café and started bringing in a contribution, so Tally and Leila had reluctantly agreed to let them go. Tally let her mouse hover over the "submit" button on her computer for a while, and then finally clicked to post the adverts. She was relieved the phone didn't immediately start to ring.

❄

'Here you go,' Tally smiled sweetly at her customer as she served another fancy coffee and piece of homemade cake. She wished she had enough spare cash to splash out on such luxuries. She smoothed down her half pinny and wiped down a table automatically as she passed, finding an easy rhythm to the work. She had been holding the fort on her own for a few weeks now, ever since Leila had given birth and been signed off on maternity leave. She had tried to resent working in the café, convinced at first that it was beneath her, but slowly she came to realise she loved it. She enjoyed her morning walk through the village and the friendly faces she would see on the way. She loved engaging with customers and looking after the place with pride, as if it was her own little business. She had tried to cling on to distaste because she had been horrified to discover she enjoyed the simple life her teenage self so easily dismissed; she had previously laughed at Leila for refusing to dream big. Simon had gone and the degree had never materialised, but Edith was still here, and her community surrounded her and her best friends supported her. She used to think she wanted a flash city life, but the trip to London had made her realise she preferred a rural life. Fenson was her home and the thought of never leaving no longer shamed her. Perhaps it's just grim acceptance, she mused as she checked the cakes for freshness, perhaps my ambition has drained away and I'm just settling for second best. She hadn't even enrolled on the degree course yet, the one she had mentioned to Simon along with a statement about not giving up on her dreams.

It wasn't acceptance that had changed Tally, it was Simon. He had finally healed her and allowed her to observe the world and her place in it with fresh eyes. Her life was no longer tainted by bitterness and fear. She had moved on and could now enjoy the consequences of what had happened to her rather than let them hang around her neck like a lead weight. She didn't obsess over impossible desires to change the past, she lived in the present, and could even see a future. She loved herself and Fenson again, her life was no longer spoilt by the events of that one night.

It was quiet for a Friday, which had made the morning drag. She much preferred it when there were people to watch and regulars to chat to. Her mum friends were due soon, which gave Tally something to look forward to. They had agreed the cafe would be the new haunt now their picnics under the tree in Tally's old garden had come to an abrupt end, with Katherine announcing the café was much more weatherproof. Tally usually managed to spend most of the time sitting with them, keeping an eye on the door, having to hop up only occasionally to tend to a customer. Since they brought in so much business buying copious amounts of coffee, cake and snacks to keep the toddlers entertained, the owner turned a blind eye whenever she popped by and found Tally gossiping with them, happy to have found a waitress who wasn't just a temp waiting for a new year of university to start. If she was lucky enough, Tally would be a lifer, just like Leila.

'Thank God, I've been eyeing up this rocky road all day,' Tally grinned when the whirlwind of mums and children arrived, and the last customer decided now would be a good time to drop his money onto the counter and leave them to it, especially since Eva had arrived mid tantrum; something to do with wearing the wrong socks.

'Grab the whole tray,' Gwen said, 'It's my treat, because I just *know* I look the best today.' She flicked her shiny hair over her shoulder to punctuate the point.

'You really do,' Tally marvelled, 'What happened?'

'She got laid, *finally*,' Susan smiled, accepting the rocky road as Tally passed it over the counter, since both other mums had their toddlers on their hips.

Tally topped up the tea pot as they settled at their usual table, smack bang in the middle of the café. 'Who's the lucky guy?' she called to try and make herself heard above the screaming. Eva was currently flinging off her shoes so she could rip off the offending wrongly coloured socks. Katherine was letting her get on with it, giving up on trying to restrain her. She had decided that if her child wanted to run around in bare feet for the next hour while she zoned out and enjoyed the rare company of adults then she was more than welcome to, Tally kept the floor spotless anyway. Susan rolled a glitter ball into the back corner of the café to lure the toddlers further away.

'It's kind of cliché, but my postman.' Gwen flushed slightly, bracing herself for the teasing.

'Oh, do you mean Gary?' Tally asked, 'I'd never met him before moving into the new house because the post box was at the end of the drive at the old place, but he really is hot.'

'It's just a shame he's called Gary,' Katherine commented.

'I think Gwen and Gary has a nice ring to it; it's kind of cute,' Susan said through a mouthful of marshmallow. 'This is amazing, by the way,' she added.

'Anna made it; she now bakes for the café. The customers can't get enough of her cakes.'

'That's good, she deserved a big break. It was criminal you kept all those scrummy baked goods to yourself before now,' Susan smiled, and it occurred to Tally that the girls had only met Anna a few times, but they cared because Tally cared, and she had told them nearly everything about her life. It was nice they were still around for her, even though she was now just a waitress living with her brother.

'How serious is it, then? How often have you hooked up?' Tally asked, bringing over the tea tray, picking her way over the abandoned socks and shoes.

'At least twice a night for the past week, isn't it, Gwen?' Katherine winked.

'We just hit it off,' Gwen smiled coyly. 'I've always fancied him, to be honest, but he finally started up a conversation; he must have guessed Ian had left, and it kind of snowballed from there.'

'That is fantastic news.' Tally perched herself on a stool and succumbed to a slice of rocky road. She didn't hear the door open behind her. 'That's one less eligible man in the village for me, though.'

'Oh, I'm not sure about that,' Susan said, stifling a laugh. The rest of them tittered.

'At this rate I'll have to marry Ned and pull pints for the rest of my life.'

'Ned's gay,' Gwen said, 'so unless you want a marriage of convenience, I really think you should hold out for someone more suitable.'

'The perfect man will turn up one day, quite unexpectedly,' Susan said, 'Things will be normal and then – boom – he'll be suddenly standing right behind you.'

'I don't think so.' Tally rolled her eyes, 'As I'm sure I don't need to remind you, the perfect man moved back to London.' She paused, realising they were all staring, with strange grins plastered onto their faces. 'What? Have I got something on my face?' She touched a finger to her lip, checking for rocky road debris.

'I just popped back for a coffee.'

Tally whirled around, nearly tumbling over as she jumped off the stool in shock at the familiar voice. She stared at Simon, wondering if he was an optical illusion. She felt immediately self-conscious of her cheesy waitress uniform, complete with high pony tail and frill around the bottom of her apron. She debated the unlikely possibility he hadn't heard her comment about him being the perfect man for her.

'Do you do takeaway? I'm in a bit of a hurry.' He glanced at his watch for effect, and she could tell he was trying to hide a smile from the way his mouth tweaked at the corners. He had definitely heard.

'Err, yes, we do takeaway.' Tally walked stiffly around to the counter to start the coffee machine, leaving the girls to exchange raised eyebrows. Eva had even decided to stop screaming. She was now joining in a toddler version of football at the back of the café, where there was a complete disregard to the hand ball rules and the aim seemed to be attempting to lick the glitter off the ball. 'Americano?' she suggested, as Simon made a play at reading the board above her head.

Katherine elbowed Susan as she bit into a large chunk of rocky road and started chewing loudly, like an annoying cinema patron.

'Latte please,' Simon corrected, dropping a fiver onto the worktop between them.

'On the house.' Tally pushed it back towards him. He pivoted his wrist and lay his fingers over hers.

'I didn't really come here for a coffee, Tally.'

They ignored the audible hush from their audience. She finally had the courage to look at him, and believe he was right, and this wasn't just a final cruel trick designed to ensure her heart was still a heap of dust. His fingers seared into her skin. He wasn't an optical illusion.

'It did seem like a long way to drive for a coffee.' She was screaming at herself to come up with something a bit more daring, but was too terrified to stick her neck out. He had been the one to kiss her, now it was her turn to be brave. Perhaps he had left some paperwork in the estate office, or had to pick up something from his old house. It would be too bold to think he had travelled all this way just to see Tally. The three pairs of eyes staring at her were distracting, although Simon didn't appear to notice the gossip-thirsty mums. He hadn't taken his eyes off her and the intensity reminded her of them standing in her bedroom and him kissing her, the window sill digging into her back. Finally, he lifted his hand and she could almost hear the groan of disappointment from their audience. They had been hoping for a dramatic over the counter kiss. Pouring the coffee seemed to take forever, especially since he was watching her so closely, it was as if she was under examination. She fumbled with the lid on the paper cup, nearly tipping the whole thing over. She pushed it gingerly across the counter, wondering if now he had his coffee, he would simply turn and leave. *Say something,* she shouted at herself and, glancing back to the other girls, they were all silently shouting it too.

'How is Camilla?' she finally asked, immediately kicking herself for asking, and in such a friendly way too, as if she cared how Camilla and her ugly car was doing. She saw Katherine shake her head in disapproval at the choice of works.

'Camilla?' Simon asked, as if he didn't recognise the name.

Does he really think I'm that stupid? Tally seethed.

'Oh, Camilla,' Simon remembered, 'you mean my solicitor, the one with the briefcase and the over-the-top car?'

'She's your solicitor?' Tally asked, and despite the instant relief, she immediately questioned if it was wise to be dating his own solicitor.

'The family solicitor,' he nodded. Then he paused and understood why Tally had asked. He narrowed his eyes at her. 'You didn't think she and I were...?'

Tally shrugged, doing her best *I didn't really over think it* act, but it wasn't fooling Simon. Tally could see Susan slapping her palm against her forehead silently, making a show of how wrong Tally had got him. Simon had just soared in everyone's estimations, since the secret girlfriend had been weighing heavily against him in public opinion, more than him leaving without saying a proper goodbye, since the kiss had been romantic enough to let him off. Tally was starting to wish they didn't know everything about it because she could guess too easily what they were all thinking which, right now, seemed to be *Tally you're an idiot.*

'I don't suppose you can sneak off for a little while? There's something I want to show you.' Simon looked at her friends for a willing volunteer, his smile easy, causing them to practically swoon.

'We can certainly man the shop,' Gwen nodded, wiping the crumbs from her face as discreetly as possible.

'I don't know,' Tally hesitated, when she should have already chucked her pinny at them.

'Go on, you won't get into trouble, we can serve a couple of pieces of cake.' Katherine waved her off, wiggling her eyebrows for extra effect. 'Susan knows how to operate tills,' she added.

Susan nodded, although Tally wasn't convinced Susan had any idea how to operate a till, she didn't even work in a shop. The three of them would probably club together to personally cover whatever the next few customers might order.

'Call me if you need anything.' Tally edged her way around the counter, nervous of not having a barrier between herself and Simon.

'We won't,' Gwen called as she left the shop, following Simon, reassured by the sight of his car parked on the side of the road outside because that made it less likely that he was a figment of her imagination.

※

'I'm sorry to interrupt your afternoon tea,' Simon said as he started the engine. Tally realised she'd left her pinny on as she clicked her seatbelt into place.

'It's fine,' she replied, her mouth dry and her tongue feeling as if it had swollen in size. *Why am I so nervous?*

'We would have mainly been bitching about you,' she added for a reason she couldn't fathom. Simon smiled wryly, seeming to enjoy being part of the conversation.

'You haven't forgotten all about me, then?'

Tally didn't know how to answer. Should she pretend she had moved on, as if he hadn't been important to her, or should she just admit she couldn't stop thinking about him, especially not that parting kiss. She was half hoping he would do it again, but half afraid he might because that would probably mean he was leaving all over again.

'Leila had her little girl.' She opted to change the topic completely. 'She was quite early so scared us for a little while, but she's thriving now. They called her Laura, and chose Natalie for her middle name.'

Simon smiled out of the windscreen, warmed by the news. 'You're an auntie.'

'Apparently so.' Tally shook her head.

A mother, an auntie, how had that happened? Inside she was just a teenager, quaking at the idea of being all alone with a boy she fancied, wondering what was going to happen next. They were winding their way out of the village and it occurred to her he might be kidnapping her and taking her to London, and if he was, she wouldn't even mind. She'd have to protest purely because he had forgotten to pick up Edith. He indicated into the estate, as if he was stopping to collect Edith from Helena, who babysat whilst Tally worked when Leila was too busy doing something with Laura to take the both of them. 'Mum is going to be shocked to see you.'

'No she isn't,' Simon laughed as they crunched over the gravel.

Tally frowned, thrown by his comment. Then the front door opened as Simon pulled up to the bottom step, and Helena stepped out in her full glory, a crisp white shirt with a high collar, tailored cream trousers, heels and jewellery that made Tally blink. Her hair was perfectly coiffed and Tally wondered if they had just gone back in time. Edith tottered out and squealed upon seeing her mother so soon, not expecting her for hours. Tally scooped her up half way up the steps for a cuddle, and Simon leaned in to ruffle her hair. She grinned back at him, recognising him as an old friend, and wondered where he had been recently.

'Mum this doesn't count as moving out,' Tally said, glancing apologetically at Simon, worried he would be exasperated to still find her parents living in the old wing, using the main entrance, clinging on in denial. Surely the new couple were itching to take possession and had packed up all their expensive furniture, settled all their affairs and finished doing whatever else it was that had kept them from moving into their new estate before now.

'Don't worry darling, we're staying in the old wing, we've grown accustomed to it, besides, now you and Michael have moved out and Simon's planned all the remaining repairs and renovations, it's much nicer, it'll soon be as much of a palace as the rest of it.'

Tally swallowed, afraid her mother had been drinking, whilst looking after her child. Edith wriggled down and then disappeared back into the house.

'Charles and Edith are in the middle of an elaborate game of hide and seek,' she explained, 'he's currently wedged into the shoe closet. She'll never find him.'

'Have I had a recent blow to the head?' Tally asked Simon.

'No.' Simon steered her into the hallway.

'I better go, I promised Anna I'd watch her cinnamon buns and take them out of the oven before they burn.' Helena tottered off in the direction of the kitchen – the grand gigantic kitchen they used to have.

'Mum cooks? Dad plays with Edith? They're in the house?'

'I can't claim credit for the first two things, but I can explain the third.' Simon pulled a folded letter from his back pocket.

Tally took it gingerly and scanned the letterhead. It was from an estate-agent based somewhere in London, with a really fancy logo. There was an elaborate signature signing it off which looked like it took far too much effort to reproduce over and over again. It looked rather official. She read the first few paragraphs, then read them again. She couldn't quite understand what it was telling her.

'You bought the estate?' she finally managed. She tilted her head to one side. 'Didn't you buy the estate off us to begin with, and then just recently sell it?'

'British Estates bought the estate off your family. I then bought the estate off British Estates.'

Tally stared. Was this good news? Did this mean that horrible couple wouldn't be moving in? It didn't explain why her parents were in such a good mood.

You live in London, she silently added, *and can't afford this place*. The estate must have been valued at millions, and Simon's father wasn't exactly the type to give his own son a bargain, not when he was getting rid of the place just to scupper his progression to CEO.

'I sold everything to afford it. My flat, the house in Fenson, the cars – except that one - my share of the business, and Mum left me a chunk of money, too.'

Tally couldn't quite compute. 'Why?' she finally asked agog. Did that mean he wasn't going back to London, surely not, if he didn't have a flat there anymore?

'I hoped that part was obvious.'

'To prove your father wrong?'

'No, although, this place will become a success, with your help, we can run it as an independent business. No corporate hurdles, no head office, no burgundy fleeces.'

'You didn't like the burgundy either then?' Tally smiled.

'God no, I thought we could go for royal blue.'

'We?'

'Don't make me nervous,' Simon laughed, and Tally sensed a moment of hesitation.

She saw it then in his eyes, everything he had just gambled on a girl he had met in Fenson. He had put his entire life – everything he owned - on the line, jumping feet first into a new future and holding out his hand as he fell, hoping she would reach out and grasp it in time. Everything he had just told her, the letter in her hand, finally clicked into place. He was waiting for her now, standing on his new parquet floorboard, the one she had walked over a million times before, to answer the unspoken question he had just asked, with potentially the grandest gesture any man had ever made. He had risked his entire future on her choosing whether to smile and nod her head or back away in horror. He had taken a chance that another man hadn't since come along ready to step onto his toes, that she hadn't fallen out of love and forgotten him. And there she was too scared to say something back in the café just in case it would be considered too bold a move.

She let out a long breath, allowing the amazement to sink in, aware it was an agonising wait for Simon, but she had a lot to process. She wouldn't have to sell the horses, she could leave Michael and his new family to enjoy their home, Edith could have a dad and she could be *happy*. What's more, she thought, letting the letter flutter to the floor so she could reach for Simon's hand, she could keep him, this man who had fallen into their lives and rattled their cages then somehow caused her to fall in love with him, and somehow decided he loved her back, enough to do something so mad as buy the estate, the most elaborate rescue plan.

'I like royal blue,' she said finally, watching the slightly fearful frown melt from his brow and his lips tweak into a relieved smile.

'In that case, I have just one more request,' Simon said, his voice muffling as he pulled her close and pressed his face into her neck.

'Anything,' Tally replied, her knees weakening.

'Can I see your room?'

❄

Thank You

Thank you for reading my latest novel. Self-published authors rely on word of mouth, so if you enjoyed reading my book please leave a review on Amazon.

Follow me on Twitter - @BeecroftHazel - my Facebook page - Hazel Beecroft Author - or Instagram - @hazel_beecroft - for updates on my horse riding and writing.

I would like to give special commendation to my two wonderful horses – Jester and Kody – and my beautiful daughter, Verity, who inspired me to expand from equestrian fiction and human relationships to explore motherhood.

Other Books out now in both eBook and Paperback:

Jump If You Dare
Thrill Of The Chase
The One Day Event (A Short Story)
After The Start Bell

Clear To The Last

A Year At Worst

Down The Centre Line

Printed in Great Britain
by Amazon